THE GIRL,
THE RING,
& THE
BASEBALL
BAT

Also by Camille Gomera-Tavarez

High Spirits

The Girl, The Ring, &
The Baseball Bat

Camille Gomera-Tavarez

LEVINE QUERIDO

Montclair | Amsterdam | Hoboken

This is an Arthur A. Levine book
Published by Levine Querido

LQ

LEVINE QUERIDO

www.levinequerido.com • info@levinequerido.com
Levine Querido is distributed by Chronicle Books, LLC
Copyright © 2023 by Camille Gomera-Tavarez

Maya Angelou quote from *Black Women Writers at Work* © 2022
Claudia Tate. Updated edition published by Haymarket Books
in 2022. First published in 1985 by Oldcastle Books, London.

Library of Congress Control Number: 2023931662

ISBN 978-1-64614-265-1
Printed and bound in China

Published in February 2024
First Printing

To my younger self and all the underserved
public school kids out there.
You are more than your circumstances.

3

The Bat

4

Rage

I saw so many adults lying to so many young people, lying in their teeth, saying, "You know, when I was young, I never would have done . . . Why I couldn't . . . I shouldn't." Lying. Young people know when you're lying; so I thought for all those parents and non-parents alike who have lied about their past, I will tell it.

—Maya Angelou

Chapter One

On Anger Issues

– Rosie

I knew from the moment Ashia Kingston popped her earbuds in that my sister was gonna slap her across the face. There was a point before every fight I've ever witnessed, where the air became motionless, and the hairs on the back of my neck levitated. It was this bright, flashy, tangible energy. Kill Bill sirens sounded off in my brain. Everything was mad static. I could feel it as soon as someone (anyone, even a complete stranger) walked into a room. Their anger was a vacuum of potential. All my attention was sucked up and concentrated into the energy tornado that surrounded them. That's when I knew that shit was about to go down.

As much as I could never, ever, never imagine my weak, gym-phobic ass in the middle of a fist fight, I had to admit that some part of me found them incredibly entertaining. And I always seemed to have a front row seat. Just my luck. Girl fights—in the locker rooms and the bathrooms and the alley behind the CVS across the street—were the best kind. Boy fights were almost always disappointing. Mostly empty threats and them putting their faces close enough to kiss. All bravado, no bite. Girl fights had story, plot, development. You had to catch up on a whole reality show of drama before the fight and stay tuned for the drama after. And they were nearly impossible to break up once someone latched onto a handful of hair.

Back in sixth grade, I overheard our principal at Lincoln Park Junior High describe Caro as a "gangster with anger issues" while I sat with her on the cold hallway floor. We laughed about the word "gangster" for at least a year after that. I mean, who says that about a child? But Mami took the anger issues part seriously, like she'd received the diagnosis from a qualified doctor and not from a corny Italian man from Jersey City who hated children. My friends from the Accelerated program, Taylor and Lovely, would giggle and whisper towards me when they realized she was my sister. So did everybody else. *Don't fuck with Caro, she's spicy, she's got anger issues, she's crazy.* Crazy Caro. They said she'd gotten into a hundred fights, but I knew she'd only been in one before. And that was only because Marco Madrigal had thrown a rock at her head outside the CVS. No one called Marco Madrigal crazy.

Caro and I never really fought, though. Because I skipped second grade, we were in the same year, but always had completely different classes. After multiple complaints from Mami over six months, the school had finally put me in Accelerated classes that November. Ten months before I'd become a high schooler. By that point, I only saw Caro in the hallway between classes where a head nod was the extent of our interaction. She had softball and track; I had tutoring and model UN. We had arguments at home, like any sisters, sure. But they usually ended with some sort of concession. I'd admit I was a little right and a little wrong (even though I am never wrong) and I'd say I'd buy her a soda next time we hit the dollar store. She'd admit that I was always right (because I am). That was it. That was the way we worked.

The thing about Caro was that, like a fluffy honeybee, she only violated others when provoked. Is killing yourself, and possibly your enemy, a bit dramatic a response to accidentally getting a hand swatted near you? Sure. But why bother an innocent bee? That's what I never understood about most of the kids we went to school with. A lot of them did things just to see what would happen, and cried when something inevitably did. Like Marco Madrigal, they fucked around and they found out.

The day after she filed a stolen items report that probably went straight into an office shredder, Caro walked into eighth-grade homeroom and saw a familiar green iPod Mini slide its way into Ashia's puffer jacket. She went through the whole first half of the school day, stewing, before telling me about it at lunch. I was honestly impressed that she held it in that long. Caro was a hundred times scarier when she found a sliver of patience to mask her anger. It was my idea to wait till we got home to tell Mami and have her yell at some secretary to get the stolen iPod back. And by the time the front doors swung open, I was the first one out on the steps. I waited for Caro's head to appear among the sea of kids. When she burst out the doors with a smile on her face, I almost thought we were home free. Until I watched something catch her eye. Well, someone.

It was a girl ahead of us who was right in the middle of a wide, boastful laugh. She was dripping with audacity and surrounded by a group of girls with shiny, flat-ironed hair.

"Caro—" the warning barely made a sound as it escaped my throat. Sometimes I lie awake in bed regretting not speaking up then. Though, I don't know if Caro would have heard me even if there weren't hundreds of loud ass kids celebrating freedom on a brisk, obligation-free afternoon.

I couldn't hear what my sister said when she tapped the girl on the shoulder. I only heard the gruff "Nah!" that followed from Ashia. The tone in Ashia's voice was really what set things into motion.

"Lemme see it," Caro raised her voice now, but still remained steady. I briefly wondered, what if she had been wrong? What if it wasn't her iPod?

"I don't have to let you see nothing. Get the fuck out my face." Ashia turned back to her friends and widened her eyes playfully. She mouthed the words, *Oh my God*. I was a little relieved that she stopped just short of calling Caro the magic word: *crazy*. That would have set her off in a snap. Caro took an annoyed deep breath. Thankfully, a couple months prior, I had walked my sister through some breathing exercises.

"Do it got the letters CDR engraved on the back? Just show your little friends that it ain't got those letters. Just show 'em." Caro spoke to the back of Ashia's greasy head. She spelled out the letters slowly, like she was speaking to a kindergartener. I remained glued to the bottom steps of the school, out of punching range.

Ashia shuffled awkwardly for a tense moment. She eventually rolled her eyes and fixed her face into a teasing grin. She turned around to meet Caro's eyes.

"So what? It's mine. Maybe CDR stands for Suck my Dick Rojas?" Ashia's friends burst into high-pitched laughter. One collapsed to her knees. Ashia beamed. I didn't even pause to question whether someone like Ashia might actually think *suck* started with a *C*. "I got it custom-made," she continued. That was when she drew a white cord out of her puffer jacket and popped the damn earbuds in. Caro's earbuds. The idea of Ashia's slimy earwax contaminating them made my nose wrinkle.

I took a reflexive step forward after Caro raised her hand for the slap. Then I stopped myself. Instead of hearing the satisfying sound of my sister's hand making contact, I saw that Caro was holding a shaking hand a centimeter away from her victim's face. The whole crowd got eerily quiet. We were collectively frozen in a memory that would burn itself permanently into my brain. In a split second, Caro retracted her hand and went directly for the prize in Ashia's pocket. That's when I heard a fist crack against my sister's jaw.

The kids around me closed in. A couple of stragglers climbed on top of the stair railings to get a better vantage point. I squeezed my way to the front of the crowd. I don't know what I thought I was gonna do. Defend her honor? Pull her back? I just felt . . . useless. It was useless to get involved and it was useless to pull Caro out of it. She always did exactly what she wanted to do.

I would remember seeing red leaking out of Ashia's nose in slow motion. It was beautiful, in a way. Like watching a massive, burning fire dancing along the horizon as it turned the world to ash. I should've stopped Caro then (or when she snatched a fistful of tracks out of Ashia's scalp) but the film playing out in front of me left me dumbstruck. I wasn't shocked at the violent act, though, or Caro's sudden fury. I was shocked at my own envy. Because I did envy her in that moment. I envied her access to that part of herself. I wondered what it felt like. I mean, to push all your feelings into your hands and just . . . do it. Just act and not think. Just feel your fist be the cause of pain and keep going and going until all your anger was just depleted. To let your insides out. Finally. Let it all out. I couldn't even stop thinking long enough to move my legs and reach out for my sister. MY sister. Someone I should protect. Especially when the girl in front of her (who had stolen her green iPod Mini and proceeded to talk shit) was kicking wildly at her shins.

Just fucking do it. Move. Help her. Stop her. Do SOMETHING. I looked on and did none of the above.

The universe or God or whoever must've been listening, though, because a violent force sent a push against my backpack. I tripped forward into the boxing ring, all my breath knocked out of me. My hands balled into fists, emboldened by random rage at whoever decided to thrust me into this. Caro's arm swung aimlessly and barely missed my face. Her other hand twisted into Ashia's shirt. I saw Caro's gold hoops sitting on the ground next to her sneakers and made a mental note to grab them. Our grandmother had gifted her those hoops.

"Say something, say something again! Fuckin' thief bitch! Say something!" Caro repeated the same phrase over and over. Her victim finally squirmed away and regained her balance.

Then I watched Ashia's grimy, square, press-on nails reach desperately towards me.

The next thing I remember, I was in the nurse's office lying down with something cold on my forehead.

"Your mother and sister are in the office next door, just rest up, honey. I'll let them know you woke up. Close this door on your way out," the nurse said. She added in a whisper, "If I leave now, I can still make *Dancing with the Stars*." And then she was gone.

I felt like I was in a bad dream. I sat up, looked in the mirror across the office, and touched the band-aid that was pasted against my forehead. There were scratches on my neck. I felt like shit. Uncertain memories flashed through my mind in blurred focus. On the counter sat a pair of gold hoop earrings. Outside the window, it was already dark.

When I closed the door behind me, I could hear muffled yelling coming from the principal's office. I stared at the door.

"That's not fair! She didn't fucking do nothing!" Caro's distinct gravel echoed through the empty hallway. "But she didn't *do* nothing!"

✿ ✿ ✿

I'd only seen my mother that angry once before. The last time Papi was home. When he gave Caro that iPod as a belated birthday present. And she packed his bags. That was a different kind of mad, though. A controlled one. This one was wild. I could feel the steam pouring out of her ears while I sat next to her on the car ride home.

When she spoke, her voice was low and calm like Caro's was earlier that day.

"I don't want you in my house. No te mereces ni eso. Lo que debo hacer es dejarte en la calle pa que aprenda. You thank God que tu Mamá es una mujer amable y graciosa. No me hables. Ni me mires. Apologize to your sister."

Mami left the car, slamming the door behind her. I looked at Caro's bloodshot eyes through the rearview mirror.

"Apologize for what? Look, I'm fine. It's okay. It's just a scratch," I pleaded. Caro was on the verge of tears. Why me? Shouldn't Caro apologize to Mami—or Ashia even? As much as the thief didn't deserve it. Caro stared at her shoes. I pressed again. "Apologize to me for what?"

"I'm so sorry Rosie. I really—I really am,"

"It's fine. I'm fine!" I repeated. Caro kept looking like she wanted to throw up. I climbed into the back seat next to her, setting off another headache. I grabbed my sister's hand. "What? What happened?"

And then she explained how Principal Rossi had been a condescending bitch and how he looked at her like she had the word *criminal* tattooed on her forehead. She didn't understand the big deal, considering Ashia was still alive somewhere (albeit probably in a hospital bed awaiting stitches). I tried not to feel sorry for her, but I did feel sorry for her parents. That must've been awful. And I wasn't sure Caro could escape the "crazy" label after sending someone to the hospital. She was given in-school suspension for the rest of the school year, of course. Four months. And then put on juvenile probation for the foreseeable future. Which meant check-ins with a school resource officer.

"I'm sorry. That sucks."

It did suck. A lot. I was already thinking about how I would have to help her catch up on her schoolwork over the summer. Though, other than that, I didn't see what it all had to do with me.

"And . . ." She looked away from me. "And apparently Ashia said you were involved, so you got detention for a week . . ." The words came out painstakingly slow. I'd never gotten detention before. Anxiety was already brewing in the back of my mind, like waves building into a storm. But there was more to it, I could see it in her face. ". . . And—I'm sorry Rosie. I'm so fuck-ing stupid. I don't know why I—fuck Rosie I'm sorry—"

"And what?" The words came out too sharp. It was hard trying to hold my sister together while I was barely together myself.

"And . . . he kicked you out from the Accelerated program. He did it to fuck with me. H-he made up some shit about your teachers talking about cheating on tests, I don't fucking know, he's a liar. But he saw on his computer that you were in that program and he just—he kept saying there was nothing he could do about it. But he was lying. He just took you out to be a dick. I know it. I-I'm sorry. It's not fucking fair." I understood the words individually, but together . . .

Caro let her tears flow into my shoulder before I could make sense of the mess she'd left behind. My thumbs rubbed circles into her back and we sat there in the car as dusk settled into night. I didn't have any tears. I didn't have any response. Not a forgiving one, at least. It seemed like I was living out some inevitability of my life. *See? Told ya!* They were gonna put you back where you belonged eventually. My head hurt and my eyes were tired. So, I walked straight from the car to my bed without eating or doing my homework. I don't think I'd ever been so tired. It was a drool-on-my-pillow, sinking stones kind of tired.

✿ ✿ ✿

When I finally finish sinking, I am standing in front of two paths in a humid forest. It is a place that will visit me for many nights to come. The path on the left has rocks and thorns, while the right one is lined with beautiful, glowing white flowers. Sometimes there's a person, like my mother, or Caro, standing in the flower path. Every time I try to reach them, I can't step onto the path. There's nothing in my way, but I just can't. So, I float with the wind on the left path, getting cuts and bruises and branches pulling on my hair, all the while seeing flowers through the trees on my right. I go deeper and deeper into this dark winding forest. The flower path always stays visible, though. And sometimes there's a ghost of me peeking through on the other side. I wonder if she's happier.

1

The Jacket

Chapter
Two

On New Churches

– Zeke

I hadn't stepped foot in a church since Ma's funeral. Thankfully, I never needed to until I got to Jersey City. When my aunt learned I could play the piano, I was drafted to fill in for their pianist who left for a cruise gig—it was more like being sacrificed, actually. I told her I hadn't played in a while. Eight months to be exact. I told her I had quit. The next day, a folder filled with sheet music was waiting for me on my mother's old bed in Auntie's spare room. It was lying next to a fresh church suit. A message from my father, keeping an eye on me from across the Atlantic. "Remember our deal."

Hanging out at the church wasn't so bad. I would never admit it to my father, but it was actually kinda nice, in an awful kinda way. From the outside, The New Testament Institute looked like an abandoned movie theater. Inside, though, it looked almost exactly like our church in Miami. Red carpet, squeaking wooden kneelers, all that. All churches seemed to be sites of worship to the same gods of gossip and keeping up appearances. Every glimpse into a group of worshippers telling as much of a story as the triptych paintings hanging behind Father Jon. All sorts of people—Haitian, Trini, Kenyan, Ghanaian, and of course, Jamaicans like us.

I sank my instrument into the background as best I could, blending into the tapestry. Much quieter than the altos in the choir who nearly busted my eardrums every practice. I don't think God was anywhere near their vocal cords. Sometimes they threw in a dash of Bob Marley along with the hymns. Switching any "unholy" words for *God* and *Jesus*. I got to hear Auntie sing. A few times, I swore I heard my mother's voice come out.

There wasn't as much in terms of theatrics, though. I only saw someone catch the spirit once and it only lasted a couple seconds. I assumed that's what Auntie was talking about when she complained about the ministry being too "Americanized." I didn't know what to do with myself when I wasn't playing.

Auntie wasn't quiet at all when we rehearsed. Church was basically her whole life. The baby she never had. Just like my mother's mayoral campaign had been hers. The whole congregation knew Miss Gale and she knew all of them and every juicy bit of news she could squeeze out. I watched how her circle of disciples doted on her as she floated throughout the building. They waited for her approval on a program layout or for her opinion on the rice and peas they served in the back room. Too much garlic apparently.

She would talk to me sometimes, but only briefly.

"How're you doing?"

"Good, Auntie."

"Hmm. Good."

She always seemed busy. Flying from one person to the next.

It took me a while to notice the stares I was getting. Even when I had small talk with anyone, it was like they were staring through me, past my face. At first, I thought they stared at me because I was a new arrival or because I was Gale's nephew. So, I decided not to take it personally.

After rehearsals, Auntie liked to call me over to show off to her friends.

"Looks just like his mother!" they would say each time, without fail. Not without adding, "Such a tragedy, God bless!" Which would eventually evolve into, "So talented! Not many boys playin' keys like that anymore, y'know?" And I would smile politely. And they would say, "Bless him, he's quiet, isn't he?" "It's them quiet ones you gotta watch out for!" And I wasn't sure what to say to that. I still hadn't been given the script all adults seemed to have.

Then, on the Saturday before school started, Auntie said she had to talk to me during dinner. It was just her and I sitting at one end of the long wooden table. Well, and her boyfriend, George, who was usually laid up on her couch watching TV. Every evening, we all sat and looked at each other, saying nothing. Like strangers. Until that Saturday.

"Can I ask . . . why you got jewelry on? Has your daddy given you that?" She asked it so suddenly, like an accusation.

"No," I mumbled with rice in my mouth. I put down my fork and looked down at my chest. "I don't know, I just . . . like wearing it, I guess."

"Hmm," was her reply.

I pulled on the gold around my neck.

"These were Ma's, actually," I elaborated. She leaned over and reached for my neck, passing the jewelry over with her thumbs. Her eyes glanced between the chains and my face, searching for something. Then she stood up and started putting dishes away.

When it was time for church the next morning, I finally saw what it was. The rings on my hands and my mother's gold necklaces and the teardrop earring on my right ear. That's what they were staring at. Nothing (and everything) to do with me.

I don't know what I was expecting. I guess I just thought— with everything that had happened, and with how old I was now (or how ancient I felt in my soul)—I guess I thought they'd be different now. After watching the way my dad changed . . . I thought the rest of them would change, too. Everything around the way I dressed and adorned my given body felt so massive before. It was everything before, so much that it drowned everything else out. Now, in the after time, it seemed smaller than ever. I kept forgetting it was even there. But, of course, it always was.

I told Auntie I wasn't feeling well and stayed home the following Sunday. The altos would have to make do without me.

Chapter Three

On Keeping It Together

– Rosie

High school had been a whole year and one semester of pure hell. Every fucking day. I had daydreams about the day I'd finally be able to leave this school with a middle finger in the air and never look back. Maybe light a cigarette and throw the lighter behind me on my way out.

The first day back from winter break started how every school day usually did: with Mami and Caro fighting. I came out of the bathroom and Mami was holding a pink razor above her head like it was contaminated with a rare disease.

"Yo hablo chino, eh?! Que lo que tu no entiende?" Mami's voice boomed loud enough to shake the Communion photos hanging in the living room. A receipt blew off our cluttered dining table and floated to the ground.

Caro was reaching desperately for the razor. She was wearing the brown corduroy skirt Mami bought her that went down to her knees. Even from far away, I could see the glisten on her calves. Mami telling us tall tales about how shaving would make the hairs grow back thicker was enough to keep my legs looking like a forest. But Caro was Caro, and she had her ways of making sure her secrets were always covered. Except this one.

"Why can't I shave my legs, though? It don't make no sense! More people gonna be lookin' at me if I got chewbacca on my knees than if I don't!" It was never good when my sister tried to be funny in front of Mami. I knew she couldn't help it, but I winced anyways. "We're gonna be late. What's gonna happen if I go out like this?"

"I don't care if you stay here all day, pero así no. You no go out así. You think you grown. Look at you! Haciéndome pasar vergüenza vestida así."

Caro looked at me incredulously for help and then back at Mami when I had nothing to offer her. I didn't understand the point of arguing, especially when I knew she probably had an outfit change in her backpack. She was extra like that.

"Vergüenza? *You* bought me this!" She tugged on her skirt. Then under her breath. "Crazy. She's crazy." She slammed our bedroom door behind her.

"Cuidao con esa puerta!" Mami warned. And then she wagged her finger and hit her with the classic. "When I die, you will think of this moment."

I rolled my eyes into the stratosphere.

It didn't matter what Caro said or however valid her argument points were. It never mattered when the two of them were so focused on representing their polar ideologies that they couldn't see they were both the exact same ridiculous person. So, it always ended the exact same. Caro walked out the front door with long khakis and the razor was delegated to the trash. I told her as we were walking to school that honestly, with her curves, the khakis were more revealing than the skirt anyways. Plus, it was brick cold outside.

January always felt like a new beginning and I was actually optimistic as we crossed the front entrance of the school. I had convinced Mami to buy me new rainbow pens and a new planner. Caro helped me put my hair in rollos the night before. I snatched it into a sleek curled pony. Not to mention, I had finally gotten my stupid pink braces off. Finally rid of the baby-cheeked version of myself from Lincoln Park Junior. I was kind of a whole new bitch.

But it was the same Westside.

I was in the same lower-level English class. The same lower-level History class. The same regular Biology class. The same regular Algebra II class. With the same room full of idiots whose go-to response was radio silence when the teacher asked a question and pointed to the answer on the board. Or giggled at the word *organism*. Okay, maybe *idiots* was a strong word. They weren't all idiots. Just mostly idiots. Most of my teachers were even bigger idiots. I guess I was an idiot, too. Because 80 percent of the time I kept my mouth shut and minded my business. And 99 percent of the time I felt 100 percent numb. Like my life was a really boring movie I was watching.

Before homeroom, I paid a visit to the guidance counselor's office. I had figured out that Mrs. Solis was in a better mood before 12:00 p.m. when the coffee was still fresh in her system. I think she secretly hated me because I came by her office so often. Still, she was my only route to getting what I wanted. A very stubborn, rocky route. I didn't even open my mouth before she put a hand up.

"Still no word from ITI. I'll let you know when I hear." She'd said the same thing verbatim before we'd left for winter break. In addition to advising me to *lower my expectations*.

"B-but Jess Warwick posted her acceptance on Facebook yesterday," I challenged her with the phone glowing in my hand. The smiling blond girl I presented to her was probably picking out her new classes as we spoke.

"She's a freshman, it's a whole different schedule. Plus she's top of her class, she's got AP credits, she's not like—it's just different. Be patient. If anything, there's always next year, honey." Mrs. Solis lifted her *Don't Talk to Me Before I've Had My Coffee* mug with a freshly manicured French acrylic set and looked past me. "Be with ya in just a sec, Marie!"

I'd had to beg her for months and scrap together three recommendation letters and save up all my wages from working at Lena's Salon and babysitting all summer. Not to mention having to somehow figure out Mami's convoluted tax papers, plus keeping up my grades, just to get Mrs. Solis to consider sending my application to the Innovation Technical Institute last semester. It was all I wanted for over a year now. Every atom of energy I had after all my obligations were met I poured into this one immovable goal. All the money that was ever mine I saved up to pay for whatever tuition was left over from the scholarships I'd applied for. Half that money wasted on application fees twice already.

I wondered if Jess Warwick was forced to do the same. I wondered how the hell she had AP credits when there was only one AP class offered and it was for seniors. I wondered a lot of things I wanted to hurl at Mrs. Solis like daggers, but I kept them hidden beneath my tongue. She looked up at me with impatience.

"Just one last question, sorry. Have you ever seen a kid get accepted to ITI their junior year?"

"No, I don't think I have, sweetie," she sighed.

"Cool." I closed the door behind me before remembering myself. "Have a great day!"

Amazing start.

And it just kept getting better.

After gym class, my own sweat broke through the gel in my hair, causing it to frizz up. I pulled a red bandana over my head to cover it. Then I had the thrill of running into Mr. Scaramucci, who had been promoted from assistant PE teacher to full-time health teacher last year despite confidently telling my gym class that girls pee from their vaginas. I don't know if all the gym teachers had a bet going or what, but they made it their mission to hang around the halls and give out pink slips for dress code violations. Caro called them "parking tickets," because they held the same level of nonsensical pettiness. They woke up every morning and chose to follow the hate in their hearts. And that morning, Scaramucci's hate led him to me. It was partially my own fault—I forgot to find a crowd in the hall to blend myself into.

"That's not appropriate," he said. I looked behind me, wondering who he was talking to.

"... What?"

He pointed at my bandana.

"This is a school, not one of your little gang things. Take it off."

Little gang things?

I was still stuck on trying to figure out what about my hair accessory was so scandalous. If I took off the bandana, I would look like an unkempt toddler for the rest of the day. I had my knockoff North Face beanie in my locker, but our new principal had added a rule that we weren't allowed to wear winter hats during school hours. Because that made sense when half the heaters don't work. Regardless, I was already sweating bricks after doing shuttle runs for half an hour in gym.

"There's nothing wrong with what I'm wearing." I stated the fact very plainly.

"It's distracting to your fellow students. This is a learning environment. It's inappr—" He put a clammy hand on my shoulder and I shrugged past him before he could finish.

"I'm gonna be late," I said. And I didn't look back. Not even when he called after me. Honestly, I kinda hoped he would forget about it. Foolish, naive Rosie.

By the time I got to Algebra II, there was a yellow slip on my desk. A Saturday. Maybe if I'd just stood there and shut up, I would have gotten a normal pink slip detention. Instead, I got a Saturday—where they sent the extra bad kids—and I shoved the yellow slip to the back of my locker, where I wanted to shove the useless tears that started blurring my vision. Where Mami would never find it.

I weighed the pros and cons of telling her for the rest of the day. I didn't tell Caro about it either. Not even when I sat with her friends at lunch. I did that sometimes, while I tried not to stare at Taylor Reese and Lovely-Marie Espejo and their Accelerated cult a couple tables down. My default place lately always seemed to be by my sister's side, even though her friends got on my nerves. We were closer and further apart than ever.

The thing was, I knew that Caro was the only person, really, who would always be there. Solid as the tiled floor beneath me. Not just because she was my sister, but because she owed me. She would always owe me.

I was about to tell her about the Saturday before her friend, Leidy, pointed a finger too close to this girl Marta's face. She kept doing it, too. I could tell the first shove was coming before Leidy even stood up, and took it as a sign to dip out into my next class.

As I walked, I heard the attending teacher blowing his whistle behind me like they always did when there was a fight. He didn't even bother stepping in to stop them. I don't know what teachers thought their little whistle was gonna do. For real, what was a whistle gonna do? Like Leidy was gonna hear it and snap back to a composed state like a ventriloquist act or a trained dog or something. Just stand up suddenly and go, "Oh my darn, was I punching you in the face? I am so sorry! Good golly, if it hadn't been for that whistle I don't know what I would've done!" Absurd.

After Stage Crew Club, I finally walked home alone with my earbuds in and my hands balled into fists in my pockets. All I could think about was how I would do it. How I would lie to Mami. I could say I was going to rehearsals for the musical on Saturday. Easy. I could even stop by the auditorium and organize the paint closet while I was there. That way it wasn't a total lie. Is lying by omission a lie? Even if she never had to know? Or would I actually be saving her some grief by not telling her? I mean, she had enough going on, really. Three jobs, two kids—one of them being Caro. Honestly, it was kinder not to tell her.

I walked past three men smoking outside the Salon on the corner of Westside and Duncan Ave and hopped up the three concrete steps on the side of the business.

"Damn, mami! You good?"

Ignoring the man with what I hoped was a stone-cold expression, I reached for the key in the pocket of my North Face coat. Another man let out a whistle. My sister would've had some smartass response to say. But she wasn't here. She was probably off somewhere with her boyfriend. I'd attempted to stall my encounter with that group of men by turning right instead of a left three blocks back. I was also taking full advantage of the fact that it was Wednesday, the "other" Lord's day. Mami was at choir practice until four. But God help us all if that woman came home to dirty dishes in the sink. I'd promised Caro I'd cover her chores before Mami got home, in exchange for a fresh five dollar bill I'd added to the coffee can under my bed labeled *Rosie's College Fund*. So, I had to come home eventually.

The final decision was not telling Mami about my yellow slip. I would simply come home, do the dishes, and keep my mouth shut. Saving myself, and my sister by default. There. All done.

I turned the key and slammed the door behind me. Every step up to the third floor brought another witty comeback to the man's catcall.

"Damn, mami! You good?"
"I'm sixteen, you?"
"Damn, papi! My dad's a boxer."
"(A slew of all the Spanish
swears I knew.)"
And my personal favorite, a lovely
hand gesture.

But it was too late now. It always was.

As soon as I closed the apartment door behind me and set down my backpack, it felt like all day my brain was unbridled static and now there was silence. An unsettling silence. But then came a familiar three-toned beep.

I unlocked the laptop on the dining table and opened my email.

Ms. Rosalina Rojas,

Due to our high volume of applicant each semester, we regret to inform you…

This feeling was not a new one. I was weary already of this damn feeling. This feeling I didn't know what to do with. This feeling that didn't quite fit comfortably in my hands. That rose like heat into the tips of my ears. It was something like anger. A quiet rage that betrayed my body's natural state and made me feel naked. So I did what I always did with anger when I had nowhere to put it. I put it in a jar in my mind, shut the lid tight, and put it on a shelf. I would stare at it from afar and let it sit for a while. And I would make a mental note to open it when I was ready. If I ever *would* be ready. Or I would pretend it didn't scare the shit out of me. Because it was a useless, stupid emotion. One I didn't have time for. Like regret or shame. One I refused to let overtake me and crash down on all I still had the chance to be.

As hard as I tried to clear them out, my mind was as cluttered with these little jars as our dining table was cluttered with Mami's mail and trash. Except there was no garbage for me to sweep them into. No way for me to tidy up whatever the hell was going on up there.

Chapter Four

On Homework

– Zeke

The first day of school was the first day of school. I didn't know what to say when Auntie picked me up and asked me about it except "Fine." She didn't ask past that. We walked home listening to the sounds of the city and avoiding patches of ice on the sidewalk. The gesture was nice, but I was too grown for an adult escort. I told her I'd walk by myself next time.

Westside Academy High School was a heavy name that sounded like it should be engraved in solid gold. But there were no uniforms or grand staircases or sculptures. Just a plain brick building, with piles of garbage outside of it. And kids who walked fast and had been there all year and knew where they were going. And then there was me. Second semester drop-in, Zeke Parish. I could go a while without hearing my full name again.

This is Zeke Parish.... Is it Zeke or Ezekiel?

Welcome our new classmate, Ezekiel Par-eesh.

Say hello to Ezeekal Parish, all the way from sunny Miami. Bet you wish you were there now, right Z?

I hadn't given Mr. Giordio permission to call me Z, so that was a fun thing to look forward to for the rest of the semester. Now I was Z. A letter.

Another fun thing was that I got lost not one, not two, but *three* times. No one had given me any instructions to go with the flimsy schedule they handed me at the front desk. In the movies, they assigned the new kid a buddy or something to help them get acclimated. Not at Westside. There were all these letters and numbers that meant absolutely nothing to me. First, I went to E202 instead of F202. Then my schedule ripped in half and I spent too many minutes looking for V115 before I realized there was no V wing of the school (it was a *W*). By the time I found W115, I was too embarrassed to go in. I just stood outside the door and waited for the bell to ring.

I was never good at school in Miami, either. That's why I went to an arts high school where all my classes were on the same floor and we took classes like The History of Bright Colors and I could just say, "Sorry, I was at rehearsal," anytime I was late, and no one batted an eyelash. It wasn't like I was dumb or anything. I just don't like rules. You poke most rules with enough questions and they just stop making any sense. A small part of me hoped a change of scenery might help me . . . I don't know. Become a different person, I guess.

But like every New Year's midnight I've ever known, neither time nor place seem to make much difference. I was mostly the same as I was yesterday. The same Zeke my mother used to say would lose my arm if it wasn't attached. It was depressingly anticlimactic.

At lunch, a girl with bright purple braids and shiny lip gloss from my Biology class invited me to sit with her friends. She acted like she'd won a prize when I said yes. Her name was something like Tiffany or Stephanie. She asked me if I was Trini because she had a cousin with my last name. I told her no, and that I was Jamaican. She asked if I was mixed. I said no, just Jamaican. Technically, Gran was from Panama, so I was part Panamanian. But I didn't feel like sharing that. It seemed like it was important information. I guess I could've lied and said I was part British or something. I *wish* I'd lied, actually. Maybe I would've had a more interesting day. I sat through thirty more minutes of them asking me questions about Miami and commenting on how I "don't talk much, huh?" Still didn't know what to say to that. I felt like in my brain I talked a lot, actually. I wish I knew how to shut up.

Towards the end of the period, the whole cafeteria dimmed to a whisper after a girl pushed this other girl against a trash can. My jaw hit the floor. It was shocking to me that nobody stepped in—not the lunch staff or the teacher assigned to monitor the room. They just stood and watched, looking almost bored. A guy came out of nowhere and shoved the pushing girl back as he helped the trash can girl, and the pushing girl shoved her boot into the guy's torso. The three of them got entangled and started getting some nasty licks in.

Shouting swear words. People cussed a lot more than at my last school. Even the teachers, sometimes. A lot of them saying words that started with *N* despite being a lighter complexion than the palm of my hand. It was more bewildering to me than offensive. My mom wouldn't let me be caught dead saying any of those words. I still couldn't. Every time I tried, her own words spun a loop in my head. *We have to be better than them.*

I wished someone would have filled me in on the obvious drama because there was plenty of it fueling this cafeteria fight. When I tore my eyes away and looked to my side, I found Stephanie or Tiffany standing on our lunch table with her phone pointed at the action. The scene didn't last very long, five minutes tops. Then the players were carried away by security officers as the lunch bell rang. The rest of the day, the fight was all anyone could talk about. I guess I could have told Auntie about the fight on our walk home, but then she would have worried. And then Dad would have worried.

They must pump sleeping gas or something into the hallways because I couldn't have felt more tired towards the end of the day. All the travel and the newness had caught up with me. I gave in and closed my eyes in Algebra II (honestly, I don't know how I was the only one—our teacher literally had the tranquilizing voice of Bob Ross). When I woke up there was a thick folder on my desk with the syllabus and the homework I had to make up. Mr. Bob Ross hadn't even bothered to wake me up, he just left the classroom with the rest of the class when the bell rang. Which was a cold move. I couldn't decide whether I hated him or admired him.

And so I was late for the third time.

When I got back to the apartment that used to be my grandmother's, I stuffed a full backpack under the desk that used to be my mother's, and stared at it from the bed I slept on that didn't yet feel like mine.

I stared.

And stared.

And stared.

Until the edges of the world blurred away.

And I wondered how I got here. Or why I'd asked for this. Because I *had* asked for this. When my dad's gran, who I'd hardly known, got sick in London, and he sat me down to talk about moving across the ocean, I asked for *this*. For him to move and for me to stay with the aunt who'd come down to Florida to stay with us from (what I thought was) New York City. So the adults in my life shifted worlds to make it happen. I hardly even thought about it. My guidance counselor had to have told me that there was more than the average homework involved in transferring to a regular school hundreds of miles away midway through the year. That the school my dad was looking at in London had a far better reputation and music program. But I didn't want a music program. That was the whole point. I just wanted to leave and be alone.

It was too much, being chained to him in that big house, with her paintings and her antique furniture and her piano where I endured biweekly torture putting on a show for her politician friends. It was too much to see it empty. It was too much to see the disappointed look on his face every day. I couldn't think of anything else except being somewhere where I could be completely alone. Where I wasn't doted on or casually therapized over what everyone seemed to think was wrong with me. Anything else, I'd thought, would be a future Zeke problem.

So here I was. Future Zeke. Staring at my backpack.

I didn't even believe in homework on a fundamental level. The word *homework* doesn't even make sense. Home is home and work is work. After six hours of working (for free), why should I do work at home? I'm not a teacher, but I gotta go home and do their job for two or three extra unpaid hours? And now they were making me do work from when I wasn't even there? It was ridiculous. I couldn't possibly give in to something this fucking ridiculous.

On the other hand, maybe future Zeke wasn't as principled as old Zeke. Maybe future Zeke did his homework as soon as he got home like a good boy. Like the son my mother wanted me to be. The person she always seemed to see that I never measured up to. The one she talked about in her campaign speeches. Maybe future Zeke wanted to do his homework on time, and join a group of friends that go out every weekend, and be decent at a sport, and go to college for something fancy, and be dumb and happy and *normal*—whatever the fuck that was.

I opened my backpack and took out the Algebra II folder. Flipping quickly through the pages and pages of foreign numbers and letters.

On the other other hand, I thought about how old Zeke had slipped through ninth grade just fine. And he came home every day, took a fat nap, and stayed up late watching reruns of *Living Single* with Gran snoring beside me.

I chose old Zeke for now.

Until it was nighttime, and Auntie was calling me into the kitchen for dinner.

Chapter Five

On Finding Out

– Rosie

As I stood over the sink washing dishes with music blasting in my ears, I felt a chill creep up my neck. It was more than just the eeriness of being home alone. There was a breeze coming in from somewhere. I put down the cup I was washing and began walking towards the hall. I stopped short in the middle of the hallway as cold trickled up my ankles. The door to my mother's room was open a crack. It was forbidden territory, but one I'd often ventured into and stolen chocolates from. I drew up the courage to push the door further, inviting a blast of icy air to smack me across the face as it made its escape.

Coño. I let out an exasperated sigh. From time to time, Mami was always sneaking a smoke in private before pretending to hate it in public. Which was fine. Well, it wasn't, but whatever. She wasn't the one who mailed the checks to PSE&G to pay the gas bill—I was. Shit wasn't cheap.

I stepped in, careful not to knock over any photos or saintly candles on Mami's dresser. It smelled like Vivaporú in here.

Ugh. There was a load of laundry sprawled across her bed along with some mail and checks from Lena's Salon where she worked on the weekends. I diverted my attention to the paint-chipped window. My fingertips clasped both bottom edges and pulled a little to the left before dragging straight down with all their strength. A tried-and-true method. Worked every time.

Dust flew up as the window slammed and the glass sent out shivering vibrations. Something moved in the corner of my eye. Saint Anthony was making a break for it, tilting back and forth. Taunting me.

In a panic, I took two lightning strides forward with outstretched arms to rescue him. My sneaker decided to stay underneath a wooden floorboard while my body soared through the dust-filled space. I managed to see that Saint Anthony had leveled himself—a miracle—before my whole face hit the uneven, wine-colored floor and the room went black.

I groaned into the floorboards.

The beginnings of a bruise were forming on the right side of my forehead as I slowly found my feet. My right puma was still wedged under the floorboard. I really didn't have time for this. A sink full of unwashed dishes still called my name.

I tugged and tugged at the sneaker, with no luck. That's when I tried prying the floorboard up. To my surprise, the whole thing came out of its place with one jerk. I jumped back. What the hell? There were wads of newspaper crammed under there. All yellowed and from a publication called *El Inquisitor.* I couldn't help myself. I sat down and reached to examine them further. My fingers felt something solid underneath the newspaper wrappings.

I gently unraveled the package and found a silver gift box. At first, I thought it might be my mother's secret cigarette stash. The lid came up and revealed something even more scandalous. Weathered photos of scantily clad women. I mean, some real baddies. Their clothes indicated they were deep in the eighties. I knew Caro would love to steal a couple of their looks and wear them today. They all wore matching leather jackets and had perfectly permed hairdos. Some of them weren't even wearing bras. One had an armful of tattoos. I ravaged through the collection, forgetting anything related to the time and space in which I sat.

There was a ripped envelope addressed to my mother. Inside was a signed picture of a young Ricky Martin with writing on the back. *Felicidades! Tu Querida Hermana, Yolanda. 342 Amber Lane, Kew Gardens, Queens, NY.* Attached to this via paperclip was a wallet-sized photo with a ripped corner, exhibiting a group of about ten of these women posing in front of some motorcycles, and what looked like a bar. I slipped the relic out and flipped it over, wondering what their stories were, and what they were doing in my mother's floor. On the back was her distinctive cursive handwriting. *Mis hermanas.* I turned it back to the front, puzzled. Then the pieces fell into place. Riding atop a shiny black motorcycle, with ripped stockings and a flower tattoo on her right shoulder: a face that looked eerily like my own. Except, it couldn't possibly be.

The front door locks clicked. My head snapped up.
Shit. Shit. Shit.

Chapter
Six

On Secrets

– Caro

Okay, red jacket! I see you! You good, mami?"

"I ain't ya mother! No me joden!"

My red Js kicked dust past the familiar three concrete steps and turned the corner. I slid my way through the narrow bricked alleyway and grabbed the plastic tote bag I'd hidden behind a dumpster. Holding it in one hand, I used the other to pull down on the fire escape ladder as slowly as possible. I removed my shoes to keep them from creasing. After expertly climbing up to the third window like the ex-athlete I was, I stopped on the platform and lightly tapped on the glass four times. Hopefully, not too loud.

While I waited, I licked my thumb and cleaned my Jordans. I knew Mami must be home from church by now. I'd really messed up this time. It wasn't my fault JJ decided to get handsy in his car on the way back from his house, after I was handsy in his house after we fought, because he was liking a random girl's Instagram post. Hopefully, Rosie had been covering, as promised. I hoped the smell of cigarette smoke wasn't still lingering in my hair. If it was, I could say it came from the goofy ass herbs standing outside who'd stared at me like I was a walking breast.

"Que lo que, loca?" Rosie greeted me at the window with a judgmental look. Always so judge-y, that one.

"Sup, dumbass?" I tossed my red shoes.

"Hurry up and be quiet," my sister lowered her voice. "Mami's home. She's already mad cause I didn't finish the dishes—"

"YOU DIDN'T—"

"SHH! What'd I just say?"

I rolled my eyes and hopped through the window. We'd agreed before school that she'd take my turn of the chores in exchange for five bucks I'd stolen from JJ's wallet. I quickly slipped off my ripped leggings and scarlet tube top while Rosie fished out a respectable turtleneck and lengthy skirt out of our shared closet. As Rosie tossed the garments, she explained the situation. When our mother had arrived moments ago, she lied that I was taking a shower. Then, she snuck into the bathroom and left the water running.

"Guao! Mira que smart!" I teased.

Mami was in the kitchen now, preparing dinner and muttering about how no one in this house ever helped her with anything. She was always talking to ghosts, that lady.

"I'll go open and close the bathroom door and then tell her you're in here changing."

Once I got it all off, I balled up and stuffed my heathen outfit into the back of our closet. Rosie, about to make her exit, paused and turned around. "Oh. And I got something to tell you." She left the mystery on the other side of a gently-closed baby pink door.

Spending half a second in suspended wonder, I exhaled before I continued changing into my third outfit of the day. *Got something to tell me?* I pulled on my nun clothes. *What something?* I pulled my hair in the bun it was in before I'd left for school this morning and sprayed some cheap, off-brand perfume into it to get the smell of JJ out. *What, was Rosie pregnant?* I wiped the lipstick off my lips—what was left of it anyways. After I processed the thought, I stifled a laugh. Like that would ever happen. You had to have sex to get pregnant.

One last glance in the mirror and I was ready for the furious force that swung open the bedroom door. One hundred and fifty-five pounds of stubborn woman stood in the doorway with two tight fists adorning her hips. I suddenly felt like a matador fending off a bull. No sudden movements.

"Cuantas veces te tengo que decir que no me cierres esta puerta?! Por dios!" Her high-pitched voice pounded my eardrums. That was her greeting to me. *Hi Mami, nice to see you! How was your day? Mine was great, thanks!*

"Sorry, Mami," I presented my most innocent smile as I fixed the folds of my church skirt.

The woman still had a scowl on her face. Her accusing eyes lasered through every corner of the room, searching for a flaw. They stopped their gaze right above my head.

"Why that window is open? Eh? U'tede no saben lo que e dinero!" I let go of the breath I'd been holding in my lungs, then turned to shut the window. "Go help your sister with the dishes. Me voy. I'm going to the súper to buy tomatoes and las viejitas from church are joining us for dinner. I want those dishes done and the table cleared before I get back, okay? Ya saben!" Mami warned me with a pointed finger before turning to leave.

I took a moment to thank my lord and savior Jesus Christ. Then, I got up to join my sister in the crowded kitchen where several pans were left sizzling on the stove. We talked while she scrubbed and I dried.

"So, what happened with your mans?" Rosie chided. Sometimes I thought I caught a hint of jealousy hidden under her disapproving tones.

"Nothing, of course. I'm a good Christian woman." I giggled through my words as she rolled her eyes. Rosie loved to roll her eyes. I knew damn well that my sister didn't wanna hear nothing about JJ. I hated when she kept me in suspense like this. "So? What did you have to tell me?"

Rosie's eyes lit up. She revealed the scandal she'd uncovered in our mother's room. The photograph of a rebellious Mami in front of a bar, with her distinctive handwriting on the back. As I pictured what she was telling me, I shook my head. It was impossible. I refused to believe it. It had to have been someone else. Mami was always telling us bullshit stories about how she was always the respectful, pious daughter of a priest. That a life in the church was our birthright, just like it was hers. And why shouldn't she expect her daughters to be just as dutiful as she was?

No, it had to be someone else.

But Rosie insisted. She glanced around the kitchen and peered out the tiny window, as if our mother's piercing eyes were hidden somewhere watching us. Then she reached into the back pocket of her loose acid wash jeans and slid out the yellowed photograph. Proof.

My jaw was on the floor. "Well, ain't that a bitch?"

I *still* couldn't believe it. It didn't even look like the same woman. By the looks of it, our holy saint of a mother was in some sort of biker gang as a teenager. She was at a bar. With alcohol. And cigarettes. And sin. And a fucking tattoo on her shoulder. How? How was that even possible?

"Are you sure she doesn't have a twin she's been keeping from us?"

"That would be a novela-level plot twist," Rosie replied. "No, I've seen her birth certificate." She'd clearly already thought about this in depth. I searched through every detail of the photo. I don't know what I was looking for. Clues, I guess. "There's more. This was attached." She took out a larger photo with writing scribbled across it.

"Is that . . . baby Ricky Martin?"

"From Menudo, yes."

My mind went in a million directions. Blackmail was the most compelling direction. The barely dressed woman in that photo had no place telling her daughter not to go out on a

Saturday night. I could save it for a rainy day. Or I could choose chaos and leak it in the church ladies' Facebook group. That could be fun.

Rosie put a stop to what she already saw brewing in my mind.

"We should just ask her about it. I know she's not always . . . understanding, or . . . truthful? But I think if we have proof—"

I shut it down right away. Naive, naive little sister. Sometimes I felt like we were on the same team, and other times it was like she was off on an island all her own.

"No way. We have the upper hand. We should—oh my god!" I whipped a damp towel across her shoulder and ignored her yelp. A smile spread across my face as the realization came. "We have to go!"

"Go where?"

I pointed to the address on the back of Ricky's photo.

"Didn't you have to write an essay about family gossip for your ITI thingy? Let's go to the source."

"Not gossip. They wanted you to write about your family history."

"History, gossip—same thing. You want the truth or nah?" It was crazy that I had to spell out something so obvious to Miss *Little Einsteins*. Information for her, security for me. At worst, a quick trip to the city and we still had the photo for personal use. I nudged my sister until I saw her big brown eyes sparkle and those little hamster wheels start turning.

There she was. My Rosie. The girl with a plan.

Chapter Seven

On Hidden Gems

– Zeke

When the sun grazed across my eyelids on the first Saturday morning after the first week of school, I squinted them open and smiled. Then I pulled my covers over my head again and dug my ass deeper into my bed. There was something sweet about a Saturday morning—especially this one. Finally, time could move slowly again.

Twice, I heard Auntie yell that breakfast was on the table. And twice I ignored her. When I heard her leave out of the front door, I finally lifted the covers and stretched my legs. I thought how Auntie must hate me. I might hate me if I was her. A kid just thrown at her, eating all her food that she paid for, can't be bothered to do anything but sleep all day. Yeah, I would hate me. I didn't want her to hate me. I was grateful, I just didn't know how to show it. She was my Auntie. She was family. Some of the only family I had left. You don't have to thank family for being family. For taking care of you. That's what they're supposed to do. But I was grateful anyway. From a distance.

I walked through the empty apartment and enjoyed the stillness. Occasionally there was a honking horn or the sound of footsteps upstairs. But there was beauty in the silence between. When life's ineffable conductor raised her arms. And there was beauty in the way the light filtered into the main room through the window, exposing sparkling dust as it floated through the air.

After I ate the fried plantins and fried eggs she'd left for me at the table, I decided to grab my headphones and do the dishes.

✿ ✿ ✿

There was nothing good on TV.

You could do your homework? Or just start it?

I laughed out loud. I was the funniest person I knew, honestly. This fucking dude.

Instead, I quickly flipped through my notebook for the old photo of Gran that I'd taped to one of the middle pages. She was standing somewhere in New York City, in front of a river, looking glamorous and young and pointing to a tiny statue in the distance. She told me it was the Hudson River and that it smelled like doo-doo. That was the word she used. *Doo-doo.*

I eventually decided to put some outside pants on. Then I grabbed my coat and my keys and stepped through the front door. And now I was out there, in the world. Like a person. Zeke Parish—human person. I didn't really have a destination in mind, I just walked in the general direction of downtown. That's what I'd done most afternoons. I'd walk around in giant circles marveling at piles of snow until I couldn't stand the cold anymore, and then I would speed-walk home.

My hands started to feel like balls of static so I stuffed my hands into my coat pockets. To my surprise, I felt something in my right pocket. When I pulled my right hand out, a twenty-dollar bill came with it. My first thought was: *Auntie.* I tried to rack my brain about whether or not she owed me twenty dollars. Or what the money might be for. Maybe she'd told me what it was for while I was asleep. So many holes in my cheese brain.

I put the money back where it was and nearly ran over a small pink child escaping their mother on the street. And then instead of turning right onto Colgate Street—like I'd done three times before—I turned left. That's how I ended up in front of Brownstone Vintage. Whoever named the store had done a great job. It looked like a storefront out of a Miyazaki film. Just ancient and ornate and brown with gold lettering.

There was an older Black man sitting at the register by the window. His eyes met mine. So, I was stuck in this now. I had no choice but to walk in.

"Afternoon, young man," his voice was rough but warm.

"Hello," I nodded towards him.

"See something you like?"

"Yea, it's a beautiful store. You the owner?"

He let out a laugh that let me know he was someone's uncle. "I wish."

My eyes drifted away to the contents of the store. There was a lot of it. It was . . . eclectic. Almost dizzying. I didn't know where to look. When I looked up, I saw that there were gold frames in all sizes pasted on the checkerboard ceiling.

"You lookin' for something?" the man asked.

"No," I put my hands up in defense. I didn't want to disappoint him, but I was sure I couldn't afford to spend any money. Especially not here. I think I saw some Picasso sketches framed on the floor. And there was a giant case of vintage jewelry beside me. "No, just . . . looking."

"Aight, lemme know if you need anything." He opened a newspaper and slid back into his chair.

I made my way around the store, trying not to touch anything. There was one aisle in the back full of church hats. I dared to flip the tag on a suede fedora that looked like something my dad would wear. Not too bad. Fifty bucks. I don't know how, but the old man must've seen me reach for the hat.

"That's from the 1959 film production of *Porgy and Bess* with Sidney Poitier. That was one of the hats he wore in the movie. A real nice hat," the old man shouted over from the front of the store. His voice carried through the aisles. I looked around for the camera he must've been watching me on, but I couldn't find it. Sydney Poitier. I recognized the name from someone in my fifth-grade class doing a project on him for our week on Miami idols. Apparently he was Bahamian and born in Miami. Like me. (The Miami part, not the Bahamian part.) And my gran was in love with him. Maybe that's why I remembered him. I flipped the tag again. Fifty bucks? Really? That was it?

I looped around the store one more time, pretending like I was really mulling over my decision. And like I had more than a twenty-dollar bill in my pocket. Then, finally, I noticed the man crouch down for something under his desk and I made a beeline for the door.

"Hold up, son," the old man's voice stopped me. I was starting to think this man was psychic or something. "Just so you know, we got a sale going on this weekend only. If you're interested." He pointed to the cardboard box on the floor next to the register. On top of a large stack of magazines was an *Ebony* cover. I couldn't resist. I *was* interested. How did he know?

Flipping through were issue after issue of *Ebony, Cosmopolitan, Jet,* and a couple copies of *New York Times Magazine.* 1945, 1962, 2004, 1956, on and on and on. I flipped through the 1965 *Ebony* and almost gasped at the pages and pages of old '50s-style ads with gorgeous Black people buying soap and Coca-Cola. I flipped through the covers of Diana Ross, and Oprah, and Sammy Davis Jr. and on and on. The kind of covers I used to imagine my own self on. I felt like I was eight years old and someone just handed me a pillowcase full of candy. I could barely contain myself. But I tried.

At the bottom of the box, I felt something hard and heavy. I brought it into view and thumbed over an intricately carved wooden ring, with a pink pendant, that matched the stone on one of my mother's necklaces that hung across my neck.

Clearly, a sign. One I hoped the old man hadn't noticed as I slipped it back in between the folds of a *Cosmopolitan.*

"How much for the whole box?"

"How much you got?"

I stepped out of Brownstone Vintage twenty bucks poorer and a hundred years richer. I just prayed Auntie wouldn't ask me about the money.

Chapter Eight

On Cute Boys in Hallways

– Zeke

During lunch, while Tiffany or Stephanie droned on about the guy she was texting, I fell into fixating over a poem I started in Miami. My arm strategically placed to cover it from the view of everyone else at the table.

What are feelings, to a Pisces.
My body cannot contain all it has survived
Of late and pulling from past
I can only hold so many opposites within my ribs
Before feeling opposed to myself.
"If you don't know how you feel, who does?"
How can you know yourself so well
I can't, I don't know why I am
I am and I figure it only from crumbs of clues
In Frank lyrics and sampled musings
I don't know why or who put them there
I don't know that I don't know

It's unbearable, the weight of existence
I am not a god, I'm just an oblivious ant
Too small to hold anything but direction
With a mission that hopefully ends with you.

. . . .

I thought about how my life so far was marked by periods of time I spent obsessing.

Most of elementary school was marked with pirates and pirate history, after I read *Treasure Island* and made my parents buy dozens and dozens more books. Crying when my mom got me a pirate costume for Halloween when I'd explicitly told her I wanted to be a mermaid. I dropped pirates as soon as I logged onto Neopets. Which led to my Sims phase. Then there was jazz, my sole escape during piano lessons modeled to worship a bunch of dead white men. And then it became the thing I could do better than anyone else. Pretty soon, jazz was all I had time for. It was the only time my mother saw me. Her perfectly poised eyes, inspecting me from the audience. Jazz was the pride in her voice when she placed a hand on my back and told people, "This is my son. He's gonna play at Carnegie Hall one day."

And then I looked out at an empty seat in the crowd one day and the pressure on my back was gone.

So, what was the point?

I snuck away to poetry slam nights and got really into smoking. Mostly for the aesthetic. Like all poets, I was now obsessed with a singular topic. Love. So for a couple months that was who I was. Zeke, the angsty poet who lost himself in other people. He was pretty exhausting. Once death visited again and I was finally completely alone, my only obsession was making life make sense.

In the hospital, I once asked Ma how she knew she was in love with Dad. It was a question I asked because I realized I didn't know who my mother was. And I wanted to know her. To redeem her. Too late, maybe. But better than not at all.

They'd met at a community college class. She said she knew something was up when her blood boiled at the sight of him. He irritated her. Always arguing the opposite point she made in class just to spite her. She couldn't stand him, to the point she knew she had given him control of some part of her. So when he asked her out, she said yes. But it was when Dad said one night that he would build her a house, and she believed him—that's when she knew it was love. And they stayed that way until the end. My mother, the badass lawyer. My father, the renaissance man turned truck driver. It was a good story. The kind I loved reading about. "Find someone who'll build a house out of their love, baby." She'd looked intently into my eyes when she said this. Like she knew something I didn't. It was a rare moment of softness from her. Too soft. For once, no trace of coercion or expectation in her voice. It was how I knew she'd be gone soon. In the darkest depths of my stomach. I just knew.

Tiffany or Stephanie reached over for my notebook and I slammed it shut.

"What are we hiding, Ezekiel Parish?" She giggled like we were playing a game.

"Nothing," I said, looking up at the clock.

"So mysterious . . ." She winked at me.

As I walked through the halls alone, I kept seeing hands enveloped in hands and longing looks between couples and friends falling over each other in laughter. I wondered if that was the key to everything. A chiseled jaw. A long eyelash. A fresh cut. Sometimes they stared back—maybe because of how I dressed or because I was new. I didn't really care. That's all I needed to form a novella-length fan fiction of us going on adventures together at three a.m. running around a park reenacting scenes from *Love & Basketball*. By the end of the first week I would learn most of their names. Martin, J, Christoph, Raquel, Zafaela. . . . Seeds of possibility I only sowed from a distance. Because I could never dare act on it. And besides, it seemed like they all already had people of their own. Entire solar systems that didn't include me.

I thought things would be different here, but the same pain in my stomach followed me from a thousand miles away. Everyone with their person or tight-knit crew. It seemed that was the thing—finding your person. I was lucky enough to have a whole person all to myself once. But now I was somehow portaled into the future and it was just me. Zeke, the loner. The part that was left over. Floating around trying to attach myself to something. Not just anything—something bigger. Life-changing, hopefully. I felt like I'd already lived a thousand lives and still I was woefully behind in this one area of being human.

Now I was in the part of my story where all the suffering was supposed to mean something. So, I walked around in this new life, waiting for something to strike me. While I waited, I had me and my fantasies and cute boys in hallways. Taking me far away from this poorly maintained building before I returned back to earth with a generous amount of late slips.

✿ ✿ ✿

The same way I never told her about the fights, I never told Auntie anything about school or the late slips. It seemed like it was my problem to handle. When I came home on Friday, she was frying patties in the kitchen.

"Almost forgot—your father sent you twenty dollars in the mail. You find it? I left a note in your pocket," she said casually, over the sound of sizzling oil.

My hand instinctively clasped around the ring on my thumb. It had been almost a week since I had gone into Brownstone Vintage. I'd almost forgotten about the money. Why did she take so long to tell me about this?

"Uh yeah. I put away the money but I couldn't read the note. What did it say?" Sometimes it scared me how little time it took for a lie to enter my brain and leave my mouth. I swear, I didn't mean to.

"Babies needa learn cursive. Dying art," Auntie muttered under her breath and kissed her lips. "He wanted you to go get a haircut for school. Told him it was a bit late for that. You should go soon." She pointed a fork up at the tight curls on my head.

I started calculating how much money I had left in the emergency envelope Dad had given me before he took off. Then, I wondered how I would make the twenty bucks back. Dad was anal about money. Even back when we had plenty of it. I waited for Auntie to elaborate, letting the air hang between us. Eventually, I caved, hoping my voice didn't sound too desperate.

"Aight, sure, I'll go this weekend. What barber's decent round here?"

"Hmmm . . ." Auntie paused as she handed me a plate of three steaming-hot patties. "Dunno about decent but there's a barber at Lena's that gets a lot of attention. Two blocks down on Duncan." She pointed to the wall on the left side of the room, as if that general direction meant anything to me.

As I was about to take my first bite, the house phone rang.

"Could you get that, nephew?"

I put the patty down, walked into the living room, and picked up the phone.

"Hello?"

I heard static on the other end, then a familiar voice.

"Ezekiel! I finally catch you!"

"Hey, Daddy. How's Grandma Lynn? How's the road there?"

"Long and black. Same everywhere. You get a haircut yet, hippie boy?"

I didn't not notice him deflecting from the grandma topic.

It felt like an eternity since I'd last spoken to my dad. After moving to London, he'd settled in with his mother and finally started training for his truck driving job today. At least that's what he'd said in our WhatsApp chats. Honestly, we talked more now that we were apart than we ever did together.

"No, I was thinking of dyeing it rainbow colors. Really go all in," I teased. I heard my dad laugh. Even through the static, his warm, melodious baritone came through. I was glad we could laugh now.

"I'm not gonna stop you, boy. Might dye my locs to match. How's school?"

"Long and boring. Same old."

"How can a new place be old?" In another life, my father was a philosopher.

"It's not like I'm in a different country. It's all the same. It's colder here, though."

"Ah, New York *is* a completely different country. You've much to learn."

"New Jersey." I corrected.

"Same thing," he said solemnly. And then there was silence. I could hear the sound of car horns in the distance. My father let out a sigh over the phone. Then he continued.

"Let me know if you need more money. And put any change you get back in the envelope." How quickly he'd shifted back into dad-mode. It seemed unlikely that I'd find a good haircut for less than twenty bucks. "Let me chat at your auntie."

"Okay." I tried hard to think of anything else I had to say to him. In the two weeks since we last spoke, it seemed like everything and nothing had happened. "Bye, Dad. Love you."

"Bye, Ezekiel. Love you more. Be good."

Good.

I was trying.

Chapter Nine

On Detention

– Rosie

When I stepped into the room listed on my yellow slip, I waited for fifteen whole minutes before the teacher—an elderly man who was half asleep—told me there was a clerical error and that I was in the wrong room. Because, of course, there was a clerical error.

By the time I finally walked into N213 late nobody seemed to care. Why would they? It was Saturday and we were in this prison of a school; tardiness wasn't at the top of anyone's mind. Though, a part of me was afraid they'd make me come back next week. Typical Westside.

Mr. Bard was attending the new detention room. He'd been my history teacher freshman year. I was a little embarrassed for him to see me here. But not too embarrassed. Mr. Bard was the kind of teacher who would play us movies for class every day if he could. He loved to use our class time to complain about how his dating life was going. There was a running gag amongst his students about the color of his ties corresponding to the way the dates went. Red meant it went well. Black meant he bombed. And a special American flag swirl was dubbed the "fuck tie" . . . because . . . you know. Again, I was only a little embarrassed.

"Finally snap, Rojas?" he asked, as he marked my attendance on a clipboard. The words didn't register at first. My eyes were lost in the clipboard wishing I could ask him to give me a receipt in case they made another "clerical error." It seemed like he was expecting a response.

"Huh?"

"It was a joke. What'd you get in trouble for? Forgetting to pay back a library fee?" I never laughed at any of Mr. Bard's jokes when I was in his class. Not even the funny ones, as a matter of principle. Drove him crazy. I glared back at him and his black tie.

"No. Apparently, I was distracting students with my "gang-affiliated" bandana, so . . . guess I won't be getting that tear-drop tattoo." I looked around the room. Five kids sat scattered around. Two of them were sleeping on their desks. Two were on their phones. One of them was holding up a magazine over his face. I thought I heard a muffled laugh.

"Ah. Of course," he said. "Well, sit anywhere you want." Mr. Bard sat back into his seat at the front of the room and slipped on a pair of oversized headphones. Of course.

I sat down near the window next to magazine boy. This was much calmer than I thought a Saturday detention would go. Still, my leg wouldn't stop bouncing up and down. I wished

I'd remembered to bring my own earbuds from home. I set out my History textbook and my notebook and my set of colored pens and highlighters to calm me down. But when I looked down at the book, none of the words stuck. I read the same sentence twelve times and all I could think was a loop of *Tu Querida Hermana, Yolanda. We regret to inform you... Tu Querida Hermana, Yolanda.*

"Yo, did you just *break* a pen? Are you, like, a serial killer?"

The boy next to me uncovered his face to reveal his shock. I could see now that he'd been reading a *Cosmopolitan* magazine. Bold choice. I looked down at the blue ink splattered on my hands. Damn. That was my favorite pen.

"No. Sorry."

"What are you apologizing for?"

"I don't know . . . for existing, I guess." I whispered. But it seemed like the boy heard me, because he chuckled. I reached into my backpack for a pack of wet wipes and started to clean my hands.

"Do I know you from somewhere? You look familiar. You got a cousin in Miami, maybe?" That's when I finally saw the kid sitting next to me. It was Zeke, the new kid. Well, the newest kid. We had so many come and go at this school, it was hard to keep track. Sometimes I walked through the hallways and didn't recognize a single face. There were way too many people (honestly, I wouldn't have minded a plague). Zeke stood out among the crowd, though. I don't know how I didn't recognize the sound of all that jewelry clinking around earlier.

"No." I rolled my eyes at his question. "Algebra II?" Zeke stared at me blankly. Was I really that forgettable?

". . . Yeah? I take Algebra II, too?"

"I'm in your class, dude. I sit right next to you. I wrote all your notes in that folder Mr. Samy gave you? Color-coded all the problems by level of difficulty? Gave you a note with my name and email in case you had questions? Nothing? You don't remember me at all?"

"Ah, you're a Capricorn."

"How did you know that?" I said this a little too loud, prompting Mr. Bard to lift his headphones and look in our direction.

"Come on, Rojas. I get it, you kids are flirting or whatever, but keep it to a whisper, please. Thank you!" Our teacher slid back into his chair and closed his eyes. If my cheeks ever decided to turn red, that would've been the cue. I looked back at Zeke with my question still lingering.

"I mean, I could tell from your whole . . . vibe." Zeke gestured vaguely towards me as he whispered out the words. "It's kind of obvious. There's a sprinkle of Aries in there, but otherwise you're textbook Cap. I'm Zeke, by the way." He stuck out a hand like he was a businessman. Which confirmed my suspicions. This kid was weird. I took his hand anyway.

"I know," I said. Duh. "I'm Rosie."

Zeke nodded before freezing for a moment.

"Wait, your name is Rosie Rojas? Like Rose Red? Red Rose? For real?"

". . . Yes." I was surprised he put that together so quickly.

He was staring at me now. "So . . . ?"

"So . . . ?"

"So, are you, like . . . good?"

Ah. He wanted to know why I just hulked out on a pen. I wanted to know that, too.

"Oh, yeah. I'm fine." I lied. Zeke nodded slowly. Then he turned back to his magazine.

"Well, this is from twenty years ago today, but according to *Cosmo*, a Capricorn might be *feeling overwhelmed by recent circumstances and having a hard time making a decision. There is a strong cosmic flow between the stars of Capricorn and the stars of Pisces. Be on the lookout for new friends.* Look at that!" A pair of chiseled dimples appeared on Zeke's cheeks.

"That seems pretty generic," I said, trying to ignore the decisions swirling in my head.

"You're not a believer." He seemed half amused.

"Or maybe I just have a brain. Name me one human who isn't overwhelmed."

"I thought you said you were *fine*?" Shit. I rolled my eyes. "And guess what Miss Rojas?"

I didn't like that. The way he said my name. We didn't know each other like that. I turned away from him and opened my textbook to a new page, ignoring the playfulness that shimmered through his eyes.

"You're not gonna guess?" He was bouncing in his seat. A drastic change of pace from the catatonic boy sleeping through Algebra II.

I pretended to read for a moment more, not giving him the satisfaction. His glare was burning a hole into the side of my head. I finally gave up and let out a sigh.

"Ok, fine! What?"

Zeke's dimples returned deeper than ever, framing his gleaming white teeth. I'd just met this kid and already he was the annoying little brother I'd never asked for.

"You're looking at a certified triple Pisces," he gloated. What a weird flex.

Chapter Ten

On Waiting

– Rosie

I picked at the dried paint patches scattered across my hands while I impatiently waited for Caro on the front steps. Killing time by organizing the paint closet and listening to Hot 97 on the old radio that lived backstage in the auditorium was almost tranquil. Just me and the janitor keeping each other company on a Saturday. I should have accounted for the fact that Caro would be late. She and Mami have never been early for anything in their lives. Once, years ago, I left for JFK ahead of them to board a flight to DR—made it all the way to my seat on the plane without them—and didn't learn until I was at Las Américas with Papi that they had missed the flight completely. My hands trembled now, as they did then. I searched my palms for leftover scraps of dried paint to fixate on.

I had hoped, for once, she'd understand the warning I gave her that morning.

"Don't be late. Seriously."

That was the plan—she was gonna have JJ pick me up from school and take us to the train in Journal Square. By noon we'd be in Queens, and by four o'clock we'd be safely back home, before Mami got back from her morning shift at the hospital and came home to change for her afternoon shift at the Salon. I wondered if I should've just left Caro out of this and walked to the bus stop by the White Castle down the street to catch the 125 NJ Transit bus. It was more expensive, though. And who knew when (or if) the bus would come. The PATH train was coming any minute now. We'd have to catch the next one.

My hands were plucked clean at this point. I checked my phone again.

Maybe this is a bad idea.

The thought skated through my mind, leaving as quickly as it came.

Sure, if Mami found out what we were doing, she'd be pissed. And maybe a normal person in a normal family would just ask their mother about the photos I found. But Caro was right (in this instance). Mami loved secrets—especially ones about family. I think she fed on them. That must be where Caro got it from, too. Like Miss Lena always said: *No se puede negar que son familia.* Truly.

Every time I asked her why she decided to come to the US with our grandmother, she said the same thing. "For better opportunities. For you girls to get a better education." I don't think she understood why I wanted to know so badly. I don't think she understood the value of the information she chose to withhold. It was my origin story. A boring one at that. It was the reason why I was here and not on a beach sipping guava juice right now. The kind of thing I'd had to write about in my application to the Innovation Technical Institute. The reason it took me months to come up with my shitty essay response to their shitty prompt this year. *Share your family story.* They probably tossed my application directly into the trash.

There was one last deadline coming up in late March, for enrolling junior year. One last chance to get them to really see me. Whoever I was.

I heard the reggaeton blasting before I saw JJ's Toyota Camry. I still couldn't believe he actually drove around in that piece of junk. And that Caro was in the front seat despite swearing she'd never see him again if he got those flames painted on the sides.

"Sup, ugly?" was his greeting to me.

"Sup, assface? You're late." I got into the back seat. JJ was exactly Caro's type—dumb, lightskin, and Colombian. His car seats smelled like cigarettes.

"Whoa! Testy! That's no way to greet your Uber driver." He winked at me in the rearview mirror. Gross.

"Sorry, sis. Perdóname pleeeeease!" Caro turned around in her seat and pouted. I rolled my eyes and leaned forward to kiss her on both cheeks.

Like a good sister, I ignored JJ's hand inching up Caro's thigh, closed my eyes, and let the car's music shatter my eardrums.

When we rolled out of JJ's car, I grabbed Caro's hand and speed-walked to the train station before she could kiss him goodbye. As we stood in front of the MetroCard machine, I felt her squeeze my hand. I turned and saw Caro's other hand pointing to the top of the escalator.

"You know that dude? He's looking over here."

I squinted up to see where she was pointing. A short guy with a beanie and too much jewelry was waving at me. Fuck me. We didn't have time for this.

"No." I lied. "Let's go." I grabbed her hand and moved us towards the turnstiles.

Caro looked at me and then back at him. She just couldn't help herself.

"Ey yo! Eyeballs!" She approached the boy at the bottom of the escalator. Zeke's eyes grew big and round. "You wanna fuck my sister or something? What are you looking at?" Why. Why would she yell *that*? Luckily the station was sparse this morning.

"Uh . . . Is that, like, an invitation? Do you *want* me to fuck your sister?" Zeke quipped back. I didn't think I was his type. My hands pulled Caro's shoulders back.

"I'm sorry, we don't usually let her out of the house." I covered Caro with my right arm as if she were a misbehaving pet.

Caro looked at me curiously with a raised brow. She spoke over my arm.

"How you know my sister?" Her tone was protective, bordering combative.

"Besides the fact that apparently I want to fuck her?"

"Yea, besides that."

"We just met like two hours ago. And she's in my Algebra class, supposedly. I'm Zeke. I like your earrings."

"Thanks. Caro." My sister turned up her chin. "You're the new kid, right?"

Great. A compliment was all it took to warm her up. Our train was arriving any minute and they were standing around, exchanging pleasantries.

"How are you even here?" I asked, exasperated.

"Uhh . . . I walked?"

I don't know why I asked.

"*Why? Why* are you here Zeke?"

"I dunno. Free country." He shrugged. "Swear I'm not stalking you. Are you guys going to New York?"

"Yes, and we have things to do and we're gonna be late so—"

"Dope! Uh, me too! I been meaning to go. Still never been." He stumbled over to the MetroCard machine, awkwardly floating a hand in the air over the touchscreen. He was like a lost puppy in a foreign neighborhood. "Uh, y'all know how to use this?"

Caro stepped in and started pressing the buttons.

"Do you know where you're going?" She asked him.

"Uh . . . yeah. Duh. Wait, where are you guys going?"

"Queens."

I cocked my head to the side and glared at my idiot sister.

"No way, that's where I was going!" Zeke's eyes sparkled in my direction.

Of course. I rolled my eyes and ignored his stupid smile. Just then, a familiar screech echoed through the station. I snatched the card out of the machine.

"Fuck it, let's just go."

✿ ✿ ✿

On the train, Zeke nudged my sneaker.

"I was right, you know." He opened his arms, gesturing towards himself. "New friend."

I shook my head. It was going to be a long ride whether we talked or not. I could stare at my phone, but I knew there was nothing in there. The messy mop of curls on Caro's head was already resting on my shoulder. I reached into my backpack and foraged for the half-finished bag of plátano chips I'd saved. I offered the bag to Zeke, and he took a handful.

"Why did you get a Saturday, anyways?"

"Got a bunch of late slips," he said over a mouthful.

Always with the brief answers, this kid.

"Already? How? It's barely been two weeks."

"I get lost a lot." Zeke had a sheepish look on his face. "Y'all's school is so confusing."

Admittedly, I felt a pang of regret for being mean earlier. It was hard being at Westside even when I'd racked up nearly two years of experience. I couldn't imagine coming into this mess in the middle of the school year. Even teachers who arrived mid-year were always on some sort of downward fall from grace, bumbling around like depressing ghosts. There must've been a reason he moved here this suddenly. It was likely none of my business.

"Mmhmm . . . yeah, took me a minute to realize the color lines on the ceiling were color-coded by wing. Red is West, Yellow is East, Blue is North, Green is South."

Zeke nodded enthusiastically. "See? Shit like that. I wish I had a guide or something."

"Send me your schedule. I'll draw you a map."

"Really?" His face lit up as the train doors opened to the first stop. Just like that, I felt responsible for him. I wondered how this boy had survived this long without me. "You know, I think you're the first person I've met here who doesn't suck, Miss Rojas."

"Stop calling me that. It's Rosie." I leaned back in my seat and let my eyes close. "But I agree. People suck."

Chapter
Eleven

On a Journey to the Center of Queens

– Caro

After two trains and bumpy bus ride, I walked behind my sister and her new boyfriend as they babbled on. I was starting to feel like the odd one out in this nerdy threesome. Rosie had said something about a Saturday, confirming my suspicion that she had lied to me about why she was in school this morning. I had gotten a bajillion Saturdays and barely went to any of them. I could've given her advice—like the fact that most teachers don't give a shit if you bounce right after attendance—if she'd only asked. Not that she ever listened to my advice. Little sisters never did.

"We here," I parked my feet in front of a narrow townhouse next to an arching bridge that was overrun with weeds. Rosie handed me her janky Sidekick phone with the photo of Ricky Martin and I read the pixelated handwriting once more, wondering whose hands it belonged to. Half the townhouse was covered in a thick lush of climbing purple and brown ivy. Paint on the red door at the top of the stairs was chipping away and a pile of untouched newspapers sat over a doormat that read: COME BACK WITH A WARRANT. There were wind chimes and crosses hanging on the slanted porch. This Queens street was dead quiet, lined with two- and three-story brick apartments with metal awnings and wide empty sidewalks. I let out a whistle under my breath. It suddenly felt like we were trespassing.

"I think I'll wait for y'all over here." Zeke nodded towards a nearby bus bench and backed away slowly. I thought about joining him. Rosie stopped him and extended her hand.

"Wait. Let me put my number in your phone, just in case."

As me and Rosie approached the door, we heard loud meowing coming from inside. I exchanged one last look with Zeke behind me before cautiously ringing the doorbell. Almost too soon, the door croaked open. Like we were expected guests.

"Por fin!" The shocked hazel eyes of a weathered lady in an embroidered red satin robe gleamed back at us. Her hair was a white halo circling around her mahogany face. She looked like something . . . otherworldly.

"Hola señora. I'm Carolina, this is—"

"Rosie. I know, I know. Ven, ven." The woman nudged us into her home and the door slammed shut behind us. My spidey senses were tingling. I was pretty sure the two of us could take this lady if it came to it. Shit, I could take her myself. She could barely walk. All her weight pressed onto the wooden cane wrapped in her gnarled hands.

"How did you know my name?" Rosie started. Always the wrong questions this one.

"First off, creepy lady in creepy house, what is *your* name?" I cut in.

"Yolanda. No soy creepy," the old woman said. "Soy tu tía! I been waiting for you, mis hijas. Están en su casa! Sit!" Yolanda stretched her arms out before us. I held my sister's eyes in mine for a moment before we followed her command. Our butts squeezed onto her plastic-covered couch. Rosie kept looking at her watch.

Our newfound tía's old bones settled deep into the worn black leather chair in front of us. Rosie stared intently at her, like she was studying her every wrinkle. I turned my head in circles, looking at all the odds and ends around us. There were vases and ceramics and wooden sculptures and stacks of books filling every inch of this place. Everything was so . . . old.

At least this woman was more organized than Mami. And she was strange, too. I couldn't quite place it, but she seemed to radiate a real *alive* energy (also the strong smell of habichuelas). She had this smile plastered over her face like a clown at a kid's birthday party. Eager to please, but kinda terrifying. Peeking out of her sleeves, I noticed a winding string of vine tattoos crawling up the right side of her neck. Like one of the girls in the photos. My spidey senses calmed down.

I realized that Rosie was waiting on me to say something. As grown as she thought she was, she could be such a baby sometimes. We had been drifting in a thick, awkward silence this whole time. I looked at her, silently asking why I had to be the one to say something. She was the one with the bougie essay questions. Rosie nudged me with her elbow. I cleared my throat.

"So . . . are you really our tía? Like blood? 'Cause, as far as we know, Mami's an only child." It wasn't like we didn't have a number of tías that weren't actually related to us. But this still seemed surreal. I had to ask. I searched her face for any resemblance. I thought I caught a bit of my late abuela in her eyebrows, but other than that she looked nothing like Mami.

"How much do you know about tu mamá y yo? How about we begin there? I assume she doesn't know you're here?" Yolanda sat up suddenly. "Ah, but first, can I get you anything? Galleticas? Quieren limonada?"

"Sure, I could go for some lemonade."

As I spoke the words, I got the sense that this place was already starting to feel like home.

Chapter Twelve

On The Jacket

– Rosie

How much do you know about tu mamá y yo?"
I watched the pain behind the smiling face Yolanda presented us when we told her the truth. That we knew less than nothing. That we'd never known her name. The pain was there, but not surprise.

We sat on her couch sifting through a stack of photo albums covered in blue dust. Stacks and stacks of photos just like the one we'd smuggled over the river. They just kept pouring out, along with the stories escaping Yolanda's lips. She just kept going and going. Explaining how family was something forged out of more than just common ancestry. How Mami was very much NOT an only child. And how we were, all of us, connected. Throwing out names I didn't recognize with little explanation, while she looked just past us, above our heads, out the window.

There was one name that did recognize—Barahona. That's where we were from. Where Papi lived. It's where Yolanda was from, too.

"I lived in a cueva there, by the beach, with my mother until I was eight years old. She wasn't a great mother. I understand now that it wasn't her fault. She was an addict. But luckily, she had a really great friend. Your grandmother. She took me in. Chachi became my sister. And when we were about your age, we started Las Rosas de Santa Cruz with some girls from school."

My eyes were lost in the photos, one zoomed in on a shoulder tattoo with the name she'd just mentioned. *Las Rosas de Santa Cruz*. Finally, my sister stopped the flow of information.

"Hold up, hold up. Mami was in a gang?"

Caro stared, wide-eyed at the photo I pointed to.

"Your mother was a very important part of the group, yes. She handled the money. She was smart and all that. Real smart. I was sort of like the leader. Only because I was the loudest, believe it or not. And the prettiest." Yolanda smirked. Her English was smoother than Mami's. "Those girls were my whole life. That's more or less the reason why Chachi left and decided she wanted nothing to do with me."

Chachi = Yaris = Mami. That much I had put together.

"But why?" Caro insisted. She beat me to the question. I was glad I hadn't chosen to get on the bus and leave without her. Her obsession with watching reruns of *Criminal Minds* was clearly paying off.

Yolanda let out a sigh and attempted to stand up, unsuccessfully. Caro scrambled to get under the woman's left side and help. I took the other side.

"Ay, gracias mijas. Follow me," she whistled, "Pato! Ven!"

I nearly had a heart attack when a tiny black ball of fur leaped down from the top of a bookcase behind me. Caro gripped into my wrist. The cat scurried to Yolanda's side and nudged her ankles. We were led into a cramped room full of stacked cardboard boxes. Yolanda pulled a string hanging from the ceiling and a single light bulb dimly lit the dark space.

"Pato, tráeme el jacket."

I eyed the old woman and wondered for the third or fourth time that day whether she was out of her mind. Caro and I watched the black ball named Pato leap up across a stack of boxes and return down with a shiny pink bomber jacket in its mouth. It stood on a box, green eyes level to its master. Yolanda gave the cat a pat on the head as reward and retrieved the jacket. She turned around to present the garment to us. Her trembling hands held it like it was made of the rarest diamonds. At first, it seemed like she was reluctant to speak. Then, like a rush of water, she let the words flow out.

"This belonged to a girl we knew. She was beautiful. She had pink hair and she always wore pink dresses. People thought she was weird, you know? Used to work at the salon on our street. A real sweet girl. We all protected her. Era la mejor amiga de tu mamá desde chiquititas. Se llamaba Rosalina." My heart jumped at the mention of my given name. I remembered a girl with pink hair from the photograph. The one with an arm wrapped around my mother. I wondered why my mother never mentioned her, and then I remembered who my mother was. "One day, I got us involved in some activities that were . . . not-so-legal with some . . . not-so-great people. Bueno, las cosas pasan, you know. We ended up getting in a fight with a group of girls from another town. And a very bad man. . . . We lost her. I'm not proud of that day."

Our new tía sullenly folded the precious jacket in her arms. She traced the seams with a crooked finger. I tried to read between the gaps in her words, but all I could make out was pain.

"After we lost Rosie, your mother never forgave me. She left Las Rosas and Barahona as soon as she could. And then I got better and went after her. But . . . well you know, I sent her letters, she never responded. So, now I'm stuck here. In the meantime, I've got Pato and this old house. And my brujería and my santos . . . La vida sigue."

Stuck. I wondered what she meant by that. And I wondered how she could afford this whole ass house.

"You're a bruja?" Caro took a step back.

"*That's* what you took away from that story?" I asked. My sister, man. The woman had just told us her friend—our mother's friend—had died when they were young. The woman I was named after. It was heavy stuff. Not to mention the whole earth-shattering news that our mother was this whole entire person before she was our mother. Before she was Mami. She was once this insane person with nose piercings and a tattoo and a motorcycle. This person who gets apologies from people she used to hold as sisters and chooses to ignore them for years and years. Who remade herself as a devout, God-fearing Christian. Devout in all ways but forgiveness. She was this Russian doll of lies.

"So, like, a potions, hocus pocus, magic cures, broohaha flying shit bruja?" Caro continued. I couldn't help but roll my eyes.

Yolanda's devious eyes returned. "I dabble in many belief systems. I'm also a seamstress and a welder. Among other things." She pulled a business card out of her chest and handed it to Caro.

Yolanda Cuevas: Cosmic Life Coach

She had the same last name as Mami. I looked at my sister and let out a short chuckle. Caro seemed stuck on the bruja thing. I was trying to picture the white-haired woman in front of us with a helmet and sparks flying from her hands. It seemed to be obvious by the contents of Yolanda's home that a bruja would live here. I don't know how my sister could be surprised. Though, I knew Caro was the type of person who wouldn't believe in that kind of thing. Me on the other hand . . . I don't know.

Zeke's astrology thing was one thing—a scam thing. But I didn't see how the ceremony that seemed to be involved in brujería was that different from the ceremony of church. Or when my mother made a gross tea for us when we were sick. Admittedly, I didn't know that much about brujas besides the fact that it was a nickname my mother gave me when my hair was frizzy. But if they were anything like Yolanda, they couldn't be all that bad.

We spent about two more hours talking at Yolanda's house. But this time she asked us questions. We answered about a hundred things the woman asked about our lives and school and music and TV. I don't think I've ever talked to an adult who asked us so many questions about ourselves. There was just something about Yolanda. She was an excellent talker. I wished I could be like that. She knew how to have a conversation and how to pull things out of people. Behind her gray hair was a fresh energy that was infectious. She talked to us like we were old friends she was catching up with. I wondered if it actually *was* magic, the way she was able to put us both at ease. The kind of magic I wish I had.

"You have boyfriends?" she asked. Then she gestured towards me and added, "Or lovers?" I felt my nose scrunch up. But Caro didn't hesitate.

"I'm talking to someone. He's Colombian." I was taken back by the freeness of Caro's admission. "He's obsessed with me or whatever. I like him."

"As he should be." Yolanda nodded. "You're young, nena. Find a thousand lovers while you can. Pero use a condom! No matter what he tells you. I won't be making that mistake twice."

Caro laughed and I shook my head in fake disapproval.

The woman turned to me. "Y tú?"

I didn't know what to say. That there was something wrong with me, and I didn't think I'd ever even had a crush in my life? That dating seemed to me like the most futile thing for any high schooler to focus on? I couldn't even open my mouth before Caro chimed in.

"Rosie's too good for boys."

As she said it, I noticed that the light was starting to dim from the windows and made the executive decision that we should leave. I'd completely forgotten about Zeke sitting outside. When I looked at my phone, apparently on silent this entire time, I saw two missed calls from an unknown Florida number. Shit. If I was him, I would have left by now. I squeezed Caro's hand and she seemed to be on the same page. When we had all made it to the front door, Yolanda's hand grasped my shoulder. She pressed the pink jacket into my hands with a quiet determination.

"Creo que e'to te pertenece," she whispered.

"Oh, no. I don't think—"

"I sewed this jacket for Rosalina when I was very young. I was a different person then. I wasn't in a good place and I don't remember what I did pero . . . bueno, tiene algo encantado. It gives the wearer special . . . powers. Creo yo. Pero solo si canta tu nombre. . . . How? I'm not sure. It's been boxed away for decades. And it has your name. It belongs to you. Entiendes? Even if it doesn't work anymore, I want you to have it."

I ran my fingers across the embroidered *R* and tried to process what she was saying to me. I couldn't decide what I wanted to say back. It felt somehow disrespectful if I were to challenge her spiritual beliefs. I remembered a YouTube video

I watched about the pseudoscience behind the health properties of crystals and the way they produce a placebo effect in people who believe in that stuff. Whether a crystal could cure your headaches or not, if you believed it did, then the result was a cured headache.

I checked my watch again.

"What kind of superpowers?" I asked. I instantly felt silly for asking.

Yolanda shrugged. "I don't really know. For my Rosalina, it was sort of . . ." She reached for the words. "No sé! Como un . . . force field that protected her and the ones she loved. As much as I try to read up on and recreate what I did, I just—I can't. It was before I had the sense to get help." Her face had a look of defeat. And a little shame. It was a weird look. This would've been the part where a bunch of men with cameras jumped out to tell me I was being pranked. But no one came. And the sky was turning burnt orange. Yolanda's eyes pierced through me. "Take it. Por favor."

I look towards my sister for an answer. She was standing behind me on the porch, head in her phone, goofy smirk on her lips.

"Is it . . . is it okay if I come back here? Maybe interview you?"

"Of course! More than okay."

I nodded and folded the jacket into my backpack. Then I kissed her on the cheek. It felt like the thing to do. When my nose brushed past her cheek, she smelled like coffee and sage.

"Bendición, Tía." I offered. There were tears in Yolanda's eyes now.

"Dios te bendiga, mija. Come back soon. Please."

I had a feeling we would.

Chapter
Thirteen

On Origins

– Rosie

The three of us were standing on the subway platform staring at a man who was struggling to drag a love seat down the stairs. Caro was recounting the time warp of an experience that was Yolanda's apartment in between chews of half an empanada we'd split from a juice bar nearby.

I had tuned her out. My brain was trying to piece together the scraps of puzzle pieces I'd just been given. Why didn't I write anything down? I had even more questions spinning around my head now than this morning. My whole being was recalibrating. It was like I had just gotten out of an intense movie only to find that it was still daylight outside. I would have to come back when there was more time.

Shit. The time.

I told myself that if Mami was home by now she would have been blowing up my phone already. But what if the reception was bad down here?

"Why aren't you wearing it?" Zeke whispered after Caro reached the end of her tale. Questions. Questions.

"Why aren't I wearing a dead girl's jacket? Gee, I don't know."

Zeke reached for my backpack. I dipped away from him.

"Come on! I would be fuckin' casting spells all over the place! You gotta use your powers for good! Or for evil. I'm down for some evil, whatever we're into. That's cool, too!"

"I don't have any powers. It's just a jacket." I said it slowly to make sure it got through his thick head. "I think she just meant that it's like, blessed, or something."

"Okay, but how do you really *know* that?"

I didn't have the answers. Honestly, I didn't know why he was still here. I was sure he'd had more glamorous hopes for his first trip to New York City. He could be on top of the Empire State Building overpaying for a keychain right now. I told him earlier that he didn't have to come back to Jersey with us, but he said we were stuck with him now. And he needed us to hook him up with a barber Jersey City. Caro said she knew a guy. Unfortunately, so did I.

And so, Zeke had stuck around. I still didn't understand this boy, but I was learning to let him be.

Caro looked up from her phone and put a disrespectful arm on Zeke's shoulder, accentuating their height difference.

"I'm with shorty. I wanna know what that thing does. Plus—" she looked around the platform, "—what better place to do some possibly weird shit than on the subway? If you start levitating, I guarantee you no one here will give a flying fuck."

She started chanting *put it on, put it on, put it on* and Zeke joined in.

As poetic as she was, my sister had a point. I couldn't keep this thing in the house. If us coming home late didn't give Mami a hernia, finding this hard evidence certainly would. I'd have to find a place to hide it. I don't know why I was so worked up about it anyways. It was a jacket. A piece of fabric.

I pulled it out of my backpack and admired the stitching once more. The faded photos of the girl who shared my name, wearing this artifact with a bittersweet smile, came to the front of my mind. It didn't feel right that I was allowed to hold it. It belonged behind a glass case. Pretty old things belonged behind glass cases where kids couldn't break them.

I took a deep breath.

My personal peanut gallery clapped as I slipped my arms through the luxurious silk lining. It fit me perfectly.

And then . . .

Crickets.

Zeke circled around me. He tapped my shoulder lightly and jumped back, startled. My heart raced for a second before I realized he was just messing around.

"Probably just static. But, let's keep an open mind," Zeke said as he rubbed his finger. I rolled my eyes.

"You want something to happen, you have to actually do *something*, Ros." Caro puppeted my arms around. Having four eyes staring at me was starting to make me feel like a fish in a tank.

"I don't even know what it's supposed to do! I told yah. Just a jacket."

"Let's see: we've got telekinesis, invisibility, super speed, super strength—ooh, try to pick me up," Zeke said.

"Absolutely not." My muscles sure didn't feel any stronger. Zeke pinched my arm hard and I punched him back. "Ow!"

"Hmm . . . no invincibility." I was getting the sense that Zeke read too many comic books.

"You can hear my thoughts? What I'm thinkin'?" Caro stared through my soul.

"No clue. And it's, *What AM I thinking?* not *What I'm thinking?*" She rolled her eyes. I thought for a second. And then I remembered that I knew my sister. "Are you calling me a bitch?"

"No." Caro looked genuinely disappointed. "I was calling you a hoe. Damn."

She was so predictable.

I looked down at my hands, willing them to show me something. They looked as plain as they'd always been. I snapped my fingers. I turned my middle and index fingers towards my wrists like Spiderman. I balled them into the tightest fists I could. Nothing. This game was getting old and I was starting to feel dumb.

"I told yah. Nothing. Let's just go."

As I said it, the ground began shaking beneath my feet. Caro's arm quickly locked into mine, bracing for what would happen next. A sudden gust of wind swept through my hair and twirled around the plastic bags and empty water bottles that were littered all around us.

Por fin.

Our train was here.

It blurred past us with thunderous noise and didn't show signs of slowing down. I waited for it to let us in, but it just kept going and going and going and going and going. Suddenly, the tail end of the train zipped past my nose. I couldn't believe it. I put my free hand up, running behind it with Caro in tow and Zeke trailing behind us.

"WAIT!" The cry came out desperately.

The train screeched to a violent halt in response. White sparks flew up from the tracks. Then, it slowly inched further and stopped again and again, rocking its passengers with each screech. It inched a bit further once more before coming to a full stop. A long pause came before the car doors finally slid open along with staticky loudspeaker noise. I turned to my sister, letting a silent question float between us.

✿ ✿ ✿

"I swear I never seen a train stutter like that," Caro laughed as we sat on our ride back. When she was like this, her laughs came out in bird noises. Zeke was clenching his stomach.

"I guess we know her superhero name—The Conductor!" It wasn't even that funny, but he could hardly get the words out.

I let myself crack a smile and sat back as the city flew by.

After fatigue started creeping in, Zeke's eyes had some sort of epiphany.

"Hey! Did you check the pockets?"

"There's nothing in my—" I started, as I felt my sides. I stopped when I realized I was lying. Something flat and square was in my right pocket.

Zeke wagged a finger in my face. "Rule number one of cool vintage shit: always check the pockets," he asserted.

I pulled out a crisp, black envelope addressed to Yolanda's home in Queens in curly white script. It was unblemished and unopened.

"Who's Wendell Rojas? Your cousin?" Zeke pointed to the sender's address in the top left corner.

"No. Our dad," Caro said, snatching the card from my hand. She was already ripping the envelope apart. I would've been more annoyed if I wasn't insanely curious as to why Papi, of all people, would send Yolanda a letter. And by the looks of it, recently. The words leaped out of expensive-looking cardstock.

YOU'RE INVITED!

¡TE INVITAMOS A CELEBRAR NUESTRA BODA!

"Your dad's getting married?" Zeke asked. I was too shocked to even register the fact that apparently Zeke could read Spanish.

"I guess he is . . ." I replied, letting out a deep sigh. Zeke looked between us and took a second to realize that this was the first we were hearing about our father's apparent wedding.

My fingers slid across the embossed letters with caution. As if doing so would unlock some kind of spell. Or make the impossible less real.

El cinco de febrero. A little over two weeks from now.

"Well, shit."

Chapter Fourteen

On Homecomings

– Caro

When we got home Mami wasn't there. Which was weird. Her car was outside.

I'd been preparing to shield myself from her, now armed with infuriating new information in the shape of the black envelope in Rosie's backpack. My sister and I, arms linked, weapon in hand, ready for battle. The weight of what we'd done today was starting to sink in, but was quickly being outfucked by the weight of what Mami had done. Fuck the old photos. I couldn't give less of a slice of a fuck about her past. She was a reformed malcriada desgraciada biker chick, so what? This lady was lying about *the present* now. She was lying in my face.

All of her lies sat crushed inside my knuckles and swiftly released into a mild calambre when I opened our door and we stood toe-to-toe with an empty apartment.

Rosie started rummaging through the splattering of papers laid out on the table in the kitchen. There were bags of unsorted groceries spread on the floor. I watched hurricane Rosie devastate every corner of the living room, turning old mess into new mess. In the center of the storm, I stood still, calculating.

Rosie was going for Mami's bedroom, like a dumbass, when we heard the familiar chime of polite laughter ringing outside the front door. She was chatting with Doña Ismerys next door. Our building only had three floors and five units sitting above the Salon. At the top was Miss Lena's place. Then us and Doña Ismerys. Mr. Bill and his wife were below us and next to them were the newest residents: the Garza kids (three elementary-aged Filipino kids who ran up and down the stairs; aka a reliable source of babysitting money).

I hated Doña Ismerys. When we were little, she would babysit us and force us to pray before every snack or meal. Somehow, she regularly found an excuse to slap my wrists with her ruler for "praying wrong" (which never made sense to me). Something about signing the cross right to left instead of left to right. Or maybe it was the other way around. Clearly, praying wasn't my strong suit. Plus, la doña always smelled like fresh-cut onions. I hated onions.

When I looked up from where I stood, with a clear view of the kitchen, I could see the thing Rosie was looking for—a black envelope sitting on top of the fridge. It nearly disappeared against its background. Suddenly, my body was on the move. I went to work as keys jingled by the door. By the time Mami turned the knob and stepped inside, me and Rosie were sitting on the couch with textbooks laid out in front of us. I let out a casual yawn, with outstretched arms.

"Por fin! Ción, Mami, where you been?"

"Bendición, Mami." Rosie gave me a look that said *tone it down.* Sure, it was a risky move, but it worked.

"Dios le bendiga, mis niñas. I went to the súper after work. Then I was, uh, dropping off an arepa for Doña Ismerys. You know. No quedamo hablando. We lose track of time," Mami explained without looking at us.

"Oh, how is she?" I pushed.

"Bien, bien. Tú sabes, tiene la presión, but hopefully she likes the arepa. I made with honey instead of sugar this time." She stood nodding awkwardly by the front door. The vibes were very off. Not that Mami ever had good vibes. Hers were usually uptight, irritated vibes. But right now, there was this thing—this guilt that hung between us. It was a delicious kind of guilt. One I didn't get from her often. It was a guilt she usually demanded from me. I wanted to squeeze some more out like wringing the last drops of juice from a fresh lime.

"That's nice. Hey, have you heard from Papi lately?" I turned to Rosie, keeping my voice light. She shot daggers back at me.

"No." Rosie hid something deadly beneath the word.

"Huh. Mami, have you heard from him? I feel like it's been a while, right?"

That's when I really saw her. That dead-tired look. Completely washed. I caught her eyes quickly dart towards the top of the fridge. Then she just stared at us. And for a minute I thought some detail of our little study setup was out of place and we'd been found out. But I watched her face twist and contemplate as she went into the kitchen. She returned with the black envelope. I didn't even have to pretend to be shocked. My brows furrowed. An unexpected, but not completely unfounded move. She was taking control. Her expression turned from tired to grave and if I didn't already know there was a wedding invite in her hand, I might have thought someone died. I prepared myself for whatever story she had for us.

"I . . . mis niñas . . . I have been battling a lot of demons lately. And I've been protecting you from them. But the Lord spoke to me through Ismerys and told me to lead with truth today, so I must listen to His word. Doña Ismerys was right. You deserve truth. And I only hope I've taught you enough to make the right decisions after that."

Que drama.

She dropped the envelope in front of us. Rosie took it and opened it, feigning curiosity. I kept my eyes steady.

"Your father sent this," Mami continued. "He's getting married. I don't agree with it, but you know your father. Terco. It's your choice if you want to speak to him or not, or congratulate him or pray for him, however. I wanted to shield you from negative . . . emotions. But . . . you girls are growing up now. I have raised you how I can and given myself to you. I have to trust you know the right answers."

Huh. Right answers. Which meant there were wrong answers. Black and white. Mami was nothing like Yolanda. Yolanda spoke like she loved without asking. Like our words were safe with her. Mami spoke in riddles that came with conditions. Always asking for something in return. She was pleading with us as if our eternal souls were on the line. Like Jesus himself had a personal stake in our decision-making. But Jesus and God had nothing to do with this. This was about *her*. Our allegiance to *her*. Everything was always about *her*. God forbid we have opinions outside of her. God forbid she be wrong. God forbid she apologize for anything. I wondered if I would ever be a mother like her. If it was just gonna happen even if I swore it never would. If something would happen to me between now and then, like something had happened to her. And then I started to get mad. Pissed, actually. Because how were we supposed to know what to look out for if she never told us what that something was?

I bit the inside of my lip, not knowing what to say back. My thoughts were clouded by the heat rising from my chest to my head.

"I thought he was already married. To you." The words came out of Rosie's mouth with surgical precision. A very good point, of course. We waited for her response to a plain fact like that. She took off her coat, tossing it over a chair. Then she plopped down on the couch between us like a bag of rocks. I felt my body tense in response. I tried not to stare at her bare arms, but I couldn't help searching for evidence of her past self. All I found was the Icy Hot patch that lived on her left shoulder.

"Technically no. We never had a formal wedding."

What a day for earth-shattering news. Blow after blow after blow. I tried my best to keep the judgment out of my face. I don't think I did a very good job. I wanted to purse my lips and roll my eyes so bad. How about *that* for a juicy bit of gossip for the church ladies?

"Wait, so—" I started.

"As I said, you are free to call him and congratulate." She lightly tapped both of our legs and stood up from the couch as if the conversation were over. But I wasn't finished. I stood up beside her.

"Caro . . . just—" Rosie whined. Now they were *both* getting on my nerves. I don't know why she always tried to stop me when I was right. What was she so afraid of? Clarity? Was I just supposed to let the woman go on speaking in riddles and acting like everything was fine?

"No, just wait a damn minute. Are we *not* going then? Is that what you're saying? 'Sorry not sorry I kept this from my own daughters—'"

"Sabe que no me gusta cuando u'tede hablan con palabras tan feas!" was her idea of a response.

"WHAT ugly palabra? Damn? Damn, damn, damn! There. So what? It's in the Bible, like, a thousand times!" I looked towards the ceiling. "Just answer the question. Are we going to the wedding or not?"

My mother's hand shot up. I flinched backward, fully expecting a slap, and cursed my body for betraying me. But her hand stood still in the thickness between us.

"Not a wedding. No estoy de acuerdo. Ya te dije. You make the right decision." She pointed her index finger at me. "When you were born, I know God sent you to challenge me. And I tried aunque sea. Porque soy tu mama. I'm positive your sister would not leave her mother, but if you disagree, Caro, hija mía . . . I can only pray for you." Mami's eyes were fogging up. Incredible acting technique, really. Comparing me and my sister was just a cherry on top. Chef's kiss.

"Ugh, don't speak for Rosie! Just be for real! Just say you don't want us to go!" I turned to my still-sitting sister. "Do you even *want* to go? He's your father, too! Say *something!*"

Rosie's eyes said *I'm sorry*, but her mouth said nothing. She shrugged and put her hands up as if the decision weren't her own. Coward. I didn't accept her apology. I'd have to find a way to forgive her tomorrow. Or maybe the day after that. For now, I shook my head.

"Wow."

❀ ❀ ❀

I slammed our bedroom door behind me and reached underneath my pillow for the prepaid calling card that was always there. My cellphone sandwiched between me and my tears. A couple buttons and thirty seconds of elevator music later, there was a familiar grainy voice on the other end.

"Pa? Alo?"

"Por fin! Una de mis hijas se acuerda de mí" I could hear his wide, toothy smile. I reluctantly allowed a smile of my own. If nothing else, you could rely on the man for jokes and an annoyingly endless reserve of bear hugs. I could feel his hairy arms now, cradling me and wiping the tears from my face. He was right, as usual. It had been too long since I last called. I had so many questions I didn't know where to begin.

"Ción, Pa . . ."

That was as good a place as any.

"Dios te bendiga, Carajita."

Chapter Fifteen

On Strange Nights

– Rosie

I stuffed my backpack into the farthest corner under my bed, where Mami was least likely to rummage around "reorganizing" things as she was known to do. For now, we were in the clear about Tía Yolanda. I was afraid Caro would blurt out something about it when she got all worked up with Mami. But she didn't. The thinnest sliver of a silver lining. Still, I didn't think she would let me keep the jacket if she found out about it. And I couldn't get over the fact that we really just went to this random lady's house. We could've been murdered. How incredibly dumb of us. Of me.

Caro had already dredged out her dinged-up lime green suitcase and placed it next to her bed, preparing for the trip she insisted on taking and had somehow convinced Papi to pay for. Just like he paid for her fancy iPhone. *With what money?* I wondered. I would go on wondering.

I sat in my bed for a while after she fell asleep, listening to the slow rhythm of her breathing synchronized with the occasional passing car and the one cricket that was always sitting outside our window. The moon outside was full and beaming down on us, like a second sun. Try as I may to empty my brain, the more I commanded my thoughts to shut up, the louder my own internal voice felt. It was like this most nights, but these past twenty-four hours left a whole lot more to think about. Most of it boiled down to one paralyzing question that seemed to haunt my life.

Stay or go?

I felt a duty to go. Then there was the moral obligation to stay and look after our mother. I also really, really didn't want to go. And why would I when Mami had given me an out? And the final junior-year ITI application deadline clock was ticking. And I probably had an Algebra test that week. And Caro was Papi's clear favorite anyways. And, and, and, and . . .

My feet rose me up to close the window blinds. The sun was on the edge of overtaking the spotlight from the full moon. Looking out the window, I froze, locking eyes with the four-legged creature that was standing in the middle of the street below me. A lone black horse with a shimmering coat. At least, it appeared slick black under the moonlight. It stood stoically like a sculpture. I thought my eyes were tricking me, until I saw its tail move. I could almost see myself reflecting off its black eyes. I wondered if it escaped from somewhere? It made me think of those horses that pulled carriages through Central Park way across the river and imagined this majestic creature racing through the Holland Tunnel. I never knew where they kept those giant horses in a city like New York. When I tore my eyes away and I looked to Caro's bed, I weighed whether this impossible scene merited waking her up. Only, after I turned back, the thing had vanished. I looked up and down the street bewildered—nothing but a fog that was creeping over empty sidewalks. Accepting defeat, I closed the blinds, already planning the horse story I'd have for Caro in the morning (that is, if she was still talking to me). Though, I probably wouldn't know whether or not this was part of the dream by the time we got to church.

✿ ✿ ✿

With a liquid steadiness, my breathing slows and my sight goes black. I feel the world turning over on itself. I drop into this tropical oasis riddled with hibiscus flowers radiating colors that are cranked to max saturation. There are endless rolling hills of guava trees and a shimmering black river cutting through the whole thing. Something about the scene is almost too perfect. It makes me nervous: like the whole scene could break and swallow me whole. I feel the heat baking my skin. Above me, a red and purple bird circles around me with its wings spread wider than the length of our apartment. I start running for the river, and the bird follows overhead, making me run faster. Sweat trails behind me. When I finally reach the river, the water is crashing wildly against rocks in opposite directions, creating a whirlpool in front of me, stirring up metallic fish weaving beneath. Swimming in the waves is a familiar pink garment embroidered with roses. I try to reach for it, but a girl with pink hair appears in my reflection. "E'pérate!" she says, her voice drowned out by the water. I jump back, then slowly inch back towards the river, seeing her as my own reflection again. It's her. The other Rosie. The girl in the picture. "Oye, pérate! No estás lista. Todo viene en su tiempo." I have no idea what she's talking about. I mean, I understand *the words* she's saying. They just aren't making sense. She's young, but she's yelling at me like she's my mother. It's kind of annoying. She has a look like she knows what I'm about to do and she rolls her eyes. So, I reach into the water again. As soon as my hand breaks through the cold surface, the bird above lets out a screech and it swoops down hard. I turn around, covering my face against the knife-sharp beak diving towards me. "Stop!" My voice catches as I try to let out a scream. "STOP!" The bird freezes. Like, *literally* freezes. Suspended in mid-air. As if someone pressed pause on a movie, its giant wings painted a multicolored blur behind it. I stare in awe. Then, I step to the side, out of harm's way. "Uh . . . go?"

✿ ✿ ✿

All I heard was a splash before my eyes catapulted open into the real world. It was early Sunday morning and I was drenched in sweat. It felt like my bed was on fire.

I rolled out and looked under the bed, my backpack just where I'd left it. I fished it out. The jacket was still there, under a crushed bag of plátano chips. I stuffed it back under, shaking off the ominous feeling burrowed deep in my gut.

My phone lit up from the nightstand. When I picked it up through squinting eyes, I saw the incoming texts, time-stamped at 3:45 a.m.

Hey, it's Zeke.

What's your birth time?

2

The Ring

Chapter
Sixteen

On Barbershops

– Zeke

Y ou're in Honors English? How—I mean, how's
that?" Rosie asked from behind the salon receptionist's desk.
She'd surrounded herself with multicolored highlighters and
sharpies and gel pens and was going to town on an elaborate
hand-drawn map of our school while my torn-up schedule sat
on her lap.

I sat in the sole barber's chair in the salon, with a black
cape draped across my neck. More than a week had passed
since Rosie and her sister and I returned from our little Queens
adventure. Now, her pink jacket was sitting in the back of my
locker after she said keeping it at home was cursing her
dreams. I couldn't tell if she was joking or not. But she trusted
me. Which meant we could be on the road to being actual
friends. The soulmate kind of friends, my gut told me.

When Rosie unlocked the salon and let us in, it felt like
we were trespassing at first. Which was not a good look—two
Black kids breaking into a building for a free haircut. But

apparently, on Sundays, Lena's opened late in the afternoon while everyone was down at the church potluck. Perfect time for the owner's goddaughter to sneak me in with the keys she obtained in a totally consensual and legal manner.

Sitting in that chair, it became clear to me just how crunchy my hairline was getting. Ignoring Rosie's line of questioning, I talked through the mirror in front of me.

"Yea, it's okay. It's English. So, when's ya boy getting here?" I pulled at my short coils, letting the split ends slip through my fingers. It was nearly long enough to braid.

"He's not my *boy*. He's Lido. And aren't you broke? You should be thankful Caro got him to hook you up. She had to promise him she'd talk him up to Lena. Knowing damn well Lena don't want that man." Her voice suddenly held the tone of a woman three times her age.

"Why, he ugly or something?"

"No, Caro used to have a crush on him in middle school. *Used* to. Not anymore. But Lena—she just swore off guys after her last boyfriend cheated on her with his cousin."

"*His* cousin? Oh, wow. You really all up in people's business like that, Rosalina? Wooow." A smile tugged at my cheeks and I got dead eyes back from the girl in the mirror. She shrugged.

"Again, Rosie." She gave me a look. "And it's just how it is here. When you spend a lot of time sitting around waiting for your mom to finish drying old ladies' hair, you get all the juice. I didn't choose this life." She shrugged and let out a yawn. I wondered if Rosie knew how funny she was without trying. I thought about the comment one of Auntie's friends made about me. *It's them quiet ones you gotta watch out for.* Rosie was a quiet one, too. And I could see right through her uptight facade. She yawned once more. One of those contagious types.

"Tired of me already?" I held in my own yawn.

"Nah," she breathed out, even though I could see the sleep in her eyes. "Church just wears me out every time. And if you don't go, they judge you at CCD and then—"

Just then, the wind chime above the glass door twinkled. In walked the most gorgeous specimen of a man I'd ever laid eyes on. Tall like an oak tree, with a crisp fade and sharp line framing glossy curls to top off his marble sculpture of a face. It was almost offensive. Unfair, really. And the first word on this man's gloriously moisturized lips was my name.

"Zeke?"

I didn't know what to say to that, still processing how such a hard-edged name could sound soft and round when wrapped in the tones of his voice. I channeled my nerves into my hands and fiddled with the ring on my finger.

"Hey, Lido. That's him right there. I think he just wants a trim and his edges sharpened up or whatever it's called." Rosie's phone buzzed in front of her. "And Caro says hi," she added in a bored tone without lifting her eyes from the map she was still drawing.

"*Thank you, Lido, my friend. You're so buenmoso y tan generoso. Qué tiempo que yo no te he vi'to. Y de tu vida? No?* None of that? Aight, I see you, lil sis." Even as I struggled to catch the words as they raced off Lido's tongue, I could tell he was teasing. So, I chuckled (maybe too hard).

"Thank you. Really." I finally spoke through the mirror. He had a face that was hard to hold eye contact with. My gaze bounced around the shop.

"Don't thank me yet, bruh. I ain't fucked your shit up yet." He waved a pair of clippers at the mirror and laughed graciously. My pulse quickened. Unfortunately, even if he did fuck my shit up, I would probably be thankful.

"Be nice, Lido." Rosie warned.

"I kid, I kid. For real, bruh, I take my shit mad serious. Even if I weren't getting shortie's number, it don't matter. It's my art, you feel me? Imma make you leave here and tell all your lil friends about me. Tell them Lido hooked your ass all the way up, aight? Trust." He put his firm hands on my shoulders. I nodded. Then, he swiftly spun me away from the mirror and the buzzing of his clippers filled the room. He leaned in close to whisper in my ear. "I'll be gentle." And if I wasn't already sitting down, that would've brought me to my knees.

I almost didn't notice that he never asked me any further questions about how I wanted my hair cut. He just went straight in. By the time I realized, it seemed too late to say anything. Halfway through, he took a phone call between his ear and shoulder, speaking melodious Spanish. And then I started thinking about my breathing and where I set my eyes and how I could try not being so awkward. I couldn't remember the last time I felt this flustered. It felt like forever ago. Though, if I was being honest with myself, I fell in love pretty much every day.

In a swift, dramatic motion, he put the clippers down and spun me around, waving off the cape from around my neck. I examined the mirror. My fingertips traced the white lines around my razor-sharp hairline. He'd even trimmed my eyebrows a bit. Damn.

"You straight?"

I was taken aback by the question. Came outta nowhere.

"Uh, no? I mean . . . it's complicated . . ."

How many times had I already done this and somehow, still, hadn't locked down a response? A whole existential crisis launched by two simple words.

Lido looked as confused as I was.

"Ah, don't even worry about the chalk, bruh. It'll go away in the shower. I'm telling you, bruh, you look fresh! Don't he look fresh, Roz?"

Looking over at Rosie, I realized my mistake. Our eyes held each other in a telepathic plane. She was biting back a laugh. I shook my head.

"No, yeah. He looks great!" she said.

I got up from my seat and held out my hand to Lido.

"Sorry, man. It looks amazing, thank you!" He took my hand in a firm shake. So, we were holding hands now. "Cool to have a barber in Jersey now."

Lido's perfect face beamed. He reached into a drawer under the salon mirror and pulled out a CD in a lime green case.

"Aight, I'll catch yah later, but hold onto this for me, aight? I also do my music thing, you know. Tryna make it out here. Give it a listen. Put your friends on if you like what you hear, ya feel me?" He handed me the CD. Just like that, I felt like I'd been lost in the desert, salivating over a sparkling royal feast, only to find it was a cactus the whole time. He gave me a fist bump and pointed finger guns at Rosie before leaving the sound of door chimes behind him.

I sat in silence with Rosie for a minute, not sure what to do with the CD that was in my hands. She broke the silence.

"So . . . straight, huh?" She looked down, scribbling a marker as she said it. It was an opening. I eyed her, trying to figure the girl out.

"Not-so-straight. But I think you knew that, for some reason."

Her eyes met mine.

"What? No! I mean its cool, and maybe . . . I had my suspicions, but I wouldn't say I knew for sure. Or didn't know. I was curious, I guess. If you wanted to share. But it's not my business."

"Right. You always mind your business." I narrowed my eyes. Rosie shrugged.

"For real, I won't tell anyone unless you want me to. . . . So, you wanna hear Lido's SoundCloud?"

An expertly maneuvered change of topic. I raised a brow.

"Is it as terrible as I think it is?"

"Worse."

Chapter
Seventeen

On Accident

– Rosie

I t was Mami's idea for me to call up the people at ITI. She'd been surprisingly calm with the news of my rejection. She asked me why they waited so long to tell me. I told her that was just how things worked. You try really hard on your grades and you fill out a form that forces you to choose between Black and Hispanic and/or Latino and you send them words you pulled out from the bottom of your stomach about how sad your life was and what your tenderest hopes were and you wait for an automated reply with outstretched beggar's hands.

I think since she was giving Caro the silent treatment, Mami made it a point to be nicer to me. Maybe for choosing to stay home. I didn't know if it really was a choice. If I'd decided on anything, it was to do nothing. Using the upcoming PSATs and the fact that Mami already paid the fee as my official thin excuse to stay.

Still, my mother said she was proud of me for not giving up on ITI and said she knew a woman from church who knew a woman who knew a woman who never even finished high school and went on to be a successful real estate agent in Manhattan. Wasn't sure what that had to do with me, but I appreciated her attempt to console me anyways. It was better than the lecture I was expecting. She said she still wanted me to apply to Saint Agnes, the all-girls school up the street. But if I insisted on this fancy school, she suggested maybe I ask them what I could do to make my application better. That seemed like a good idea to me. Something to do, at least. A place to start picking up the pieces.

The morning after Zeke's haircut, I called a number I had called a dozen times before while I waited for Caro to finish getting dressed for school. Even though I hated talking on the phone, I knew calling was best. If I emailed them, it was fifty-fifty whether they'd even bother to respond. Their jazzy hold music played while I waited for Caro to come out of the bathroom.

"Innovation Technical Institute Admissions Office. Brenda speaking. How may I help you?"

"Hi Brenda. Not sure if you remember I actually spoke with you a couple months—you probably don't remember. Forget it. Anyways . . ." I took a breath. "My name is Rosalina Rojas. I go to Westside Academy in Jersey City and I submitted an application for the spring cycle. Linda Solis should have sent over my files. I was wondering if maybe one of your counselors could send over any feedback they had? Like what's missing or, I dunno . . . like what can I do better?" I asked.

There was a long second of silence on the other end. Then I quickly added. "You know, if that's okay, to ask. I mean, if it's not a bother—"

"Rosalina Rojas. R-O-J-A-S or is it R-O-H-A-S?" said Brenda.

"With a J. I said. Rosalina is R-O-S-A-L-I-N-A then R-O—"

"Sorry, hun. I'm not seeing an application from you in our system. I would contact your guidance counselor to make sure everything's in order. You can look at our website for the requirements. Anything else I can help you with?"

The ground shifted beneath me and a sinkhole swallowed me into it. She'd said it in a cheery tone as though she'd plunged a knife through my chest and somehow solved all my problems.

"What do you mean my application's not in the system?" Caro finally emerged from the bathroom and was about to say her usual slick shit before I put my hand up in face to stop her. I continued with a phone pressed to my shoulder, trying to keep myself steady. Trying to keep my fire and panic locked in the jar. I could feel it slipping out like smoke regardless. "Rosalina Rojas. R-O-J-A-S. Can you check again?"

"I checked, hun. Sorry. You're not coming up for this semester's apps. I can take your name down and email in case anything changes." This woman was a nonchalant wall whose energy only fueled my panic. I gave her my information and when she told me to have a nice day, I hung up the phone.

"Yo, you good?" Caro asked, brows raised. They were the first words she'd spoken to me since our trip to Queens.

"I'm fine."

✿ ✿ ✿

That morning, when I stopped by the guidance counselor's office again, Mrs. Solis wasn't there. Probably hiding from me. I asked the secretary where she was and the blond-bobbed woman's one-word response was, "Out."

So, I checked my phone for reception for the fiftieth time in the hallway. Finally, after a billion years, I loaded up a snapshot of the rejection email I got from ITI last week. *Due to our high volume of applicant...* And it was on that fifth read I finally noticed the typo. Then I noticed the sender address.

<lsolis@gmail.com>

L. Solis. As in *Mrs.* Solis. As in the one woman who was not here to face my wrath. The woman who had been brushing me off for months. The woman who was not there to answer my many, many questions. It was direct from her. That Mrs. Solis. From a personal account.

I reread the email one more time. I didn't know what to do with this information. I could've been wrong. On the slim chance some other lady from ITI had the same last name and first initial. Unlikely, but possible. Stranger things had happened. And if it *was* the very same Mrs. Solis, what could I do about it anyways? Maybe it was protocol to send student rejection letters via guidance counselor personal emails. Maybe. So, I shoved it down and kept it moving.

"Something about it just . . . smells funny. I dunno. I just . . . don't get it. Like, why?"

We were in Algebra class (or what was left of it). Zeke leaned back in his chair, nodding.

"I mean it happens. I've had plenty of rejection. I used to have to jump through hoops for auditions all the time at my old school. Until . . ." His chair wobbled backwards and then he crashed forward. "Until I just stopped. There just . . . I guess there wasn't a point anymore. So I bombed all my auditions on purpose. It actually felt really great. Powerful."

I gave Zeke a glare that I hoped was worthy of how batshit he sounded. How could you be proud of failing on purpose? He was truly an enigma. And besides, that wasn't what I meant. I was talking about explicitly *not* failing.

"Why do you even wanna go there so bad? I've been to two high schools already and I can tell you a school is a school is a school," Zeke said, twiddling his pencil between his fingers.

"I just do," I responded, trying to finish the extra credit worksheet Mr. Samy handed out. Mr. Samy, who left class early that day, after complaining that he was overworked and underpaid after he was pissed about missing his lunch break for a faculty meeting. His absence meant class was a free-for-all. At least for the next ten minutes before the bell rang.

"What do they got over there that y'all don't have here?"

"Money. For one." I looked up from my paper. "They also have the best engineering program for high schoolers in the state according to the *Washington Post*. You know, 99 percent of their students go to college. Isn't that crazy?"

"Sounds fake. Wait, you wanna be an engineer? That's what your passion is, like for real?" Zeke was gnawing at the eraser end of his pencil now and it made me want to crawl out of my skin. I made a mental note not to borrow any of his pencils in the future.

"What do you have against engineers?"

"Nothing. It's just so . . . basic."

"Well, I'm less concerned with passion as much as I am with money. So, I'm *going* to be a civil engineer. Or an architect. Or both. I'm not great at the drawing part yet, but they have computers for that now," I said.

"Not an expert, just a former art school kid, but I think you're pretty good at drawing. And I totally know what a civil engineer is . . ."

I ignored his compliment.

"I didn't either until a lady in a pink suit came for this career week program in middle school—they would have a bunch of people come in to present and we could sign up to spend a day with them at their jobs. Anyways, this lady had Legos. I love Legos. I still have the set she gave me. And she told us she was a civil engineer. I went with her to her job. She said she loved to organize things and help cities work better. She had this fancy suit and a Prada bag—which I looked up later and it was worth like three thousand or some shit. She was just . . . cool." I shrugged. "And that was it, I guess. I don't know. Everything made sense. I knew that's where I was supposed to be."

"That's kinda dope. Wish they did that at any of my schools. The closest I got was getting to play with the Miami Symphony Orchestra, but that was just, like, a couple of us. A career week would've been—"

"Well, they didn't do it for the whole school. Just the Accelerated kids. Back when I was in the program."

Zeke nodded slowly, taking in the information. A group of our classmates had started a paper airplane contest. One flew its way past us, landing gently on Mr. Samy's vacant desk. I went back to my worksheet. Except now I wasn't thinking about quadratic equations, I was thinking about the dope civil engineer lady and Mrs. Solis and her fucking lies and my brain was making loops around different theories on why anyone would do something like that. Why would she do something like that? Did she do this to everyone or just me? Why me? Could I even do anything about it?

Then Zeke pulled me out of my head when he whispered, "Isn't that kinda fucked up?"

"Isn't what fucked up?" I whispered back, not finding a connection. Unless he could read minds.

"That they only did that thing for the Accelerated kids? What if the other kids wanted to do career week or whatever? What if they wanted to skip school to visit people at their jobs? Or learn what a civil engineer is?"

I thought for a beat.

"They didn't. They would be in Accelerated if they did," I decided. It sounded like the right thing to say. Zeke was taken aback a bit. Sometimes I forgot he was new here.

"What does *that* mean?" he said.

"I just mean ... you know, like, kids in Accelerated really want to go to college and pay attention to boring presentations and shit. If they can only do it for a handful of kids, it should be them." Zeke's upper lip grew more incredulous with every word I spoke.

"*You* really want to go to college. *You* pay attention to boring presentations and shit. You're doing a worksheet right now you don't even have to do. And you're not in advanced classes— or Accelerated or whatever the hell . . ." I wanted to stop him and tell him that I didn't count. That I was different. That my situation was different. But he kept going. "And why can they only do it for a handful of kids? That just doesn't seem fair."

I turned to look at him. At his soft face and resolved eyes. He wasn't being combative or trying to irk me as per usual. He really cared. He was asking a genuine question. For real. And waiting for a genuine response.

"I don't know," was my answer. Because I was realizing that I didn't. I didn't know a fucking thing.

Chapter
Eighteen

On Buzzcut Girls

– Zeke

I was in Honors English when I first saw her. Luckily, this was one of the only classes in which I regularly found myself sitting up, wide awake. Raising my hand, even. Occasionally. Each time to my own surprise. Unlike the first floor of Westside Academy, which seemed to follow a penitentiary theme, the second floor—where all the honors and advanced-level classes were—was brightly lit with white walls and Mac computers lining every room. Old models, but still. Macs.

She must have introduced herself to the class at some point after she walked in with the note she laid at Mrs. Shapelli's desk, but I couldn't hear a thing. I just watched her take her place at the empty seat beside me in the back of the classroom. The place where new students were exiled to. I stole looks at her the whole rest of the period. She was wearing combat boots, a distressed crop top, off-brand Louis Vuitton–patterned leggings, and several layers of silver necklaces. Hanging loosely off her shoulder was a worn-out leather satchel. She looked like she just stepped off from a photoshoot for *Paper* magazine. Her eyeliner was sharp enough to slice a hole through my heart and a septum nose piercing rounded out the symmetry in her face. On top of her head was a tied-up pink scarf crowning a buzzcut pink scalp that glowed against her skin. If a stranger walked into our classroom and had to pair up students like a matching game, she and I would go together. For sure.

"If a person—any human being—is told often enough, 'You are nothing. You account for nothing. You count for nothing. You are less than a human being. I have no visibility of you,' the person finally begins to believe it. Does anyone know who said that?" Mrs. Shapelli asked us. There was the usual silence. Then, buzzcut girl's hand passively lifted halfway up. Shapelli nodded in her direction.

"Maya Angelou."

She said it boldly. Like there wasn't an ounce of doubt in her mind.

"Yes, actually!" Our teacher didn't even try to hide her surprise. "And do you know why—"

"She was talking about the state of Black people—specifically Black men—in the US and how the propaganda that they were being fed by white media was affecting their self esteem as well as the higher rates of incarceration in the prison system—which back then was, and today currently is, modeled after the slave plantation of the 1800s and needs to be abolished, like, yesterday."

Everyone stared at her now.

"Damn!" someone whispered. This elicited a round of murmurs and giggles. "What is she *on*?" I heard from another corner.

"Uh, sure, I think that's . . . part of it. Love the Malcom X spirit." The fist Shapelli raised up somehow felt wrong in my spirit. "But for today's class we're actually talking about the way that Holden in *Catcher in the Rye* feels his life is nothing. Like his life is meaningless. Which I think we can all relate to sometimes, right?"

Buzzcut girl scoffed.

When she got up after the bell rang, I scrambled to get my bag and stuck out my hand.

"H-hey." I said. She didn't seem to hear me. "Hey, I'm Zeke." I raised my voice a bit. "I sit here, next to . . . you." The words trailed off. I wondered how to get my mouth to stop forming tragically inept noises. She just glanced at my hand and didn't respond, which didn't help. I took my hand back, accepting the sting of her curve. "Uh, I really—I liked what you said earlier about the prison system. I thought that was really . . . smart." Her brown eyes narrowed to a sharp point. For a moment I couldn't breathe.

"Did you? Nice. Well, maybe next time share your thoughts with the rest of the class, Zeke." Her words cut through with a glare that left me no choice but to feel ashamed. I didn't even know what I was ashamed *of.* She picked up her satchel and walked away.

Chapter Nineteen

On Small Miracles

– Zeke

We were walking out of lunch when it happened. Rosie was still venting something about that bougie school she wanted to go to. She did this a lot in the short time I'd spent with her. I tried to follow along but I was also still trying to figure out this map she'd given me. Possibly the nicest thing anyone's ever done for me. It was extremely thorough. And very colorful. Mostly shades of highlighter pink. Like the Doc Martens buzzcut girl was wearing that day.

"Okay, I thought about what you said about career week and all . . ."

"Uh huh . . ." I folded up the map, equipped with a general direction and blind faith.

"I think I get what you mean. And I guess I agree, maybe a lot of kids don't even get the chance to explore their ambitions, that's fucked up. BUT, like . . . I don't know. What are they supposed to do? NOT reward certain kids for working harder than other kids? Everybody gets a cookie?"

"Uh huh . . ." Now, I was thinking about buzzcut girl and her necklaces and wondering if they held meanings like mine did as I twisted the ring between my fingers. This was not good, not good at all. It was too soon for me to already be this gone. I was outer space gone. Nope. Not good at all.

"I guess you can say maybe the metrics they use for who's working harder are like rigged or something. And sure, even if I do fucking everything they want me to do, like, what's the point? What's the point if people like Solis can just—"

"Here we are again, Rojas." A stern voice interrupted her.

Before I knew it, we were standing right in front of a grown-ass white man wearing basketball shorts in the middle of this freezing winter. A gym teacher, I assumed. Rosie's nostrils flared in an almost reflexive response. The crowded hallway had thinned down to emptiness. The hairs on my arms were on high alert and I wasn't sure why. It felt like I wasn't allowed to exist in this space at this given time. Like everything about me was wrong.

"What did I say about these distracting clothes of yours, little girl?" he continued. The way he said "little girl" made me have to hold down vomit. I tried to figure out what he was talking about. Rosie's sweater looked fine to me. She couldn't have looked more covered up. "You can run along, young man. No reason for you to be late to class."

"I think I'll stay right here, thanks," I said. He gave me a look like I'd said something wrong. I stepped behind Rosie's shoulder.

127

"Again, Mr. Scaramucci, sir, there's nothing wrong with what I'm wearing." I could see Rosie was on the verge of a breakdown. Her hand was balled up so tight I could see a vein about to pop out. The same hand I once watched explode a pen. A beyond obvious idea came to mind.

"You know what?" My arm wrapped around her tense shoulders. "Actually, babe, didn't you leave your jacket in my locker right up here? She can just put that on, right?" I pointed to my locker, just ahead of us. Scaramucci gave us another scrutinizing look before reluctantly nodding and gesturing for us to show him the locker. I walked ahead and turned the combination lock. Scaramucci followed close behind me. Didn't he have actual work to do or something?

Under my breath, I whispered to Rosie, "What's this dude's problem?"

Out of the corner of my eye, I saw her hold up a pinky finger. I choked on a laugh.

"Thank you. You're a lifesaver," Rosie said as I handed her the dead girl's jacket. She slipped it on and I watched her shoulders get broader and her back get straighter. The confidence looked good on her. Really good. She zipped it up all the way. "So, we good here?" She cocked her head to the side, preparing for a fight.

"Just . . . try to follow the dress code next time, Rojas." The gym teacher's keys jingled as he turned on his heels to leave.

"I mean, I *was* following it, but okay," she replied with a sunken look in her eyes. What was she doing? Her words made him turn back around towards us. If eyes could kill, his would've sliced right through us.

"Excuse me?"

"I said . . ." She took a brazen step forward. "I *was* following it, just like I do every day. Why don't you just admit it doesn't matter what I wear? That you target students you know won't fight back because you have some sort of power complex and you get off on giving out pink slips?"

And with that, Rosie was gone. I didn't recognize the ball of wrath that had taken her place. Honestly, a part of me was living for it. Also, slightly terrified. Mr. Scaramucci was left rooted in place with his mouth hanging open. His hands were vibrating rapidly at his side.

"I-I . . ."

"Just admit it!" Her words rang out through the empty hall with the force of an incantation. It didn't sound like Rosie's voice. It sounded like a song being played from another room. Gliding through the walls like a sinister leak. Suddenly, everything felt weighed down and heavy. The air in Miami moments before a rainstorm. I watched Mr. Scaramucci's eyes steady and the confusion quickly flow out of his body. And then the impossible happened. He listened.

"You're . . . right," he said. "I feel insecure about getting promoted when I didn't deserve it, so I overcompensate by trying to show off to my boss by targeting female students. You disregarded my authority last week. I've been looking for a reason to put you in your place ever since." The words flew out of his mouth like a shotgun. Now my own mouth was left hanging. A hand flew to cover it up.

"Apologize." Rosie demanded.

"I'm sorry. I'm sorry for interrupting your day and trying to upset you. You didn't deserve that. I wish I could make it up to you." I watched a thin line of blood trickle out of his left ear and run down his neck.

The curl on the edge of Rosie's lips seemed pleased with his response. I couldn't help but wonder if she was hurting him somehow. If he was in pain, he sure didn't show it. All I saw in his eyes was fear. Rosie took a step forward. Her eyes inspected Scaramucci's glossy green stare, looking for something. A fault in her spell, maybe? She looked down at her own hands in wonder. Then, she shrugged and turned to me with a devious smile. She leaned down to whisper.

"You wanna skip class?"

I looked between her and the man still standing frozen in front of her. Whatever demon had taken control of Rosie's body still somehow seemed to remember that I was her friend. At this point, I'd forgotten we were even at school. The late bell cut through the hallway's silence to remind me. I considered her question and nodded. She turned her attention back to her subject.

"You're gonna fill out a form to get us out of class for the rest of the day. But first, you're gonna get me a meeting with Principal Ordena." She was so . . . resolute. Like she knew what she wanted and how to get it. Like nothing and no one could stand in between her and that want. It was mesmerizing.

Scaramucci nodded his head and began walking ahead of us. Our very own police escort.

"Are you . . . okay? I mean, why are we going to the principal's office? Voluntarily?" I asked.

"I have some questions I want answered," was her response. I had about a dozen questions I wanted answered, too. Like what the hell was going on? "Maybe whatever this is . . . maybe it can help me." Her voice was cooled down, yet I watched flames dancing beneath her eyelashes.

I was slowly beginning to understand. Something was going on with this enchanted jacket. It was feeding off her unbridled anger. Or maybe she was feeding off of it. Whatever was going on, I knew that look in her eyes. It was a look I'd seen countless times before on many a white woman in a retail store.

Rosie was speaking to the manager.

Chapter Twenty

On Rose Thorns

– Rosie

The first time I remember my silence being rewarded was in kindergarten, in Miss Pat's class. It's one of the first vivid memories I have. Weird how some things stay with you and others leave. It's also one of the first times I remember an adult (who wasn't my parents), yelling at me. To her credit, the class was on a sugar high from eating Oreo cookies for lunch that day. The blinding wall of noise created by twenty or so kids having too much fun had reached a boiling point. It seemed like I was the only one who heard Miss Pat pleading with us from the front chalkboard to sit down and be quiet. I looked at my classmates in awe of the wild spirits that possessed them. That they could so easily forget that we were in a school.

Something switched in my brain and I remember thinking, "Would anyone even notice if I behaved?" I doubted it. So, my six-year-old self conducted an experiment. I folded my hands, sat at my desk, kept my mouth shut, and stared straight ahead. Mere minutes later, after Miss Pat resorted to flickering the lights on and off and shouting that we should be ashamed of ourselves, she took a breath and added that my classmates "could stand to act more like Rosie, who has been quiet this entire time." She made the whole class apologize to me. And I got a shiny Tinkerbell sticker that day.

Standing in the middle of the hallway with Mr. Scaramucci's heartbeat in my grip, I had possibly never felt better in my life. It was like I was truly in my body and in complete control of all that surrounded me. Sweet, sweet control. If I concentrated hard enough, I could probably convince the air to let me fly. It was incredible. Every step of my sneakers strutting down the hallways was filled with divine purpose. Who knew all it took for my life to fall into place was for everyone to do exactly what I asked without question?

When we got near the school's front entrance, I flung open the door to the main office and directed my attention to Rishi, the student worker guarding Principal Ordena's door. I knew Rishi as one of the few members of Stage Crew Club. Besides Mrs. Shapelli (the drama and English teacher who regularly flaked on our meetings) there were only four of us, so it was hard to miss him. He was our lights and sound tech. Like me, he expressed that he was only there for an extracurricular to put on his college application. But it wasn't like Rishi and I were friends. More like colleagues. He looked up from his desk, inspecting us through ringlets of jet black hair. His hazel eyes rested on Zeke.

"Hey, Rishi. We're here see Ordena. Scaramucci sent us," I said.

"Do you, like, have an appointment, orrrr...?" Rishi responded. He was twirling a pen between his fingers. I pressed the ringing in my ears down into my clenched fists, calling on whatever force had immobilized a grown man in the hallway moments ago.

"Open the door." The command echoed through my head. I waited for Rishi to obey, but he just stared back at me blankly. Unlike the empty, glassy stare I'd seen before, Rishi's lively eyes were lit with confusion.

"Okay? Open it yourself. I don't get paid enough to stop you, babe."

I blinked twice as the force slipped from my fists. I reminded myself that Rishi was not the enemy and I let out a slow breath.

"Fine. Thanks." Zeke sat down in the waiting area. His leg bobbed up and down with the speed of a sewing needle. "Uh, you can stay here. I'll be right back," I reassured him. I saw the worry in his eyes as he fervently nodded back at me. Then he pulled out a magazine from thin air, suddenly the same aloof Zeke from detention. If only I could make him understand how little he had to worry about. I had this. I had never been more sure of anything.

When the heavy wooden door creaked open, I crossed the threshold and stepped into a forbidden land I'd only heard about through my sister's complaints. I never thought I'd actually find myself here unless it was to claim some sort of award. Just as she described, it was far from glamorous. Everything was dark wood and in sore need of dusting. The walls were littered with boxes of papers blocking empty built-in bookshelves. Well, not completely empty. Behind Ordena's slicked back hair were lonely copies of *The Prince*, *Freakonomics*, and *The 48 Laws of Power*. His desk was covered in knickknacks, including a ceramic apple and wooden bird that kept bouncing back and forth. And then there was Ordena himself. The man who'd vowed to get Westside Academy "back on track" while his wide face was plastered over the local newspapers. Recently trending on local Facebook groups for rolling up to school in a convertible electric blue Porsche. He was almost a myth. A mascot. A school of thought personified.

The man had just set down a corded phone when I walked in. It felt like I was interrupting something. Without another word, I kicked the door closed behind me, sat down in one of the chairs in front of him, and crossed my arms. He looked at me, through narrowed eyes. Then he pressed a button.

"Uh, hey, Rishi. What did I say about letting people in my office, buddy?"

I heard Rishi's crackled one-word answer come out of the speaker.

"Oops."

The principal's jaw clenched. He turned to me.

"I'm sorry I don't have time—"

"My name's Rosie Rojas, sir. I think you'll find you do have time. Especially for your favorite student." I smiled at him and leaned forward, adjusting the collar on my jacket. I watched the same glaze that had covered Scaramucci's eyes creep over his.

"Of course, what can I do for you?"

Great question. What should I have him do for me? I didn't even know where to start to unravel the tangled mess that was my stunted ambitions. Here was the man with the power to change all that. Here he was sitting in the palm of my hand and my mind had suddenly gone blank. I thought back to the confusing emails from that morning.

"Where's Mrs. Solis?"

Principal Ordena's back straightened. He looked through me as he gave his answer.

"Unfortunately, Mrs. Solis is no longer employed here."

If I wasn't already sitting down, I would have had to take a seat. In my phone I had screenshots with evidence that she possibly screwed me over and never sent my application to the school I was supposed to be at this very moment. That's the hypothesis I had settled on. The main reason I decided to march down here was to find that lady and give her a piece of my mind. Come to find out, someone had already done it for me and taken her out, before I even got the chance.

"L-like she was fired? For what?" I felt the thread between my words and his glazed eyes dissipate. Ordena's face grew tense.

"She was found . . . mishandling funds for students . . . among other things. The authorities are looking into it. It's not much of your concern . . . This is strictly confidential."

My brow furrowed as I read through his words. Mishandling. Like mixing up a couple zeroes or like . . . stealing?

"Hmm . . . well," I continued. "She was my counselor. Someone who was supposed to HELP me. She said she sent over my application to ITI and I think maybe she didn't. I think she lied about it and never did. Someone needs to tell me WHY and then get my application in as soon as possible. With a *glowing* recommendation. And full refund for application fees. Unless you'd like me to look into what Mrs. Solis has or has not allegedly stolen. I'm sure the PTA moms would love to know."

To my surprise, Ordena laughed. "You really are a hard cookie, aren't you?" I didn't laugh back. Because nothing was funny. "Sure, I'd be happy to put in a request. And I'm sure *if* we find out where she put the funds, we *might* be able to get that back to you. But—" Why? Why was there a *but*? There always seemed to be a *but*. Why couldn't things be easy for fucking once? "But, it's highly unlikely. And you should know, it's not up to me, Rosie Rojas. It took me a minute, but I recognize your name now. You see, your file has to go through a board process in order to approve school recommendation. And that tainted record of yours . . . is a nonstarter."

"W-what tainted record?" I felt my voice breaking. As I spoke, he started typing at the archaic brick of a computer in front of him. This was the first I was hearing about this so-called "board process". "I get straight As. My GPA is a 3.8. I have perfect attendance. I won second place in the Spelling Bee last year. I'm president of the fricking Stage Crew Club and I started an annual event where students volunteer at my mom's hospital last year. You can ask any of my teachers, I—"

"Your file indicates that you had a level-five infraction two years ago at Lincoln Park Junior High? Which puts a permanent discipline notice on your record. And it says here you got a Saturday detention recently. I don't know if something's going on at home, but I'd suggest you focus on your studies, honey."

My right eye started twitching when he said the word *honey*. I kind of felt bad for him for a split second. Because I knew he thought he was just doing his job. But the cracks were starting to come through and I could see that he actually thought he was doing something more than his job. He thought he was teaching me something. He thought he knew me. He really, really thought this. I couldn't keep the bitterness I'd been suppressing for years inside any longer.

"Focus on my—so that's just it, then? I'm a nonstarter? Someone from YOUR staff fucks up and I don't even get a chance? Do you KNOW how much I've done for this shithole just to get nothing in return?! I don't have any fucking friends. I go to school, I raise my hands three times per class for a participation grade, I go to Crew Club and volunteer, and then I go home and do my homework. I've done THREE group projects by my fucking self just this past year alone! I was stuck in remedial math last year despite getting the highest grade possible and STILL your "board process" refused to put me in advanced classes. I don't belong here! I don't! Last week I got up and taught my fucking biology class by myself because you forgot to hire a sub! Focus on *my* studies? Really? That's your advice? Why don't you do your fucking job?"

When my voice reached its highest peak, I felt the last thread connecting us finally snap.

Ordena shook his head, floating out of the trance as he blinked, still slightly high off the truth serum my words seem to have imparted on him. He crossed his arms and leaned forward. Then I watched a blanket of darkness fall over him as he tilted his broad chin to a 45-degree angle.

"Imma be real with you for a sec, alright? Because you remind me of my daughters." The shift in his tone was jarring. I gave him nothing back. Because no, it was not okay. None of this was okay. He was holding my future from me and he didn't even know who I was or that, as far as I was concerned, the acceptance letter was already mine for the taking. I had put in the work, so it was mine. And he was making me beg. I really thought bringing up Mrs. Solis and the PTA would have ended this conversation. Hell, the enchanted pink threads on my back alone should've ended this conversation. Instead, I found myself drowning.

"Alright, listen. I understand the situation wasn't necessarily your fault, and I can see you're getting upset." He continued in the tone of a condescending father. And that's when it clicked in my brain. Why his attitude towards me seemed so alien, yet so familiar. Why the chair I was sitting in felt like it had turned to cold stone. I realized that he hadn't been listening to a word I'd been saying this whole time. He didn't see me as equal. It didn't matter that I was newly sixteen or that I could list every US president in chronological order from memory. He just saw this little girl. He just saw one of his daughters. What the fuck was I supposed to do about that?

"Sorry you feel this way, but you just need to change your attitude about this, right? I'm sure you feel like you're different, you're special, you're the exception, or whatever they're telling children these days. It's just not realistic. Everyone can't be . . . special. More often than not, we don't get what we want. Así es la vida. One piece of advice I hope you can take: remember this world doesn't owe you anything. Not a damn thing. This school doesn't owe you anything. You have to *work* for everything. By yourself. No one's just gonna hand it to you."

I narrowed my eyes. I wanted to chuck the stupid wooden bird on his desk at his useless forehead. *This school DOES owe me. A fucking lot.* The words weighed at the bottom of my throat. Mrs. Solis owed me. Scaramucci owed me. They had a responsibility to owe me their best behavior. *I* was the kid and *they* were the adults. Water was pooling in my eyes, painting a portrait of the patronizing man in a blur and warbling his voice. By now, the power I'd held when I first walked in here was smaller than a grain of sand. He was still talking as the first drop made its reluctant escape onto my hot cheek.

If he noticed my tears, he didn't seem to show it. His words sharpened into focus again.

"All things take time. You kids these days are too impatient to understand that. Remember, I've been where you are. We're on the same team here." He pointed to the Argentinian flag on his wall, as if it meant anything to me. Then Ordena pulled out a drawer. "Best I can do is give you this pamphlet and recommend you ask someone at ITI about other options. I hear they have a killer summer program." As if I didn't have five copies of the same pamphlet and the scholarship page memorized. As if the summer program wasn't four thousand American-ass dollars without scholarship opportunities available. I let the pamphlet hang limp in his hand.

"You're gonna regret not helping me." The words broke my voice and sounded pathetic coming out. It was all I could think to say. He gathered up a stack of papers in response, straightening them out. Then he sighed and I wondered what the fuck there was to sigh about.

"Truthfully, right now, I have much bigger problems to deal with. And you, young lady, are nothing but a thorn in my side. If you want me to help, you're gonna have to give me a better reason to. Hopefully, I don't find you in my office again. I suggest you get back to class."

I turned away from him, slowly reaching for the bronze door handle that conjured my distorted reflection. My mind was still frantically searching for the right words to cut him with. Nothing was coming to mind. And, like always, it was too late now. Always too fucking late.

"And one more thing," he continued. I refused to face him. "Crying doesn't solve anything. It wouldn't kill you to smile."

I slammed the door behind me. Not nearly as hard as I meant to.

Chapter
Twenty-one

On Waiting

– Zeke

Y ou're Zeke, right?"

"Yup." I didn't bother looking up.

Sitting in the waiting area felt like when Gran left me at the grocery store checkout line while she went to grab a missing item. The line growing shorter and shorter and the prospect of small talk rapidly approaching. Between magazine pages, I held the permission slip that released me from student obligations for the rest of the day. My golden ticket. Just as mystical and ominous as Charlie Bucket's.

"I'm Rishi," said a floating voice.

"Cool." I tried to focus my eyes on my magazine, to keep him from looking suspicious.

Just like when I waited at the bus stop in Queens, I was fully aware of my own autonomy. I mean, I was free to go. I had the ticket. I could just go. But I knew my ass would stay right where it was. By now, Rosie must've known I would do whatever she asked and followed wherever she led. Without her using whatever she'd used on that asshole gym teacher. Because that's how I was. I didn't resent her for it. If anything, I resented myself for allowing everyone to treat me like a doormat.

A muffled yelling pierced the silence of the office from the other side of Principal Ordena's door. My heart jumped to the memory of Rosie's unrestrained energy taking hold of the bleeding man in the hall. If she did something to Principal Ordena that would be very . . . not good. Super not good. Maybe I should step in to help? Who knew what she was doing to him.

"Your friend is very . . . loud."

I nodded.

Moments later, the door swung all the way open, as if from a sudden gust of wind. Rosie motioned her chin up for me to follow her. I could make out lines of dried salt water that decorated her face.

"We're done here. Let's go," she said. As though she were possessed by my mother.

I stood up to follow her and dropped my voice to a whisper.

"Uh, where to?" I don't know why it mattered.

"Queens."

Like I said, wherever she led. Though, if she was thinking what I was thinking, Queens was probably one of the better places to go. It was the source of the code that would hopefully defuse her bomb. A place for guidance. Assuming she wasn't looking for more fuel to add to her explosives. Which was . . . a possibility. I figured we'd cross that bridge when we got there.

My body followed her as she stomped out of the office. Just before I closed the door behind us, a bright voice stopped me.

"Nice talking to you!" Rishi waved at me from behind the desk, his smile unrelenting beneath striking honey-colored eyes. For some reason, I kinda felt bad. It felt like I'd gotten the script wrong again.

". . . Yeah. Sorry. Bye."

Chapter Twenty-two

On Broken Jars

– Rosie

When we arrived at Yolanda's, she was shuffling a train of people out her front door. It was a weird range of punk fans, artsy folk, and yoga types. All expressing their praise for the gray-haired, flowy-dressed woman at the door as they made their exit. It was a curious scene. My newfound tía looked exactly the same. Except for the specks of dried paint and clay now stuck in her gray halo.

"See you next week!" Yolanda hunched over her cane yelling after the crowd. And then, to Zeke and me, "Come on in, chicas!" She said it with the same warm tone she'd worn on our last visit. Like we were expected guests. Always welcome.

"Bendicíon, Tía." I kissed her cheek.

"Am I a chica?" Zeke whispered behind my ear.

"You are an honorary chica, if you like," she whispered back to him. "Uh oh. Y esa cara?" She pinched my cheeks in her hand and inspected my eyeballs.

Then she guided my back into her living room, where I sank into the plastic covers, holding tight to the string I was about to unravel. I'd gripped onto the sleeves of my pink jacket the whole ride over, like the handlebars of a rollercoaster, afraid of what would happen if I let go. It felt as though my bones would turn to ash if I dared take it off.

Zeke was still standing by the door. His eyes darted from Yolanda to the otherworldly contents of her home. A plastic sheet was laid down on the living room floor. Spread newspaper and wet clay figurines covered her kitchen table. At this point, I'd stopped asking questions about how exactly Yolanda made a living and figured it was none of my business.

"It's alright, I don't bite."

"Uh, hi. I'm Zeke. Rosie's friend. You don't know me but I know you. . . . Nice to meet you, ma'am."

"Of course I know you! You sat in front of my house like a chicken. But it's okay. Chickens come when ready. Sit." Yolanda walked into her kitchen.

Zeke directed his shocked eyes to me. My shrug said *I told you, so.* Then he squeaked his butt beside me, hands itching towards the golden tarot cards sitting on the coffee table.

"And your sister?" Yolanda asked, returning from her kitchen with a cup of tea. I'd almost forgotten about Caro. On top of everything else, my sister's stubbornness had been grinding my nerves lately.

"I don't know. School."

"Mmm . . ." She looked into her teacup as she stirred her spoon. "Our sisters are all we have. Remember that." When her eyes lifted to meet mine, they were like a swirling dark portal to another dimension. But I hadn't come here to talk about Caro. And honestly, Yolanda's aloof nature was starting to get on my nerves, too.

I tried explaining what had happened at school. "I came here because—" There weren't any rational words to explain it. I reached and reached, but my brain was still tinted with different shades of red. "I came here because I thought you might . . . I-I need . . . I don't know. I don't know what happened. I feel like . . ."

"Okay, sí, sí. Te pusiste la jaqueta, your emotions amplified your energy power, which, by the looks of your new aura, seems to yield control and influence? Or it did . . . earlier. Now, the light is waning. Stretched. Like . . . rubber band. Almost broken. You don't know how to snap it back. Am I right?"

My face felt hot when I looked up at her, processing the new sensation that was coursing from my heart through my fingertips. I nodded.

"I just need to—" I unclenched my fists and looked at the crescent-shaped marks in my palms. "If I could just get it back, I could fix everything. I could get him to *listen*."

"Aht, aht." Yolanda slowly set down her teacup. She bent into the leather chair in front of us using her cane for support. "Slow down. Todo a su tiempo. We'll get to that soon. Right now, I need someone to bring a couple of those statues in the kitchen. And, right behind you, Ezekiel, hand me that jar. The blue one."

I blinked. How, when Yolanda clearly understood the gravity of how monumentally shitty I was feeling, could she ask me to do chores for her? How could she ask me to do the same thing Ordena demanded of me? To wait. I looked to Zeke, who was already obeying, handing her a jar of hydrangea blue paint which had clearly once held Gerber baby food. His eyes were glued to the woman with intrigue.

"You teach a ceramics class here?" Zeke asked timidly. It was as if my problems had left the room entirely.

"I do. A weekly community class." Yolanda turned to me, expectantly. I finally sighed and got up to follow Zeke's lead.

"How much does that pay?" I asked from the kitchen, begrudgingly giving in to the change in topic.

"My class? Nothing. It's free," she said.

I could hardly feel the slick statues I cradled carefully in my numb hands. There were dozens of these miniature figurines creating a scene at the kitchen table. Modeling various winged cherubs and baby cupids.

"That seems like a wasted opportunity. You don't even sell these? I could do it for you." *Save up for the expensive college I'm never getting into*, I thought.

I heard Yolanda's chuckle from the other room. "Qué niña más capitalista." She said it like it was a bad thing.

I chose the smallest three to bring back to her. Then I sat down. I waited for her to tell us what to do next or to at least answer my question. And when nothing came, I filled the empty space with an outpour of ramblings.

"So, what happened was . . . Ordena—he's, just—he's insufferable. And incompetent. All of them are. You know they fired Mrs. Solis? The lady I told you about who was holding my application? He told me they fired her 'cause—guess what? She was stealing money. Fucking, of course she—I knew that bitch was shady. Never liked her. Both of them are just—ugh. Fuck, I mean why even take a job at a school if you don't even like childr— Like why make everything so hard? Why don't they want to help me?"

Yolanda put her hand up to stop me. I hadn't even noticed the speed of my heartbeat until then. My lungs gasped for breath.

"Slow." Yolanda contrived a paintbrush out of thin air. She pointed it towards me. "Paint. And breathe, nena." She took a large gulp of air and blew it out. I could smell chamomile with hints of cinnamon flowing out of her.

"I don't know how to paint this." I took the paintbrush in one hand and held up a tiny terra-cotta-colored cherub in the other. Its balled-up cheeks looked like they were blowing a gust of forceful wind.

"You paint sets for the play." Zeke piped up. He reached for a cherub of his own.

"Musical." I corrected. I couldn't help myself. And besides, that was different. I knew how to paint a flat surface, not a moldable, moist, three-dimensional one. As a rule, I did not like doing things I knew I would probably be bad at.

"Yes, exactly. You know how to paint. Keep in mind, when I finish firing them, the clay will turn white and the paint will dry a bolder color. Now, paint. You too, Ezekiel."

So, we sat quietly, taking turns dipping our brushes into the blue, and we painted these chubby babies. All different shapes and sizes. Some had wings. Some held instruments. Some were crawling. Some were running. Some had misshaped proportions. Some were wrapped in delicately gathered clay made to look like fabric. One was completely naked. I sparingly painted the blue where I thought blue should go, in their clothes and the things they held. Zeke went rogue and painted hands and hair blue and inscribed curling designs into their arms. He asked loads of questions about how ceramics worked and if Yolanda was allowed to put a kiln in her backyard (according to the city, she wasn't). After the blue, we moved to a pale lavender that Yolanda assured us would dry fire red. I had to admit, Zeke was right. This felt just like my tedious and solitary afternoons painting set panels in the auditorium.

"Won't your students be mad that we messed their pieces up?" Zeke asked her.

"They'll be fine. Ceramics is the art of letting go. These are the first attempts. Next week they will try again and they will make better attempts. That's the lesson. That's life." She held up a clay statue with comically oversized ears as she said this. Then she let it slip out of her hands and crash into a soft lump on the floor. "Oops!"

I'd hardly noticed when Zeke got up and started a Héctor Lavoe album on an old-school record player Yolanda had lying around in another room. It mixed with the sounds of squawking geese in the distance.

I took a lot longer than him to finish painting my half. The numbness trickled out of my hands. My thoughts settled as the wide and uncertain newly magical world reduced to just the people sitting in this dusty room.

As I painted the final tiny winged figure, Yolanda grabbed her cane, lifted up from her leather chair, and plopped down on the couch next to me. She gently dabbed a solution at my sleeve, where a splatter of paint had landed. Then she motioned for me to take off the jacket. I peeled it off slowly, immediately feeling naked. After crisply folding it in two, she let it drape off her knee and gave it a pat. By some miracle, I was still in one piece.

"Now," she said, putting her other hand on my knee. "How do you feel?"

I thought for a second. How did I feel? When Mami asked me questions like that, my response would usually be a shrug. Or *fine*. Or *I don't know*. And Mami would say some variation of "If you don't know how you feel, who does?" before shooing me away. How do people know how they feel? I think I was usually the last one to know. It was only now that I could put a word to the emotion that had paralyzed Mr. Scaramucci in the hallway and propelled me into Principal Ordena's office.

"I was really angry before. Like really, really pissed. Like old anger. Months of bottled up bullshit. It was the first time I think I *liked* being angry. Or it liked me, maybe? But I don't like it now. It got . . . heavy. I mean, I feel better now. I can breathe a little. But . . . still. There's still something . . . living there inside. I think there always was."

Yolanda nodded knowingly. Then she carefully plucked out her words.

"It's good to be angry."

I set down my clay figurine, momentarily stunned by the complete opposite of what I'd heard all my life. From the moment I entered kindergarten it was always, *violence is never the answer.*

"I don't know about that." I disagreed. "It's stupid and makes me feel stupid. I don't want to be angry. I want to be a nice person."

"No, not stupid. Would you have come to my door weeks ago if not for your anger?" I considered her question. Probably not. She nodded again. "When you've stopped being angry, you've stopped caring. You are human, mi amor. Your emotions and your body are working as they should. It's *good* to be angry. Anger is not bad. It is like fire. It is a result. And like fire, if used properly, it creates change." She took my hands in hers, ensuring her words held weight. "When did it stop feeling like change?"

It sounded weird to phrase it like that, but I knew what she meant. I thought back to the moment my tears disobeyed me, retracing my steps to see where it went wrong.

"It was fine until Ordena laughed. Something about the way he talked to me . . . I think my anger reached, like, a tipping point. And then I started feeling everything slip as he kept insisting what I was asking of him was impossible. It was like this wall I couldn't get past. And then at some point it felt like the power transferred to him. He started saying these horrible things. He called me *tainted* and a *nonstarter*. And then he told me—you wanna know what he said? *The world doesn't owe you anything*. Pshh." I looked out the window and watched gray clouds rush over the sky. My nose scrunched itself up. "I think that was it. Yeah. Like I was this . . . baby . . . like I didn't already know that *all things take time*." Yolanda reached for my face and wiped away the tears that had apparently been falling as I spoke. Stupid tears.

"Time is a tool of compromise, and man is a creature of adjustment." Yolanda said, looking past me. It took me a while to connect the words to their meanings. "I read that somewhere . . . I can't remember, déjame ver . . . ?"

Zeke nearly gave me a heart attack when he popped his head in from the next room, hand grasping the door frame. "Louis Lomax. *Ebony* magazine, volume 20, issue 10. I wrote that one down. Straight fire." I gave him a scrutinizing look before I choked out a laugh.

"What the fuck, Zeke?" I felt a smile redirect the streams on my cheeks.

"What? I read."

"It can't be with the same brain that didn't know what 8 times 9 was," I teased as I wiped my hands over wet eyes.

Zeke shook his head through a suppressed smile. He kissed his lips. "Just when I thought you had a soul."

Yolanda chuckled and fixed her eyes on the light reflecting off his hand.

"You're absolutely right, Ezekiel. Very good! And I like that ring of yours."

Zeke twiddled his fingers in airy waves. His dimples made another appearance. "Thank you, Auntie—wait, can I call you Auntie?"

"Call me what you wish, chica. As I was saying . . . time can heal wounds, but only if those wounds have been given the proper attention."

She was talking to me, but it felt as though she were voicing a reminder to her own self. A familiar curiosity awoke in me. I got up and reached for my backpack. This wasn't exactly the reason I came to visit her, but now felt like as good a time as any. I pulled out a fresh yellow notebook I'd picked up at the dollar store before meeting Zeke for his haircut. I'd been carrying it with me everywhere ever since. The first page now read: *The Rojas-Cuevas Family Origin Story*.

"I don't know if you remember, but the last time I was here, I asked if I could come back and interview you." I handed her the notebook.

"Of course," Yolanda said, taking it from my hands. "I'm not *that* old, hija mía. My memory still works fine."

Ordena seemed to have momentarily sealed my fate with the ITI application. I might not even need to finish the new essay anymore. So, what was the point? Leaving the notebook empty, though. . . . It seemed sad somehow. Like giving up on something bigger than ITI. No matter what I did with the information, I'd already opened the box. I had to know what was inside.

"Right. Well, I kinda wrote down all my questions in there. We don't have to get to all of them today, but maybe we could—"

And then, right as it felt like we were finally getting somewhere, my Sidekick rang to the tune of "Lip Gloss" by Lil Mama. A relic from my questionable decisions as a middle schooler. The screen glowed with a photo of Caro as a toddler with baby carrots stuck up her nose. She hated that picture. Guilt shot through me with every buzz. It was already three o'clock. In all the confusion getting trapped by my own rage, she'd dropped to the bottom of my list. I didn't really want to talk to her right now. But if she'd worked up the nerve to drop the silent treatment and return my call . . .

I asked where the bathroom was and excused myself.

Chapter
Twenty-three

On Liars

— Caro

I was assaulted by Mami at the buttcrack of dawn to get my hair done that day. Being awake that early should be illegal. Unlike her and Rosie, I refused to use the conditioner Mami had laced with relaxer, preferring the volume of my natural curls. Where they could blow dry their hair straight in an hour or less, once I was forced into a salon chair against my will, I needed a solid four or five hours to get the same effect. To make things worse, that morning I was greeted with a lovely blood stain in the bathroom. Which was just great. The sun wasn't even out yet to pre-warm my salon chair.

Still, I knew for some reason, if I dared cross onto our home soil without my hair in the freshest, silkiest, most deep-fried hair ... I don't know. Maybe the embarrassment of being unpresentable in front of complete strangers would give Mami a heart attack or something. She also had to be the only one to touch my hair, of course. Apparently, Lena and the other vie-jitas at the salon didn't know how to do it right. *They don't get the roots*, she'd said once. As if she didn't know that as soon as I stepped off the plane, the humidity would undo all her hard work anyways. I think she took it as some kinda challenge. Like if she passed a hot iron through my hair enough times she could beat mother nature at her own game.

She didn't talk, but I felt her sharpness through fingers that violently massaged my scalp and twisted my head from side to side. One particular tug of her comb through my knotted curls felt like it might've been on purpose, actually. Though if I found a bald spot tomorrow, my mother would probably be more heartbroken than me. Like a child, Mami would never intentionally damage her favorite doll. Which is what I was. Well, maybe not favorite. So I didn't mind the silence she filled with 1010 WINS humming out traffic updates from the radio at her station.

Papi had transferred some money for me to get a cab to JFK later this afternoon. But JJ convinced me to let him drive so we could pocket the money for a date. As far as I knew, Mami still didn't approve, and wasn't planning on helping me pack or get there. Rosie was still on my shit list. At the very least I had JJ. It was gonna be my first time on a plane all by myself; I just had to figure shit out on my own.

I winced as Mami pulled the last rollo tight to the nape of my neck and stabbed my scalp with a rusted bobby pin. She pushed my shoulders under the dryer and handed me a bowl of oatmeal. I wasn't gonna ask for an apology from her or nothing. If she wanted to apologize, she already would have. So we spent the morning in a standoff, waiting for the other to make a move. I even held my tongue when she burned the tip of my ear with the iron. The bitter smell of burning hair filled my nostrils.

Before I stepped out the door, she finally broke her silence.

"Cuidao con el dengue. Ponte el repelente pa lo' mosquito. As soon as you get to your father's, wrap your hair into a tubi, como t'enseñé. Don't forget. And call me when you land."

When I got to the school parking lot, a rando wearing a beanie and a spiked collar was talking to JJ outside his car. She walked away when I rolled up on him. I took off my oversized hoodie and changed into the cropped Juicy tracksuit I'd had since I was twelve years old. It cut off just below my belly button now.

"Who was that?" I asked him.

"Ionno. Some girl. Never seen her before." He was leaning one shoulder against his beloved Camry, looking past me. While I looked in his rearview mirror to adjust my lipstick and fix my hair, I felt my jaw tighten. I hated dealing with my hair when it was like this. All flat and long and limp. It almost reached past my boobs. Like a mermaid. Because I wasn't used to it, I constantly felt like something was touching my arm, then boom—hair. And then there was the other thing, with everyone staring at me and feeling the need to tell me how much *better I looked this way.* I checked my teeth one last time in the mirror before turning back to my boyfriend.

"What'd she want?"

"Who?"

"Who do you think?"

"Ionno! I think she got a crush on me or something. Told her I wasn't interested. You look bomb though." He wrapped his arm around my waist and tugged me roughly towards him. *A crush on me or something.* I knew that was his version of a joke. I wasn't laughing. He stayed liking other girls' pictures on Instagram and I was getting tired of complaining about it. I didn't want to be that girl.

"I like your hair, mamas." He took a bit of it and twirled the limp strands around his meaty fingers. His eyes softened to a desire I recognized too well. In an animalistic burst of energy, he leaned in and took a bite out of my neck. It tickled. I couldn't help but giggle as I shoved him off of me. Then he slid his hand down my ass pocket like he used to do when we first started going out. And we walked together.

The first time I saw JJ was in gym class at the beginning of last year. He was tall. Taller than me, which was rare. I'd been looking down at most people since the fifth grade. And for some reason looking up at him made me want to find a way to touch his bronze, unblemished face. The next day, I got the girl who sat in front of him during exercises to switch seats with me. And then at lunch, his goofy ass sat next to me. And a couple days after that, I followed his crew to Bruno's, the pizza shop he worked at. I got Rosie to tag along. We told Mami we were studying at the library.

Everyone thought JJ and me were dating way before we actually were. We were always touching each other and shit. We called each other *bestie*. I would trace letters in his back with my fingers and make him guess what I was saying. After his shift, I'd offer to brush waves into his hair and set it with a silk scarf while he shouted at his *Call of Duty* game. Eventually, he started calling me *wifey*. I let him. Then I'd come home to endure Mami's wrath, but it was worth it for nights I spent cheesing into my phone under the covers.

One afternoon, last summer, hanging out at the pizza shop quickly turned into night, and before I knew it I was following his crew to the corner of Grove and 1st Street at this empty lot where they had ATV races sometimes. It was loud as fuck and everything was filled with smoke. That was the first time I got really drunk. I almost lost my voice cheering JJ on as he beat the rocks outta this other kid in the monster truck–sized ride he'd borrowed from his older brother. Something about the way he was waving this big ass Colombian flag while beating his chest and hanging out of that ATV just did something to me. My heart started beating fast between my legs. And then he scooped me up and took me for a ride. He started kissing me hard and fast and with a purposeful tongue. I told him how I'd never done anything like that before. I just told people I had, and they believed me. He wanted to do more, but I told him I wouldn't without a condom. And without him calling me his girlfriend first. I don't know why I said that, I just did.

The next morning he sent me a screenshot of his changed Facebook status and we walked into school together with his hand down my ass pocket.

Just like it was now as we crossed the metal detectors.

"Relax, boo." He kissed me softly at my locker and whispered in my ear. "Not too much, though. You look hot when you're jealous."

His rough voice felt like a fly buzzing in my ear. I punched his left shoulder and then he skipped off to class. Even finer from the back than from the front. If only he knew how to keep his beautiful mouth shut, he'd be perfect.

As I turned the corner to my homeroom, I nearly collided into the brick that was Officer Matt, who insisted I call him by his first name. Like we were buddies. Every time I saw this balding man, who wandered the halls as a constant reminder of how easily I could be put back on probation for something as dumb as talking back to a teacher, my heart started running a marathon. I couldn't even look at the makeshift police station by the gym. I'd only been subjected to that place once. Once was enough. Officer Matt just felt like being near a frayed wire. He was so . . . unnecessary. It didn't matter that he smiled a sickly sweet smile and told me to "stay out of trouble." It didn't matter that, to my knowledge, I'd done nothing wrong (yet).

I didn't see JJ again until third period, when I texted him to meet me in the south wing girl's bathroom on the second floor. There weren't as many officers on the second floor. Still, we almost got caught. Then we were at it again at fourth period when we met at our spot in the east wing janitor's closet.

At lunch, the attending teacher—who'd obviously never heard of having fun before—had to tell me to get off his lap. So, I made do playing footsies with him the rest of the time while my girl Leidy filled me in on the Facebook drama of the day. People said I talked fast, but I'd never heard anyone talk as fast Leidy did. Her bottle red natural curls in a messy bun on top of her head, bouncing back and forth as her words picked up steam. She talked like the world was ending tomorrow. Apparently, the girl she was beefing with—Marta—had photoshopped her face onto the Wendy's lady and captioned the post "go back to work, lady" in her latest clapback. Which, I had to admit, was pretty funny. Even if Leidy didn't think so. Still, if I wasn't working on leaving my hoodrat ways behind, I too would have molly whopped that girl the way Leidy wanted to. If it wasn't Marta, though, it would've just been someone else. Leidy once told me that sometimes she just spread lies about people when she was bored. She was nuts. As long as she kept my name out of her lies, though, being friends with her was, at the very least, entertaining.

"What is she even mad about?"

"Girl, I don't even remember. I think I called her dog ugly or something. How was I supposed to know that lil bitch died, or whatever?" Leidy said. I snorted milk out of my nose as she continued pleading her case.

"Damn, Leidy! You a savage." JJ laughed, his deep voice cutting through the cafeteria chatter. He addressed the rest of the table. "She finna be at your funeral looking down at the casket like, 'Bye, ugly!' Is that how it is?"

Leidy nodded, keeping ten toes firm on her argument.

"If you ugly then, yeah! That's how it is! You want me to lie?" She shrugged, looking to me for support.

JJ lost it, howling and banging the table. He could be so loud sometimes.

"Control your man, Caro. He embarrassing you," Leidy said.

"He always embarrassing me. Imma still stick beside him." I took his cheeks in my hand and shook his squished-up face.

"Goals, honestly. If ya don't win best couple this year that shit is rigged!" Then Leidy grabbed my arm and said, "Oh shit! Almost forgot!" She dug her elbow into me. "Did you hear about . . . you know . . . your bestie being back?" Her eyebrows raised, expectantly. I tried to think about who she could possibly be talking about. My eyes wandered to the table next to us, where my sister was sitting with Zeke, quietly writing in a notebook.

Leidy's lip curled. Then she whispered in my ear. "Turn around, on the left, by the vending machine. Pinky."

The realization hit before I saw her. Instantly, my mind went back to the parking lot this morning. Back to the girl JJ was clearly lying about. I saw the back of her pink head, her neck wrapped in a spiked leather collar. She was sitting with the girls from the dance team. I was still lost, though. How was she my bestie, exactly? I gave Leidy a curious look, waiting for her to elaborate. After a moment she said, under her breath, "Oh, you don't recognize her?" I asked who it was. "Guess." I hated when a bitch made me guess. I wished she would just tell me.

"I don't know, fuckin' . . . Rihanna?" I rolled my eyes at her. "For real?"

I looked closer, watching the girl stand up and throw away her trash. From the side, I could see something in the rounded corners of her nose that was vaguely familiar, beneath all that makeup. It was on the tip of my tongue.

"Jesus Christ, it's Ashia! From your middle school? Ain't you used to fight her?" Leidy hissed at me. I barely heard Leidy after she said the name. *Ashia.* Of course. My ears grew hot just at the memory of her. Of her nose crackling beneath my fist. Of her slick hair slipping between my fingers. Of warm blood sprinkled on my cheeks. Of my tears seeping into specks of her blood as I stared at myself in the school bathroom and furiously scrubbed my hands clean. A high-pitched ringing tone overtook my hearing. "She goes by *Ash* now. I go to CCD with this girl from her old school who swears she's some kinda witch. Like a real one. She put a curse on this kid at their school who got hit by a car."

Leidy choked out a laugh as she finished and I tried to smile to keep the bitterness out of my face. I kept one eye on the pink-haired girl for the rest of the lunch period. It felt like that shit went down a century ago, and yet here I still was letting just the sight of her affect me like this. Honestly, it was embarrassing. I kept trying to let this old version of me go and she kept fucking showing up.

After lunch, I had gym class. Which I didn't feel like doing today because in addition to the ringing in my ears, my period was rearranging my insides. If I gave my gym teacher that excuse, she would say some shit like, "You know what's good for cramps? Exercise." So, I "forgot" my gym clothes. You could do that three times a semester and still pass.

I sat on the bench and watched everyone do their exercises, winking at my man when he shot me a smile during sit-ups. One of the six gym teachers blew their whistle.

"Listen up! Boys are moving to the gym class next door and the girls from next door will be coming here for us to play— drumroll please . . . pin guard!" My favorite game, pin guard. It was basically dodgeball, except they banned dodgeball years ago after kids kept getting sent to the hospital, which is the point of the game. Only with pin guard, the point was to hit the bowling pin at each end of the court. If a couple kids got hit in the process, then . . . oh well.

Another teacher explained that they decided the boys were too rough to play with the girls last time. Hence, the gender split. I'd gotten the winning hit in that last game and two whiny boys complained that I cheated, so it smelled like fresh bullshit to me. Just my luck that I had chosen to sit out today. Could've used the stress release.

JJ blew me a kiss goodbye. I pretended to catch it and pelt it back at him. He dramatically pretended to get shot in the heart as he bounced out the door.

And then, of fucking course, Ashia's pink scalp walked in. A whistle blew again.

The next thing I knew, through no fault of my own, our gym teacher was pointing at me and yelling "DETENTION!" All I'd done was pass a stray rubber ball from the bench back into the court and it happened to hit Ashia in the head and she happened to fall over. Not my fault the girl had a weak center of gravity. I turned away when she snapped her head up in my direction. But not before catching a pained look in her eye.

"Keep it up and you'll be back on probation, Rojas!" They always came at me with the probation threat. I hated that it always worked. My hands started shaking. I folded them under my arms, fixing my face into a pout. When everyone's eyes finally detached from me, I defiantly grabbed a spearmint gum out of my bag and popped it in my mouth. For that, I was stopped on my way out of class and told to pay a visit to Ordena's office.

I'd been met Ordena a couple times before, of course. And the guy before him, and the guy before him who'd only lasted a month. At this point, I was sure the chair in his office had my assprint engraved into it. Comfortable. Like a memory foam mattress. No way nearly as bad as the police station. It had been a minute, though. I'd been keeping things pretty lowkey.

"Another Rojas. Not good." Our principal wagged his finger at me. Not sure how I felt about him using my name as a verb.

"It was an accident." I shrugged.

"There's no such thing as an accident. You know who said that?"

I stared blankly at him.

"No guesses?"

"I don't know. Some dude who never made no mistakes? Ain't you boutta tell me?"

"It's *aren't*, not ain't— Please—" He shook his head. I smiled. It was too easy. "Anyways . . . Freud. I believe it was Freud who said there's no such thing as an accident. Okay? The point is . . . accidents are avoidable. And in a functioning society, they will not be tolerated. That's why we do not tolerate accidents at Westside Academy. So . . . think about that when you're sitting in detention."

Every time Ordena talked to me I thought some guy was gonna pop out of his closet with TV cameras or something. Always talking in corny quotes and nonsense monologues like the white teacher in a movie whose very presence was a gift to the "underprivileged" kids. Like they were doing charity work. Sometimes I wondered what the fuck a principal even did. The amount of time I'd spent in his office, I could probably do a better job than this oily ass man.

After staring at me for a full minute, he dismissed me and said he better not see me in his office again (even though there was a 90 percent chance he would).

After school, I complained to JJ about him as we walked down the front steps.

"Maybe try not hitting bitches you don't like next time. Count to ten or something." His pea brain always seemed to skip the listening part and go straight to half-assed solutions.

"It was an accident! As in, I didn't mean to hit her! And I ain't forgot you were talking with her this morning." I pressed a finger into his chest. He rolled his eyes.

"Oh my god! I already told you! Ionno her! Never seen her before in my life!" But as much as I wanted to, I still didn't believe him. His phone buzzed in his hand and he forced out a breath. His shadow crept over me when he kissed me on the forehead. "Aight, I'll hit you up later."

I twisted his black t-shirt as he turned towards the parking lot.

"Whoa, whoa, whoa. *Later?* Hello?"

"What? I don't got time for this. I gotta go handle some shit with my cousin."

So now he was rushing me. Unbelievable. He really forgot.

"You was 'posed to drive me to the airport in an hour." I widened my eyes at him, trying to jog his memory.

"Ah, shit. Was that today? Which airport?"

"JFK." I'd already told him this. If I grabbed his phone right now, I was sure the textual evidence would be right there.

He closed his eyes and pinched the bridge of his nose. Thinking.

"Wait . . . I thought your pops gave you money for a cab or something?"

"You said to pocket the money and you'd take me, member? Fuck! Forget it!" I pushed him away from me. His phone buzzed again. "Go! Don't worry about me!"

He hesitated before kissing my stiff hand and then he was off. Fuck me. Guess I was walking home, then. I wrapped my coat tight. Icy gusts of wind blew strands over my lips. My frozen fingers tried to pull hair out of my tongue.

My shivering hands pulled out my phone to text Rosie. No response. I pulled out my chapstick. Thinking. Waiting.

Like a dummy, I waited on the steps for a whole five minutes, searching for her in the crowd of kids pouring out into school buses, pickup cars, and the CVS across the street. Until they dwindled down and the afternoon patrols started handing out jaywalking tickets and breaking up groups. Cold whips smacked me across the face and made my eyes water up. Still no Rosie. Now the clock was ticking for me to figure out this cab situation on my own. I didn't even know what number to call. Mami had made it clear she'd be no help. Fuck.

My feet started for home as I pressed the phone to my ear, waiting for Rosie to remember she had a sister. Wherever the fuck she was. Probably with her new best friend. I almost thought she wasn't gonna pick up, when on the tenth ring . . .

"Hello?" Rosie's voice was hushed.

"Where the fuck are you?!"

"Kind of a long story."

Now I was worried. She usually wasn't this vague. At least not with me.

"Come home. I'm leaving soon. . . . Unless you forgot, too?" I said, trying not to sound as desperate as I felt.

"Leaving where?" So she *had* forgotten. First JJ, now the one person who was supposed to have my back, no matter what. I put her back on the top of my shit list. "Your flight. Oh shit, shit, shit. I'm sorry, Caro. Wasn't JJ supposed to take you?"

I took my phone out of my ear and took a breath.

"He bailed. Just—just get home. Text me the number of the cab company Mami uses. I'll wait for you so we can say good-bye." There was silence on the other end. I rolled my eyes. "What?"

"It's just . . . it might be a while. I'm in Queens with Zeke. I don't know how long—"

"Why the fu—Wait. Are you at Yolanda's? Without me?"

". . . Yes. It's a long story. It happened so quick, we ju—"

"Whatever." I stopped her as I narrowly avoided an ice patch on the sidewalk. I pushed down a lump in my throat. "Goodbye, then. I'll tell Papi you were sorry you couldn't make it."

I was about to leave it at that and hang up when I heard Rosie mutter something on the other end.

"I wouldn't say I'm *sorry.*"

The phone smashed back into my ear. The nerve on her was fucking astronomical. I bit my tongue between my back molars. How could she be so selfish? And then I asked her what I'd really wanted to ask her ever since we'd gotten the wedding invitation in the first place.

"How come you got beef with Papi, anyways?"

Chapter
Twenty-four

On Fathers

– Rosie

How come you got beef with Papi, anyways?"

I didn't answer Caro immediately. It was a question that had lingered in the air between us for years now. Even as casually as she tried to phrase it, I could feel pressing down on us like an anchor.

"How come you don't?" I shot back.

"Because . . . he's our family? I guess he got flaws but, like . . . everybody got flaws. I got plenty of flaws. But he got good shit, too. Like always answering his phone . . ." That felt pointed. ". . . and teaching me how to throw a punch the right way . . ." I wasn't sure teaching Caro to punch was such a good thing. ". . . Y-you can't just throw people away."

"Okay."

"Okay . . . ?"

My eyes rolled a full three-sixty. "Okay and? I guess he got good shit like whipping us, too, right?" I didn't mean the words to bite as much as they did. But that's what she was fishing for. Teeth. Now she was getting ready to growl at me with hers.

Fuck. I really didn't want to talk about this right now. Not like this. Especially not over the phone. Papi was always a sore subject. I'd just spent the past couple of hours focusing on regulating my emotions and now I was completely spent. My brain was begging for a nap. I had no filter or room for anything but harsh truth.

"Whipping? The fuck you mean whipping? I never saw no whipping."

Sometimes I hated Caro as much as I loved her. Sometimes I really thought she'd say any crazy thing, as long as it was the opposite of my thing.

"Pow pow. La correa, la escoba, pela'o, la chancleta. Whatever you wanna call it. It's not that ambiguous. He beat us . . . sometimes . . . like . . ." I was reluctant to say the *b* word. What other word was there for it? For the mark above my ear from when I couldn't learn to throw a baseball perfectly like Caro. Or the spackled hole behind the Communion photos hanging in the living room.

"Psh!" Caro kissed her lips. "*That's* what you're mad at him about? That's nothing. It's just his . . . culture. That's what parents are supposed to do. It's just discipline."

"To Mami?" I would be damned if my husband tried to dique discipline me. That finally shut my sister up. For a moment, at least.

"That's between them two. Nothing to do with me."

Somehow I knew Caro would think that, but it was still wild to hear the words come out of her mouth. It wasn't just her—it was our family, our school, our town. The prevailing attitude was to keep your eyes on your own paper and mind your business. I was an expert at minding my business, too. But with Papi, I could only do it for so long. And then I was punished for it.

"Besides," she continued. "I'd rather have the shit slapped outta my ass every now and then. Rather that than be walking around like those crazy ass kids screaming at the grocery store." Caro chuckled. Her weak attempt to lighten the mood. I took the phone off my ear and stared at it incredulously.

"What? You disagree?" Caro's voice crackled amidst the pause, as if she could see the look on my face. I shook my head incredulously, wondering when the obvious would hit her.

"You think YOU not a crazy ass kid? Are you joking?"

I regretted the words as soon as they escaped my lips. Caro sighed. Then there was a long pause.

"Wooow, sis. Know what? Nevermind! One day imma be gone. You'll be sorry then, huh? Forget you, then. I'll figure it out myself. I don't need you to get to JFK."

Ugh. Never could take the same energy she dished out. I tried to backtrack as my legs paced back and forth in the small emerald-tiled bathroom.

"Can't you just wait half an hour? I can go with you? Just wait for—"

The phone clicked on her end and crackled dead.

Qué drama. Good thing I packed Advil this morning.

Chapter Twenty-five

On Origins

– Zeke

Hey, Auntie—Ms. Yolan—Ma'am . . . can I ask you a question?" I took Rosie's place on the couch while she took her phone call.

"Lo que tú quieras, papi" Yolanda's dewy eyes gleamed and I took that as a yes. It was scary how much she reminded me of Gran. Black and regal. Charming accent and all. She even smelled just like her. Except she had this expansive energy that I couldn't quite put my finger on. It felt like talking to an oracle or a soothsayer. Someone who traveled in from another time.

"Don't tell Rosie, but . . ." I put a hand in front of my mouth to divulge my secret. "What do you do when the person you like . . . maybe doesn't like you back? Or they don't act like it?"

"Am I right to say this person is not Rosie?" She raised a brow and pointed a thumb towards the bathroom.

"Yeah—I mean, no, it's not her. I mean, she's cool and all, but . . . no it's another person. It's kinda new."

"Good. Mhmm. Well, seems like you already figured some of that out."

"What do you mean?"

She picked up my hand as though it were an inanimate object. "An eternal lovers ring! Sixteenth century, by the looks of it. Very unique band. Central American. Made of anacagüita. Panama tree. Where did you find this one?"

"Panama tree? Really?" An ache in my chest made me hesitate before adding, "My gran was Panamanian, you know? Weird. She used to read cards for people at her retirement home."

I don't know why I'd felt the need to mention that last part. Yolanda nodded slowly. And then, like it was nothing at all, she said, "You're still hurting."

Her words cut through me, stirring feelings I thought I'd buried deep beneath soil a long time ago.

I took my hand back, ignoring her statement and twisting the carved wooden ring on my index finger so that its pink pendant shimmered by the window light. "Um . . . I found it at a vintage store in Jersey City. Why? What's *eternal lovers* mean?"

Yolanda put up a finger. She reached under the couch and pulled out a small wooden box with a red heart painted over it, beneath a lingering layer of dust bunnies. She cracked open the box as if proposing to me. A thin layer of turquoise-colored dust then escaped the box and blew into my eyes. After rubbing my face, I looked down at the ring in my own hand that matched the one in the box. Except mine was pink and this one was a blueish green. But it was the same wooden band and design. I took off my ring and put it next to the one she just showed me.

"I knew I kept this thing for a reason. Finally found its purpose," she said. "I can tell you the story if you want." Her expression turned giddy. I was more than happy to change the subject away from Gran.

"If I *want*? Girl, if you don't—yes! Storytime, please!"

So she told it to me, eyes dancing off the light of the stones.

It started with directing my attention to the inscribed symbol of two birds carved beak-to-beak on the inside of each of the bands.

"This is the eternal lovers symbol. The story goes: a long, long time ago when there were once two lovers..." she recounted. What followed was something like a long poem, vivid and far beyond my grasp. I didn't fully follow everything, and sometimes she slipped into Spanish, but I hung onto her every breath. Her calming graveled voice painting a fairytale scene.

✿ ✿ ✿

There were once two lovers—a daughter of the sun who was a carpenter, and the son of the moon who was a weaver. When the son visited the market, he saw the woman working and was impressed by her skill, so he sewed a bracelet for her. In return, the woman carved a ring band for him. However, her father disapproved of their affection and hid her away, throwing the ring into the ocean. The weaver disguised himself as a sea bird to gain her friendship, but her father shot him with an arrow.

Devastated, the woman devoted herself to nursing the bird back to health. As he recuperated, the woman prepared salted codfish to celebrate. Cleaning the fish, she found a silver band in its mouth and realized that it was the same one her father had thrown to sea. The bird then transformed back into her lover. They immediately snuck away to get married. Her father was shamed throughout the village. After that, the gods put the lovers' souls into river stones marked with this symbol, reminding humans that love was free, belonging to all, and not to be guarded away.

✿ ✿ ✿

"It looks like the maker of this set meant them to fit together," Yolanda said, adjusting some mechanism within these tiny pieces. She snapped them together, like a magic trick, so they interlocked into an infinity symbol. "Likely to be brought together for a powerfully destined wedding day." Then she pulled to release them again, like a magician.

"Until then," she held out the two separated rings in each of her palms, handing them to me, "powerful objects need a powerful vessel. They chose you for a reason. You should keep these together. The energy of these stones grows weaker when they're apart. They balance each other."

I couldn't help but believe every word she said. Well, not the part where she called me a powerful vessel. That was a stretch. The balance part, though, that made too much sense. No wonder I'd been feeling so unbalanced lately. I was wearing the stone wrong this whole time and I hadn't even noticed. Finally, a reason for my tired, aimless state. Something to blame.

I took the rings, placing one on each index finger. Wind chimes twinkled outside. Even though the windows were closed, I could have sworn I felt a breeze graze my skin and raise the hairs on my arms. Looking down at the rings sitting next to each other—two perfect fits—I felt a shift inside. Like a puzzle piece finally slipping into place. I felt so . . . present. Like I was finally alive.

I put my hands into fists, admiring my knuckles. Magic love rings. I couldn't help but let out a short laugh. So, I was basically the Green Lantern mixed with Cupid. Honestly . . . kinda sick.

"There you go," Yolanda's soothing voice affirmed. "I wouldn't take them off if I were you. Not until you regain your own internal balance." She ran her eyes between the chains and my face, searching for something. Maybe the same thing Auntie Gale always seemed to be looking for. Though, Yolanda's eyes lacked her judgment.

"We gotta go. Bye, Tía!"

Rosie's voice broke through my dissociative trance and I instinctively dug my newly adorned hands into my pockets. She sounded urgent. Suddenly, the world fixed its axis to revolve around her again. Her sneakers creaked the floorboards on their way to the front door. I squeezed the old woman's hands in gratitude before attempting to get up to follow Rosie. She held onto my palms, pressing into them for support as she brought herself up. So, I walked the woman to the door.

"'Pérate." Yolanda reached out for her niece.

"Sorry, I just gotta—" Rosie explained.

"One. You forgot to ask for my bendición. And two . . ." She took a labored breath. ". . . you believe that effort leads to guaranteed results. But that is not always the case. Protect yourself, first. That goes for both of you."

Yolanda shifted her attention to me. Rosie nodded quickly, still eager to leave.

"Bendición, Tía."

"Bye, Auntie," I offered.

"Remember what I said! Powerful objects need a powerful vessel! Be careful!" Yolanda called after me from behind the red door. How could I possibly forget?

Chapter
Twenty-six

On Missed Flights

– Rosie

W hen I got home, it was too late. Caro was gone. Her flight would be leaving any minute now. Our room looked like a tornado had gone through, scattering her clothes across both our beds. I'd been home by myself without my sister more times than I could count, but this felt different. Like she'd died or something. Even though I knew she was perfectly fine. The air was tighter without her being on the same continent. Everything was too . . . quiet.

On the coffee table in the living room, a new pile of junk had appeared. Decorated with some unused napkins, a broken phone charger, and some mismatched socks. Mami's piles had a way of spreading like a fungus.

I popped in my earbuds and got to work on my side of the bedroom. It was hard to come to terms with all that had been happening lately. All that had happened just that day. I didn't even want to think about the classes I'd bailed on. Or all the homework I had to do. The flame of spite burning through my heart from Ordena's words was still shining bright. I tucked it away into another jar until I knew what to do with it. For now, my brain was on autopilot, organizing pieces of mess into their righteous locations.

Our floor was nearly visible before I noticed an empty box of pads thrown in the trash can. As usual, Caro and I were synced up. Luckily I kept a secret stash in my sock drawer.

For some reason, when my mother came home from work, I expected her to ask me about Caro. But she didn't. She didn't even ask me how school was, or if I'd even been at school. Instead, she shoved a freshly printed page in my face and asked me if it made sense. It was a letter she'd written to her boss.

Dearest Nancy,

I been working the front desk at Dr. Mulberg's office for now over five years. During those years, my coworkers have tell me that I am a very reliable, efficient, and responsible worker. I have never missed a day of work. Now that Patricia is in maternity leave, her responsibilities have fallen to me in her absence. But I still stay with a salary of $12 per hour. More, the cost of living has been raised. I write to you to ask that you do the just thing and put me in consideration for a promotion and that you raise my salary for at the least $15 per hour.

Thank you.

Sincerely,
Yaris Cuevas-Rojas

Utterly exhausted, I pulled out my red pen and sat on the couch, correcting her grammar. Starting with adding *have* between *I* and *been* in the first sentence. I could read through her words and clearly see where she had translated sentences straight from Spanish. To be honest, it worried me sometimes that Mami and her limited English were just out in the world without me. I wondered what she was like. If her coworkers always understood her. If she always understood them. If anything got lost in translation out there like it did in here.

"Ya." I handed the sheet back to her. She inspected my notes.

"Es 'on maternity' not 'in maternity'? You sure? No suena bien eso."

"I'm sure," I said. "Also . . . I think you should ask for more money."

She shook her head.

"We can't be greedy." Then she kissed my forehead. "Gracias, mija linda."

She made too much rice for two people that night.

Chapter Twenty-seven

On Valentines

– Zeke

The first night I spent with my eternal rings was the first night that I actually got some decent sleep since landing in Jersey City. Not as much as I would've liked. Never enough. But beautiful, deep, nightmare-free sleep nonetheless. I forgot what I dreamed about seconds after waking up, but it must've been sweet because I woke up smiling and immediately shot out of bed. Light filtered into my bedroom and the sound of geese heralded like trumpets in the distance. The first thing I did was stare deep into the stones on my hands and dissociate from reality for what felt like ten minutes. I was suddenly feeling really grateful. Stepping into something new. Like I'd been waiting for life to find me under my covers and now I was getting up to reach out for life all on my own. Grateful at all I had survived to make it here.

My latest obsession was filling all my free time reading through threads of astrology memes. So, that's what I opened my laptop to. It occurred to me to enter the search terms

"Yolanda, Astrology, Tarot, Bruja, Queens" and, to my surprise, at the end of the first page of results, there she was. This earnest older lady with a white halo doing readings in her poorly lit apartment. The last video was from two years ago. She had a whole series of lessons called "Astro-logic 101: Finding Your Intuition." I sent a link to Rosie along with a single exclamation point.

Two hours later, she responded with one word.

Whoa.

I typed back. *I'm OBSESSED with her. Do you think she'd adopt me if I asked?*

Typing bubbles appeared.

Stop stalking my tía. You're gonna be late again.

Which I took to mean, "please, Zeke, watch every video she's ever made and ask Auntie to let you borrow her credit card to buy a textbook and then instead buy Yolanda's self-published book to learn more about this 21 Divisiones business the woman keeps mentioning. And then go to her community Facebook page, where she posts daily horoscopes, and go on a deep dive in the comments section where her fans interpret her words. And then be late to school again for the hundredth time despite waking up with the sun and get in trouble for being on your phone too much in homeroom while you deep dive some more."

The latest Yolanda fan frenzy was about the blood moon lunar eclipse in Taurus and Venus in Cancer aligning while Jupiter was turning direct to Pisces that was coming soon on

Valentine's Day. According to *blkgirl_moonstars*, it was "a recipe for passionate, spontaneous, new romantic beginnings. If you remain focused amidst distractions, you will be rewarded. Act too soon, and your shadows may resurface." From what I could garner, for me, specifically, all signs pointed to drastic change and new love entering my life from familiar places. Sign me the fuck up.

As a cherry on top, Auntie Gale told me at breakfast the next day that George wanted to take her to the Poconos for Valentine's Day, if it was alright with me. I told her I was pretty sure I'd manage just fine. Then my thumbs got to work texting Rosie under the table. Filling her in on my plan to help the universe along.

When February 14 finally rolled in, I floated into school with a flower I'd bought from a woman selling them across the street. My face slipped behind Rosie's open locker, a shoulder against the wall. When she slammed it shut, I met her surprise with batted eyelashes.

"A rose for a rose," I said dreamily. Rosie smirked and took the unthorned stem from my hand. She looked at me expectantly with her eyebrows raised. Here I was, bearing gifts, and this was the thanks I got? "What? Why you lookin' at me like that?"

"This . . ." She dropped her nose into the pink petals. ". . . is a carnation."

"Okay, sorry I'm not a . . . flower . . . doctor?"

"A botanist."

"You get the point. *Thank you, Zeke. What an adorable gesture.*"

"Didn't you say Pisces was the sign of delusion? I'm starting to see it now."

I put a hand over my chest. "How dare you? My rising is in Sagittarius, you don't know me. I'm a complicated being!"

"Whatever. Thanks. I don't think anybody's ever bought me flowers before . . . Or *flower*. No *s*." The disrespect.

For the fifth day in a row, she was wearing the pink jacket, which had now migrated from its old home in my locker to a new home in hers. It was basically her uniform now.

"You're welcome," I said. "So, how much longer is Caro gone for?"

Seeing the look on her face, I immediately regretted bringing her sister up. She was only on my mind because people kept whispering her name. Something about her pelting a dodgeball at some girl's head.

"Not sure. A week, I think."

"You don't know when she'll be back?"

"As far as I know, she didn't buy a return ticket, so . . ." Her voice trailed off. Family drama was familiar territory. I decided it was best not to pry further. Especially not on a glorious day like today.

I looped my arm in hers. We walked down the hallway chained to one another as newly familiar whispers hovered over us.

"Damn. Well, I'm jealous. She's on an island and we're here. I could use a beach day. My skin is ashy as fuck over here.

You should see this skin in Florida sun. All glowed up like a Jergens commercial."

Rosie pulled out a travel-sized bottle of lotion from her bag and offered it to me without hesitation.

"Bitch, is there anything you don't have in there?" I asked her.

"My hopes and dreams," she sighed in response. It occurred to me that Rosie would probably make a great mom one day. With the entire drugstore supply she seemed to keep on her at all times.

I turned to look at her sullen face with a raised brow and suppressed smile of my own. Then I shook my head.

"Awfully ungrateful for a girl who just magicked her way into straight As for the past week." I wiggled my fingers in her face. She slapped them away.

"It's not magic if I deserved the grade." Rosie pursed her lips. Great to see that she wasn't letting all that power go to her head at all.

"Sure . . . anyways . . . speaking of dreams, we all set for tonight?" I asked.

Rosie pulled out a clipboard from her Mary Poppins bag. The top page was some stage manager checklist for the play. She turned the page to reveal our party checklist. In bubble letters, she'd written "Z & R's Angels & Demons Party" at the top of the page. It was decorated with doodles of wings and pitchforks. At this point, I was convinced that there was an extra hour in the day that only Rosie knew about. Almost all the items on her list were checked off.

"I just have to collect the rest of the money from people. Facebook headcount is only twenty-something, but luckily you're new and everyone wants to know what your house looks like. So we'll probably make even more bread." It also helped that everyone was in a trance, fawning after her and that jacket lately. As if she didn't notice.

"Can we throw the money on a bed and do snow angels like in the movies?"

"No."

"Aw!"

"You're on snacks. I've got the decorations box ready in the auditorium."

"And Lido is dropping off the booze at six." I held up my hand for a high five. "Go team! Let's get litty in the name of love!"

Rosie brought up the carnation in her hand to fist bump my high five. A petal fell to the ground behind us.

Kind of amazing how a bunch of people I didn't know were coming to my current home in a couple hours and I wasn't freaking out even a little bit. I'd even finished all my homework early the day before since Rosie introduced me to the life hack of doing all my homework during lunch. Genius. I felt free as a bird.

The rest of the lunch period was spent observing my friend and the growing crowd that surrounded our table.

"Oh my god, I love your hair!" A passing girl gasped. "How do you curl your hair like that?"

"Uh, water?" Rosie's head was buried in her work as usual. She was actively trying to ignore the 24/7 stares and endless questions that seemed to come ever since that day in the hallway.

"Yo, are you two dating or can I get your Insta?" A familiar face I'd admired in the hallway looked her up and down. Rosie couldn't have been less interested.

"Where you got that jacket from?" Another girl chimed in.

"Girl, your handwriting is SO neat! I'm so jealous!"

"Hey, it's Rosie, right? Can we get a selfie?"

It went on and on. I took the opportunity to hand out mini flyers for our party. Rosie started biting her nails while flipping through *Crime and Punishment*.

Despite their cheery questions and waves of compliments, I could understand her discomfort with her new fan club. The feeling of phone cameras pointed at us was nice at first, but it was starting to feel kind of claustrophobic. At the very least, a boundary was being crossed. Like Rosie was an exotic animal at the zoo and, by proximity, so was I. Their eyes were drunk off her presence with just a taste of the same cloudiness she'd yelled into Mr. Scaramucci. I watched Rosie's pen break a tiny hole through her English homework. My right hand drifted over hers. She looked up at me with annoyance in her eyes and tension in her jaw. I leaned in to whisper.

"You're hulking out again." I took the pen from her hand.

She pursed her lips in disgust and scoffed at me. "It's not my fault these idiots won't get off my dick."

"Whoa, language!" I teased, poking her. "Not everybody besides you is an idiot."

"Shut up and give me my pen back," she mumbled, gently snatching it out of my hand. Only Rosie would get handed a free pass into universal likability and act like the world was out to get her. But her meanness was no match for my new Zen attitude. It was clear to me that her words were a paper-thin front for what was actually bothering her. So I gave her the pen.

"If only you knew someone with a magic jacket that made people do what she asked them to," I whispered the obvious. She froze and put her pen down. We exchanged a long look as a crowd closed in on us. A bright flash harassed us from someone's phone. Then I watched in awe as she climbed on top of our lunch table, lording over us all. Excited murmuring directed the whole room's attention to us.

"Um..H-hey, everyone!"

"We can't hear you, queen!" A voice in the back of the cafeteria shouted out. Rosie cleared her throat.

"HEY! Can everybody shut the fuck up for a second?!" Her voice boomed with the same unique dual-tone pitch I'd heard before. A little more focused this time. The room was instantly sent into radio silence. Even the lunch ladies and the attending teachers stopped chatting with one another. I tried to open my mouth to express my amazement, but my lips felt like they were super-glued shut. Panic took over. I tugged at Rosie's pant leg. She looked down at me with horrified eyes. "My bad, dude, sorry. Not you."

My mouth flew open, gasping for air. But the rest of the room remained under Rosie's spell. She continued with a fierce determination.

"Okay! If you didn't give a shit about me before two weeks ago, I need yah to leave me alone for the foreseeable future! Got it?" She paused. Everyone remained still. "Nod your head if you got it!" A chill ran up my spine as a sea of zombie-like heads obeyed her. Rosie climbed off the table and sat next to me again. She turned to look at the silent cafeteria room that was clearly awaiting her next command. Her hands made a grand motion. "Go on. As you were."

With that, the room snapped back into reality at its normal volume. Unnecessary scream-shouting, crinkling wrappers, squeaking sneakers, and heavy lunches slushing into the bottom of garbage cans.

"Well, that was fucking terrifying," I said, searching through faces in the crowd that talked around us as if we were invisible.

"Thanks." She yawned and stretched her arms above her head. "Phew. This thing always made me so tired after. I might need to take a nap before the party." Then Rosie scribbled on in blissful anonymity.

I eventually turned my attention to the buzzcut girl sitting across the room. She was sitting with a group of sporty-looking girls that she didn't seem all that engaged with. More than anything, I wanted to ask Rosie to use her powers on Ash to figure out whether or not she liked me. At the very least, to get her to come to our party. But that meant admitting out loud that I wanted her to come. Which was cringe. Not to mention, using Rosie to force her to come felt like it landed somewhere on the unethical behavior spectrum. But maybe I was just overthinking things.

I had nervously offered her a flyer in English class yesterday. When I asked her if she thought she'd be able to make it, she shrugged. *I don't know, maybe.* And what did that even mean? Was she trying to be chill, but saying yes, she would be coming? Or was she just trying to be polite when no, she was obviously busy? Without Ash there, it seemed like the whole thing was useless. Like the stars wouldn't do their job properly. I looked at my rings and reminded myself to have faith in the vague prophecy that had foreshadowed this day.

Focus, Zeke.

With five minutes left in the lunch period, I got up to throw away my trash. As I walked, my ears picked up on a song that was building in the room through voices without origin. First a whisper, then a low percussive rumble: *Penis.*

Penis.

         Penis.   *Penis.*

PENIS.

                          PENIS!

It felt suddenly like I was in a weird cult initiation. It occurred to me briefly that this could be a bizarre aftershock from Rosie mind-controlling everyone. Which could be very, very bad. My neck snapped back and forth, trying to decipher the meaning of this seemingly random ritual. I returned to my seat, nudging Rosie's shoulder.

"What the fuck is going on? Is this you?" I asked her.

Rosie blinked, drifting out of homework mode. She looked at the clock and then back at me.

"What do you mean?" She started putting away her books.

"PENIS!!" A shout cut through the general noise from two tables down. I pointed a casual finger in that direction, a bewildered look on my face. Rosie's face sunk.

"Oh shit. Not this again."

"What? Why is everybody saying *penis*?" I insisted. Suddenly, something white blurred past us. It landed with a splat on the wall next to Rosie's face. A cup of mashed potatoes.

"Someone's starting a food fight. It's a warning," she finally explained, before quickly addressing the rest of the room with an outstretched hand. "NO ONE HIT ME! I swear to . . ." No one paid her any mind. She had, of course, explicitly told them not to just minutes ago.

All at once, as if on cue, a thunderstorm of milk cartons and square pizzas and broccoli and chocolate pudding cups and mashed potatoes rained down on all of us. My body instinctively crouched down and hid underneath our table. I dodged a splattering of chocolate milk that crashed down on the floor in front of me. I had to pick today, of all days, to wear a white polo shirt. Bloodcurdling screams and unidentifiable objects filled the air. Brown sludge with sliding sneaker prints quickly spread across the tiled floor. Everything was garnished with smooshed up flower petals from the Valentine's Day stand. Lunch ladies and teachers were nowhere to be found. At the table above me, Rosie was still sitting, motionless. She crouched down and looked at me with a brilliant smile on her face. A face which remained spotless.

She offered me a hand. "Come on."

I couldn't begin to express my undying gratitude as she shielded me. Like a spy making it impossibly past a wall of bullets, we made it all the way to the door in one piece. My white shirt pristine and Rosie's jacket shining like new.

Another miracle.

Chapter
Twenty-eight

On Parties

– Rosie

Because there were so many kids at Westside, most gossip never made it past individual friend groups. You had to do something really wild for anyone to give a shit. But when someone did, it was the topic of every conversation for the next twenty-four hours. And today's news cycle was about JJ's best friend, Marco, possibly getting sent to juvie for starting the food fight. Allegedly. The whole point of the penis game was to anonymously distribute the blame, but Marco was an easy scapegoat. The officers in the school all knew him by name. It was hard for anyone to say what had actually happened. By tomorrow, for sure, the details would change.

No one seemed to notice that I had made it out unscathed. If they had, I would've probably been a prime suspect. Principal Ordena didn't even notice as he angrily strutted past me through the halls, flanked by police security. The loudspeaker had broadcast his voice the moment the bell rang and a flurry of dripping wet students filled long lines to the bathroom.

"*A REMINDER THAT DESTRUCTION OF PROPERTY WILL NO LONGER BE TOLERATED AND WILL BE MET WITH IMMEDIATE DISCIPLINARY ACTION. ZERO TOLERANCE. THERE WILL BE CONSEQUENCES. I REPEAT: ZERO. TOLERANCE.*"

He sounded so frantic and desperate that rather than invoking fear, most students standing in the halls laughed in response. I felt a bit of pride for whoever had started the food fight and their ability to fuck up Ordena's day. While all the confusion was still causing a palpable frenzy, I took the opportunity to dip into the main office. I assumed it would be empty. It wasn't.

"Sup?" Rishi held up a peace sign, barely looking at me. He was wearing a pair of giant headphones attached to a portable CD player. "You hear about the food fight?"

I thought for a moment, looking him up and down, wondering how he might be of use to me. Before lunch, I'd spent most of the day planning and playing Ordena's words on repeat. I combed through them, searching for something I could use. A starting point. Yolanda's lecture about my anger floated behind like a stubborn ghost. *Like fire, if used properly, it creates change.*

"Do you happen to know where I might find some of Ordena's accounting files? Of the charter-school-application-money nature?" I asked. Rishi took the headphones off his ears, puzzled.

"Huh?"

I decided to cut to the point. My fists clenched up and I focused on pressing all my desires into the back of my tongue. I looked into his eyes, intently.

"Get me Ordena's accounting files. Now, please."

Rishi's eyes glazed over for only a moment before he blinked it away. His brow furrowed as he stared back at me. Then he folded his arms across his chest.

"You can be really bossy, you know. And not in a girlboss way. For real, you don't need to do all that."

I took a step back.

"Wh—I . . . do all what?"

"Use your big cult leader voice. You can just ask, y'know?" He pulled out a drawer and handed me a box of files. "Just bring it back when you're done."

I considered his words, unsure of how much he really knew. It felt like he'd pulled back the curtain on something. Like he'd found a hiding spot only Zeke and Caro had known about. I slowly reached to accept the file box. My eyes narrowed, suspiciously.

"Thanks?"

"Whatever," he said. Before he put his headphones back on, he added, "I heard you were throwing a party?"

"Uh, yeah. You should come . . . if you want. Zeke's posting the location on Facebook later today. It's five bucks for booze. I don't know if you drink. If you don't it's—"

He added a five-dollar bill on top of the box of folders.

"I don't," he said. I looked at him with newfound curiosity. His headphones slid back over his ears. "There's always people that drink and don't pay. It's not a big deal."

I was stunned by his act of altruism. Rishi held multitudes. Who knew? Maybe Zeke was right. Not everybody at this school was a complete idiot.

✿ ✿ ✿

The only parties I'd ever been to in my life—apart from moments spent waiting in JJ's garage with Caro and his friends—were family parties. And the way I saw it, the best part about those parties was the setting up beforehand and the cleaning up after. Occasionally, depending on the host, the eating part was pretty good too. But everything in between was just me and Caro and all our cousins sitting in a bedroom, with the door acting as a barrier between us and the dog-whistle screeching of our mother and aunts on the other side. Every new screech drawing a knowing look between Caro and I. Oh, and don't forget clammy-handed uncles trying to rope one of us into joining them on the dance floor. Wild teen-movie dancing had nothing on the elaborate elder Rojas-Cuevas routines. It was like a rave in there. Someone would turn off the lights and light up a disco ball that arrived straight from the seventies. And the ground would tremble under the weight of sliding heels. The worst part, by far, was the part right before the cleaning up. The part where I knew I didn't want to be there anymore, and I had to wait out the whims of others before it was finally over.

That was what was so great about hosting my own party. Well—co-hosting with Zeke. I could end it or exit when I wanted. And I was (mostly) in control. I'd even convinced Mami to let me take the car that night to what I told her was a "school dance." Which wasn't a lie, really. I was working on not lying to her as much. It was too much to juggle all the little lies along with the big lie of Yolanda and my jacket. And it was much easier not to lie without Caro there. I needed a break. So, I wasn't really lying about the party, just . . . bending the truth. And omitting the fact that my permit only allowed me to drive while an adult was present. It *was* a school dance in that people from school would probably be dancing. So, not a lie. I told her I didn't know when I would be home. Which was also true. "I trust you," she'd said. "Just be safe."

I arrived at Zeke's aunt's apartment with the box of dollar store plant vines and flower bouquets and Cupid decorations that were possibly used at a previous stage adaptation of the 1996 *Romeo + Juliet* movie. Lido was already there helping Zeke unload cartons of liquor from his car. We'd decided early on that this would be a no-beer party because we both agreed it tasted like battery acid. Besides, I didn't like to drink (usually). In my mind, it would be a classy, sophisticated affair. Like a college party.

From outside, I could hear Lido's music blasting over a speaker. In between, Lido was rattling off the details of his elaborate workout routine. Poor Zeke. He gave me a pained look as he passed by with a box of Tito's.

I held the front door open for him, trying not to gawk at the evident old-world luxury of Zeke's aunt's apartment. The place was huge. There were floor-to-ceiling windows and intricate crown molding and a fireplace. It was the kind of brownstone that used to cost pennies and host Harlem Renaissance–style community art gatherings before suburban white people started snatching them up and raising the rent. It was crazy how this whole different world was waiting here, just blocks from my own.

I handed Zeke our bulging cash envelope to pay Lido with. He looked me up and down.

"Is that what you're wearing? Please tell me you're pulling a Caro."

So rude. I looked down at my button-up thrifted flower-print cardigan, covering a red turtleneck, covering a black slip dress that, yes, I'd borrowed from Caro's secret closet. She would probably wear it without the cardigan. My pink jacket was in my backpack. It didn't match my outfit. I don't know why I'd brought it if I wasn't planning on wearing it, but it seemed like a security measure at this point. I conceded and took off the cardigan and turtleneck, revealing my bare arms.

"What? I was cold," I explained. Then I reached in the box and took out a sparkly devil-horned headband. "There. Done." I gave Zeke a twirl.

"Moderately better," he said, pulling out part of the cash. I stuck my tongue out at him. Zeke had texted me three options for his outfit. He'd gone with the revealing silk white top and bleached white jeans to remind the world that he was, in fact, Jamaican. I looked down at his bare feet.

"You're one to talk Mr. No Shoes."

He wiggled his toes.

"Rosalina, girl, you know I'm allergic to shoes."

"Again. Rosie."

"Sorry. Rosie." He would learn one of these days.

Lido counted the cash while we bickered. He eyed the envelope. "I got other stuff, too, if yah interested . . ." His eyebrows wiggled suggestively. "Twenty bucks a dime?"

Zeke's puppy eyes looked at me, asking for permission. Personally, I hated the smell of weed. But this was his party too. I shrugged.

"You can do whatever you want with your half of the profits," I told him, trying not to judge. "I, for one, am not a heathen."

He grinned, handing over the extra cash. "Well, maybe *I* am." Lido discreetly handed him a plastic Mentos container that was clearly filled with weed. I don't know who he was trying to be discreet for. It was just us.

"You sure your aunt's not gonna be mad you're throwing a party at her place?" I asked him, eyeing the abstract painting above the fireplace.

"I don't think anyone in my family could be mad at me if they tried," Zeke said. "At least not outwardly."

I switched off Lido's music as soon as his car drifted away. Much to Zeke's appreciation. "I understand why your sister stopped having a crush on that guy," he added, grabbing a decorative red garland. Lil Wayne's "How to Love" was first up on our playlist as my celestial "Angels and Demons" vision started coming to life around us. It was a pretty nice vibe. We talked while I stood on a ladder and fixed rows of fake flowers to the ceiling. Zeke concocted a bucket of hibiscus-flavored jungle juice in the kitchen.

"Zeke, what do you want to be when you grow up?"

He shrugged.

"I feel like that's such a weird question, 'cause like, when is someone grown up? At eighteen, twenty-five? And why do you have to be one thing? When I was a kid I wanted to be a merman. Then I wanted to be an orchestra conductor. Then a psychologist. I change my mind every day."

"What about right now? What do you want to be?"

He contemplated for a minute, gazing out the window.

"I don't know. Right now I just wanna be . . . alive. Wherever I am. So, here. In Jersey City. With you."

I rolled my eyes and pressed on. "But what about, like, your future? Where do you want to be tomorrow? Or the day after that?"

His eyes stayed lost in the window.

"I guess where I see myself in the future . . . I'm like this happy eclectic older version of me, with just a little bit of white in my beard and amazing hair. And I live in a really old building in Brooklyn with my stupid hot partner and our dog and we go on a morning walk every day. And then for money I own a tea shop that sells old records and I give people tarot card readings on the side. I guess I just want to be . . . free. To be whatever. You know?"

I stopped what I was doing to look at him. For someone who "didn't know," he seemed to know an awful lot. I'd never heard anyone our age talk the way Zeke did. Like the scope of life's possibilities was infinite. In recent days, it seemed like the dark cloud that usually hung over his head had lifted. I was kind of jealous of the friend who had once wallowed in bitterness alongside me. The one who scrawled out long depressing poems next to me during Algebra.

"What?" he asked. I shook my head and went back to my task.

"You know, I used to think you were a quiet kid."

"I can be."

I laughed. "I wish you *would* be."

He threw a napkin at me. "Shut up."

"So . . . no plan, then? Just vibes?"

"Yup," he said with a smirk that quickly soured into a somber mood. "I used to follow a plan. It wasn't mine. I think maybe everyone does that sometimes. It's not all that great. Why set yourself up for failure when the world is full of shit you can't plan for?"

"Isn't astrology all about plans and predictions?" I challenged, pointing a plastic flower in his direction. He nodded slowly, considering my theory.

"I think it's more about . . . possibilities," he concluded. Zeke was a certain shade of wise when he wanted to be.

I considered my own question for a moment.

"Well, the first thing I remember wanting to be was a dolphin. I don't know why. I just wanted to live in the ocean and I read somewhere that dolphins were really smart, I think. I read about sonar and all that. I thought it meant they could, like, read minds. So, I wanted to be a dolphin." I examined the flower I'd just finished hanging. "But then I was pretty sure I wanted to be a teacher. Then a civil engineer. And now a civil engineer who's an ITI valedictorian. But it feels like . . . I don't know . . . like God is telling me to adjust my vision board? If that makes sense?"

"I feel that," Zeke nodded. "I say we go back to merman and dolphin. At least we'll still be friends." I looked at this warm-hearted idiot and realized he was right. We were friends. Good friends. Maybe the best friend I'd ever had. Ew. I could feel my heart turning to goo.

Then the doorbell rang. Outside, there were still threads of sunlight hanging on. Zeke's head whipped around to look at me, momentarily disoriented by the sound. He tentatively got up to open the front door.

"I'm hella early aren't I?" I heard the low voice beyond the hallway.

"Uh, yeah. It's fine. Come on in," Zeke said. "You can help us set up."

Zeke walked down the hall, stepping into my line of vision. A hardly recognizable Rishi trailed behind him, dressed head to toe in a straight-out-the-bag Party City vampire costume, complete with a cape and fake blood on the corners of his mouth. I guessed it was his version of a demon. His oversized backpack really sealed the trick-or-treater vibe.

"Uh, it's . . . our friend . . ." Zeke searched for a name.

"Rishi!" I said, saving him. I climbed down the ladder and gave him a quick hug. "You came!"

Rishi stood awkwardly for a moment, his eyes examining the floral decor around the living room.

"It looks dope in here." He pointed to the miniature bluetooth speaker sitting on top of a bookshelf. "Uh, so . . . I didn't know if you guys had a DJ, but I also got speakers strapped to my bike. Just in case, you know . . . the sound quality . . ." He let the rest of his sentence die off.

"Oh my god, that would be great!" I said. "Just set it up wherever."

"Also," he continued, reaching into the backpack on his shoulder and pulling out a large boxy black device. "Brought this from the tech room. It's a smoke machine. Seemed fitting—like, I don't know, if maybe—" He wiggled his fingers into jazz hands.

"Oh, fuck yes!" Zeke's eyes lit up. He pointed finger guns back at Rishi. "Perfect ambiance, dude! Remind me to get you some shots later!"

Rishi smiled back, golden eyes beaming. He didn't mention the fact that he didn't drink and it didn't seem like my business to bring it up.

The three of us continued setting up and I started to wonder if all this effort was worth it. If people would actually come. If my silver tongue had maybe worn off by now. Honestly, I would have been happy if no one came and it was just us the whole night. Like I said, this was the best part.

After a while, Zeke went to his room to finish his angelic glitter makeup. By the time he emerged donning a pair of heart-shaped sunglasses, a couple people had started trickling in. His radiant dark skin glowed shades of blue in the dim lighting as light bounced off the white carnations in his hair. Then, all at once it seemed, the whole place was packed with figures swaying to DJ Rishi's Jersey club mixes. The loose crowd tightened as his mashup of "Chicken Noodle Soup" with "Hollaback Girl" brought out the synchronized choreography. It seemed impossible that the floorboards could hold this many people. I looked around in awe. It worked. We did it. We had made this happen from nothing. I had made this happen.

It was a study in human behavior really, the way most of the girls chose slutty angel costumes and the boys came costumeless or donning low-effort devil horns. Two Polish boys from the hockey team had painted their bare chests with red paint. It didn't take long for their musty sweat to fill the air. So much for a sophisticated affair.

I watched Zeke bounce from group to group, playing spin the bottle, laughing like the sun itself. He came over to give me a sloppy kiss on the cheek. An overly affectionate drunk.

But I was happy for him. He deserved this. He deserved the adoring looks he was getting from people who were finally seeing him for who he was under his moody exterior. He deserved the unbridled joy in his eyes. But something about sitting around on the couch holding a red cup of cranberry juice that I was passing off for liquor and watching teenagers making out in different corners of the room was making me feel more alone than ever. Not to mention the fact that occasionally someone would walk past and wonder out loud, "Whose party is this again?"

A crowd formed around JJ and his friend Marco, who'd decided to show up with girls from another school. Marco gestured wildly while he recounted his encounter with the cops at school. "I kept telling them they was hurting my fucking hands and shit. This SRO motherfucker had the audacity to tell me, 'If you're not acquainted with the juvenile justice system, son, you will be very soon.' So, I spit in his bitch ass face. They playin' with the wrong one." His audience cackled and cheered along.

My head pounded louder than my heart as the speakers rattled. It wasn't like I was invisible without the pink jacket. People—boys—still looked at me. Though their attention was more out of curiosity than actual interest. Like they were trying to figure out where they knew me from. The ceaseless adoration they'd pestered me with earlier in the day, reduced to a whisper of déjà vu. A couple boys followed their drunken curiosity far enough to ask me to dance. But I just wasn't in the mood for any of it.

All I could think about was the box full of accounting files that was sitting unopened in the trunk of Mami's car. *The world doesn't owe you anything.* Instead of chilling me out, the red cup only amplified Ordena's words. *The world doesn't owe YOU anything.*

I looked back at Zeke, dancing carefree and alone while Rishi bounced at his makeshift DJ booth hyping him up. Zeke's theory on aiding the universe along seemed to be coming true. He'd given in and listened and allowed himself to want. And now he was riding high on the wave that the universe manifested as a reward. Maybe I, too, was allowed to want more.

I stumbled up to my feet, grabbing onto Caro's friend, Leidy, for balance. Then I made my way to Zeke and tapped him on the shoulder. I had the sudden feeling that what I had to tell him was urgent.

"You were right!" I yelled over the music.

"Huh?!" He leaned down and put a hand behind his ear.

"You were—" Somewhere, glass shattered like a bomb, bringing the whole party to a stop. The crowd wrapped around its perimeter like a naturally parting river.

And that's when I saw her. She was wearing combat boots, a ripped-up white t-shirt dress, and several layers of silver necklaces. Hanging loosely off her shoulder was a worn-out leather satchel. Behind her, a pair of giant feathered wings. Crowning her head was a bejeweled white headband. A buzz-cut pink scalp peeking out underneath. I had seen that pink head bouncing through the halls several times. But only from the back. It was only now that I truly saw the distinct contours of her face.

"Ash." Zeke gasped, a surprising tenderness in his voice.

Ashia.

Chapter
Twenty-nine

On Strange Nights

– Zeke

I t took me a moment to feel the magnetic energy that was clearly flowing between them. Intoxicated eyes in the crowd glared back and forth between the two girls, waiting in anticipation. A couple of stray whispers relaying information that I was obviously missing. The tension in the air thicker than a bowl of my grandmother's porridge.

And then Rosie cut through it, breaking the staredown as she made quick long strides past Ash, roughly checking her shoulder along the way. She grabbed her things. In a snap, Rishi threw on "Crank That (Soulja Boy)" and the party went back to normal.

"Where are you going?" I asked, running after her.

"The library," she said.

"What?! You're just bailing?"

"Sorry. Bye." Her voice sounded like sandpaper as she choked the words out. I hadn't seen this shade of her before. I struggled to focus on a reason for it.

"B-but it's almost midnight. Aren't they closed?"

Rosie threw her pink jacket over her shoulder, defiant.

"Not for me."

Rishi stepped in from behind me, holding out his hand to her.

"Whoa there. Car keys, please." That hadn't even occurred to me. She asserted that she was sober. Rishi took out a light from his keychain and flashed it into her eyes. He seemed to believe her. "Alright, call me when you get home, then. Stay safe."

Then he went back to his station and turned the music back on. It almost drowned out the sound of the door slamming shut behind her. I couldn't believe she could just leave like that. I considered ending the party right there. Telling everyone to go home. But . . .

Ash.

She came.

"Sorry about the spill." I spun around and there she was. "I'm such a klutz sometimes. I-I didn't see it and I turned—"

"Don't even worry about it," I said, putting my hands up to stop her apology. Behind her, I could see Rishi already procuring a broom from somewhere and cleaning it up. "You came."

She crossed her arms and took a deep breath. "I did. But—" She looked unsure for a moment. Which was weird. In the short time I'd known Ash, she was the least unsure person I'd ever met. Then she took a step towards me. And I got lost. She smelled like fresh-cut flowers in a sitting-room vase. "Is Caro here?"

I narrowed my eyes. Caro? What did she want with Caro? Was that why she came? Because she knew we were friends? My heart sank a little. Then I remembered today's horoscope. *Focus.*

"Uh, no. She's on vacation. Wanna drink?" I offered her a hopeful smile.

"Oh." Ash looked down, embarrassed. "Uhh . . ." Surely, she hadn't gotten all dressed up just to chat with Caro. It was my house. My party. I took her hand.

"Come on."

I led her away from the noise, to the backyard, where I poured out a cup of Coke. After I handed her the cup, I wiggled a bottle of rum in her direction, telepathically asking if she wanted some. She hesitated before tipping her cup forward.

"Fuck it," Ash said.

We sat and talked. I watched the usual spikiness behind Ash's eyes melt away with every sip. A series of laughs brought out the novelty of her unique snorting noise.

"So," I breathed. "How do you know Rosie and Caro?" I tried to make it sound as casual as possible. She shifted in her seat.

"It's a long story."

"That's okay. It's a long night."

She let out a nervous laugh.

"Maybe one for a different question."

I nodded.

"Fine. New question. Did it hurt?"

"Did wh—" I reached over and touched a feather on her wings. She grimaced. "Oh. When I fell from heaven. Ha, ha."

"For real, do you just keep angel wings on you at all times, or you got them special just for me?"

I couldn't tell if she wanted to punch me or kiss me. Then she shook her head and laughed, taking a sip of her drink.

"You're not what I expected, you know that?"

I let out a satisfied exhale as I realized . . . I did it. I was *doing* it. I was talking to Ash. And she didn't hate me. We talked about Mrs. Shapelli, who we both agreed was corny. "Mad corny" according to her. I liked the way she said it. I asked her what her sign was. *Pisces.* Her birthday was five days after mine. Her moon in Taurus. Aquarius rising. She knew all about astrology. As if I needed to be convinced any further that we were soulmates. We were moving back and forth like liquid fascination and I hardly noticed the space between us growing smaller and smaller.

When my knee bumped against hers, she excused herself to go to the bathroom. I sat twisting the rings between my fingers in her absence, trying to figure out what we should talk about next. Five minutes later I heard JJ's unmistakable baritone voice booming from inside. My fingertips suddenly grew cold.

"Nah, nah! It landed on Ash! Don't run away now, shortie. Truth or truth?"

I turned around, seeing the back of her white wings. A circle had opened up to surround her. Behind the glass doors, smoke drifted to conceal and reveal bloodthirsty faces in the crowd.

"C'mon! You gotta play!" I think that was Marco.

"I got one: is it true you're a dyke?" JJ asked. I could make out his shark teeth even in the near darkness. My whole body suddenly tensed up.

"Ay, yooo!" Marco's obnoxious cackle didn't help the mood.

"Fuck you, JJ," Ash said. She turned towards me and I could see the fresh shine in her eyes. Without another thought, I stood up, a sudden protective anger fueling my rum-soaked tongue. The backyard door swung behind me. I grabbed the empty wine bottle from the middle of their circle.

"You." I pointed the bottle in JJ's direction. "Get outta my house, please." I stared him down. The incredulity in his face was marvelous (and a little terrifying, in a *what's this dude gonna do* type of way). I instantly remembered how much taller he was than me. He looked around the room for support. Then he shrugged.

"Whatever." He took the hand of a blond girl I'd never seen before. "There's no beer here, anyways. Pussy ass party."

That one poured salt over an antiquated wound, but only for a half a second. Before I realized that I was wearing glitter on my face at a Valentine's Day costume party. It *was* a pussy ass party. Fuck him for coming here expecting any different. I put the bottle down.

After JJ left, the chatter of the party went on as though nothing had happened. I led Ash back outside and we sat some more. For a minute, I was afraid she'd bounce too. But she didn't.

"Sorry for treating you like shit in English class. I kinda feel a little bad now," she said, before taking another sip.

"Only a little?"

"Only a little, yeah." She pinched her fingers. I laughed. "But for real, though. I just have this armor, you know? I guess I got it from moving around and going to a bunch of schools. It's not you. I just . . . hate my life." She was trying to push some sort of pain away with levity, but I felt it emanating off her anyways.

"You live with your dad now, right?" I asked.

"And my stepmom. I hate it there." She sank down in her chair and nodded. I saw her eyes go somewhere else. Then she pursed her lips. "Honestly, I kinda miss living with my grandma in Ridgefield. She had all these dope records and photos 'cause she used to be a photographer. All over her house, just mad photos from the Newark Riots in the sixties. She was friends with all these Black Panthers in the city. Like, she was really just out here. Plus, her food was really bomb. Ugh . . . I miss her banana bread so much. I don't know what she put in that stuff. Crack, probably."

"My gran used to make this dulce de frutas fruit cake thing. It sounds gross, but, trust, I have dreams about it. She used these spices she shipped over from Panama. She refused to use anything else. I tried to get her to teach me how to make it before she died, but she never used any measurements. She just . . . knew how much of everything to put in. She said she could feel it. I'd kill a man to eat that dulce de frutas again. Oooh, right after a bowl of her sopa de pata." I realized as I said it that I hadn't talked this much about Gran dying with anyone before. It kinda felt nice. Not sure if it was the alcohol or something else, but my chest felt warm.

"You're Panamanian? No way." She brushed the back of her hand against my arm as she playfully hit me. I tried to act like her touch didn't send electricity down my whole body.

"Not really. Just a quarter."

"Still counts. I'm half Haitian, half Saint Lucian. As my mom used to say, 'all island gyal.'" She wiggled her hips adorably. Then she laughed again, putting her hands over her face. "Oh god. I'm so drunk right now." The edges of her words started blurring away.

"Are you still cool with your mom, then?" I don't know why I asked. Immediately, the goofy atmosphere shifted. She opened and closed her mouth several times, grasping for words. I put up my hands. "Or—never mind. None of my business."

"No, it's just . . . she sorta just floats in and out. She won't give up custody of me. Not that I want her to, but . . . sometimes I kinda do. Like, I feel bad about it. But then I don't. . . . Sorry, that didn't make sense."

"No, no." I put my hand over hers, sealing the gap between us. "I get it. Trust me. Kinda how I felt when my mom got sick.

She was really . . . overbearing. It's weird 'cause like moms are supposed to be everyone's favorite person, but . . . she just expected a lot out of me. She was trying to take over the world and be a bigshot politician and everything. So I had to match. Be her brilliant gifted son. This . . . puppet. Who wore little suits. And when I didn't want to be that, it all kinda blew up."

Blew up was an understatement. It was the fight that still kept me up at night. Where she said she would disown me for refusing to uncross my legs on stage. And I allowed her to push me to yell, *Go ahead! Please! Go find a straight son! It's not me!* Which didn't make things any better. It didn't get me an apology. It didn't make her see me. It didn't do a damn thing. ". . . And then she got sick. And then . . . she . . . died."

The last three words wrestled their way out of my mouth.

"Oh shit. I'm sorry, Zeke. That's . . . yeah. That's heavy."

"Thanks. I mean, I'm fine now." I recognized the worn-out lie as soon as I said it. I looked down at the cold ring that was touching her warm hand. "Or I'm not, but I think I will be."

She poured us two shots, spilling white rum everywhere. Ash's giggling was infectious.

"To shitty moms."

I lifted my cup.

"To shitty moms."

Some of the rum spilled out the corners of my lips. We started laughing at absolutely nothing. My chest ached.

I didn't know I was crying until Ash started wiping my tears away with the corner of her thumb. With an unexpected force, she leaned into me. And then . . . I closed my eyes. I leaned into her. Breathing her into the center of me. Brushing my lips against the softness of her flower-scented face in quick, fluid motions. Giving into want. Thanking the stars and the universe and Venus and Jupiter for this magnificent day. Hoping it would never end.

She pulled away, gasping for air. Pins and needles pricked my mouth in the spaces where her tongue had escaped.

"I'm sorry, I didn't mean to—"

"It's okay," I said, trying to reassure her.

"I've never kissed a boy before."

"Okay . . ." I tried to hide my surprise. "Do you want to stop?"

Rather than answer, she crashed into my orbit again. And again. And again. Despite the fact that this was everything I wanted, each time sent chills cascading in waves down my body and rang warning bells through my head. Because I'd come to learn through fire that peaks always have downfalls. And life always swung on a cruel pendulum. It was only a matter of time.

✿ ✿ ✿

After I washed my face and kicked everyone else out, Rishi helped me carry Ash to my bed so she wouldn't get drool on Auntie's cushions. I figured I'd take the couch. He'd taken off his costume, donning a white t-shirt and jeans. There was still a trace of the fake blood he'd had around his mouth. It was just the two of us left conscious, now. This was the part I was supposed to be doing with Rosie. Cleanup. Her favorite.

I was weirdly comfortable around Rishi. I'd only briefly interacted with him before, but I could tell he looked different somehow. Or maybe I was just bad at noticing things. I couldn't put my finger on it. We set Ash's lifeless body down and Rishi pulled my comforter over her. She groaned and curled up like a baby in the fetal position.

"Isn't that yours?" The question sounded like an interrogation. He referred to the pink stone ring that had drifted from my left hand to Ash's somewhere between our bodily entanglement. I vaguely remembered her commenting that it "looked soooo pretty."

"Uh, yeah. It's my lucky ring. She borrowed it," I yawned.

"Oh," he said. Rishi's deep tan arms glowed purple under the twinkling lights as he tucked Ash in. He turned to meet my gaze. "What? Do I have something on my face?"

I realized my eyes had settled on his arms just a bit too long. Now they were sleepily set on his jawline. Shit.

"No, sorry, you just look . . . different, maybe?"

Rishi covered his face, a light panic flashing over his expression.

"Sorry, I didn't have time to shave. It grows in pretty fast. Why? Does it look bad?" He ran a hand across the dark stubble.

"No, no. You look . . . nice."

"Thanks."

"No, thank YOU, dude. I literally don't know what I would've done without you here."

He looked sheepish, chuckling as he scratched the back of his neck.

"Sure, no prob . . . *dude*." Again, I felt like I'd gotten the script wrong. Did they not use the word "dude" over here? Maybe it wasn't the right word to convey my thanks. I mean, I really was grateful. Without Rosie here, he'd become one of the only people I felt tethered to at the party. And he'd been so nice to me this whole time, while I'd been distracted trying to convince Ash she was my soulmate. And he was still here. It felt like I owed him something.

We stood awkwardly for a while until Rishi shook his head and laughed again. Which made me laugh. "Uh, is it alright if I head out?"

"Yeah, of course! I guess I'll see you at school?"

Rishi nodded. He grabbed his backpack and hesitated. Then he unzipped it, reaching inside for something.

"Um . . . almost forgot, sorry. My parents told me never to enter someone's house without a gift. So . . ." He handed me a fancy-looking box of chocolates. "They're a Syrian brand. It's stupid. It's fine if you don't want—"

"Holy shit, thank you! Seriously, I'm gonna eat this whole box by myself."

He laughed again. "Cool."

"Cool."

"Bye again."

I waved as he stepped out the door. From the window, I watched him bike away and get swallowed into the night. The dude was kind of a loner—unattached to anything concrete. It was familiar to me. Or, at least, what I used to be. Though, there was always a souring taste of misery to my solitude, where Rishi seemed to find a joyful sort of freedom in it.

"Bye again," I said to no one.

Chapter Thirty

On Strange Mornings

– Zeke

D on't leave. I haven't . . . thanked you," Ash yawned from my bed. Her wings were set down in front of my closet. She was merely a human now. "You're . . . a nice guy, Zeke." Her words blurred into one another before she slipped back into a coma. I knew she was half delirious. She probably wouldn't remember it. Still, she may as well have told me she loved me. That's how good it felt to hear.

A nice guy. Maybe I could be.

I turned off the light. The silence rang loud in my ears. My internal body temperature was about a thousand degrees. The digital clock on my nightstand blinked at 2:16 a.m. When I opened the window a crack, I could hear a cricket chirping outside beneath the eerie red glow of the blood moon eclipse.

My hand instinctively reached to fidget with the pink ring that was usually on my left index finger. A warm grin tugged at the corner of my lips when I found nothing, thinking about

Yolanda's prophetic words. I didn't feel so unbalanced anymore. I felt pretty great, actually. That must've been a sign. That it worked. That Ash was my soulmate, whether she knew it or not. It didn't matter if she knew. I knew. And that was enough.

I looked deep into the stone of the ring that was left, noticing new patterns glowing under the gray sky. The orb shifted from light blue to varying shades of purple. I could vaguely catch myself in its reflection. I slipped off the ring to examine it further. That's when I noticed the letter *Z* etched into the inside of the wooden band. Like a tiny Zorro had gone in between my fingers and left his mark. I shook my head. Yolanda must have put it there when I wasn't looking. The ring slid back in its place.

Leftover glitter stained my fingertips. The makeup had been a bitch to get off my face. I think I'd accidentally gotten industrial-strength clown makeup from the drugstore. It would probably stay beneath my fingernails for all eternity. *Worth it.* I thought to myself. It was a satisfying feeling to start the day believing in the magic of possibilities and ending it with a pink-haired girl sleeping in my bed.

I took out my phone and saw zero missed calls or texts. Not even from Rosie. Guilt swept in for waiting this long to see if she was okay. And for ignoring the weird vibe that was obviously brewing between her and Ash. I wondered if I should tell her that we kissed. Or that she was in my bed. Our friendship was still fresh and delicate. I couldn't afford breaking it. I would tell her eventually. Maybe.

My fingers floated above the keyboard. I typed and deleted. And then typed again. Send.

Hey! You get home alright?

A minute passed. No reply. She was probably fine. If she wasn't, I was sure I would know somehow. I would feel it. Like I had felt it coming two times before. She was fine. I would see her tomorrow and she would explain.

I closed the door behind me and grabbed one of Auntie's crochet blankets. The split second I set my head on the couch pillow and my eyelids met, I heard a knock coming from my bedroom door.

My chest jolted up and I backed away as far into the couch as it could. For a second I considered that I had imagined it. That maybe it was the sound of my own heartbeat. Or the old radiator. Or one of our neighbors rolling out their trash. But then there it was again. Louder.

¡Bang, bang, bang!

This time, the apartment began shaking with each aggressive pound. It was undeniable now. Not just paranoia. Someone was in the house with me. Auntie was gone. I was alone. The only other person here was a comatose Ash. Maybe there was a straggler from the party. But why would they be knocking at my door so urgently?

¡Bang, bang, bang!

I thought the door was about to break into a million pieces. The doorknob rattled in the attack's aftermath. I stood up, desperately reaching around me, and grabbed a candlestick from the faux fireplace.

¡Bang, bang, bang!

I could faintly make out a frantic scratching noise. Like an animal clawing away at the wooden door. With my candlestick at the ready, I tiptoed towards the door. My hand hovered above the doorknob, twitching.

¡Bang, bang, bang!

As fast as I could, I pulled the door open and propelled my arm forward.

"Zeke!" The sound of her cry stopped my strike midair.

She stood there in the dark, face wet with tears and deep crimson dripping off the fists at her sides. I flipped on my bedroom light. After a moment of utter shock and my eyes adjusting, I saw the deep cuts she'd scraped into the wood. Bits of wood scattered on the floor, mixed with fresh blood and half a broken nail. The wooden band around her finger was soaked. She was breathing loud and sharp. Her white headband thrown aside on the ground in a pile. Once peaceful brown eyes now surrounded by black veins.

"Ash . . . what . . . ?" I looked into the clouds that had drifted over her eyes. Nothing was behind them. She leaped on top of me, wrapping me tight in her arms and legs. I almost fell backwards. Her hand clasped in mine, knocking our rings together. Ash felt like the sun. Her bloody nails dug into my back. Her mouth kissed my ears, whispering the same word over and over and over again:

Zeke, Zeke, Zeke, Zeke.

My head was pounding painfully now as her heartbeat stabbed through me, a quarter second behind mine. Never before had my name sounded so much like darkness.

❀ ❀ ❀

By the time the sun came up, I had tried to unlatch my rose-colored ring from Ash's bloody hand at least twenty times. It wouldn't budge. Not even a little. It was like her skin had started growing around it. Attached to her the same inexplicable way she seemed to be attached to me.

With her legs still wrapped around me in my bed, I could feel her heart slow down. Mine continued a drum solo in my chest. I wasn't sure whether or not her deep sleep was a good sign. A fuzzy fact floated in the back of my mind about someone dying in their sleep when they had a concussion. What were the signs of a concussion? And what was the point of anything at all if perfect nights ended in blood anyways? My dry eyes stayed fixed on the broken door. I knew I had to move. Do something. Anything. But I couldn't. I just couldn't. No matter how much the command berated my mind, my limbs felt like a bag of rocks.

Just. Fucking. Do it.

I willed myself to no avail. Where would I even go? What would I do? What if I only made things worse? And as much as I hated myself for thinking it, sitting here in bed with her was kinda... nice? A kitchen with all burners on and all windows and doors locked shut. An unbearably hot summer day when nothing was the only thing to do. Nothing but the two of us just lying here together. Away from the rest of the world.

I mean, it wasn't exactly what I had in mind when I'd called her my soulmate, but that didn't change the fact that she still smelled like flowers beneath the metallic taste of blood. It didn't change the fact that I was happy she was in my bed. That she wanted me. Even if she was like . . . this. Like a . . . love zombie.

Oh god. I was back to hating myself.

I wiped dried blood off my neck. She cuddled me closer.

You need help. That one was familiar. I was so used to silencing that mousy voice in my brain these past few years that I almost couldn't make it out now. It had dimmed to a flicker like a need that had not been properly fed. *You both need help.* This time, the voice grew a little louder. I looked down at the drooling girl in my arms whose pain I'd caused. At what happened to people who were unfortunate enough to love me.

"We need help," my lips admitted beneath a whisper. Ash stirred beside me. "I need help," the voice said a little louder.

✿ ✿ ✿

At seven in the morning, many hours before Auntie Gale would be back from her trip, I stood outside of a red door in the frigid cold with a shivering girl's breath warming my neck. A hoarse voice continued a hushed refrain: *Zeke, Zeke, Zeke, Zeke…*

Ash's body was as close to me as my mother had once been. So close she was miles away. So close she was choking me.

229

For the first time since my previous visits, I looked into the side alley and noticed a giant graffiti mural sprawled across the bridge that cradled the townhouse in front of me. Crowded and arrogant, its bubble letters read: *Hell Gate.* Like the universe, once working in my favor, was taunting me.

Wind chimes rang, accenting the horror scene that must have greeted the sleepy old woman with a cane who opened the door. The washed-out blood moon eclipse was waning to a sliver as she motioned her cane inside her home.

"You kids ever heard of calling first?"

My head hung low. I was still catching my breath.

"I can't get the ring off her," I launched in, as if that was my only problem.

My heavy body sank into the couch with Ash happily cooing in my arms. She refused to look at Yolanda. "I should never have put it on her. Stupid, stupid—"

"Tranquilízate. That part is easy." Yolanda opened a drawer in her kitchen, took out a jar, reached her bare hands in, and slathered a salve over Ash's knuckles.

"Nooo!" Ash whined. "Zeke!"

So, she knew two words now.

Yolanda clasped her had around the ring bearing finger. She tugged at it while I pulled Ash's hand in the other direction. With a pop, it finally slid off. Lingering beneath was a black line tracing a gash in her slim mahogany finger. Ash began to cry.

"No, no, no!"

We both ignored her whimpering.

"Huh," I said, catching my breath. "I guess it *was* easy." For some reason, I'd expected something bigger to happen then. But nothing did. Ash was still breathing down my neck.

"Coconut oil," Yolanda said, licking the rest off her fingers. "The next part will not be so easy."

"What next part?"

Yolanda examined the black mark between two pinched fingers. I suddenly felt stupid for not thinking of something as mundane as coconut oil before I hopped on two trains and a bus. Then I noticed what the woman was looking at. A lightning streaked mark that almost looked as if it was moving across her hand. Like a rippling ocean. Expanding.

"Try standing over there." She pointed a thumb at the other side of the living room.

I knew what the result would be before I even stood up. Ash tugged on me and let out a blood-curdling shriek that was too loud for this time of morning. My head split in pain as she leaped into my arms again. I let out an exhausted sigh. The magnitude of my fuckup was beginning to show its full form. What now?

"It has gotten into her blood," Yolanda explained.

Before I could ask what *it* was, I was holding the body down as Ash's limp arms were tied to the headboards in Yolanda's bedroom with white strips of fabric. She shook the bedframe with a carnal intensity. Struggling to break free. Yolanda tightened her reins.

"Once the tie is severed, it can never be tied again. In any capacity."

"W-what tie?" Yolanda shot me a look. "OH . . . what, like . . . she won't be my . . ." It felt childish to say the word. *Soulmate.* A word that now felt like a fantasy. "Like never? Never never? Will she at least . . . like me?" My chest began rising and falling rapidly. I reconsidered things. "M-maybe, we can—"

Beeping of heart monitors deafened my ears. I was back there again. Holding my grandmother's hand moments after being told she'd be coming home. Feeling every nanosecond like another prick of blood. Asking for another chance.

"Listen to me." Yolanda took me by the shoulders, giving me a gentle shake. My eyes remained fixed on Ash, whose whining spurred my compassion. And my own desire to find another way to make this work. To make us work.

Yolanda doubled down on the assertion in her voice. "Listen, Ezekiel. You have a remarkable amount of faith. But you are holding onto something you never owned. Obsession is *not* love. One person is *not* enough to close the hole in your heart. But it's not too late to fix the problem in front of us. We must act. Now! Draw out the darkness before the rest of her blood is infected."

I was too afraid to ask what the hell she meant by all that. What would happen if it infected her blood? Hopefully my expression did enough to convey my confusion without betraying the fact that I was absolutely shitting myself. The sharp look in her eyes was crystal clear. Whatever was happening, it was bad enough that I was better off not knowing what would happen if we failed.

Yolanda put a candle with an image labeled *Santa Ana* on her nightstand and set it aflame with a match, using the remaining fire to light a two-finger-thick cigar. I felt utterly useless as her calm storm orbited around my stationary body. Her hands moved fast and with a laser-focused intention as she gathered the necessary ingredients. Palm branches and thyme and incense and oils she flicked over Ash's forehead. She crushed a thin, leafy plant with a small pink flower and stuffed the mixture into the girl's mouth, causing her flailing legs to instantly relax. Then she poured a trickle of rum on the hardwood floor and hovered the cigar around the room. I looked down at the tall drum she'd placed in front of me.

"I don't know how to play it."

For the first time since I'd witnessed her, the old woman's face grew impatient. She struck down her cane.

"You are a musician."

She didn't know how wrong she was. There had to be another role for me. I frantically searched the room for excuses, and, finding nothing, I shrugged.

"I play piano. Not drums."

"You are a musician and a poet and so much more, Ezekiel. For this to work, we must make an offering. Art is not like love. There is no wrong way." I heard her say it in my grandmother's voice. That's when I remembered Yolanda's warning the last time I saw her. *I wouldn't take them off if I were you. Not until you regain your own internal balance.* And I was reminded, once again, how the pleading pain in Ash's eyes was caused by my hand.

Yolanda's knees slowly bent before the bed. She picked up a small silver bell and let its sharp ring vibrate, signifying the start of something. Ash's still body arched slightly away from the bed. Yolanda set her elbows beside the girl's knees in a prayer position. The old woman's voice began building into a song, floating in a language indiscernible to my ears. Not Spanish. Something else. Infinitely warm and ancient. Filling the room with reverence, like an organ in a church. As if by their own command, my hands began tapping along, following the lead of her melody. Suddenly, I was no longer afraid. I could feel the music cutting through my fear as I watched it blaze through the convulsing body laid in front of us.

"Zeke, Zeke, Zeke . . ." Ash continued gasping the tired refrain until the veins in her neck popped. "W-w-wait! No! Zeke! P-p-p-please! I-I love—" I squeezed my eyes shut. The volume of her words lowered by the beat that had overtaken me from within. So I played on.

3

The Bat

Chapter
Thirty-one

On Sisters

– Rosie

After several outgoing phone calls, I drove loops around Newark Liberty International Airport with my knuckles clenched over the steering wheel until I finally saw Caro's signature lime green suitcase shining amidst the frenzied darkness. I hardly recognized her. More than once, an official-looking traffic attendant wrecked my nerves by knocking on the window and asking me to move Mami's car. Each time I prayed they wouldn't ask for my nonexistent license. I hated airports with an undying passion. Caro wordlessly loaded her luggage into the trunk and plopped into the passenger's seat.

"You came," she said, inspecting her nails. Her hair was braided into large box braids, pale scalp highlighting slightly darkened brown skin. She looked brand new.

"I did. Mami wanted to come too, but she's cooking. Enough food for a small country. I hope you're hungry," I chuckled, letting my nerves escape.

"How was your flight?"

"Fine. I almost missed the plane 'cause I couldn't find that tiny stupid ass visa ticket."

"Ah, you should've tucked it in your passport," I suggested.

Caro let out a terse grunt.

That was the first silence.

✿ ✿ ✿

Earlier that morning Mami and I organized Caro's laundry and took either side of her quilt as we made her bed. Mami had gotten up early to put pernil in the oven for slow cooking. I could already smell its aroma filling our apartment.

"Your Confirmation is coming up. You're the first one, big deal. We haven't talk about it." Mami was terrible when she was trying to be casual. Confirming my undying devotion to the New Testament Institute and its statue of the Virgin Mary wasn't exactly at the top of my list at the moment. Nor was the fact that I was doing so before my older sister. I should have followed her lead and flunked my CCD exams.

"Yeah. I know all my prayers," I had assured her, wondering where she was going with this.

"Aha ... bueno ..." I wished she would just come out with it already. "Las viejitas— We thought since there are six boys and six girls in this year's class ... and the procession involves you walking in partners, it'd be nice to pair you up for pictures. We even got money for a photographer y todo eso."

I sat down on Caro's bed, processing.

"You're setting me up with someone. With a boy."

"No, no . . . bueno, te estoy preguntando. If you want . . ."

"So you didn't already pair me up with someone?"

Mami's eyebrows spread and her eyes averted mine. She sat down.

"You did," I said. ". . . Without asking me. And if I don't want to?"

"Cómo que 'I don't want?' What you mean? Qué es eso? Of course you want."

"Of course." My throat was slick with sarcasm.

"It's just for the pictures, mi niña. He's a nice boy." She put her hand over mine and I slid it back. She let out an exasperated sigh. "His family is coming over with him. They're very excited. Don't you think it will be nice? A handsome boy on your arm? And one who is already saved? Imagínate if you're the only one without a partner, the pictures just wouldn't look . . . right."

I ran my head through the prospects. All the boys in my CCD class were less than underwhelming. I glanced at the backpack that was sitting at the foot of the bed across from me. My mother's words turned to shapeless sound.

I knew that this is what she did. This is what made Caro hate her so much. *It wouldn't look . . . right.* That was all she seemed to care about. How things looked. What other people thought of her and her baby dolls. What me and my sister wore. Where we sat at church. How I did my hair.

I knew *why* she cared so much about it. It was like a security blanket she clung to for safety against a cold foreign country. It was what she thought would save her. It was what

I used to think would save me, too. But I also knew better now. I knew that posing for perfect pictures meant swallowing tiny shards of glass every day until your insides exploded. And then being asked to apologize for the blood you spilled.

✿ ✿ ✿

Caro turned the radio on while I figured my way out of the airport's maze. I turned the volume down. Once we hit the highway, I looked over at my sister, waiting for her to regale me with stories of her trip. Insights on the new stepfamily I'd never met. Pictures of the beach to make me jealous. Anything. Instead, she reached for the radio volume again, turning it all the way up. "Bills, Bills, Bills" by Destiny's Child shook the car seats. I turned it back down and pulled Mami's oversized black penny coat close to my chest.

I didn't expect being apart from her to be so . . . weird.

"So . . . you still mad at me?" I asked.

She crossed her arms.

I pressed on, reciting the script I'd prepared. "I'm sorry I wasn't there to take you to the airport that day and that I left you hanging with Mami. I kinda tried to find last-minute plane tickets actually, but . . ." I looked over and noticed the moonlight reflecting off her tense jawline. "Nevermind, that doesn't matter. I just . . . froze, I guess. It had nothing to do with you. I just . . . I didn't want to leave her."

"So you left me. Got it." There she went again. Us versus Them.

"I didn't mean to. But you're right. . . . I'm working on it. I mean, I won't be praising Papi anytime soon, but . . . working on it. No matter what, from now on, I'm always on Team Caro first. Pinky promise." I brought stretched my pinky towards her, still holding the wheel. After a couple seconds of renewed silence, I added, "And I should've called you more."

". . . Or at all."

"Wh—I literally called you yesterday!"

"Not enough." She reluctantly wrapped her pinky around mine.

With that, my sister turned the radio off. Muffled sounds of car horns and the whoosh of wheels flying past us replaced the music. Out the corner of my eye, I saw her bite down on her lower lip.

Then, she said: "It's whatever. I'm not mad at you anymore. And you weren't totally wrong about Papi." Which was the last thing I expected her to say. She must've seen the shock in my face. "Long story," she added, which seemed like an incredibly unfair thing to do. Just dangling a morsel in front of me and leaving me dry.

"Did something happen? You look . . . different. Not just the hair, just . . . you've changed I think." I don't know how casual I managed to sound. Whatever it was that happened, it had clearly brought us on the same side of the line drawn in sand many years ago.

"People don't change."

"I've changed," I said. I felt her eyes inspecting me as I faced forward, focused on the simple objective of getting us home. She kissed her lips.

"Yea, right."

I gestured towards the car I was currently driving.

"Okay, okay," she conceded. "I'll admit driving this thing even though you think it's against the law is pretty surprising for you. I'll give you that."

"It was only against the law coming here, when I was alone. I can drive with a permit if there's a driver in the car with me. So, I'm good now with you here," I corrected her.

"They gotta be twenty-one and experienced some years in driving, though. So . . . still illegal." She reached over and pinched my cheek between her thumb and pointer finger. "You must really love me." I shrugged her off, almost swerving into the car in the next lane.

Her gloating smile lit up the dark car. She was right, for once. I let out a sigh.

"I do love you, Carolina," I admitted beneath my breath. I wanted to take the words back the moment I let them leave.

"Ew!" Caro shrieked. Her dumb bird laugh threatened to shatter the windows.

"Right? That felt wrong. Ugh! I take it back." A shiver ran down my spine as I shook the words off my shoulders.

"Who are you and what have you done with my sister? You make it sound like I'm boutta die or something." Her laughs subsided into a bitterness. After I turned off the Parkway and onto our exit, she mumbled something at her nails. "I care for you deeply, too, or whatever."

I pretended not to hear her, letting the words linger for a moment. The car made its way around the corner of Westside Ave, onto our street.

"You're not gonna hug me now, are you?" I teased, a smile tugging at the corners of my lips.

"Ew. Shut *up*."

Ahead of us, a small crowd of three dark figures huddled underneath the streetlight shining over our apartment. I slowed down the car. The sharp smell of cheap cigar smoke leaked into the car. One of the men sat in a folding chair parked precisely in Mami's parking spot. They hadn't been there when I left. I pulled up next to them and rolled down Caro's window.

"How you pretty ladies doin' tonight?" The man sitting on the curb flicked the red light of his cigarette in our direction. Caro turned to look at me. I sighed and opened my mouth, but she beat me to it.

"Hey sir, you mind movin' somewhere? You're kinda in our spot," she said. Her voice was loud and firm. Instead of moving, the man looked up at his friends and chuckled.

"Oh, wow! I ain't know we had spots on the block. What's this one worth to you?" His sanguine smile spread in the night like a Cheshire cat. I put a hand on my sister's arm.

"I can just park around the corner," I tried.

"You know what? It's boutta be worth my fist in your ass!" Caro unbuckled her seat belt and reached into her backpack, pulling something out. Before she could get out of the car, the man lunged towards us. One of his friends emerged from the stoop behind him.

"Maaaan, kids these days got no respect!"

"Who you think you talking to little girl?"

The sitting one had got his hand halfway through the open window by the time I swung open the driver's door. I planted two feet on the concrete.

"Stop!" I put up a hand, trying to find myself. They obeyed, standing frozen with their mouths hanging limp. Caro's head peaked from behind one of them, bewildered. "All of you, go! Walk into traffic!" The gaggle of men slowly dragged their legs into the street, walking towards the busy intersection at the end of it. The lights of a pickup truck approached. I put up both hands, stopping them. "Wait, no! Just . . . run three blocks that way! Now! And stop harassing teenagers on the street, you fuckin' weirdos! Get a life."

At a snail-like pace, the men nodded and followed the finger I had pointed towards the empty lot at the end of Duncan Ave. After a few seconds, they picked up the pace to a jog. After the first block, the shortest man slipped on a plastic bag and fell down. But he got up just as fast and caught up with the others. I held down a laugh, sticking my numb hands in the pockets of the black coat I was wearing.

Caro stared off at the goons as the darkness engulfed them. Then she stared at me, meeting my smile with scrutinous eyes and an anger that quickly fizzled out into caution.

". . . You . . . how?"

I unbuttoned the coat and pulled away to reveal the pink fabric underneath. A million emotions raced across my sister's face as I watched her put pieces into place.

"You . . . you've been wearing that the whole time?" It wasn't the first question I expected from her. I laughed. She raised her voice an octave. "Not funny. What the fuck, Roz?"

"Sorry. No—I mean yes, I've been wearing it."

"So, it works. And it makes people . . . do that?" She pointed down the street with what I now realized was a small baseball bat in her hands.

". . . Yeah. Well, anything I want, I think."

"You . . . on Mami?" An unexpected air of betrayal flashed over her face. Okay . . . she figured that one out pretty quick. Not as slick as I thought I was. Still, I only felt a little bad about it. How else was I gonna get that woman to let me take the car? "That's so . . . reckless. What the hell? How do I know you ain't used it on me?" Caro pointed the bat to her chest. She seemed really concerned all of a sudden. I rolled my eyes and walked past her, closing the car's passenger door.

"That's what you're worried about? Relax. I'm not a monster. And besides, I've got super embarrassing news for you, bro." I hopped back into the driver's seat, pulling the car into reverse. "I have a working theory that . . . it doesn't work on people I actually like." When I finished parking, I added a brief addendum to myself. "Usually."

When we dragged her luggage up the stairs and I pulled out the apartment keys, I could still feel Caro inspecting at the side of my face. Before I turned the key, my sister's phone started buzzing and ringing notification bells like crazy.

"Is that JJ?" I asked, trying not to take a peek.

"No," she murmured. "Just the service finally kicking back in. A bunch of missed texts and ca—wait. Who's 'Bounce underscore That underscore Ash'? What the fuck?"

Her mood shifted drastically. She frantically pressed a thumb into her phone. I realized that while I'd been waiting for my sister to fill me in on her break, I should've probably been filling her in on all she missed. But before I could figure out where to begin, the key in my hand drifted away from us and the door swung into our home.

"Language! Asi e como u'tede saludan a la gente? Y eso?" Mami had brown sauce smeared across her brown cheek and brows that furrowed along a signature wrinkle.

"Who's ustedes?" I asked, rolling the luggage past her. I kissed her on the cheek even though I'd seen her less than two hours ago. "Bendición, Mami." I gave Caro a look. If the two of them didn't call a truce, I didn't know how much longer I could take it. It was hard enough with everything else that was on my mind lately. They stood in front of each other awkwardly for a moment.

"Bendición, Mami." Caro finally said. Before she could give the woman a kiss, Mami's arms had overtaken her tall body, pulling tight. Like she might never let go again. "Okay, okay. I can't breathe, Mami. Ya, ya." My mother released her grip.

"Mi niña, cariño, amor de mi vida! Dios te bendiga!" The woman's smile faded a bit as she ran her fingers through the ends of Caro's braids. I watched her mouth open and close slightly. I cut in.

"Doesn't her hair look so pretty, Mami?"

Caro pulled her braids back, giving me a confused look. Mami nodded slowly, holding her tongue. Then she clapped her hands together before changing the subject. "Okay. I make your favorite. Fritos con pernil. No onions. Y molondrones. Y arroz blanco. With the concón. También compré ese katchup dulce americano that you like."

I knew it pained Mami to make that plain white rice, even though it was my sister's favorite. No sauce, no habichuelas, no peas, nothing. Caro looked up at the ceiling, searching. Then she came back down.

"*Katchup dulce americano?* You mean barbeque sauce?" She chuckled and I saw bits of my sister shining through cracks in her shell. Finally. Her eyes met mine, shaking her head. She pointed a thumb at Mami. "Dique *katchup dulce.*"

"Ay, ya! You know what I mean. Come. A comer," Mami said. Caro had already plucked a piece of pernil with her bare, unwashed hands and was scarfing it down. I tried to slip past her into our room, but Mami stopped me. "Y ese coat?"

Shit. I froze. My eyeballs shifted to Caro for help. She had *I told you so* sitting in her pursed lips. I could see now how that could be annoying. Everything was suddenly so still, you could hear a slice of bread hit the floor. Then, her look shifted as I prepared my response and clenched my fists.

"Oh, nah! Don—" Caro started, food still in her mouth.

"*What coat, Mami?*"

After a moment, I watched a cloudiness flash in and out of her eyes. My mother blinked back at me, anger building in her tone. "What you mean 'what coat?' Ese coat. That's mine, no? Qué tú tiene . . ." Her eyes narrowed. I felt my heart trying to escape through my chest. "Take it off. Now."

". . . No?" I tried. I knew it wouldn't work. It only made her more angry. Caro's head rolled.

Mami stepped to me, grabbed the zipper at my neck, and yanked it down. The truth laid out before the three of us and my string of untruths came unraveled. I turned away from my mother. When I looked to my sister, she was sharing a longing look with the uneaten feast laid before us, about to go uneaten for a while longer.

Mami grabbed me by the shoulders.

"That. Is. Not. A toy." Each word fell like another bomb off her lips. "Where did you get this? What did you do?"

Chapter
Thirty-two

On Insomnia

– Zeke

I dreamt a poem with open eyes
but the details are fuzzy

It was about anxiety,
No it was about funerals,
No it was about perseverance,
No it was about the way I think I am

going crazy
And I can't sleep
when my head is full of half scribbles
and questions like, what even is soap?

I remember

There were a whole lotta fruit flies picking on my heart
swarming and feeding on love's bittersweet decay

The Girl, The Ring, & The Baseball Bat

I stand still
still there is a claw on my throat
And the consequences of moving are
between life and up to death

Up to* I know
there is a whole lotta pain between life and death
To be half alive or half dead, can't decide
whether being good is worth the stillness

Yet again I am still
And close my eyes

Hoping the words don't fade from my lids

Chapter
Thirty-three

On Shattered Glass

– Rosie

Two days after Valentine's Day, Zeke still wasn't at school.

On day three, I saw a pink head sticking out of a locker on my way to Stage Crew. The same girl with the pink hair this dude was going on and on about at lunch, I realized. But I wasn't listening then. My fingers gripped the sleeves of my pink jacket.

"Where's Zeke?"

Ash's face scrunched up. "Who?"

I blinked. "Z-Zeke." Her face was still blank. "You have English with him. You were at his party. Zeke Parish."

"Why would I know where he is?" she scoffed.

I couldn't tell if she was fucking with me or not, but I stuffed the urge to swing at her into my pockets and walked away. It was a stupid idea, anyways.

✿ ✿ ✿

Mrs. Shapelli didn't show up to stage crew rehearsals again. She put me in charge. While I told the actors to practice their blocking with the set, I took out the thick binder that had been weighing down my backpack. Printed scans of newspaper clippings from the library, Post-It notes, and the important bits I dug out of the accounting files Rishi had given me. I went through the scraps of insight again.

According to the files, there was money from the budget allocated for "Hardship Application Grants," but I didn't see any evidence that those funds were distributed anywhere. Not to mention the astronomical portion of the school district budget that went towards "Correctional Operations" aka the School Resource Officers aka the police station housed within our school. And then there were the transcripts from the bi-monthly school board meetings.

From a meeting a year ago, a mother spoke out about her concern over the resources disappearing more and more each year.

> *"I've got three kids and one laptop. What happened to the grant for the computer lab you all were talking about? Why are we letting these schools with PAYING CUSTOMERS, like Saint Agnes, and DePaul, and ITI pull larger and larger amounts of money from the money the district is supposed to give to its public schools? If those fancy rich people don't want their kids touching ours, why don't THEY pay for it?"*

I could feel the mystery woman's mama bear energy through the page. She wasn't wrong about the 15 percent of the district budget that went towards non-public schools. That was compared to the 0.01 percent that went towards health services. Or the 0.003 percent that went towards the school libraries. Like *all* the libraries. An insane 5 percent went towards school resource officers, who apparently weren't even required to go through any training.

I flipped to another one from a state-wide exposé on state testing that interviewed an expert on Advanced Placement programs from Princeton.

> *"The screening tests for most talented programs have proven time and time again to be faulty and biased. There is rarely such a thing as a divinely gifted child from birth, and yet we continue to foster this outdated idea and segregate children. We know now that that is not the way our brains work."*

I highlighted a new Ordena quote I found in the same article where he answered for cutting all the AP programs besides AP Calculus.

> *"We always want to help our most talented students succeed, but unfortunately with our budget and the large number of low-income black and brown students at Westside, we don't have as many talented kids to put into these courses."*

There was something about that quote. The way he linked *black and brown* and *talented* and made them opposites. I drew an arrow back to the previous quote.

Then there was a testimonial in a newspaper from a parent I somehow knew was white.

"I pay very high taxes in this city, and I do it gladly knowing that my kid goes to a quality school. Not a failing one. He works very hard, and he deserves to be rewarded for it with as many opportunities to thrive at ITI as the district can offer. If we're saying its got to go to one school or the other here, I mean… come on. It's obvious."

And a very old article about criticism over ITI's low admittance rate of Black students with a quote from one of its teachers.

"Diversity is a lovely idea, but we don't believe a child's success rate will be determined by the child that is sitting next to them, whatever race. We believe in individual responsibility."

It was so vague I had to read it back three times.

I thought back to my conversation with Zeke when I told him about ITI. *Why do you even wanna go there so bad?* Why *did* I want to go there? Because someone told me about it? Because of a pamphlet? Or a statistic? I wasn't sure I even belonged there. Why did I want a place that probably didn't want me?

Looking over the accounting files one last time, I made a decision. For maybe the first time in my life, I decided I knew who I wanted to be and I wasn't gonna wait for permission to be her.

I was taking my own shit back.

Chapter
Thirty-four

On Rough Landings

– Caro

When I got off the plane in Las Américas International Airport, greeted by a row of women in spinning traditional white dresses flanked by men in linen guayaberas playing instruments, I winced. And I wondered if tourists actually liked that shit. It lost its charm after the first time. That job must be mad annoying. Dancing for tired strangers. Like we were at fucking Disneyland or something.

When I made it to customs, I was greeted by two lines and a whole existential crisis. An airport attendant saw me gawking, trying to figure out where I belonged. He asked me "Dominicana?" And I said yes, but no, but yes. He pushed me into the foreigners line. I paid twenty dollars for a tiny visa ticket I knew I would immediately lose and made it through a quick interrogation at customs. If Rosie was there, she would have thought of someplace safe to put it. I slipped it into my pocket.

I walked on until I reached the familiar smell of fresh coffee and pastelitos. When I turned a corner, I was immediately engulfed by hundreds of screaming fans surrounding a wide runway and waving their signs at me and the trickle of travelers following behind. All screaming for their people. Reunited in fits of tears and bear hugs. Above us, a giant *Bienvenidos!* sign was flanked by chirping birds. At the end of the runway, by the exit doors, I watched taxi drivers pouncing on tourists. My eyes glazed over, overwhelmed as I quickly approached the end of the line. Not a single face was the one I was looking for. It occurred to me then that anyone could just jump out of this crowd and snatch me away and no one would know. Who would know to look for me?

Before hitting the exit doors, I dodged a man trying to take my bags to a taxi and pivoted towards an airport cafe. *Look like you know where you're going, bitch. Stop looking lost. Stop looking like a tourist,* I told myself. I dug my phone out of my backpack. It was still on airplane mode. I meant for it to stay that way unless there was an emergency. Who knew how many hundreds of dollars would get added to Papi's phone bill if I tapped on that tiny button? Who knew if I'd even get service. Was *this* an emergency? Lost at the airport by myself, even though my father assured me he'd be here? The way this whole trip was going, man. No one around to drop me off, no one here to pick me up. Pathetic.

I went to the wifi settings and watched the free airport wifi show up. I could message Papi via wifi. There. A solution. A sigh of relief escaped. Then hope dwindled away as the slow wifi loaded and loaded and loaded and loaded.

You could get a taxi to the address on the invitation, I briefly thought before remembering I only had fifty American dollars left. What was that, like five hundred pesos? How much would a cab ride to Barahona be? It was a long ass drive the last time I remembered going there. My mind ran through my options, trying to find the right one.

I was wondering how Mami managed to exchange her money for pesos before she got here when I suddenly heard someone call out my name.

"Carolina!" The voice came from a tall, lanky woman with a mouth full of shining pink braces and bottle-blond hair wrapped in a tubi with bobby pins. Almost as tall as me. With a significant bump in her stomach popping out through her maxi dress. I'd never seen her before in my life. She looked like half the elementary school teachers I'd ever had. I turned my neck around, wondering if she was talking to someone else. She approached me, stretching her hands out for a hug. "Carolina! Hellooo?"

"Uh . . ."

"You don't recognize me?" I ran through the cousin roster in my head. Maybe a tía I'd met once when I was little? But she spoke English. None of my tías in DR spoke English. None that I could remember. "Fernanda?!"

"Oh! Right!" Still nothing. I nodded, feigning recognition.

"Your father sent me to get you. It's so nice to finally meet you! Wow, pero tú ere un mujerón! Sorry, you speak Spanish? My English is not so good." Before I could say anything, this stranger trapped me into a hug. My brain started making calculations, trying to figure out what angle this woman could possibly be scamming me from.

Fernanda. I'd read that name before. I glanced at her stomach again. *Oh.*

"Uh, yeah, un chin!" I lied, trying really hard to match her enthusiasm. Technically, it was my first language, but I'd come to realize through many failed Spanish classes that I didn't speak Spanish as much as I spoke Mami. "Sorry, I'm a little tired. So . . . you and Papi are . . ." There was too long a pause that I waited for her to fill. I felt like I was handling a lit firecracker.

"Are . . . getting married!" She brought up her hand to show off the small silver ring on it. "Sí, sí! Ay! Don't tell me he didn't tell you!" She put her hand over her mouth.

"No, yeah. He—he did. That's . . . why I'm here."

She let out a cackle and put her hands on her knees. I wanted to ask her how old she was, but that seemed like a rude thing to say. She couldn't have been more than ten years older than me, though.

"Ah okay! Good! Haha! Bueno, por ahora, tenemos muchísimas cosas que hacer. Tamaira esta cocinando la cena. You know Tamaira, right? Maybe no, haha! Sorry, tu pai no me a dicho mucho de ustedes. And your sister? Tú ere la má vieja, verdad?" The way she talked so fast with that weird boujee accent and slipping between languages was making me dizzy. Like the translating machine in my brain was working overtime. I had to keep pausing to take in the information.

"Yea—yes! I'm the oldest. And . . . uh, she couldn't make it. School stuff. Un . . . examen."

"Ay, qué pena." She pouted. "Well, let's go! I'll tell you more in the car! Vamos!"

I guess that meant we were just flying straight past the fetus-sized elephant in the room. Got it.

As soon as I crossed the threshold of the airport exit doors, I felt nature take course and the falsehood of my straightened hair reveal itself. By the time we made it to her black SUV, long strands were stuck to my neck like seaweed. I could feel the waves forming at my roots. Thank god the car had functioning air conditioning. It was nearly a four-hour drive to Papi's place in Barahona. And just driving out of the airport on its own felt like two hours with Fernanda beside me. Once we hit the streets of Santo Domingo, she immediately started swerving in and out of oncoming lanes. I buckled in.

"Has he shown you the house? You're gonna love it!"

"House? Nah, last time we came he was living in an apartment above that garage he used to work at. I forgot the name of it . . ."

"Ah, no, no. Eso ya hace rato. When your father proposed I told him we had to have a house first. Claro. Yo no sé comó el aguantaba to' esa bulla! Imaginaté! Me and Lesi above a garage with all that boom, boom, boom? Ay, no. Lucky my father—he's in, ah . . . you say construction? Development? Anyway, lucky he had the perfect place for us. Well, almost perfect. I would've preferred a place in Santiago, where my family is from. Pero you're gonna love the house. Una belleza! I designed it myself. Soy arquitecta."

I nodded, trying to process at a million miles a minute. Slowly, the meaning revealed itself as I carved out the words from her string of sounds. *Aguantaba*. To put up with. *Belleza*. Like Nuestra Belleza Latina. The beauty pageant. *Arquitecta*. That was an easy one.

"Uh . . . Lesi?"

"Lesika. My daughter. She's with Wendell's mother now. They're meeting us at the house."

"Oh. Your daughter. Right." No big deal. I sat back in my chair. She turned to look at me.

"He *has* told you about Lesika?"

I gritted my teeth into a smile.

"Of course, of course!" Just like he told me a stranger was coming to pick me up from the airport. "Can't wait to meet . . . her."

"It's okay if we make a quick stop by the súper? Still so much to buy for the wedding."

Our quick stop turned into an hour detour at La Sirena. We left with an SUV filled to the brim with grocery bags. And a five-gallon water jug between my legs.

✿ ✿ ✿

Once we left the city and hit rural dirt roads, Fernanda told me to be her lookout for goats and cows. Which added a new level of stress as I held onto the ceiling and simultaneously had to scream and point when one crossed our path. Not to mention the potholes that threatened to take my tall ass out. Thank god there was still a bit of daylight, at the very least. By the time we hit the Barahona checkpoint, where the soldiers didn't blink twice before letting us pass, the sun was on the brink of setting.

We slowed down in front of a wide, half outdoor colmado and a jungle gym surrounded by a low wall with a winding mural. Across the road was a field of plátano trees. I could tell they were plátanos by the broad, wavy leaves I'd once plucked on the shoulders of my father. A shirtless man in gray basketball shorts appeared from the field and pulled open a swirling iron gate. As we drove into a narrow dirt path he'd cleared for us, I could see lumps of underdeveloped plátanos peeking out under the tree leaves. The biggest one no more than the size of my iPhone.

The rocky path turned, and so did our view of a large house at the center of this humble plot. *The* house, I realized. Fernanda's house. Papi's house. Papi had a house. A whole ass house. With land and a long winding driveway. Like people in the movies.

It was two stories of ivory with yellow trimming on the windows and clay Spanish roof tiles. A balcony hung over the wooden double doors that crowned the entrance. If not for the patches of dug-up dirt and cardboard boxes surrounding the front, it could be featured in a magazine above the caption *money*. Our car pulled up into a separate gated area alongside the house.

"Wow," was all I could think to say. I suddenly wondered about the mess I'd left in my shared bedroom with Rosie. And whether there was still a leak beneath our bathroom sink.

When we got to the open-concept kitchen, a feast was already laid out across a long dining table. A ham in the center flanked by different kinds of rice and sweet and black plátano maduros. It smelled incredible. And everything looked so . . . new. Tufted white dining chairs that belonged on the *Real Housewives*. Marble columns separating the spaces above sparkling white floors. Out of all the rooms I saw, peeking around, the kitchen felt the most lived-in.

A small woman emerged from one of the bathrooms and startled Fernanda and me. She couldn't have been more than two or three years older than me. Her skin was the same shade as mine, only it was marked by purpled scars along her arms and legs. She hung her head before Fernanda.

"No te dije que usaras el baño de afuera?"

"Perdón, señora," Tamaira said. As if Fernanda's request was at all reasonable.

Tamaira nodded towards me and went to work cutting an avocado on the marble counter. Her dark hands transformed before my eyes into the hands of my mother at her old job. Into *Powerpuff Girl* reruns on Saturdays when she would sit me down in front of a stranger's TV and conjure silent obedience before women who looked a lot like Fernanda.

Beyond the kitchen was a doorway covered with an opaque plastic sheet. Everything from the walls to the kitchen table to the porcelain figurines on the windowsill was coated in a thin layer of blue dust. I felt it tickling my nose and let out a sneeze.

"Salud," Fernanda said. I thanked her. "We're still finishing with construction. These guys. Ay, so slow. Never build a house in Barahona, Carolina," she warned. As if I would ever be in a position to use that advice.

"Your room is there. Hope it fits okay. Your father described you as a little girl, I had no idea . . ." She gestured up and down. When I saw the room, I saw what she meant. Against the wall was a short bed fit for a toddler. Over the window was a string pinned with hanging photos. All of little Lesika. One with Papi and her at the beach, smiling. "Sorry the other rooms aren't finished yet. It's okay?"

I nodded reluctantly and set my luggage into a corner. Fernanda went back to overseeing Tamaira in the kitchen. Finally alone for a moment, I got the feeling I was forgetting something.

A shriek echoed through the house and nearly made my heart stop. I followed the sound to the front door, where a glossy-haired little girl was climbing into an electric toy truck. In front of her was the man himself. I waited for him to notice me.

"Bendición, Papi."

He jumped up in surprise and pulled me into a side hug, barely giving me a glance. Like he saw me all the time.

"You met Fernanda?"

"Yeah, we're besties now."

"Mmm . . ." He nodded, still looking at the little girl. Then he called out to her. "Te gusta, Lesi? Tá jevi, no e' verdad?"

"Sí! Sí! Sí!" She rode circles through the dirt. My father beamed. The motorcycle he'd driven in on was still emitting smoke.

A minute passed before he finally eyed me up and down. "Well, look at you!" He planted a wet kiss on my forehead. "Llegó la Carolina de su pai, coño! Welcome home!"

✿ ✿ ✿

At dinner, I found myself staring at the ring on Fernanda's hand.

"So, how long have you been . . . together?" If that's even what they were calling it. Fernanda smiled. "Ay, cuánto son? Two years? Two and a half?" I nodded, trying to do some math.

"So . . . how did you do it?"

Papi gave me a curious look, searching for meaning. "I thought they woulda taught you that in school by now. You know . . . when a lady and a man really love each other, or sometimes only kinda like each other, really . . . they get together and—"

"Okay! Diablo! Not what I meant. How did you do it, like how did you propose?"

"Ah!" He laughed. Then he clasped his hand over hers. "Bueno, dile tú."

Fernanda smiled. "It was nice and simple really. He didn't even have a ring yet, but we were walking and talking en el malecón like we did on after our first date y . . . pues, he just got down on one knee, and before he could say anything else, I said yes!" She giggled. "I just knew it was time."

"I think you knew before I did, amor." Papi leaned his forehead against hers. "Pero, sí, here we are. A wedding and more to come. Dios sigue bendiciendo."

So it was his. I took this as an opening to bring up the subject of Fernanda's stomach, asking how far along she was. Six months, it turned out. About eight or nine long-distance phone calls ago.

"Didn't I tell you last time we talked?"

"No. You didn't." I didn't feel like voicing my opinion in front of all these strangers.

"Well, you got here in time for the good part. Ya que tá to con el wedding, we can finally pick a name for him."

"Him? The doctor said—" Fernanda protested.

"Let me dream, mi vida. Carolina, any suggestions?"

The last thing I wanted to do—right after licking the crusty bottom of my chancletas—was help my father and the woman I'd just met, who would become my stepmother, choose a name for their secret baby.

"How did you choose my name?" I asked between delicious mouthfuls. I already knew the story, but I asked for it anyway. I glanced at Fernanda. "Or did Mami choose it?" Mami never failed to remind me of it every time we went grocery shopping.

Papi cleared his throat. "Uh . . . pshh! No! I worked very hard for that name. Your mother was throwing a fit over her constant cravings. Se puso absolutamente loquísima. It had to be the one specific kind of rice we got from this restaurant. I ran around a hundred corner stores in New Jersey trying to find her that damn white rice and when I came home for the third time, todo un tiguere, feeling like a real man. Por fin, her face lit up and she said 'That's the one! That's what the baby wants!' So I said, 'Pero ahí tá! La Carolina. Like the rice.' And that was it. Decided."

After dinner, I collected my plate and a couple of stray cups and made my way to the open kitchen area.

"Mamita, no. No, no. Deja eso. That's what Tamaira is for. You're offending her. Siéntate. That's why we have help." The way Fernanda was snapping irked me. Ignoring her, I picked up the dinner plates anyway and silently helped Tamaira wash up in the kitchen. Bits of blue detergent powder stuck between my fingers.

If only my mother could see me now. Doing chores outta spite. Back in Jersey, I would have gladly let Mami or Caro handle the cleaning if they offered. Not because I was lazy, I just . . . I liked to pretend. If you're a girl and you pretend to do things badly, people do things for you. Like the two old men on the plane fighting over who was gonna help me with my carry-on luggage. I guess I didn't see the point in doing work someone else was willing to do for me. The way I saw it, my future involved me looking pretty and lounging glamorously beside an in-ground pool. Why mess with that vision, you know?

"Sorry," I said to Fernanda. "I'm not used to having a maid."
Nor was I used to talking about said maid as if she weren't in
the room. Neither was Papi. Or at least, he didn't used to be.

Fernanda kept calling after me.

"It's okay! Really! It's normal here, todos tenemos ayuda.
No pasa nada. Siéntate, ya!" This lady would not let this go,
Jesus Christ.

"Really? Everyone? Tamaira do *you* have a maid? My bad,
I ain't know." I looked at Tamaira next to me as I said it, realizing immediately that I had made a mistake by speaking in
English. But I still caught a smile curl the corners of the girl's
lips. I smiled back and offered her a clean plate.

"Ay que asco! How is society supposed to function if we
don't let the help do their jobs? They take pride in that. It's . . .
all they have sometimes, you know? Wendell cariño, explí-
caselo!" Out of the corner of my eye, I saw my father clasp his
hand over Fernanda's hand.

"If she wants to clean, let the girl clean," he whispered. I
could still feel the tension emanating from my future stepmother as I dried the last plate.

I didn't want to be there anymore, so afterwards I sought
refuge in one of three bathrooms in this empty house. When
I looked in the mirror, I saw what this island had done to my
hair. It looked like I'd walked through a carwash made of bal-
loons. I got to work in the shower, undoing hours of my
mother's labor in seconds. Ice cold water washed the travel off
my face.

By the time I emerged with a towel wrapped around my chest, all the lights were turned off and Lesika was sound asleep in her bed. In my bed, actually. Everything in the house had gone uncomfortably still. All I heard was the sound of crickets and bachata in a far-off distance. I wasn't used to sleeping this far away from the party. The door to the master bedroom was locked, though I could hear Papi and Fernanda murmuring a conversation on the other side. All I could make out was, "Esa niña ta bien extraña. Nigun cariño pa la gente." That was from Fernanda. Apparently, she thought I was a weirdo. Which was an insane take. I'd been nothing but nice to her. At least, to her face. "No e culpa della. Así e que son to la gente de Nueva Yol." That was my papi. Apparently, he didn't disagree with her.

I grabbed my bag out of Lesika's room, settled on the couch, and adjusted my expectations.

Chapter
Thirty-five

On Strange Family

– Caro

My first morning in DR, I woke up to the soothing sound of Papi's three stereo systems blasting his Los Toros Band CD. I knew it was the same CD he had when we were little because the first song always skipped ten seconds in. Lesika's claps and squeals cut through the music.

My eyes opened just enough to see that someone—probably Papi—had brought me back to Lesika's tiny ass bed. I groaned into her Hello Kitty–printed pillow and folded it over my ears. My face was drenched in sweat. In the earliest hours, I'd heard heavy footsteps walking in and out of the house. Drills and machinery and heavy things falling every five minutes. It didn't feel like I'd slept more than an hour.

"Weeppaa!" Papi was shouting and slamming together pots in the kitchen. Oh, my Papi. He was a crazy man. But his light always shone brighter in the mornings.

I tried to shut the world out for another five minutes more before I finally gave in and touched my feet to the cool tile floor.

My first stop was the closest bathroom, but there was a man with a toolbelt crouched down in there. My father let out another shout. So, I headed for the kitchen.

"Oye! La Carolina linda de su pai! She has risen!" He pointed his spatula up to the sky. "They are fixing the plumbing this morning. No hay agua por ahora, but there's a bucket in here if you need. Buen día!"

"Buenos días," I mumbled. No water. Great. Loved being drenched in sweat in the morning. Who needs showers? "Isn't it a little early for music, Pa?"

"Ya casi son las 12, sleeping beauty," he said, which seemed impossible. I squinted through the iron bars in the kitchen window, looking for the position of the sun. Being here was always trippy. If the Bermuda Triangle was a black hole where shit disappeared, I think the rest of the Caribbean must have been something like a time warp. Hours contracted and expanded with the breeze.

"You want a salami with your eggs and mangú?" I felt forgiveness flowing out of me with ease as I watched him spin through the kitchen in a white tank top.

"Of course I want a salami, Papi. Thanks." I kissed him on the cheek.

"Yo quiero *más* salami!" Lesika slammed her little hands on the dining table. Bits of the chewed-up food already in her mouth flew through the air.

"Buenos días to you, too, Lesika," I said. She responded by sticking her tongue out at me, which made it very hard for me not to start my day by throwing hands with a six year-old. Before meeting this tiny terrorist, I'd considered having kids when I got older. So much for that. I pulled out my phone and tried to refresh my incoming messages. I tried again and again and again. Nothing was happening. "What's the wifi?"

"El wifi se fue," Lesika said. I didn't understand what that meant.

"What?"

"Fichi took the hotspot with her this morning. She'll be back soon. You can use my phone if you need," Papi explained. Fichi. That's what he called Fernanda. He slid over my breakfast plate.

"Oh," was all I could say. I didn't feel like telling him that I couldn't check for JJ's texts on his phone. I flipped my phone over and fidgeted with the tablecloth. It was thick and white with an intricate lace placed over it. It was the kind of white that meant that someone was responsible for keeping it that way. When I dipped my salami in ketchup and took a bite, my face puckered up when the sugar hit the back of my molars. I *knew* I forgot to pack something in my luggage. American ketchup.

"So what's the plan for today?"

"Bueno . . . la suegra is taking Lesika off our hands today. Fichi is at a spa and then she's going to dinner in a fancy restaurant with her girlfriends, aya por el malecón. I'm sure she would love to have you." I didn't mean to curl my upper lip, but he seemed to catch it. "Pero, of course, si quieres . . .

you're more than welcome to join me and the guys. We're going to the cancha for the big boxing match tonight."

I only went to the cancha when I had a cousin to accompany me because it was filled with the same typa dudes that hung around outside Lena's. But my cousins were all away at school now. However, if the alternative was hanging out with my father's fiancée ...

"Uhh ... I don't know ..."

"Hablen españooool, señores!" Lesika commanded us, slamming her hands once more. Her tiny, bewildered expression was honestly kind of hilarious. I could tell she was dead deadass, though, so I swallowed my laugh into a cup of fresh-squeezed chinola juice.

Papi leaned down to kiss his future step-daughter on her pale forehead. My heart tightened. "Tienes razón, princesa. Hablamos español!" *Princesa.* The word reached back through distant memories of my chubby legs hanging off his broad shoulders. He set down my mountain of a breakfast plate. "So? Qué dice la Carolina?"

"Yea, sure, soun—" Lesika shot laser beams at me. "I mean ... sí ... mejor voy pa la cancha. Suena ... chévere?" I wasn't sure if I was using the word right.

"Muy bien! Chévere!" My father's rounded laughter bubbled out of him. Not even midday, but he still raised a bottle of half-drunk Presidente and poured me a cup of my own. I washed it down gladly.

Chapter
Thirty-six

On Overgrown Rituals

– Rosie

Three days before Caro's return, I was sitting on the couch, avoiding the looming list of chores Mami assigned me by checking my text messages for the fifth time that day. The same message from Zeke hung over me since the night after the Angels and Demons party.

Hey! You get home alright?

Now with a string of my unreturned texts below it.

> *I'm fine.*
> *Are you sick?*
> *Sorry about the party. It's a long story. Can I*
>   *call you?*
> *Pls pick up. Starting to worry. Stop being a butthole.*

It wasn't long before Mami actually handed me a mop and requested my assistance. She was like a manic fly every year around this time. Like a ritual. Only this time, doubly intensified. She buzzed from one room to the next, cleaning up one space by creating a mess in another. Everything she touched landed in a specifically chaotic spot. And she had something on the stove at the same time. The only way to avoid a meltdown was just to not get in her way. That's where Caro almost always went wrong—getting in her way. When Mami started cleaning the bathroom, I snuck into the kitchen and turned down the heat on a pot that was boiling over. Then I got back to the mopping.

When we were nearly done setting up the living room, I sat at the table, cutting flowers over a newspaper. Hurricane Mami was winding down. I waited for an opening.

"Is it okay if I ask you something?" I paused and picked at my nails. Mami looked me up and down, curiously.

"Claro. Anything you want, mama."

"Did we come to the States because you wanted to get away from Papi? What happened with you guys?"

The first thing I saw on her face was shock. My mother set down the Hefty bags she was stuffing into a closet and put a finger on her chin for a moment. The longer she thought, the more I expected her to lie to me again. Or tell me to get back to work and stop asking questions. But then she opened her mouth.

"Nos mudamos por lo que estaba pasando con el government y la economía. Y por u'tede. So my girls had a place to grow. A place I didn't have. A place that wasn't . . . no sé, like . . . a trap. Pero, I want you to know that what happened between me and your father had nothing to do with either of you. You or Caro. We just . . . las cosas pasan. We grow. We become different people. We have different values now."

I nodded, holding on to the same courage that pushed the first question out into the open.

"So you don't hate him? It's okay if you do." *Because I do*, I wanted to say. She sighed. I could tell she really wanted to say the right words. She spoke slowly and deliberately.

"I never had any hatred towards your father. I don't agree with his choices. Your father was a man at war with himself. I was only tired of getting caught in the crossfire. Not my battle, pero I kept getting hit. So I had to leave before I became at war with myself, too. And you *know* how I love myself." A bittersweet smile rested across her lips. As I listened to her talk, I felt myself becoming lighter somehow. Like I had been a fish swimming my whole life in a murky pond, and, finally, the water was being purified.

"You do have flawless skin, Mami," I laughed. At the very least, her obsession with other people's opinions kept her looking on point at all times. Even as she was digging through a garbage bag on the floor like a rabid racoon.

"I know! Who else is gonna keep me looking this good? Solo el dios mío. Not a man. Y ahora tiene otra pa joder y yo me quedo con mis niñas. I wouldn't want it another way. . . . Pásame eso?" I handed her another garbage bag.

"I love you, Ma."

I said it because it was true. Suddenly, I realized that I really didn't say it enough. Mami looked at me then like she was gonna cry. I wished she wouldn't. If she cried, I was gonna cry.

"Y yo a ti, mamita. Y yo a ti. Te amo, te amo, te amo." She trapped me into a hug. I feigned my own discomfort as I tried to escape. But honestly, this time I didn't mind being trapped.

She hugged me until the doorbell rang. It rang again and again until we finished stuffing months of unsightly stress out of sight. Slow and steady, the church ladies started filing into our living room with their rosaries in hand. There was a shift in the air this year compared to last year. They weren't as somber and only five of them wore black. The rest wore regular clothes. I even heard Doña Ismerys laugh. And no one shushed her.

After I finished organizing the flowers at the altar in the living room, I set out a tray with plastic cups of lemonade and felt a buzzing in my leg. Zeke's name illuminated my face. He was calling me. Like an old person.

Who called people without notice?

I was so pissed I nearly dropped the phone. My hand frantically shook the locked door handle to my and Caro's room. Locked, of course, because Mami had converted it into a makeshift second closet. The key was somewhere in the kitchen.

"Fuck," I whispered, and prayed the old women couldn't hear me.

My phone kept buzzing. I opened the door to Mami's room halfway, hitting a stack of black garbage bags on the floor. My torso squeezed through and closed the door behind me.

"Hello? Zeke?" Just that iota of physical effort had me out of breath. Silence greeted me on the other end. The possibility briefly occurred to me that Zeke had gotten into a horrible accident and someone else was calling to spread the news. In which case, I was starting to regret calling him a butthole.

"Hey. Sorry I disappeared."

Oh, thank God. I really wanted to be mad at him. Instead I just let out a long-held breath in relief.

"It's fine. I'm sorry about leaving the party. And calling you a butthole, even though you kinda *were* a butthole. I just thought you were mad at—"

"Don't . . . don't worry about it. Listen, can I just—can we hang out? You busy?"

I turned towards my mother's bedroom door, where I could hear the church ladies giggling on the other side.

"Uh . . . no. Not busy. I mean my mom's having . . . like, a party? I guess? But I can tell her I invited you! You do own a rosary, right?"

"Oh. Sorry, never—"

"No! Come! Come! I'll be mad if you don't come, really."

There was a pause on his end.

". . . Okay. See you soon then."

As soon as I clicked the phone off, I remembered Mami's number one rule. *No boys in my house.* Did Zeke count as a boy?

Chapter Thirty-seven

On Being Overwhelmed

– Zeke

I wasn't surprised when I heard a knock on my bedroom door and heard my father's voice.

"What are you doing here?" I sleepily asked him from my bed.

"Nice to see you, too. Only got on a ten-hour flight, no big deal. Don't mind me, didn't mean to interrupt your sleep," he said. Ten hours? Fuck. I groaned and sat up, wishing he *was* interrupting my sleep. Then maybe I wouldn't feel so dead-tired, like I'd been awake for an eternity now.

"Hi Dad, nice to see you. Why are you here? Did something happen to Grandma Lynn?"

"Why you think I'm here?" He crossed his broad arms. I surely hadn't asked him to come. It took me a minute.

"You didn't have to come. Like I said over the phone, I'm fine."

"You missed school. You not playin' keys." He was so *serious*. It was creepy. "Your auntie says you been locked in here all week."

278

"She lies."

"Mmm . . ." He looked around the room beneath thick black glasses. At all my empty water bottles and the half-eaten dinner plates on the floor. Then he stared at me in that way he liked to sometimes. His dreads hung just below his chin, hairline receding in all the same places I remembered. Peppered beard trimmed shorter than before. I didn't know what he wanted from me. "Get dressed. Go somewhere," he commanded, shutting the door behind him to mark his point. This was the closest I'd come to being in trouble in over a year. I didn't mind it much. At least it was something.

"It doesn't have to be you. Just make sure he talks to someone," I overheard him say to my aunt in the kitchen. The first someone I could think of was Rosie.

✿ ✿ ✿

I arrived outside of Lena's Salon and sent off a text.

Here.

Even though the front door was open, I waited to be let in.

This was the first time I'd let sunlight hit my skin in days. The relief in Auntie's face when I told her I was going out was a little embarrassing. She was right to call Dad, and I should've probably been spending time with him instead. But I couldn't help feeling like a problem everyone had to solve. Again.

Minutes passed. Two women dressed in all black brushed past me and opened the door. I looked around me before following them into the building. It was a lot smaller than Auntie's place.

"Just ten minutes! We've got Jefferson's rez next. These things always drag on too long," said one of the women in black. They stopped at a unit on the second floor. Where tambourines were making music along with the rhythm of chanting voices. Even in Spanish, I recognized the gospel music.

When I peeked my head in, I saw women in dark colors sitting in the living room, on the couch and in folding chairs. All facing towards a coffee table by the wall with the giant framed portrait of a grizzled Black woman wearing a mean scowl.

Immediately, I knew I was in the wrong place. The absolute worst place.

A woman with fabulous skin and a collared dress buttoned all the way up the neck was standing at the front, leading the chant.

"Santa María, Madre de Dios. Ruega por nosotros pasado— pesos— pasando . . ." She stuttered, searching for a word.

"Pecadores!" the crowd called out.

"Sí, sí!" She laughed slightly. "Ruega por nosotros pecadores. Ahora y en la hora . . ." She stopped and locked eyes with a woman in front of her. The tambourine stopped. "It's crazy. I've never forgotten a prayer since I was a girl. You know, my mother would lock me in our outhouse when I would say my prayers wrong. She was . . . a tough woman." She stared into the portrait beside her. "That I would forget a prayer . . . today of all days—bueno, not today, ya u'tede saben . . ."

The women nodded solemnly. She stared back at them. Then she focused back on the wooden rosary beads turning in her hands.

"Bueno, its been some years and I don't usually talk much at these, pero now I'm thinking . . . como le dije a la Doña Ismerys, I been through a lot of loss in my life. Starting when I brought home a baby goat from my abuela's campo. I called him Rico. Snuck him in my father's truck and got him all the way home without my mother noticing. Bueno, the next morning, she nearly split my head from my neck. Threw Rico, el pobre, back in the truck, and forced me to eat chivo for dinner." She shook her head, lips pursed towards something lost to time. A dry laugh escaped her. "I'm sure there were moments of compassion in between the years, but out of everything, that's what I remember. Chivo. That's how I remember her."

Discomfort turned to bewilderment throughout the congregation.

"Esa mujer sí que odiaba los animales." A frog-like voice opened from the crowd.

The fabulous woman chuckled, shine building in her eyes.

"If that isn't the truth . . ."

"I saw her kick a dog onto a train track once. Just like that. Como nada."

Chatter and laughter nervously built in the room.

"She'd probably eat a baby kitten if you gave her some adobo."

They were all laughing now.

"The last thing she say to me . . . *Yaris, tienes que comer más aguacate. El doctor en el tele says it can help you lose weight.*" Her hand outstretched to the older woman ahead of her for support. The older woman nodded.

"She was something!"

"En verdad, yo no aguantaba a esa mujer, no."

"Bless her, that woman was wretched!"

My body was transfixed. My eyes dry. And then I saw Rosie. Holding a pink rosary. And she saw me. Her face colored with pity. And I couldn't breathe. So I ran.

✿ ✿ ✿

My head hung between my knees over the concrete steps. That's as far as they took me.

"I'm so sorry! I should've told you it was an hora santa thing, I just didn't know how to explain it. It's not usually like that. Usually wayyy more boring." I didn't know what *hora santa* was, but I knew the shadows of death when I saw it. A memorial service was the last thing that I needed explained.

"Are you okay?"

Where to begin answering that question. Was anyone ever really okay, or did they just hide it better than me? Were those women laughing in there or were they crying? Were *they* okay?

I took a deep breath.

"I didn't cry at my mom's funeral."

"Oh." She conjured up a long pause. I felt her eyes examining me. Waiting for something. I felt like running all over again. Then, finally, she followed it up with a shy, "Really?"

My hands fidgeted and tugged at the space where my ring had been. I nodded, feeling a rock push against the walls of my throat.

"And then . . . at my gran's funeral . . . I couldn't go. I was just locked in my room for days."

Rosie sat still for a while, not seeming to know how to properly hold the information. Shit, *I* didn't even know how to properly hold it. I'd been holding onto it for so long now. I was tired of carrying it alone.

A single tear fell on my cheek and I quickly wiped it clean.

With every second of silence, my teeth ground deeper into each other. Finally, she said, "Do you regret not going?"

"Not really. I think my gran would've understood. But my mom . . . I don't know."

"You feel guilty about it." Her words seemed to reach out for me. She took my wrist in her hand to stop the fidgeting.

"Not so much guilt as . . . I think I've been really mad at her, actually. My mom. Which sounds ridiculous. But yeah, I *am* mad at her. For leaving like that. Like she just up and left mid-sentence, before she could properly . . . and then at the funeral I was supposed to like, praise her? Not that she was a monster, but she didn't seem to . . . like me? Or like . . . she never *saw* me? And I just—I don't even know. I'm not making sense. I'm sorry."

"No, I feel that. Sometimes I hate my dad for leaving us. But then I'm also not mad because everything feels . . . easier? Without him here. You know?" I nodded. Rosie quickly shook her head. "Not that—like, obviously it's not the same at all as with your mom. I can't even imagine. I just—"

"It's better to be apart than to be hurting each other."

We sat with the weight of the words for a moment.

"Yea." She wrapped her arms around my stiff shoulders. "Exactly."

"Exactly," I repeated.

"You hide things too well, Zeke," Rosie said. "I don't like it. It makes me sad."

"I don't mean to—"

"I'm not kidding. If I ask if something's up with you, *tell me*. Please. I want to know. I mean it!" Rosie released her embrace and forced herself into the nook of my neck. It felt nice. Warm. "Dumbass . . ." she added, under a shaky breath, punching my shoulder.

"Okay, okay! God, you're corny," I sniffled, pulling her away. "I feel like I'm in an afterschool special. Why are *you* crying? Ew, please stop crying." I felt an indent appear on my left cheek, soaking up the rivers that were pooling on my own face.

"You first."

"I can't," I laughed softly. "I'm a water sign."

She hooked her arm into mine and grinned back at me.

"And I'm your earth sign."

I felt my heart swell. It seemed miraculous to choose someone and have them choose you back. I'd known there was a compassionate soul beneath Rosie's militant facade since the moment we first met. All it took was my mental breakdown to finally draw the humanity out of her.

As my tears dried, I picked at the tiny plate of finger food she brought with her. A small diamond-shaped ball of fried dough filled with spiced beef was the first thing I'd eaten all day. I moaned as I chewed, feeling the notes of cumin and turmeric sparking my tongue. There was something else in there . . . mint, maybe?

"This is amazing!" I mumbled through a mouthful. "Your mom made this?"

Rosie shook her head.

"No, it's from 2Moons. The Syrian diner on the corner. With the spinning blue sign. My mom likes their quipes, so she keeps a bunch in the freezer and tells people she made them."

"Honestly, respect that. Also, your mom is literally gorgeous. Nothing like you described," I said, shoving another ball into my mouth. Rosie tapped her foot nervously and peered back at her front door. "You should go back. I'm sure she needs you."

"It's fine," she lied.

"Go." I removed my arm from hers and tapped her hand. "I'm gonna head home. I'll be okay. Promise." She gave me a concerned look. Then she gave in and stood up, turning back towards the room full of half-grieving, half-laughing church ladies. But Rosie put an index finger in my face to scold me.

"Text me when you get home."

I wouldn't come home for a while, though. And I wasn't planning to. I just needed time. So I did what I always did. I went for a walk through the brisk, dry afternoon as the pink sun let go. My still-unacclimated hands shivering as the temperature steadily dropped. Until the faint warmth of a spinning blue sign glowed down on me.

✿ ✿ ✿

Through the glass, I spotted an ebony Steinway near the front door. The door made an embarrassingly loud slamming noise after I opened it. The place was empty. No one in any of the lush teal booths. No one at the podium in front. No one at the back counter.

Before I knew it, my fingers were grazing the ivory keys, unsure. As still and unadorned as they'd been during my last concert. When I looked out at an empty seat in the crowd.

A hand appeared next to mine and slowly poked at the piano, playing the beginning of "Heart and Soul." I looked up, surprised to find the boy in an apron beside me with a towel draped over his shoulder. I chuckled and joined the duet. Old Zeke would have made fun of something so truly basic. I couldn't help but shift the last notes of the song into the bridge of another song.

"Whoa! What was that?" Rishi finally asked.

"A song."

"By . . . ?"

"Zeke Parish."

"You're joking! You compose, too? That's insanely cool! I only know like two songs on this thing." He started poking at it again. My ears started bleeding. Then he found the note he was looking for and slowly poked out "Axel F," aka the Crazy Frog song. I nodded, laughing.

"You work here?" I asked him.

"No, I'm just cosplaying as a busboy ... for fun." He ran a hand through his curls. "Not funny. Uh ... yeah. My family owns this. So I have to be here." He threw the towel off his shoulder and dug his hands into his jeans.

"You're Syrian? I thought you were Black—or ... mixed?" I felt incredibly, unbearably stupid. What a stupid question.

"Nope, just plain Syrian. Some Afro-Syrian on my dad's side. There's Black people everywhere."

"Oh. Right." I nodded.

"So ... did you come here for something besides the piano? We're kinda closing. Not to be rude, or anything." Of course they were closing, duh. I'd just waltzed in, like an idiot.

"Of course, sorry. I was just eating these ..." I motioned the shape with my hands, trying to remember the name. "Kibbles?"

Rishi chuckled. "Kibbeh."

He untied his apron before hanging it on a hook behind me, stretching his arm across. I instinctively took a step back, but the smell of sandalwood on his neck lingered.

"My mom left me some extra. But I am dying to get outta here, if you wanna eat outside? I know a spot."

"You want me to come with you? Yeah, s-sure. Yup."

✿ ✿ ✿

"You look kinda rough," he said to me. We walked his bike through a path until the pavement gave way to cobblestones. Rishi's backpack was looped around the handlebars.

It was remarkable how he seemed so sure of where he was going.

"Like a good kind of rough? Like Shemar Moore in a Tyler Perry film rough?"

"Sure, let's go with that." He smirked.

I shook my head. "I think I just need a good night's sleep. Like if I just had fifty or so hours, uninterrupted, that'd be perfect."

"Same. Is that why you haven't been in school? Too busy not sleeping?"

I looked down.

"Sorta." I didn't feel like elaborating any further. Thankfully, he dropped the subject.

"So . . . what are you always writing in that little book?"

"Why do you wanna know?"

"Is it your diary? Is there anything about me in there?"

I refused to answer him.

"Okay, stay mysterious."

We walked on for a moment, in a strained silence. At a fork in the path, we turned right.

"Is Ash in there?" He was looking up at the starless sky.

"What do you mean?" I struggled to force the terror out of my voice.

Rishi passed his left hand over the back of his neck. Again, I saw a peek of those deep tan forearms. Something troubled his expression.

"I saw you guys at the party. Outside. Looked kinda steamy," he said. "She's pretty. If you like that sort of thing."

"Oh."

"So . . . ? What happened? Are you guys together? Or was it just a one time thing . . . ?"

Exactly what happened was still unknown to me. And I didn't know where to begin.

"No, nothing happened," I stretched the truth as far as it could go. "Also, I'm pretty sure she hates me now." I was more than pretty sure. Another person added to the list.

"Oh," he said. We let the silence hang in the darkness a moment more. Then he did a little skip and pulled out his phone.

"How about I make you a deal?" He handed me an earbud. "You show me yours, I'll show you mine. Promise not to judge?"

I looked him up and down, wondering what could possibly be on the other side of those earbuds. Unlike Lido, I actually had proof that Rishi had decent music taste. I was a little scared to take the earbud.

He hit play and summoned radiant notes of an acoustic guitar that glittered overlapping melodies. Building to a warped crescendo, crashing into cacophony before turning sweet again. It instantly conjured images of a fairytale. Like the rain scene in *Bambi*.

"That's actually really good," I said.

"Psh! *Actually*?" He took his earbud back. I laughed for the first time in a while.

"It's very good. Sorry, I used to be in a music program at an art school. I've heard some dogshit stuff in the past."

"Ah, explains the piano skills. What kind of music did you play?"

"Used to be jazz, mostly. My own stuff."

"Used to?"

We came upon a grassy area with a shadowy jungle gym to our left. Rishi guided us past it, turning in. There was a warbled noise I recognized, beating like a heartbeat in another room. I stopped. Déjà vu rose inside me from a part of my brain I couldn't quite place. I stuffed my hands in my pockets, feeling for the rings I'd left there.

"Why do I feel like I've been here before?"

Rishi stopped ahead of me. He spun around.

"I mean, it's Liberty Park. Lots of people come through here."

I was pretty sure I hadn't, though. I would remember seeing this much nature all in one place. The grassy fields went as far as I could see.

"Come on! Wanna see something cool?" Rishi turned around and jogged into the park. I followed behind, feeling swift winds cutting past my face. Until I realized I knew exactly where I was.

"Tada!" Rishi stretched his arms before the blinding New York City skyline stretched out behind a railing. Except it wasn't in a movie or in the distance, it was right there. With us. Its roots laid bare below, emerging from the edges of the island it sat on. A boat with flashing lights floated behind the proud boy in front of me. "And if you kinda squint you can see that green lady over there." He pointed past the skyline to an island with a large brick building on it.

"Is that . . . the Statue of Liberty?"

"Yup." His eyes were glowing. "This is actually where immigrants used to pass through in the olden times. They had to come through Ellis Island, which is technically both in New York and New Jersey, but most of it's in New Jersey. Some stayed here, some went to New York or other places."

I took in the scene with awe. When I looked down, the water reflected glittery moonlight. "Wow." Rishi locked his bike to a nearby bench.

"Don't think you're getting out of our deal," he wagged a finger in my face. A greedy palm was set out before me. "C'mon. Give."

I had never shown anyone my poems before. It was honestly embarrassing. I was sure any adverse reaction would crush me. Especially today. My eyes searched for a way out of this. And then they caught onto the shape of a tall, angular building. Finding something far more valuable. I made a frame with my fingers and squinted.

Then I slid the notebook out of my pocket and flipped to one of the middle pages. I held it up to Rishi under the glow of a park lamp.

"That—that's my grandmother," I started. "When she was young. She used to live here, in Jersey City. For a little while. She was always talking about it. My aunt bought her old apartment. That's where I'm staying now. I-I thought she took this in New York, but it was here. Right here."

"Whoa, that's wild! You can still see the Twin Towers there, I think." He laid his fingertip over the photo and I felt myself flinch backwards. Rishi hesitated, looking hurt more than disappointed. Then he sat on the bench with his arm hugging the back. He let out a sigh and motioned for me to join him. "Does she still live in Miami?"

I bit down on my lower lip. Then I sat down, facing the scene of my grandmother's past. And my present.

"No. I mean, she used to live with us, yeah. But she died. Two years ago today, actually."

"Oh." Rishi's voice was barely audible. "On your birthday?"

My head whipped to face him. His brow was furrowed. "How did you—"

"I may have stalked your Facebook." He looked bashful. Under the lamplight, I could see a rosiness overtake the tip of his nose. "Sorry. That must've really sucked." I knew the script here. I was supposed to say *thanks*. But I didn't feel like it. Because it was currently sucking now. Only now it was the kind of dread I could breathe through. The kind I could, for once, see a light at the end of. A light painted in heavenly skyscrapers.

"I'm really tired," I said. My head slipped down and rested on his shoulder.

"Well, I'm starving. So . . ." He reached into his backpack and pulled out the food I'd forgotten all about. He offered me a ball of fried dough. "Happy Birthday!" A sleepy smile spread across my face. "There he is! There's Mr. Dimples."

"Thank you."

I could feel the thickness in my eyelids flutter them open and closed. Soft waves rolling over the cold rocks below us. A thickness taking over my body with ease. Setting me into a sleep my limbs had been craving for several days now. And I was more at ease than I'd been in too long a time.

Chapter
Thirty-eight

On Shattered Glass

– Caro

I t amazed me how different the town was from when I last left it three years ago. Before we got to the cancha, my Papi loaded me onto the back of his prized motorcycle and took me for a quick tour. I clutched onto the front of his shirt and felt the ground pass beneath my feet. The curls on my head escaped into the breeze, growing wider by the kilometer. I admired the new row of dress shops that appeared on the narrow market street. There was construction near the malecón for some resort. And there was a giant *Barahona* sign near the sand for tourists to take pictures at (I made a mental note to go back there). Past that was a brand new Pizza Hut that also seemed to also sell Helados Bon ice cream on the side.

Some things were still the same. We passed Papi's old apartment, and the all-white facade of the Hotel Casa Larimar, and the Cervezas Liquor Store, and the TROPIGAS where one of my cousins worked, and Pretty Esquina, where

Marciel (my childhood hairdresser) was sitting outside in nothing but a cheetah-print bra and jeans, twisting a young girl's hair. My dad whistled at her and she waved as we passed by.

We followed the sound of five-foot-tall speaker systems and cheering until the sounds culminated at the gated entrance of the cancha. Papi put down the kickstand between the rows of other parked motos. I glided my finger across the vehicle's shiny black frame.

"When I'm older you're gonna buy me a moto, right, Pa?" I shouted above the noise.

"You want a moto?" He laughed and tucked my head into the crevice under his arm. Then he kissed my forehead. Now that we were away from that house, he was like a different person. "Your mom would kill me if she saw you driving one of these things."

"Not if I promise to wear a helmet."

"A ti no te pega nigún helmet." He was right. I was too cute for helmets. Plus it would mess up my hair.

"Pshhh! Did Mami wear a helmet when she used to ride motos at my age?" My mind projected images of the photographs in Yolanda's house. I didn't remember any helmets— then again, they probably weren't invented back then.

Papi shot me a pointed side eye and I realized that my mother wasn't the only one keeping secrets about the past. I bit my tongue between my molars. He pursed his lips, carefully considering his words.

"...At first, no. No, she didn't...but I think she wishes she did. That's probably *why* she'd kill us both."

I searched his near-black eyes for answers. Without my intention, my messy ass question was something of a test. An invitation for him to join my team against hers. But, like Rosie, he was a wall. And unlike Rosie, he was still my father. So I turned back to the motorcycle and tugged on his arm like a toddler.

"C'mon! You know I would look so good on a hot pink one. We could keep it here in your garage. She'd never have to know!" I was only half joking. But I could totally picture my ass zooming through the barrio. Salt winds of freedom gliding across my taste buds. Damn, I looked good.

"When you turn eighteen, we'll talk, mami." My father laughed. I pouted at him. "How bout I promise to give you lessons while you're here?" There was a 99 percent chance that he'd forget his promise by the end of my trip. But I didn't care. I smiled so big my cheeks hurt. He tucked a curl behind my ear and threw his arm around my shoulder and we made our way to the bleachers.

We were greeted by a crowd of men whooping and whistling and lifting up overflowing cups of golden beer to a smoky night sky. My father was the youngest of thirteen brothers, eight of which were here for this bachelor party (or as multiple people throughout the night would call it, "The Retirement of El Tiguere"). I hadn't seen most of them in over three years. I was glad I came, my tíos knew how to cut it up. Every time they got together, I was sure there was a new one I'd never seen before. Today the new face was named Enrique, who had five strands of jet black hair combed back with hard gel. He looked much older than Papi.

"Carolina de lo más caro! No me digas! Y esta princesa tan alta?" Tío Nino was my favorite tío. Shock and fascination colored his deep umber face. I was almost as tall as him now. He pulled me into his huge, brawny arms.

"Bendición tío," I said, before turning to the rest of them. "Bendición *tíos!*"

They raised their bottles and plastic cups and offered scattered chants of "Whey!" "Oje!" and "Dios te bendiga!" With a whistle, the boxing match started and a giant brown bottle of Bacardi made the rounds. A man with a blue jersey and a man with a pink jersey emerged from opposite sides of the court, meeting in the center.

"Who are we rooting for?" I whispered to my father.

"My money's on Fernandez." He pointed to the one in the blue jersey.

The match itself was actually more exciting than I thought it was gonna be. Both the boxers were scrawny, but whip-fast. The only gear they had on were their gloves and the sweatbands on their heads. After one punch, I shot up with my hands over my mouth as red spit sprayed across the court. The crowd roared with satisfaction. I clapped when the blue fighter got himself back up.

Papi handed me the bottle of Bacardi, the rum already swimming in his eyes.

"Voy pal baño. Hold this for me, will ya? Don't let your Tío Nino get ahold of it!" He winked.

As soon as my father left for the bathroom, Enrique took his seat next to me. He leaned into my ear.

"Tú no te recuerda de mi, verdad?"

I shook my head no.

"So, how old are you now?" He asked me in warbled Spanish.

"Dieciséis."

"Guao! Diablo, pero, you young girls are looking older and older, huh?"

I nodded slowly. Not sure what he meant by that. Minutes passed like molasses. By now the boxers were both covered in bruises and it wasn't looking good for Cuevas, aka blue jersey, who was catching his breath.

"Where'd your pai go?"

"Baño." I looked to the entrance that Papi had left from. As I looked back, I caught pink jersey's right foot tripping blue jersey. I flinched and yelled "Whoa! Hey!" along with the chorus of groans from half the crowd. Another whistle blew.

"Tú tiene novio?"

If I lied and said no, for some reason, I figured he wouldn't believe me.

"Yeah." I kept my eyes on the match.

The second I said it, I wished JJ was here with me. I wished he could meet Papi and come over for dinner and we could be a regular degular family. I wished Papi would come back from the fucking bathroom already.

That's when Enrique put his thick hand on my ass and gave it a pinch. I felt every muscle in my body tense up. At first, I was stunned by his audacity, a thousand percent certain I must be imagining it. That I'd just been bitten by a mosquito. That if he was trying something, somebody, somewhere in the crowd around us would stop him. But nobody did.

"What do you and your boyfriend do together?" His voice fell to a slither. I looked back at the rest of my uncles, all distracted by the match. I looked back at the entrance, waiting five whole seconds before . . .

In one motion, I smacked his hand away, stood up, and twisted back his pinky. He yelped like the injured dog he was. I sensed the crowd around us turn their attention to the scene. I could have sworn, in my peripherals, I caught a couple phone flashes pointed in my direction. A couple of my uncles ventured closer and attempted to pull me back. Mostly though, people were laughing. Always fucking laughing . . . never doing shit. It was happening again and again. Even here, in this place where no one knew me or my past. How many times was this gonna keep happening? What the fuck was I doing wrong?

The thin-haired man pleaded with me beneath his outrage.

"Don't. Fucking. Touch. Me." I tried my best to keep my voice level, but the words still came out like shards of glass.

"Ay! Coño pero—" Enrique pulled his hand back, trying to break free from my grip. All I needed was one quick snap in the right direction and ...

"Carolina Rojas! Pero bueno!"

My father appeared beside me, stern dad voice all the way on. I dropped the pinky.

"Esa niña ta loca!" Enrique had the nerve to say before he scurried away.

My father dragged me towards the exit, his arms hanging heavily as they pulled mine. He stopped in the space between the bleachers, grabbing me by the shoulders.

"Are you okay?"

"I'm fine. I'm sorry." I bit my lower lip.

"It's okay. Diablo qué buena forma, I'm proud of you!" He raised his hand for a fist bump. My brow furrowed in confusion, but I dapped him up. "Okay," he said calmly. "I mean, you're gonna have to apologize to your uncle."

"What? But he—"

"Lina, please, I have such a headache already. He's an idiot, he gets on my nerves, too. I get it. But things are different here. People don't have your books and fancy schools. He doesn't know any better."

My jaw clenched. I felt a familiar fire rising up.

"I-I won't fuckin—"

"Just, take a minute. Breathe, nena. Cálmate. Smile! It's a party! Have a drink! Say you're sorry. Y ya. ..." He looked around me and then back at the bleachers. "... Wait, where's my drink?"

I glared at him for a beat. The nails under my fists dug deep into my palms, searching for blood. Then, like a retreating ocean wave, I gave up. Because what was the fucking point? I wasn't going to fight him. I wanted to fight a lot of people; I didn't want to fight him.

"It's under the seat," I said.

"Ah, perfect." My papi pressed his sweaty face to my forehead and went back to our party. Just like that. Like nothing happened.

❁ ❁ ❁

Tío Nino and I had to carry my comatose father back home, stopping twice to let him relieve himself. We walked past everything and went back to our corner outside the rest of the town, turning right at the payphone and straight until the plátano field.

"Tienes que darle paso con lo de Enrique. It's not his fault. He's my brother but he's thick in the head. He gives you trouble again, you leave it to me, okay? You alright?" my uncle offered when we got to the front door. I dug through Papi's pockets for the keys.

"I'm fine," I said, trying different keys. I couldn't look him in the eye.

"Bueno, por lo menos you got the Rojas fighting gene. E'ta familia tiene mujere fuerte," he nodded with pride. I tried to recall when anyone fucking asked me if I wanted to be a mujer fuerte. Finally the right key clicked into place.

Surprisingly, we got there before Fernanda got back from her bachelorette party. One of my other tíos arrived on Papi's moto. I thanked him. Tío Nino kissed me goodbye and hopped on.

"We'll bring it back in the morning!"

They could keep it for all I cared.

I tucked Papi into bed and set a cup of water on his bedside table.

"Your tío said you got a boyfriend?"

"Uh, nah . . . I don't—"

"It's okay if you do. But you know my rule: yes alcohol, some drugs, no sex. Your mom talked to you about that?"

The extent of Mami's talk happened on my twelfth birthday when I got my first period. Six words. *You can get pregnant now. Don't.*

"He's not one of those afro-americanos, right?" I didn't like the way he said that. Another thing I didn't know I wasn't allowed to do.

"No, Papi. He's Colombian." I took off his right shoe.

"Does he got a gun?"

"Huh?"

"He a drug dealer?"

Jesus Christ.

"No, he's not a drug dealer." Just a dumbass. "He works at a pizza place."

"Good, good. Pizza good." His voice drifted. I took off his left shoe and swung his legs over the bed. He was snoring by the time I turned out the lights.

In the now-working bathroom, I splashed cold water over my face and chugged down a cup of water myself until my throat stopped burning. Then I went back to my kiddie room and checked my phone for wifi again. Still nothing. Not even a lick.

So I pulled up a chair and sat on the porch. And I listened to the crickets. And the muffled sound of a bachata bassline from far beyond this place.

And then I stepped out the front door.

And I walked.

Chapter Thirty-nine

On Origins

– Caro

Using my phone as an address book, I tried to call Rosie first.

The payphone rang and rang and rang. I could picture Rosie looking at an unknown number and silencing her phone. Which is exactly what I would do, too. The ringing ended in a long dial tone. I hung up the brick of a payphone and picked it up again. Spending my last peso coins.

JJ's phone was next. It rang three times before the phone clicked. I sighed in relief.

"Hellooo?" It wasn't JJ. It was a girl's voice.

"Uh, sorry. Wrong number."

"Yo, gimme my phone!" I heard JJ's voice in the background. The blood that was fresh in my ears began bubbling up again.

"Who is this? Is that JJ? Put his ass on!"

"Shit," the girl whispered. "I think it's Caro."

"Tell her she got the wrong number! Hang up!" JJ's hushed voice grew frantic.

"I said put his ass ON!" I growled.

"Sorrywrongnumber!" The phone clicked. And the dial tone rang again.

My iPhone slipped out of my other hand and cracked against the floor of the booth. I closed my eyes and tried to remember the breathing exercises Rosie showed me once. My thumb pressed down over one of my nostrils. Then I rushed air through my body in one big inhale. I switched my thumb to cover the other nostril and exhaled until I felt like a deflated balloon. When my hands stopped shaking, I opened my eyes.

Taped on the fingerprinted glass beside the phone box was a flyer with an arrow drawn on it. *Wifi Gratis. Mar y Sol Cafetería.* I snatched the flyer. My legs fueled by pure determination to figure out who the fuck that girl was and to unload my fists into my tongue.

I turned back into town. Past the Hotel Casa Larimar and the Cervezas Liquor Store. Past old women picking up bottles off their front porches and locking up their homes. As I walked on, more and more lights began to flicker off. The brightest thing in that darkness was the glowing sign of Mar y Sol Cafetería. The lights were still on. And a bartender was still serving drinks to three patrons sitting outside. One of which was a crying woman in a red dress slumped over the counter. I watched her look up through watered eyes and point in my direction.

I twisted a hundred eighty degrees. Ripples of heat floated over me. The smell of smoke and burnt rubber hit the back of my nostrils. I could see somewhere far down the main road where a fire was building in a line, like a wall. When I squinted, I could see people tossing car tires and liquid into it. All wearing white. Spinning in dancing circles. No more than ten people, circling in and out of each other. It was some kind of protest. Or celebration. I swore I caught the shape of Tamaira's hair wrapped up somewhere in there. But it was too dark to tell for sure.

I looked down at my phone, letting its fractured glow illuminate my face. The restaurant's wifi popped up. My thumb hovered over the join button.

And then I realized I didn't actually want to talk to JJ. I didn't want to talk to anyone. Especially not anyone with a penis.

So I closed my phone. And I kept walking.

❁ ❁ ❁

Somewhere between Hotel Casa Larimar and the oceanside malecón, concrete rolled up and down like a soft wave beneath my sneakers. A gust of salty air dropped the temperature about thirty degrees. Out of the pitch black of night, a crack of shimmering blue light drew a thin path ahead of me, leading towards the sound of a crashing ocean.

"Oh, hell no," I mumbled, taking a moment to look around me for someone, *anyone* to witness this with me. To prove I wasn't fucking losing it. But the only signs of life sang in the croaking of a frog and the rustling of leaves. I whipped around and the ground directly behind me was as normal as ever. The blue path started at my feet. It was for *me*. Someone—*something* was fucking with me. I knelt down to look at the shimmering line close up. My fingertips grazed the light, passing through it quick as air and leaving a faint residue of blueish green dust on my hand. I brought my index finger between my eyes, trying to figure out why it looked familiar. Of course, it was familiar. It was the same stuff that coated every surface of Fernanda's house.

It was late and I was in a strange place that was doing strange things. Rosie would've gone back to Fernanda's house. I should have gone back to Fernanda's house. Logically. But my legs had plans of their own. They couldn't help themselves.

I followed the light where the concrete bled into sand, past that, through the abyss of the late-night beach, up a set of stone steps behind a curving lime tree. At this point, I thought, what the hell, I've made it this far. If I die, at least then I'll know. I climbed up stairs that wound and wound in a spiral up the side of a cliff.

As I climbed, I thought of my mother's mother chastising me and Caro when we were little. When she let us stay at her house. Maybe the only clear memory I had of her. Striking the side of my thigh with a wooden spoon after finding us playing tag too close to the cliffs. "Didn't I tell you not to play in those cliffs? Malcriadas, la dos!" I felt her grip on my wrists now.

When I reached the top of the steps, I stopped to catch my breath. The shallow cave ceiling grazed the top of my head.

Suddenly, I felt like I was being punked. Here I was, at the end of a path drawn in magic fairy dust, believing in shit. Believing I would find something here.

Instead, the path was gone and all it had led me to was a cave.

"Hello?"

I didn't know who I was expecting a response from.

I ran my fingers along the cave walls, humid and icy, searching for a button, a door handle, a hint of the blue light that was guiding me moments before. Anything. But nothing happened. I groaned. My breathing was still pacing from the climb. I leaned my forehead against the cool wall in front of me with my eyes closed, feeling my anger and frustration drift out of my toes and through my fingers. Then I took in a lung-full of air, and slowly, slowly, let out a breath into the stone.

When I opened my eyes, the cave was lit up with the warmth of a sun that wasn't there. In front of me, where the cave wall had been, was now a moving image straight out of a painting. Endless rolls of hibiscus flowers and guava trees and a shimmering black river running across it. I couldn't help but let out a gasp. Above me, a red and purple bird soared its wings wide where the cave ceiling had been. It was like the IMAX theater I'd seen on a field trip to the Liberty Science Center in elementary. Where the ceiling ended, behind me, was the same plain night I'd just been in. A view of the black ocean beneath the cliff, occasionally highlighted by moonlight as waves came and went. Disappearing into the horizon with the rest of reality. In front of me, a fantasy.

I decided I might be dreaming. If I *was* dreaming, then I couldn't die right now. Alternative option: maybe I was already dead. In which case, again, I couldn't die twice (at least I thought so).

So, I let my right arm drift into the cave painting, watching it glow with a faint blue light as it crossed the threshold. My fingertips felt like they were passing through sand, tiny grains falling down around me as I entered this new world.

It was all so . . . real. All the colors of the land in this picture were turned up to a thousand. I picked at some grass on the ground in front of me. That's when I noticed the figures floating face up in the black river. I let out a gasp. There were at least twenty as far as I could see. One of them was wearing a pink jacket. Like Rosie. And then I saw the curve in her nose and realized it *was* Rosie. In what looked like a peaceful slumber. And floating next to her was Zeke. Neither of them looked dead, just . . . floating. Glazed in a thin layer of shine. I felt vomit building up inside as I considered how any of this was possible. My arm reached out to try and grab her but then—*whoosh.*

A neon pink bird swooped down and landed on my wrist with painfully sharp claws. I quickly drew my hand back, and the next thing I knew a fire started from the field's horizon and began speeding towards me, engulfing everything in its path. The sudden danger knocked me off my feet and left me flat on my ass. As the fire crossed the threshold, visible waves of heat danced through the cave, snaking up the ceiling before disappearing into blue smoke and returning the space to darkness. Just like that, the fantasy was gone. I sat still for a while as my eyes adjusted.

"Bitch . . . what the fuck?" My voice was barely audible in the cave and still I could hear a slight echo.

I saw a shape in the dark, jutting out of the stone wall in front of me. It looked like a club—no, a bat. A baseball bat. A child-sized one. I crawled over and put my hand on it. Immediately, a ring around the handle glowed with the same blue light that had led me to this spot. I gripped hard and pulled it free from the rock it seemed bound to. I pulled it up to the moonlight, examining the craftsmanship and feeling its weight in my palms. It was a wood that was smooth as velvet and glided through the air like butter. I twisted it around and noticed a name etched into the bottom of the knob in cursive. My thumb glided across it.

Carolina.

Chapter
Forty

On Weddings

– Caro

I spent the morning of my father's wedding chained to the toilet, hating myself for drinking that tap water the night before. My face still felt hot and clammy no matter how many times I splashed ice water over it. Since the night I spent in the cliffs, I figured I was at least a little out of my fucking mind. My body was the last thing I had any semblance of control over, and now even that was turning on me.

It continued turning on me as I plastered makeup on my face and painted my lips red. As I held onto the sink for stability. As I projectiled my insides and reapplied my red lipstick. As I pulled up my tights and pulled them back down when they squeezed my guts too tightly. As Fernanda came to the bathroom and asked if that was how my hair was staying.

"Can't you at least brush it?"

Can't you at least brush it? I did an impression of her in the mirror. Like I gave a fuck about my hair.

My head stayed foggy even as I gripped Papi's arm and walked him down the aisle of the church behind Lesika's bouncing flower girl dress. And passed a tray of tiny gold coins to the priests like I was told to do. All the while, I held down the constant urge to throw up despite running on an empty stomach. Seeing Papi kiss Fernanda with visible tongue at the altar absolutely didn't help that urge.

The party walked through town, creating a festive procession as we filed into the half-finished front yard of Fernanda's new house, trailed by a stream of bubbles in the air. I downed some ginger ale and a box of saltine crackers. For a moment, my stomach settled. I watched my Papi be his loud and unbridled happy self while the sun faded to pink. Just when I thought the worst had passed, the karaoke machine was rolled out along with speakers as tall as I was. Tío Nino started wailing "Mi Niña" by Los Toros Band while pointing dramatically to his wife. I sat at a table and laid my split head in my arms.

The entire day felt unreal. Like life was happening all around me in a video game simulation and someone else held the controller. I was just being pushed along from one moment to the next. Until somehow I got to this moment, listening to my drunk father explain his theories why he thought it was important to be selfish in life to get what you want. He kept wagging his finger in my face, like he really wanted me to remember what he was saying. I kept the rotating glasses of champagne away from him and rubbed on my temple.

"La vida e corta, mija . . . too too short. Too short to spend it fighting with a woman over . . . money . . . or whatever."

I laughed. Finally, I interrupted his monologue.

"Who were you fighting over money with? Fernanda?"

I looked up at the big house that was clearly in her name on her father's land. And back at the reception tables decorated with extravagant white flower bouquets that the women around us were sneaking into their purses. And then down at the white gold chain hanging off my father's neck that wasn't there the day before.

"Huh? No ..." He took another swig of a drink that had appeared outta nowhere. "Yaris ... what a mess that was. You know what that does to a man?"

I removed my hand from his back, unsure if I heard him right.

"You ... fought with Mami over money? ... Is that why you left?" The question left a lump in my throat.

"I didn't leave nothin' ... I wouldn't ever. ... People say men are selfish and unemotional but ... I've never met someone more selfish than your mother ... perdóname pero ... it's just not right ... it's just not right." I couldn't exactly disagree with his character assassination. We were talking about the same lady that wouldn't even drive me to the airport out of pettiness.

"What's not right?"

"It's not right for a wife to keep things from her partner. It's just not right ... I don't care if ... I don't ..." I opened my mouth to remind him that Mami wasn't technically his wife when he took another sip of his drink and I took the cup away.

He didn't seem to notice. "Todo ese dinero. Sin decirme nada. Like she was just gonna up and leave me one day . . . all planned out without me . . . it's not right."

I didn't want to ask. Not really. I wasn't sure I even wanted to know.

"What dinero?"

He was getting real worked up now, shaking his head from side to side. His eyes were glassy and red.

"All in that maldito blue box. Y despué pa tener ganas to be mad at *me* . . . nah, it's not right . . . not right."

I thought back to a little over three years ago. The last time Papi came to visit us in Jersey. A slammed door woke me up in the morning, and when we had breakfast, Mami sat Rosie and me down in her super serious voice to tell us things were going to be tight for a while. She asked me if she could sell a couple of our things. Including our TV and Rosie's laptop and my iPod Mini. The one with my initials on it. But I wouldn't let her. I was such a bitch to her; I just wouldn't let her.

"Qué pasa, amor?" Fernanda appeared like a ghost in white. She grabbed Papi's shoulders. He wiped his sleeve over his eyes.

"Nada, nada, bella." He pulled his wife down for a very wet kiss. "Hermosa." He kissed her again, getting her lipstick on his face. "Esposa." She giggled. He slowly pulled himself out of the chair beside me. Just like that he snapped back into his new self. "Let's dance!"

He took Fernanda to the dance floor. Watching them spin was making me dizzy. The scraps of information I'd just been fed swirled through my mind in a blur. I wanted to vomit again, but my empty body wouldn't let me. So, I got up and went to the kitchen to hang with Tamaira, nearly getting run over by Lesika who was busy terrorizing the yard with her toy truck. Tamaira was spinning in circles, fielding requests from Fernanda and her mom and friends left and right.

"More, ve allá con los bizcochitos, por fa?" Tamaira immediately asked me. I obliged, taking the tray of cupcakes I'd helped her make the day before. As I made the rounds outside, my Tío Raúl gripped my arm. Tío Raul was closest in resemblance to Papi, with the same sunken black-brown eyes and wide nose and closely shaven head of black hair that never seemed to gray.

"Carolina, you made this? It's delicious!" he said. He took a huge bite, getting frosting on his beard. "Guao, pero ya ésta se puede casar, ah, Wendell? De una boda hasta la próxima, ah?"

God, were they all like this? I had heard my uncles say that phrase about my older cousins ever since I was little. I remember giggling at the prospect of my young cousins being ready for marriage. Marriage seemed almost like a fairytale then, like Santa or the tooth fairy. It was only now with the phrase directed towards me that it made my stomach flip. Like it was the 1900s and I belonged to my father. His property to sell off to another man for a high price, if I could cook well enough and my nose was thin enough and my hips wide enough and my smile sweet enough. As if my every move were an audition.

My father shook his head and laughed. "Con cuidao!" he teased. "Esa es la niñita!"

"Ha! Niña? Un mujerón!" This came from the dark corner of the room where Enrique sat nursing a jumbo bottle of Presidente. He hacked out a laugh. "Look at her hands! Like gorillas!"

"I know you're not talking!" Papi shouted from the dance floor.

"That's it? You not gonna defend me?" I asked my father, putting a cupcake in his hand. It didn't come out as jokey jokey as I meant it to. I had to keep reminding myself I was supposed to be supporting him today. That I would do this one thing for him, endure, come home, and forget this trip ever happened. But the man was trying my last nerve. I couldn't keep it in any longer.

"No seas brava. It's just an expression. Take it easy, relax. Toma," he handed me a fresh beer. I couldn't imagine where he'd gotten another one from so quickly. Just the thought of it was already making me nauseous. I declined. "What, are you sick?" He arched his brow, inspecting me closely for the first time all day.

"Maybe," I conceded, my brow still furrowed.

His smile disappeared. He nodded towards the house.

"There's aspirin on my dresser. Matter fact, get me some, too."

I stomped my way there.

I pulled open the first drawer of the dresser and saw something big and square and Tiffany blue peeking out from under a bunch of paper receipts. By the time I cleared the receipts and pulled it out, I'd forgotten about the aspirin. When I turned the thing around in my hands, my fingers traced over Mami's distinct scribbles and scraps of numbers written in Sharpie. I opened the lid off the box and somehow I already knew what was inside. For maybe the first time in my life, it suddenly dawned on me that my father was just a man, after all. I calmly put it back and covered it with receipts again.

And then I was in the kitchen, where Tamaira was cleaning up.

"Estás bien?" the woman asked, wiping soap off her apron. I nodded.

"Te ves muy linda con ese peinao." I don't know why I said that. It came out so robotic. What I really wanted to ask was if she was the woman whose hair I saw dancing with the fire that night. But I couldn't ask her that. She had her hair pulled to one side now and white flowers pinned into it. It looked nice. So I felt like telling her. Tamaira looked just as confused as I did.

"Gracias . . ."

A silence made me feel like I might be for real, for real losing it.

"I'm gonna go lie down."

And then I was back in Lesika's room. As soon as I shut the door behind me, the bass that had been shaking the house subsided to a low rumbling.

I opened my luggage and traced my name engraved in wood. Feeling the bat beneath my fingers, I gripped the handle tight, and swung timidly at the air. A rush came over me.

Suddenly, my body was mine again. My headache was gone. And finally, I could think straight and (maybe for the first time in my fucking life) do the math. Which was a problem. Because I was putting two and two together. But I was also putting three and three together. And four and four together. And so on and so on.

I swung again. Hearing a mystical *whoosh* noise as the bat sliced the air.

And this time I made contact. Crashing into a row of porcelain dolls with the precision of a knife. Too precise to be an accident.

Only stopped for half a second to consider whether or not I felt like a piece of shit. Turns out I didn't.

I kept going. Again and again. Then I waited to catch my breath and for my guilt to settle in. Until . . . the dolls were there again. On the windowsill. Somehow, I'd known they would be. I reached out and touched one. Solid. Like new. With my free hand, I swiped a finger across the blue dust on the barred window. My eyes inspected the same iridescent residue that had led me to the bat in the first place.

"Right. Of course. Why the fuck not?" I whispered to no one.

And I picked up the bat again.

4

Rage

Chapter
Forty-one

On Overdue Apologies

– Rosie

*W**here did you get this? What did you do?*

What had I done? So much. Too much. A cup overflowing with foolishness. I'd let my stupid, stupid, stupid ego make me feel like I had a scrap of control over my life. Left my half truths and half lies unattended. Believed in magic. Failed again and again.

The three of us stood outside a red door in Queens, breathing out white clouds, and mourning the memory of the meal we'd left uneaten. A portion of it was sitting in a box of tupperware wrapped in the Shoprite bag Mami was holding. Like we were there for a friendly, neighborly visit.

"Chachi. Right on time." The smile wrinkling Tía Yolanda's cheeks made my stomach turn. It was laced in an optimism that my mother was seconds away from crushing to a pulp. I wanted to tell my tía I was sorry. Not in the way that people usually say they're sorry. Like they were getting rid of something. But that I was really, really fucking sorry. She'd trusted me with this precious thing and I'd abused it. I was more than sorry. I was ashamed.

Mami brushed Yolanda aside, walking past her and into the house as if it were her own. Like she'd been here before. I could smell roasted chicken and garlic from the front door. Mami tossed my pink jacket over a chair and set down the bag of food on the kitchen table. Caro and I remained by the front door.

"Estás cocinando." The corners of Mami's mouth turned stiff.

"Yes. I was expecting company. Sancocho seemed appropriate. I see you brought rice."

Caro stepped inside the old woman's house. "Oh, thank god! Food!" Mami put up a hand to stop her. My sister put a hand over her stomach, but she didn't step any further.

"We won't be staying long. I just came to return your little gift. And to say goodbye."

"Chach—"

"No." My mother spoke as if she were scolding a child. Like Yolanda was one of us. But Yolanda didn't seem to take offense. "No. I know restraint not your strength, but you don't get to put my daughters in danger to get my attention. I ask of you just one thing. Not them."

"They came to me." Yolanda was ice cold.

"Then *call* me," Mami hissed. "I am their mother."

"You forbade me from calling, Chachi. Remember? This was destined to happen. You can't keep running. There must be an end. Now or in death."

"Don't." Mami pointed an accusatory finger. "Don't talk to me about death." Her church-lady facade was starting to fracture.

"Death is not a bad word. And you'll remember we both lost a sister, hermana mía."

"No. I did. *I* lost. Y tú no ere ninguna hermana mía. No empieces con esa porquería."

Yolanda put her hands up and made her way to the stove. She stirred a long stick over a bubbling caldero.

"We will eat. And we will talk." She gestured towards the table in the kitchen. "Por favor, mis niñas . . . don't be rude. Sit." Caro slowly inched towards the table and sat down. I walked behind my mother, unsure. Caro motioned for me to sit down. So I did. Mami's eyes looked too lost now to spark fear in mine.

"Every day since I lost my sister to your ego, there is a Bible verse I have turned to again and again over these years. Luke 21:16–17." I knew the numbers well. They were the lotto numbers I was asked to retrieve for her from the corner store. Every time. *"But you will be betrayed even by parents and brothers and relatives and friends, and they will put some of you to death, and you will be hated by all because of My name.* I used to think that about you. That my life was cursed because of my faith in you. I *believed* in you. In your miracles. But you are not a god. Eres una diabla."

"Si soy una diabla, tú también eres una." Essentially, *I know you are but what am I?* It was becoming abundantly clear that this woman really was Mami's sister. "But you know very well that demons . . ." Yolanda calmly began pouring out her broth over bowls of rice she'd set out. "... do not bleed. I have bled plenty." She looked Mami in the eye. "For you and for her. And I loved you. Love you still. Will go on loving you. And like the ones in your stories, I have asked forgiveness. Though you feel your holy book does not apply to me, I will be here still. Because I know you, Yaris. I know that you need me to find peace as much as I need you."

There was the slightest twitch in my mother's eyebrow.

"We don't *need* you," Mami's voice nearly broke. I wondered who she meant by *we*. She wagged a finger in Yolanda's face. I'd never seen my mother this close to putting her hands on somebody outside of arguing with a Walmart cashier. "You are *not* my sister."

Yolanda's nostrils flared. She let out a bitter suppressed laugh, keeping her face regally composed.

"You are stubborn as ever. All those years living in the same house, taking care of each other, and I'm not your sister?" She dropped her stirring stick, meeting Mami's eyes, their faces mere inches apart.

"I told you that night. I told you not to let her near him. And you let her go. You let him touch her. You let your own— And for what? For a high? Was it worth it?"

Yolanda turned away from her. I could tell Mami had landed a blow.

"I was sick, Chachi. And I am sorry. Trust me, I am. More than you know. But we're family. And I'm different now."

"Ay, sí! Just like Papá was different. Every Año Nuevo. When he swore off drinking, like you. Ay, so different. You are all the same. That's why I couldn't raise my daughters there. That's why I had to leave. They're ALL the same. . . . No, you're worse. You *knew*. You knew and you still . . ."

"And I hated myself. And I got worse. What do you think happened after you left? Or do you still not want to know?" Yolanda's voice dropped to an electrified whisper. Mami's eyes narrowed. I stole a glance at my sister, wishing I had a paper and pen. And a paper bag to breathe into. Caro offered her hand. I took it, gratefully.

"W-what are you talking about?" Mami breathed. Yolanda went back to stirring on the stove. She took a deep breath.

"Fine," she began. "You think I followed you here just because I wanted to? Who do you think he turned his anger to when she was gone? After you destroyed his things and left? Who do you think picked themself up and spied on him and got him locked up?

"They tried to kill me. That's what I kept trying to tell you while you kept running. That I needed you. And you left me for dead. You gave up on me. I am here because I escaped. Just like you. Only I did it alone. You believed in me? I am here today because of my faith in *you*, Yaris. Because I believed you. *Comadres, hasta el fin.* Right?"

It was quiet for an unbearable eternity. I watched tears beg for release in the corners of my mother's eyes. As fast as they appeared, she blinked and they were gone. Her face turned back to stone.

"I will say a prayer for you, Yolanda. For the last time, leave me and my family alone. Vámonos." Mami commanded us to our feet with the force of a military general. But neither of her daughters obeyed her. "Que nos vamos! Ahora!"

"No." The word slipped out of me like an impossibility that twisted the shadows of my mother's face. I steadied my voice. "We want to stay." Mami stood still as a wild deer before me. I felt the air buzz with an energy I'd watched Caro conjure more times than I could remember. And then, with a final crack in her brow . . . she broke.

"Mira, muchacha de la miércole!" She prepared her right hand for a strike, and I fought every instinct within me that said to cower. Instead I pushed back the chair and found myself standing up. All on my own. My chest centimeters from hers. In all my life, despite all Caro had done to disobey her, and despite her fits of anger, my mother had never laid a finger on either of us. Even at the height of her worst storm, the worst she'd ever done was slam a door or lock us in our room. I felt the heat of Caro's breath hit the back of my neck.

"I don't belong to you. Neither does Caro. We're not pets you can train." I hoped the hatred in my eyes was as potent as the hatred in hers. "Do it. Hit me. Will that make things better? If I let you keep pretending?" Instantly, Mami's hand retreated back to her side. Her eyes spun into foamy ocean waves.

"Oh, shit," I heard Caro mumble.

"I'm sorry I can't lie the way you want. And I don't care. I forgive you. I always forgive you, even when you don't ask me to. But you keep lying! You think we don't feel it, but we do. I mean, you told us you were an only child! You kept her from us! You kept all of this from us! If anyone should be mad, it's *us*!" I felt myself swell into a crescendo. Then all the strength I'd pulled washed away into a whisper. "Why did . . . why would you do that?"

Mami's ankle buckled and she stabilized herself by placing a hand on the kitchen table. Yolanda approached her to help, leaning into her cane. With one look, Mami stopped her. An entire history she'd spent my whole life burying passed in that look between them.

With hell-fueled stomps and a door slam behind her, one hundred and fifty-five pounds of stubborn woman—gone.

✿ ✿ ✿

"I don't think she's coming back." Caro said through a full mouth. She was alternating between spoonfuls of Mami's leftovers and the fresh sancocho Yolanda had served.

"She'll be back." Yolanda was washing pots in her sink and dropping scraps of bone to her cat now. Her face was turned away from us.

"What if she doesn't? What if we're just . . . stuck like this?" I moved around pieces of cilantro in my stew.

"We'll be fine. She's just being dramatic. I'll call JJ or we can take the bus back." I wanted to tell her it was too late to take the bus, but that wasn't even what I meant when I said we were stuck.

Yolanda checked the gold watch on her wrist.

"She'll be back. Not long now." I thought back to what the woman had said when we'd first arrived. *Right on time.* I watched her hold up five fingers. Then four, three, two . . .

The front door clicked.

"It's not safe to leave your door unlocked, sabes?" a tired voice said. "Maldita bruja, coño . . ."

Yolanda leaned back from the stove and kissed her lips twice. "Pato. Ahora." The black fuzzball scurried behind her and climbed up a chair. He let out an urgent meow. Mami entered the kitchen and then took two steps back, as if something had struck her.

"No . . . no puede ser . . . Pato?" The kitten climbed down and walked slow circles around my mother's legs before rubbing against her. Mami crouched down on her knees, petting it, and examining its fur. She held the nametag on its collar in her hand. "Pero . . . how . . . ? What did you do?"

Yolanda took a deep breath before wiping the corner of her eye. Then her laugh filled the room with an all-encompassing warmth. "I didn't do shit. He came back. Don't you remember? You made him that way. To always return home. You were always the most powerful of us." Now Mami was chuckling too.

"I was eight years old. I didn't *make* anything . . . I only . . . I only wished . . ."

"Wishing, making, manifesting, speaking . . . your intention was the same. He came back. Just like you."

"Wait, manifest like magic? ... Mami ... knows about your brujería?" I whispered to Caro.

"Psh! I invented brujería," my mother whispered back. Like it wasn't earth-shattering information. Yolanda laughed and shook her head.

"Ay, please. Like your *brujería* isn't just cosmetic." She pursed her lips and blew in Mami's direction. My mother's shoulder twitched. She slipped her jacket off her shoulder, revealing the sprawling tattoo from the photo, now visible beneath her Icy Hot patch.

"How did you—"

"It's been a long time. I've been practicing."

"Put it back," my mother warned. Yolanda rolled her eyes and blew out again. The ink vanished in a flash, like newspaper in a bonfire. I looked to Caro, whose expression mirrored my awe. Only hers quickly turned devious.

"Oh, you gotta teach me that!"

Sitting on the floor, Mami dug her face into Pato's neck and closed her eyes. She rocked him back and forth like a baby, purring at him. I almost didn't recognize her in that moment. "You came back. You really came back."

✿ ✿ ✿

We sat in the music of clinking spoons and my sister's loud slurping for a while. It was an unspoken agreement between us that we would wait for her to break the silence. Eventually she did.

"So . . ." Mami started. "You have the jacket . . . what about the rings?"

"What rings?" Caro looked back and forth between our mother and auntie.

"They're safe."

"What rings?" Caro asked me this time. I shrugged.

"Safe where?"

"I tried to get rid of them. They came back. They're safe. Don't worry."

"Fine. And . . . the bat?"

"Is still in Barahona."

I looked to Caro's suspiciously quiet face. What bat?

"How do you know its still there?" Mami asked.

Yolanda let out an exasperated sigh.

"I think I would have felt something if it moved. It was a part of me for a long time."

Mami nodded slowly, considering the information.

"Okay."

She put both her hands flat on the table. I had no idea where she was going next. It was like watching a wild panther and waiting to see if it was going to strike or take a nap.

"I've thought about this moment for a long time. About how I would yell at you and break all your things and tell you to stop sending letters."

"Yaris—"

"Let me finish. I've thought about this for a long time. A long, long time. Held onto it. Like a machete slicing through my hand. But I realize now . . . I was the only one holding it. So I was the only one bleeding." Mami took Yolanda's hands in her own. Her eyes shone with a pain I'd never seen before. "I may not fully forgive you yet, but I forgive me. I hope one day I can learn to let go. I-I don't want to hold this any longer."

"Gracias, Chachi. Solo deseo que tengas paz. Really. I promise you, I worked on change for many years. With every fiber of my being, I have. AA meetings twice a week. I never miss, te lo juro." She held up a pinky.

Mami looped her finger in her sister's and held it there.

"I'm sorry you had to do that alone." Then she laughed. "You know, I've been seeing a therapist. If you can believe it."

"You what?! When?" Caro coughed on her food. She crossed her arms. I exchanged a bewildered look with my sister. Mami shook her head and laughed again.

"I know. She told me I should just tell you girls, but I ... it's so ... silly. Yes, Caro. I started after Mamá ... you know. Doña Ismerys agreed to see me after work on Wednesdays."

"Ismerys? Doña Ismerys is a therapist? They gave that lady a license? Like a for real doctor? Since when?"

A puzzle piece sunk into place then. "She used to be a marriage counselor at the church, right?" I asked. I remembered a post-sermon announcement about her retirement one Sunday. Mami nodded.

"She's been my guardian angel. I don't know how I'll ever be able to repay that woman. From when I first came, solita, not knowing anyone ... and she helped me take care of you two ..." I couldn't picture Doña Ismerys with angel wings any more than I could picture my mom, present day, wearing spandex on a motorcycle. "Not to mention help me deal with your father . . ."

"Ay, how is Wendell? Still a selfish piece of shit?" Yolanda cheerily remarked. She got up and fished through her fridge.

"Bueno . . ." Mami started. She raised a brow towards Caro and me.

"Don't hold back on my account. I just came back from his wedding with that lady. I got stories." Caro cracked her knuckles. "Oh! And guess who's pregnant?"

"Oye! Now we're talking!" Yolanda took out a brown bottle and knocked the cap off by smashing it against the corner of the table.

✿ ✿ ✿

All the sancocho had vanished.

"Okay, spill. Tell the truth. When did Mami lose her virginity?"

It was nearly two in the morning now. Which meant it was Sunday. A church day. Caro was on her third beer, Mami was on her second, Yolanda had downed a couple maltas, and I was nursing a cup of red wine. I figured I might as well take advantage. We'd never drank with Mami before. Obviously, I hardly drank at all. Alcohol was gross and the smell reminded me of Papi laying on our couch. The closest we'd ever been to this bizarre situation was when our cousins snuck bottles at family parties. Adults getting lit in one room, kids in another.

Each knowing the sins of the other. Neither bringing it up in respectable conversation. Now, in Yolanda's kitchen, the veil was broken.

"Caro!" Mami slapped my sister's arm.

"TMI. I honestly don't want to know." I covered my ears with my fingers. Yolanda's mischievous smile sparkled.

"How old are you again?"

"Yo-yo! Callada!" Now my mom slapped Yolanda's arm. Yolanda winked at me.

"Got it. Say no more, Tía. I feel you," Caro said.

"So, does this mean I can get a tattoo?" I said, surprising myself.

"Since when you want a tattoo?" Mami looked at me curiously.

"I don't know. Since now, I guess. You have one. Yolanda has a bunch. It's just art." I shrugged.

"Me too! I want in on this!" Caro squealed. "I'm thinking Tweety bird below my back."

"No! No tattoos." Mami rolled her eyes. She looked towards Yolanda, who was suppressing a smile. "Look what you've done."

"Why not? Qué va pasar? Se acaba el mundo?"

"Como uno se presenta hace bastante importancia en este mundo. You would not know about that. You don't know what they're like. You have not had to keep a job and support two kids. They take one look at you, and that's it. That's how the world works."

"Ha! You sound like your mother! And you act like I'm a beggar porque tengo tatuajes. You're eating my food, no? In my house?" Yolanda reached for Mami's bowl, but my mother pulled it back, digging further into the leftover corn on the cob from her sancocho. Caro and I watched on as though we were kids at the zoo. Absolutely enthralled by the scene. If I squinted my eyes, it was almost like my mother was a regular person. "Ah, y entonce!" Yolanda's smug smile was almost giddy. She crossed her arms and leaned back in her seat.

"You care too much about what people think." Caro pointed her beer at Mami. She said it so plainly and out of nowhere. I knew she'd been sitting on this one for a while. "You should stop caring so much and just let us decide for ourselves."

Yolanda wagged a finger at her in agreement. "The girl is right."

Mami was stunned for a second. But she wasn't mad.

"I just want people to see you, mi vida. Without judgment."

"By judging us before anyone else can? That sucks. Makes me feel like I'm not good enough the way I am. Like I can't decide for myself." My sister was getting a little too real in front of company. Though, I guess Yolanda was family now.

"Okay . . ." Mami chewed on her lower lip. "I see . . ."

"That's her way of saying she's sorry," Yolanda explained. She took a sip of her malta.

Caro huffed and settled in her seat. "I don't need sorry. Just stop doing it, then," she mumbled. The air was staticky between them.

"So . . . tattoo when I turn eighteen, then?" I offered. Mami rolled her eyes again. I could see now how that might be annoying for people. She looked to Yolanda for help and groaned.

"Okay." She nodded slowly. Then she held up her beer. "Pero no antes de los dieciocho. Y nada de Tweety bird. Nothing too big. I have to approve."

"Yesss! That means I'm getting mines first!" Cato shouted. I marveled at my sister's mood shifts. She slid me a low high five. "And then I'm getting a moto!" She was trying it now. I could tell by her raised brows that she knew it, too.

Mami shut that one down real quick. "NO. No motos."

Chapter
Forty-two

On Waking Up

– Zeke

I don't think there has ever existed another human being in the history of the world with as much on their mind as me. From the moment I opened my eyes in the park and felt the source of the warmth that had sustained me, I knew I was fucked. Extremely fucked. Because the sun was coming up and he was still there. And I could hardly bear it.

"You fell asleep," Rishi said, softly. "My dad's here to take you home."

"Sorry." That was all I could think to say.

"It's okay. It seemed like you needed it."

In the back seat, I prayed it would be different this time. That the darkness I'd only just tucked away wouldn't reach him. I didn't think I would survive if it did. I couldn't do it. Not again. I couldn't hurt another person.

Chapter
Forty-three

On Busted Windows

– Caro

I stood across the street from Bruno's Pizza staring through passing cars and glass windows. My head was still pounding from the most bizarre hangover I'd ever experienced. Made even more bizarre by the fact that my mother had woken me up past church hours with an aspirin, a cup of tomato juice, and a kiss on the forehead. I didn't even have to lie to her about where I was going (only what I was going there for).

Beneath a star-shaped *2 Large Pies for $20* sign, my eyes tracked the movement of a freshly cut fade and mop of hair leaning over a blond figure standing at the cash register. And a tongue that traced misbehaving lower lips. The girl he'd been talking to walked out the front door, turning back to give him a wave. I looked down at my cracked phone and took out my earbuds. Why were boys always such sluts after a measly haircut? The whole thing was honestly so . . . boring.

His mouth moved in slow motion as it widened into a familiar smile and I repeated the same mantra I'd sung over and over again on my way over here. *Don't be that girl. Don't be that girl. He's not worth it. Don't be that girl.* Still, I felt the heat emanating from my Michael Kors bag with each step my black Nike trainers took towards the pizza shop.

The wind chimes on the glass door rang just as a blue-haired employee emerged from the back with a cardboard box in her hands. We both stood still. Her fearful eyes letting me know I'd caught her in something.

"Ashia," I finally said, making no attempt at hiding the acid in my voice.

"It's Ash now."

"What are you doing here?" It was a stupid question. I couldn't think of a better one. My eyes glanced towards the paralyzed boy at the register.

"I . . . work here?"

"Ayoo, babe! W-when'd you get back? Why you ain't call me?" An even stupider question. He knew why I hadn't called him. He walked around the counter and took a step towards me, but I reached into my bag and stopped him. Pointing my bat at his big ass forehead.

"You—" I said.

"Whoa, whoa!" He put his hands up. I felt my eyebrow twitch as I took one step forward.

"You said you ain't never seen her before."

Ash slowly set down her box.

"Baby, I—"

"SHUT UP!" Fuck. I was being that girl. He was making me be that girl. I held up my phone with my free hand. "That

your t-shirt on her Instagram? Because people seem to think
it is."

"I can explain. You weren't answering my calls. She works
here. It's not like that. I—" I waited for the explanation that
never came. Whatever would come out of his mouth next was
sure to be a lie. That's what they did best. Lie, lie, lie. Blame
their lies on the world for not trusting a liar. He looked to Ash
for help. She'd backed herself into the wall. I kept my bat
pointed at my soon-to-be ex-boyfriend and turned my attention to the girl who'd ruined my life years ago.

"You alright, Miss Thing? Looking a lil dizzy over there,"
I said.

"I'm good." Ash's nose flared.

"Uh huh. I see you still ain't learned to stop stealing my
shit?"

Her face curled in disgust. "One—didn't know this asshole was your boyfriend. And two—you can have him. He's
not my type."

JJ let out a bitter laugh. "You fucking wish," he whispered.
"Prude bitch."

Before I could figure out what that meant, Ash stormed
into the back room. She returned with a small blue USB stick.
She held it out to me.

"It might be my *prude bitch* hormones making me see shit,
but I'm pretty sure there's this tall dude that keeps showing
up on the cameras in the storage room with Leidy Ale every
couple days and deleting the footage. But . . ." Ash turned to JJ
with pity. ". . . he was too dumb to delete the backups." She

shrugged and shook her head. Then she grabbed her JanSport from behind the counter and walked towards the door. "Like I said, you can have him."

"Don't listen to that bitch, Caro. This is stupid. You know me, I care about you. Why would I do some shit like that? I don't even like Leidy!" I stared at the USB in my hand. More proof I didn't want or need. But why, out of everybody in our overcrowded ass school, did it have to be my best friend? Did they both hate me that much? Why would he do that?

"Why would I do that? Huh?" he echoed. Then he reached out and grabbed my wrist. And I thought back to that night in his ATV. Back to his hand in my back pocket. Back to our afternoons in his stupid car. The car that was sitting just outside this shop. With the stupid fire decals I could see through the windows.

I looked at him then. Really looked. And I thought about what Mami said at Yolanda's house. About realizing she was holding onto an anger that didn't belong to her anymore. That she was the only one bleeding. I hadn't realized what that meant until now, looking into this dumbass's hollow eyes. A thin smile spread across my lips.

"I really liked you," I said, holding his pathetic gaze.

"Caro, amor . . . let's just talk about this tomorrow. Please."

I set the USB on a checkered table and turned towards the door. Then I closed my eyes and took a deep breath.

"Don't talk to me again," I spat.

Before I closed the door behind me, I heard his deep voice mumble, *These bitches is crazy*. And there it was. That fucking word again. Without a second thought, I walked up to the gaudy Toyota Camry out front and swung my bat through the side mirror. My palms were on fire. The delicious, life-breathing kind of fire. The kind that stars were made of.

If that's what he wanted me to be, I was great at crazy. No, I was fucking excellent. A goddamn professional, even. I swung into the passenger's side door, making a sizable dent. Then I busted through a window. And then another window, and another window. Sending grains of glass flying through the air along with any remaining fucks I gave. Because that's what crazy really meant. Not giving a fuck. People absolutely *hated* it when you decided not to give a fuck. I punched out his stupid colored lights and drove all the strength I had down into the hood. Releasing much more than just a disappointing little boy. My blood pulsing through me and into the bat as though it were an extension of my arm.

After what seemed like an eternity of unfiltered bliss, I made my way back to the side mirror where I'd started. It was back in its place. Like new. Like my rage never touched it. I stopped and pressed my hand against the crushed metal. Feeling it, slowly but surely, slide back into place like sand. Bright red flames faded into original rusty brown.

"Whoa," a girl's voice said through the ringing in my ears. When I looked up, I saw Ash pushing back the door against a desperate JJ, locking him in. She had stars in her eyes while he was kicking and screaming and yelling behind her. I couldn't help but laugh. He backed up to charge at the door and she turned a key and set down a cinder block. JJ's shoulder crashed into the solid window and bounced backwards.

I watched the pink-haired girl approach the car. She looked me up and down. *CreeeeeeEEeee!* A harsh squeaking noise rang out like nails on a chalkboard.

"That . . ." Ash's chest rose and fell with quick breaths. ". . . was for saying I had dick-sucking lips when I started working here." She spat down at the sidewalk. Then she wiped the red paint off her spiked rings and grabbed my hand. JJ's lanky arms were beating down the door. My mouth hung open. "I think we should probably run now."

Chapter
Forty-four

On Old Friends

– Caro

Isn't it weird how we used to be friends? You know, before . . ." Ash made an explosion with her hands. We were sitting side by side on the edge of the sidewalk three blocks away from Bruno's, catching our breaths. I focused on the bat I was spinning between my legs. I imagined my ex-boyfriend's car looking like a junk car with a thin scratch on the side. I nodded.

"Member in fifth grade when we did that talent show dance to 'Work It'?"

She pursed her lips. "That . . . was not school appropriate. Ionno who let us do that."

I couldn't help but let out a giggle at the thought of us shaking our ten-year-old asses in booty shorts to Missy Misdemeanor Elliott. "On some true shit, I don't even remember why I hate you." My palms pressed into gravel as I leaned my head back. I closed my eyes.

"Something about me stealing your iPod?" Ash winced.

"Aight, I do remember. I was just tryna be nice. But since you brought it up . . ." I turned to face her. Her expression hardened.

"I-I don't even know why I did that. I was, like . . . really into stealing back then? From stores, from school, from my parents . . . it was a weird time. It didn't have anything to do with you. It was really dumb. It's embarrassing. I tried to find you on Facebook and apologize once, but you had me blocked. Which . . . understandable. I'm sorry."

For some reason, when she looked me in the eye, I had to look away. It made me feel weirdly naked. She was laying bare an old wound, but it was hard to be mad at her for it. Especially after what she'd just done. She kept going.

"I know I was wrong and everything. But after our fight really fucking sucked. Like online and everything. Again, I shouldn't have taken your things, but people were on there wylin, calling me all types of names."

"Yea, me too." She looked at me with pursed lips. "What?"

"*Me too?* I recall your caramel ass being called crazy and hot and people complimenting your right hook, meanwhile *I* was ghetto and ugly."

"Really? That sucks. Sorry, I didn't kn—" I caught the lie as I said it. "I mean, I guess I did kinda know that. I think I just didn't want to know that."

"It's fine. I'm good." Ash took a deep breath.

"I guess I'm sorry for beating your ass or whatever," I said. "Wooow."

"Well, I guess I can unblock you now . . ."

"Good," she said. We sat awkwardly for a minute.

"What happened to your hand?" I nodded my chin towards the lightning streaks of faded purple along her ring finger.

"Honestly, I don't even know. It's a long story."

Instead of telling me about it, we somehow started talking about Leidy. About how I should have known she was dogshit from the moment I met her in softball tryouts (back when I used to do sports). Leidy almost caught these hands when she put her grimy Cheeto fingers on my scalp, talking about "Oh my god! I love your curls! How do you get them like this?"

"Ugh, I hate it when they do that. That's why I shaved my head." Ash rubbed her hands over her buzzcut.

"No way. Word?"

Ash nodded. She made a fist and tugged at what little hair she had.

"Bitches don't got nothing to pull in a fight, see?"

I wasn't sure if her crazy ass was joking or not. But I started laughing. And then suddenly I was laughing a lot and I couldn't stop. Because it really was such a ridiculous idea to shave your whole ass head just to get the upper hand in a fight. Only she would do some shit like that. I could hardly breathe.

When we finally stopped laughing, I got an idea.

"You ever wear wigs? I think it'd look nice on you. Not that it doesn't look nice as is."

"Nah," Ashia shook her head. "I wanted to once, but my moms wouldn't give me the money for a good one. She was kinda mad that I shaved it. And I don't really miss having hair, anyways. I didn't like who I was with it."

I thought back to the two seconds of disappointment that flashed on my mother's face when I came home with box braids. I couldn't even imagine coming home with a shaved head. If I did, Mami would probably kill me, have a heart attack, die, and then resurrect us both outta our graves to tell me she didn't like my hair before killing me again.

"You don't live with your moms no more though, right?"

"I guess you're right."

"Soo . . . ? You wanna go try on wigs at the Beauty Supply on Main?"

"Sure. Sounds fun!"

She got up from the stoop and reached down, offering me her hand. I took it. Me and Ash Kingston walking down the street. Life was wild.

Chapter Forty-five

On Keeping Watch

– Zeke

First I was at school on a Saturday, and now I was at school on a Sunday. This was blasphemy.

I'd been sleeping so good until Rosie's three-way call with Caro woke me up, asking us to help her out with something. Caught a dream so lovely and vivid I was questioning reality. She had a lotta nerve pulling me away from the comfort of my bedsheets on a Sunday afternoon. Winter didn't seem to be releasing her grip, but today, at least, the sun was out.

Her hair was in two braids and she had the pink jacket on when I got there. She was sitting on the front steps.

"Your mom let you keep it?" I asked, taking a seat next to her.

"Nah," she said. "It just appeared under my bed again." Her voice was hollow, like she was somewhere else.

"Are you sure that thing isn't haunted?"

Not even a chuckle. Was it my turn to be worried about her?

Moments later, two figures started walking towards us from down the road. I saw Caro before I saw Ash. Her pink

347

scalp was dyed baby blue now. I didn't know it was possible for her to look better. All the scars from our night together had vanished. She looked like a miracle. A martyr resurrected.

"She's cool," Caro said, exchanging a meaningful look with her sister. Rosie didn't look so convinced. There was still that same spark in the air between her and Ash.

"Let's just go." Rosie took her sister by the arm. "She can stay here with him and keep watch. Or go home, if you want."

Ash looked me up and down. I studied her face for a poor opinion of me. Instead, she held up two nonchalant fingers and greeted me with a shy smile. I sent her a wave back.

Rosie pounded her fist against the locked school doors.

"How are you planning on getting in?" I asked her.

"Jacket."

I didn't really see how that was helpful in this particular instance. What was she gonna do, ask the doors to open?

She kept pounding until eventually, a tall janitor opened the door. Her words glazed over his eyes and he obeyed her command to step outside and not move an inch while she kept the door open with her foot. Poor guy. The name on his uniform was *Bob*. Poor Bob.

"Text me if you see anyone coming." She gave me my orders and entered the school. I held a flat hand to my forehead in a military salute.

"Ma'am, yes, ma'am."

✿ ✿ ✿

It took about five minutes of awkward silence between Ash and me before Bob broke free from his curse. His eyelids fluttered first, sending a chill down my spine. Ash was surprisingly calm. I wondered why she was with Caro. She barely looked up from kicking her Doc Martens against some rocks. The man's fingertips started twitching next.

"A temporary spell? Really? Amateur move." Ash shook her head in disapproval. I couldn't tell if she was joking or not.

Within a couple seconds Bob was back to normal, looking at us all confused.

"Shit, shit, fuck." I reached for my phone, but my hands stopped themselves. A warm tingling sensation charged through them. I swore I saw my two eternal rings emanate a slight glow. Like something was being activated.

"Who are you kids?" his husky voice whispered. The glamour was clearly still lingering a little. I followed Bob's eyeline.

Across the street, outside the CVS, was the same short woman I'd bought the flower from. She was ringing a bell every couple of seconds, looking for customers.

"You should buy all her flowers and ask her out," I said. "I think she'll say yes."

Now in a different kind of trance, his head turned to me. And then back towards the flower woman. He took a deep breath. "You think so?" There was an innocence and an eagerness in his eyes. Lost, like the effect that Rosie's words had, but a little different. A little more honest.

I gave him a pat on the shoulder. "Absolutely, king. Go for it."

He straightened his shoulders and made his way down the front steps. Imbued with a new confidence.

My thumbs grazed over the rings between my hands, trying to figure out what the fuck had just happened. Wondering if I had actually done something or if I was being delusional again.

"You've got magic, too." Ash said it in such a monotone voice. Like it was the plainest thing in the world.

"Not really?" It wasn't me that had magic. It was the rings. But I'd assumed they were neutralized if I did what Yolanda said. If I kept them together and focused on myself and tried to avoid another major fuckup.

"How did you know he liked her?"

"I don't know. I just did."

"What if he comes back? How do you know she's gonna say yes?"

"I mean, it looks like it . . ." I pointed towards the flower woman, who planted a kiss on the tall man's cheek.

"Huh. Look at that. Straight people." Her upper lip lifted in disgust. I narrowed my eyes at her. "What?"

"Nothing."

✿ ✿ ✿

"So . . . how've you been?"

Ash raised a brow at me. "Fine?"

"Good. That's good." I fidgeted with my rings, trying to diffuse the awkwardness between us. This was everything I'd been dreading every day I spent alone in my bedroom since that night. The thing I was hiding from. My heart pounded outside of my chest. "I texted you before and you left me on read, which is fine. I just want to say again, I'm really really really sorry you got hurt— It was an accident. I didn't know what I was doing, but I still should have never— I don't know why I— It was all my fault—" The word vomit kept rolling off and getting trapped in my throat.

She put a hand up. "Stop, stop. Seriously." I couldn't help but notice the scar that was still on her hand. "I don't remember what happened, clearly somebody put a hex on me or something. Not a very good one. Up until now, I thought it was maybe Rosie. But I'm fine. I'm not hurt. I took all the precautions, did all the sage, nothing's wrong with me. I swear. Look." She flipped her palms around in front of me. "See? I'm all good, dude. Breathe."

"Sorry." I barely registered what she was saying, but I knew that much. I was really sorry.

"Stop saying you're sorry. I've fucked up magic plenty of times. I get it. It's not your fault. If anything, *I'm* sorry for jumping on top of you at that party. I didn't even ask your consent first. God. Sorry if I gave you the wrong idea."

She wasn't making any sense. What precautions? Not the first time? I remembered then that there was a rumor about her being a witch. And now she was somehow apologizing? For what? I searched through her inscrutable face. There was a pain swimming through it.

"Wait, what?"

"I was kinda . . . using you. That wasn't cool." If she was using me, I was for damn sure using her, too. "Look . . . I think you're cool and all. I like you. But . . . I don't think I'm capable of liking you as more than a friend. That okay?"

After all that had happened that night . . . she was apologizing to me? For something as silly as not reciprocating my stupid crush? The word *capable* stung a little bit. So did the possibility of her not enjoying a kiss I'd spent days preparing for. But on a scale of that to what I'd done . . .

"Wh—is that . . . ? Yeah, that's fucking okay!" I sighed through the words, completely lost and baffled by how we'd gotten here. She sighed in relief and put her hands over her stomach.

"Oh, thank god! That's been stressing me out all week. I thought I broke you or something."

"Nah, nah . . . if anything, I broke myself. I'm pretty good at that."

I told her about my visit to Liberty Park and Ash filled me in on her day with Caro. How she'd helped her get back at her boyfriend. And they ran off together. My hands felt warm again as she showed me a picture on her phone of the two of them in church lady wigs. I picked my jaw off the ground.

"You . . ." A smile spread on my face. I poked her ribs. "Wow! Ash Kingston!" She snatched her phone back.

"I have no idea what you're talking about, sir." What a terribly bad liar she was. How did I not see this coming?

"Girl, you could have just said that from the beginning. I was over here questioning my kissing skills! Did you ever tell her?"

Ash looked at me like I had an elephant trunk growing out of my forehead.

"Why not?"

"I don't know how they do shit in Miami, but those are the kind of feelings I'm tryna keep to myself. Besides, I think if she hasn't gotten the hint from . . . you know . . ." She glanced down at her outfit. "It ain't happening."

I looked down at the silver chain hanging on her neck and thought I caught the smallest bit of hope in her voice. I shrugged.

"You don't know. Maybe she's got an idea but . . . she's not trying to be rude making assumptions." From my short time knowing her, it was clear that Caro was a bit self-centered, sure, but she wasn't blind.

"And *maybe* she'll beat my ass again. *You don't know.*"

Just like that, scary Ash was back. I shook my head and thought for a moment. I didn't mean for it to come off like I was pressing her so much. It was up to her, really. I guess I felt strangely like I recognized fragments of my old self in the fear hidden beneath Ash's rough exterior. Like I was supposed to help her.

"Aight. Well . . . thanks for telling me." I put a hand on my heart. "I mean it. Really."

"Technically, I didn't tell you anything." Ash looked at me with those big brown eyes for a moment. She grabbed my hand

and squeezed it tight. And I felt really really lucky then. "Thanks for not being a dick."

"I don't know about all that." I laughed. My voice caught itself mid-laugh as a memory I'd tucked away resurfaced in my mind. Instantly, I felt like crying into Ash's arms. But that didn't seem fair to her. We weren't exactly there yet. Instead, I looked up at the gray sky to keep the tears at bay.

"What is it?"

The sparse clouds spread just enough to reveal a ray of sunshine beneath. A vague familiarity tugged at the corners of my brain. I realized then that this was her doing. I felt it like a cool breeze tickling the back of my neck, rushing beneath my bones and propelling me forward.

"You know what my gran said when I came out to her? She said, *Good. When you have no more secrets—to yourself or anyone else—that's when you're free.*"

"Your gran sounds like a real one."

"Yea, she was."

Chapter Forty-six

On Sticks and Stones

– Rosie

"Wait, wait, wait!" Caro tugged my arm back when we entered the empty school. "No idea why you need to get to Ordena's office, but in case you're planning on some illegal shit . . ." She pointed up at the red light emitting from a camera in the corner. We both ducked by the front doors.

"Shit," I said. I hadn't thought about the cameras. No one would really check them right? Or if they did, maybe we'd just look like students coming in to work on something. Nothing nefarious there. I wasn't planning on stealing anything that wasn't already mine. Still, the crime documentary watcher in me was telling me not to leave any loose ends.

Before I could say anything else, Caro pulled out that same small bat from somewhere in her pants.

"Wait, Caro—" It was too late. She had already launched it in the air and hit her target. The camera fell to the floor and smashed into pieces. It would be impressive if I wasn't so mad at her impulsiveness. First, she brought fucking Ash Kingston here, now this? She was gonna ruin my whole half-baked plan. God, I wanted to strangle her. "Why would you—"

She held up a timer on her phone. I was still confused.

"I don't think it caught us. Just wait. It'll come back."

"What do you mean *it'll come back*?! You smashed it! You can't unsmash things! That's not how physics works!" I hissed at her.

"Why are you whispering?" she asked. "Just wait." I gave up and crossed my arms.

After two minutes, the thing was still broken on the floor and I was ready to give up.

"This is stupid. You can't just smash your way through everything!"

"And you need to smash your way through things more often! Sometimes that's the only option. I'm sick of people acting like it's never an option. It is! And often." An exhaustion mixed with resoluteness rose in her. I didn't know what to say to that. "Look," she pointed to the cleared floor in front of us. The broken camera was gone. "Two minutes thirty. Let's go."

She threw the bat again. Finally, my father's softball training sessions when we were little were going to use. We scurried across the hall into the main office. My hand frantically tugged at the door handle. Locked. Fuck.

Caro didn't hesitate. She smashed in the door window and opened it from the inside.

"Stop being so loud! What if someone hears?" I stepped inside and closed the door, as if that would make a difference. Thankfully, Ordena's office was unlocked.

"Oh my god! Make up your mind!" Caro sighed. "You're just like her sometimes." The words fell over me like an axe cutting through a tree. Unyielding and unfair.

"I don't have time to fight with you. We don't have time for—"

My sister picked up the ceramic apple on Ordena's desk. She handed it to me along with her bat. "Here. Break it."

I ignored her and turned my attention towards the cabinets under his desk. What I'd come here for. It had to be here. I knew it somehow. He was just dumb enough . . .

"Break. It." Caro insisted. "Do it. It'll come back. It's just stuff."

My fingers hesitated. It would be a lie to say the offer wasn't enticing. But the stopwatch was still running.

"Do it!"

At first, I did it just to make her happy. Quickly, I snatched the bat's handle from her out of spite, and I threw the ceramic apple in the air nonchalantly. But then . . . it exploded. Dust and rain and unbridled indulgence. Like miraculous confetti. I couldn't help it. I felt something. So I swung again.

And again.

And again.

And again.

This time for me.

Knocking away all the junk on Ordena's desk, breaking through solid oak. Feeling something shift within. Years of believing in a place that would never believe in me. Years of bottled-up rage washing over my pesky judgment. Until all of it was just static nothingness. All pushed into my hands, rushing through the bat, and just . . . out. Finally out.

"Whoa," I breathed. My chest felt paper-thin.

"I know, right?" Caro let out a laugh. She crouched down on the ground and picked up something shiny out of the rubble. A silver key.

My hands got to work turning the office inside out, looking for the matching lockbox. Caro scrambled beside me. I found a drawer holding a large black safe deposit box with a label that read "Retirement Plan" and slid the key into place. Inside, there were envelopes and envelopes of money. All labeled by student name and marked "RE: SOLIS, APPLICATION FEE." It wasn't just ITI applications. They were sorted by type. School apps, college apps, PSAT courses, SAT courses, AP test fees, Tutoring services, and more. Some of them were dated back ten years. I had to admit, I appreciated how organized it all was. The only compliment I would ever pay that useless guidance counselor. Too bad Ordena stole all her shit. I found the envelope with my name on it and took it out. What I came for. My money.

"Let's go."

"That's it? Take the whole thing!"

"I—" That wasn't the plan. But I was struggling to explain why not. *That's stealing,* a voice inside wanted to say. *He stole this,* another voice said.

"You have to take it. Trust me. If there's one thing I regret, it's not taking that stupid box when I had the chance. Take first, ask questions later. C'mon, we've only got twenty seconds left!"

I lifted the box up, about to close the drawer, but then I saw something else lying underneath. Something better.

Chapter Forty-seven

On the Best Laid Plans

– Rosie

I n the parking lot of the CVS across the street, I explained everything I'd found out about Ordena and Mrs. Solis. About how I had my suspicions that they were doing something fishy when I saw that email from Solis' email address and wondered what the hell she'd done with the money I gave her for my application—and now I knew the truth. And I had proof. Hundreds of envelopes sitting in that safe deposit box in his desk alongside accounting files with his signature that didn't add all the way up. Dique *and I'm sure if we find out where she put the funds, we might be able to get that back to you.* Bullshit. Electric-blue-porsche-driving absolute bullshit. He didn't fire her because she was stealing funds. He fired her because he wanted the money for himself. No honor among thieves, I guess. Who knew what other shady shit Ordena was doing?

I looked back in the direction of the school. Then at Zeke's fidgeting hands.

"How did you get the janitor to disappear?"

Zeke and Ash exchanged a look.

"It's a long story," he said. "What'd you guys find?"

When I opened the box in front of Ash and Zeke and slipped out some bills, they both let out excited gasps.

"Okay, glad I came. We get a cut, right? Wait, is this shit clean?" Ash asked. Of course she wanted money. Didn't do shit, but she wanted money. I cut a searing glance towards Caro.

"Not sure how clean it is. Possibly stolen. And then . . . re-stolen? I guess? But that's not even the best part, actually. I also got these." I showed them the pictures on my phone.

"Not to be rude, but how is a list of names better than money?" Zeke whispered.

"It's proof that he—"

"Holy shit, are those goons really tracking students based on "criminal likelihood"? Is that even legal?" Ash stared intently at the documents.

"Yes . . ." I wanted to be the one to say it, but okay. "It seems like it's spearheaded by Officer Matt and Ordena. They put us on a list and sell the list to the county. And they—"

"They track it using our fucking grades? And our home life? And then we're just put in this system? Before we even do anything? This is some dystopian shit." Thank you. It *was* some dystopian shit. And I had been the one to dig it up. Not Miss Honors English. She could stand to back up a little.

"Are you done?" I asked her. Zeke and Caro both glared at me. I collected myself, reminded of who the enemy was. I handed over the phone. "I got the first couple pages of the list if you swipe right."

Caro stopped counting money and snatched the phone.

"Wait, am I on that shit?"

"You are. So am I." I motioned a hand. "So are you, Ash," I added.

"What? But she's a straight A student?" Zeke interjected. I nodded. So the fuck was I. It didn't seem to matter.

"It's because of our disciplinary record and 'family life,' whatever the fuck that means."

"Sounds racist," Ash said. I found myself agreeing with her.

"Okay, solutions. What should we do now?" I proposed.

"Ooh!" Zeke raised his hand. I pointed to him. "I vote we ask your Aunt Yolanda for a bottle of poison. I think she's cool enough to give it to us. Couple drops in his cup. Boom. Shitty principal gone. No more cop school. We take the money and go to Disney World." Zeke clapped his hands together. About as useful as I expected.

"Murder? For real?" Caro said. "Why don't we just get him fired? Even if he's working with the cops, like . . . he was stealing money from kids right? You have proof with this and the mathy math and papers and shit? How is that not prison?"

"It won't make a difference. The cops will protect him or the school board will protect him. Even if they don't, the next guy is gonna keep the same list and make the same shady deals with the cops. None of it makes a difference," Ash said. She was almost as annoying as I was in her delivery, but she was right.

"I'm with Ash. That's kinda why I kept this to myself until now. It's so . . . hopeless. Like . . . what can be done then? Should we just put the money back and keep our heads down?"

"Pshhh! We definitely *not* giving that damn money back," Caro cut in. "I mean if anything, I'd rather give the money to the people that got their shit stolen."

Zeke pointed at her, nodding. "I'm with that. Let's do that."

It wasn't a horrible idea. Seemed pretty obvious actually. Their names were on the envelopes and everything. It would be the easiest thing to do. And yet . . .

"I'm not saying no to that . . . we should do it. It's just—I don't know. Its more than just the money. How do we make sure this doesn't just keep happening? Plus, I just feel like Ordena deserves worse? Like I wanna embarrass him without getting caught. Is that crazy?"

"Mmmhm. Not crazy. You want revenge," Caro said. Revenge wasn't the word I'd use per se. Justice had a better ring to it.

"Wait . . . they still haven't caught the food fight guy yet, right?" Ash asked.

"Or girl," Zeke corrected.

"Or girl." Ash brought her hands together over her lips. I saw the wheels turning in her head. "They let Marco go and haven't caught whoever started it and they probably won't, right? Because . . . ?"

She waited for us to answer her question. Caro and Zeke looked at each other, hopelessly.

"Because of the penis game," I whispered. Ash's eyes locked into mine.

"Exactly. So . . . ? We have the money. We have the power. And they don't know it." I liked where she was going with this. I liked it a lot. "Let's play the penis game."

"Soo . . . chaos?" I said.

"Chaos."

Ash fucking Kingston. Who knew?

Chapter Forty-eight

On Locker Runs

– Rosie

W e had three hours till curtain call. Maybe two until the buses started dumping elderly folks into the auditorium. Still plenty of time. But far less than we had a couple weeks ago when we'd set the plan. The only thing slightly worrying me was how easy it all was. By theater superstition, smooth dress rehearsal usually meant a disastrous show. But shows only had cheap magic tricks on their side. We had the real thing. Hopefully.

Ash was stuffing lockers on the wall behind me. She was wearing head-to-toe army print topped with a black beret. It was a little on the nose for my taste. We worked beside one another in silence. She only broke it once.

"Did you know that JJ's fights might be on his permanent arrest records? He was complaining about it once at work. So like if you get in trouble as an adult, it shows up that you were a previous offender and you're then more likely to get arrested again and get a harsher charge. Even scumbags like JJ don't deserve that."

I didn't know what to say to that. I didn't even know the SRO officers had the legal right to arrest us until recently. It was true that JJ was a scumbag, but I wasn't really surprised by the information. So I just mumbled, "Yeah, fucked up." And we went back to silence.

I heard Caro's sneakers squeak before I saw her running around the corner. Her braids flew through the air. She smashed down the camera in the corner and kept running.

"Good work team!" She shouted past us.

"Shhh!" I held up a finger. Ash saluted her.

"Bruh, you guys could not be more different," Ash laughed. I didn't entertain it. I just wanted to finish this so we could move on to the next step of the plan. It hadn't really felt like I was completely in my body since the moment I found the money and that list. Everything we were doing now felt so . . . crucial. It felt like my entire future was on the line. And at the same time, completely hopeless. My whole adolescent life, reduced to a name on a list. It wasn't just ITI or Ordena—it was everything. The whole thing. It was everywhere I looked now.

I felt Ash's eyes rest on my back. "Do you hate me or something?" *Shit. Here we go.* Her voice sounded so . . . hurt. It was weird being alone with her. I didn't understand why, but Zeke insisted I keep an eye on her. It seemed to be my default role, keeping an eye on other people. I looked up at the moldy ceiling before I turned around. Trying to figure out how to explain that it was a feeling far more complicated than just hate.

"I don't hate you."

"Then, what? You're still pissed about what happened with your sister? I mean, I thought we squashed that . . . unless . . . does *she* still hate me?"

I rolled my eyes.

"No, Caro's obsessed with you. It's annoying." It was true: she kept showing me her daily outfit posts on Instagram as if I cared. I caught a smile in Ash's mouth before her face went back to confusion. I thought I was being mature by just acting cordially with this girl, but I couldn't help it. There were still residual weeds of something in me that wanted to punch her in the face. Wanted to blame her for things she had little to do with. "Can I ask you a question? How did you get into Honors English? 'Cause I can't find a way, I've tried everything."

"Is *that* what it is? That I'm in Honors?"

I shrugged. Surprise colored her face. Then, she softened.

"You're obviously not the first one to wonder why I'm there," Ash sighed. Suddenly, I felt like horse shit for even asking. An apology caught itself in the bottom of my throat. "Honestly? It just carried over from my old school. They were more hippie dippie and we were allowed to choose all our courses. But it's not that great. Mrs. Shapelli tries but she's still, you know . . ." She pointed to the palm of her hand. "But wait, I thought you wanted to go to ITI? That's what Zeke—"

I shook my head. "Not anymore. I've been thinking about where they get their money from and how they decide who gets in. It's messy. The deadline for junior-year applications already passed. I'm done trying. If they don't want me, I don't want them."

"I feel that." Ash nodded. "I mean, I don't think you should let them convince you that you're not good enough for them. But I also don't think the only way out is to beg for them to choose you. There has to be another way through." Watching her speak then, casually dropping her wisdom, I considered how Ash might make a dangerous president one day.

"That's what I'm hoping, too. But, like . . . what, though?"

"I dunno, but I think I'd rather just take community college classes like my cousin and do dual-enrollment next year. Start college early. Get the fuck outta here, y'know? But that's me. You do you."

I blinked, dumbstruck. Dual-enrollment. All these years of effort. Why didn't I think of that sooner? It was a way around the mountain that had loomed over me all these years. It was the kind of information that should have been delivered by my dumb guidance counselor, not the girl I used to hate. I wanted to take Ash Kingston by the shoulders and shake her.

"What?" Ash asked. I bit down my excitement and saved it for another day. This first. I turned back to the lockers.

"Nothing. W-what do you want to go to school for?"

Ash turned back to her task, too.

"I wanna be a teacher. A good one, though."

"I think you'll be a good one."

"Thanks. What about you?"

I paused with a wad of cash in my black-gloved hands.

"Actually . . . I don't know anymore."

Chapter
Forty-nine

On the Day in Question

– Caro

A nother round of Shirley Temples, my good sir . . . And some disco fries for the table!" I waved a fifty at our waiter at 2Moons, feeling like a fucking king in our booth table. "For your troubles."

Rosie tried to get me to chill out, but it was no use. I was mad hype. If this was a mob movie, I was the mob wife showing off her brand new fur coat. I mean, why not celebrate? This was our greatest piece yet. I mean chef's kiss level.

First, the drop. I was on camera-smash duty, running from wing to wing to make sure all bases were covered. Rosie, Ash, and Zeke were locker runners. Stuffing lockers with xeroxed copies of the list, a petition to remove the school police station, a five dollar bill with 'Lost and Found' and Ordena's phone number printed on a post-it. All a part of my sister's elaborate plan. According to Rosie's math, if each locker got $5, we'd still have $10k left plus our party profits. The idea for the party came a few days before, when we were scheming in the auditorium while we helped Rosie clean the stage for her show.

"A ten a.m. matinee? That's so wild. How many people usually come to this?" Zeke asked.

"They bus like ten old people in from the nursing home," Rosie answered. "It's been a while since we've had a good turnout though. I think the last time this place was full was for *Grease*, but Mrs. Shapelli might've been gassing it. You could probably set someone on fire on stage and no one would notice."

Zeke stopped sweeping. "How much are the tickets? And when is the auditorium free?"

"Five bucks. Pretty much empty after two. Why?"

"You have keys. We have stage. Rishi has tech. We've done this before, it worked, we made a profit. This is it! This is the thing!"

"You wanna use Ordena's money to throw a party? How does that help us?"

"You said chaos. We need bodies. This is it! Not just *a* party. A mega exclusive one. Rich ITI, Catholic school types only. Trust me, I know those kids. I've been there. They'll throw bags at this. *Serious* bags."

And Zeke was right. They did. All we had to do was stand outside Saint Agnes and whisper to one string-haired blond guy about a top secret party. Those fuckers acted like Westside was Disney World. Just the right amount of danger. Watered down drinks. Confiscated phones and a faux security pat down. We didn't even need fancy decorations or good music. Zeke gave explicit instructions to play a loop of top forty tracks from five years ago.

We ended up with enough money to Scrooge McDuck–style swim in.

Then, we kicked them out. Left the school cleaner than it was when we got there. Boom. If there was one thing my sister was gonna do right, it was come up with an airtight plan. If there was one thing *I* was gonna do, it was not get my ass caught.

They did what I knew they were gonna do—call all their suspects. As expected, they had nothing. So, every student became a suspect. Rumors swirled that the culprit was a rando from another school who came to the party. Which was perfect. An announcement was made that they would be calling the entire school into the principal's office one by one. All they had were two Instagram stories of the auditorium party from Miss_Leidy95 that slipped through the cracks. Which put her in the line of fire. Unfortunately. Thoughts and prayers for her, of course. Wild how karma be handling my shit sometimes.

But the school didn't have nothing on us. Not a scratch anywhere near Ordena's office. No evidence of a break-in. Even if they had something, we had Rosie and her jacket. All I had to do was impart my hard-earned wisdom on the art of not snitching and telling authority figures to fuck off.

Now for the moment I'd been training them all for. I tapped a spoon on the glass of my fresh Shirley Temple.

"On all counts of breaking and entering?" I asked my fellow co-conspirators.

"Not guilty, your honor." Rosie was beaming. I'd never seen her so happy.

"Not motherfucking guilty. On all counts of stolen property?"

Zeke took a wad of our cash from Rosie's open backpack and used it to fan himself.

"Sorry, what property, your honor? Are you admitting to stealing money from children?" he said, batting his eyelashes.

"On all counts of trespassing school grounds and engaging in partying?" I continued.

"I believe the defense will find a signed permission form from the defendant saying we could host a *Sleepover Night* social function to raise money for the musical. Sorry if the defendant is incompetent, your honor." Rishi threw a towel over his shoulder and squeezed next to Zeke on the opposite side of the booth. He waved a copy of the permission form in question. These nerds were starting to grow on me. We were really gonna make it through this squeak-clean and scratch-free.

"On all counts of stolen funds, conspiracy, fraud, and being a general bootlicking asswipe?"

"I do believe that's a question for the defense, your honor." Rishi quipped. I gave him a high five and let out a cackle. "Oh shit, and guess who called Ordena's desk asking for a statement? News4NewYork, bitch!" We all exchanged giddy looks.

"No way!" Rosie squealed. "Fuck, what'd he say?"

"Nothing. Told me to hang up on 'em."

"Holy shit, that means we finna be on TV!" I grabbed my sister's arm. Then I turned to Rishi. "Also, sidenote: don't call me bitch, bitch. I don't know you like that."

"Yea, I was gonna say," Ash said, looking at Rishi sideways.

"Fair, fair," Rishi conceded, putting his hands up.

"Also, hopefully *we're* not on TV, Caro. Again, I don't know nothing about this," Ash continued.

We all exchanged questioning looks for a beat. Then we all spoke at once.

"I don't know nothing neither."

"Me neither."

"I ain't seen shit."

"Nope."

"Innocent, your honor."

Chapter Fifty

On New Beginnings

– Zeke

S o you don't play piano anymore?"

"Nope."

"Like, at all?"

"Nope."

"Why not?"

"I just don't. I tried, a couple months ago. But . . . I decided it's best if I don't."

My chest tightened. Not at the reminder of my past, but at the obviousness of my incapability. There had to be better words out there. I promised myself I would find better words later. One day.

"Do you miss it?"

"Like . . . kinda? But not really that much? I've just always done it, so I never really thought about it. I'm kinda more into writing right now?"

"Ah, your little notebook. You always like writing?"

I actually used to hate it. It felt like a chore before I came here with a head full of contradicting thoughts and a new body.

And this feeling that I could be anything I wanted if I wrote myself that way. It felt like something close to immortality.

"Nah. I haven't done it very long. Outside of English homework. Maybe that's why I like it. I don't know. Something new."

"Something new."

We stayed at 2Moons until closing. And then, one by one, our crew disassembled. Until it was just Rishi and I. And he was complimenting my rings. I was sitting comfortably in their warmth. A slender woman in an apron marked "Kiss the Chef" crossed the threshold into the dining area to serve us homemade hot chocolate. They were served out of the prettiest mugs I'd ever seen. Beside each was a small pack of cookies wrapped in Arabic script. Immediately, I was starstruck.

"I'm a big fan of your work, Mrs. Saab." I stuck out my hand for a handshake. She took it enthusiastically.

"Thank you!" She bore a striking resemblance to her son. Thick curls framed her face and wild bangs sat above the same golden eyes. "Is that him?" I heard the woman whisper into Rishi's ear. Then she turned to me. "Big fan of yours, too. You play piano so beautifully. I can pay you to play for customers, if you're available. Or you can tutor my son—"

"Okay, bye, Ma!" He shoved her away. She waved me goodbye as she made her forced exit. I couldn't help but smirk at their interaction.

"Does your mom think we're like . . . together now?"

"Whoa! Ya sleep on a park bench with a guy once." Rishi put his hands up.

"Just asking. I've never done this before." I took a sip of my drink. The rich, dark chocolate was thick and luxurious. I closed my eyes for a moment. They were gonna have to drag me out of this place.

"Done what? Liked a guy?" Despite the bold assumption, I felt him retreat a little.

"No, I've done that. I haven't . . . been . . . together-together with anyone before."

"Oh," he said. He took a sip of his drink and started mumbling. "Well, neither have I. But I feel like I've been pretty clear since day one. I came to your party early, like a white person." His eyes searched my face. "Do you . . . want to be together? With someone?"

Someone.

"Do you?" I volleyed back, trying to find some cover under all the transparency he usually hid in humor. He huffed out a quick irritation.

"I don't get you."

"I don't get me either. What am I missing?"

He laughed.

"You come off as annoyingly chill, but you're kinda all or nothing, huh?" Rishi asked. He seemed slightly pissed off. I'd never thought of myself in those terms. Seeming chill definitely used to be a priority of mine. "How do I know I'm not just a rebound?"

It took me a second to realize what he meant. How things must look from his perspective. Ash was the last thing on my mind. I thought for a moment, studying the tiled blue-and-white ceiling.

"I guess you don't. But I don't think you are. So . . ." I looked back at the boy in front of me and rested my head on the back of my hand. "I guess we'll just have to find out."

"I guess we will." He took a sip of his chocolate.

"So you *do* want to find out?"

He cleared his throat.

"Can we just—go slower? We're in high school. It doesn't have to be so . . . end of the world. Why don't you just start by asking me to hang out first?"

He was making good points. But why did *I* have to ask *him* out?

"Okay . . ." How did regular people do this? How did a human ask another human to spend time together so that they may or may not recreate a dream I had? "What activities do . . . you want to do?"

He rolled his eyes. "Do I have to do everything here?"

"I mean, I'm down for whatever."

"*Whatever.* Ugh! I hate people like that!"

I chuckled. "I guess I'm better at this when I'm drunk."

"Or sleepy."

"Okay, but like . . . what do you *like* to do? Besides DJ teen house parties?"

He pursed his lips for a second before crossing his arms. "There's a jazz festival in Brooklyn next week." Okay. Very up my alley. He raised his eyebrows and examined his nails. I waited for him to finish his statement. And then I realized. Right.

"Rishabh Saab," I lowered my tone and put my hands in prayer position. "Would you do me the honor of going on a very gay, very romantic date to this jazz festival in Brooklyn next week that I just heard about two minutes ago?"

"I don't know, I'd have to check my schedule."

I looked at him. And he looked at me. And we held there a while until I was the first to break. I downed the rest of my hot chocolate, feeling the heat as it passed through me while thick whipped cream cooled my lips. We watched a police siren drive past the diner window and flood the place with reds and blues. The colors contouring the curves and valleys of his face. Drawing out streaks of brown highlights that ran through his thick hair.

"You did kiss me on the forehead while I was asleep, right? Or did I dream that part?"

I regretted it as soon as I said it. I was only 80 percent sure it was a dream.

Rishi gave me a curious look and I knew I had given him too much of myself. He looked towards the kitchen, checking for something. Then he reached over and swiped the residue off the corners of my mouth with his thumb.

"Did it feel like a dream?"

Questions, questions. I fought the urge to close the space between us.

"Kinda."

And then, like a dream, I found the warmth of his breath flowing in and out of mine. I was still shivering, feeling his soft curls brush against my eyelids like velvet. I found myself raising a hand against his chin, kissing back. He couldn't have been physically closer to me, but I pushed myself closer still, fearful that he would change his mind and the moment would end. Until we were crushing each other, precise and sweet. With an assuredness that seemed to surprise us both.

A pleasant surprise to see those unwavering, dark-rimmed golden eyes before I finally broke us half an inch apart.

"I thought you wanted to take it slow?

"Starting now."

Chapter
Fifty-one

On Nights With Friends

– Zeke

I don't get what your big deal is with the bagels. It's just bread."

"You tried one? With the Taylor Ham? Where?"

"Right here, this coffee place. Uh . . . lemme see . . . Dunkin' Donuts?"

"Dad!"

"What?"

"Dunkin' Donuts? Really? That's not what I meant. They have Dunkin' in Miami. It's not real food. You've had it before."

"Don't think I have," he lied.

He was such a dad, I swear. Down to asking a million questions over *Living Single* just so he could hear me talk. I knew I was really gonna miss having him here. I don't think I missed him as much as I should have the first time. An announcement over an airport speaker crackled on his end of the phone.

"You should go, you're gonna miss your flight."

"Still time if you wanna change your mind. Come with me."

"Like I said, staying till graduation. See you in July. Bye, love you, Dad."

"Love you more, Zeke. Remember, you call me."

✿ ✿ ✿

We were sitting at Liberty State Park. Rosie, Caro, Ash, and I. Listening to far-off sounds of more geese than I'd ever seen in my life. Our legs stretched out on a field of grass beneath the night. I had gotten here first, sending out a bat signal out to see if anyone would join me. Rosie arrived twenty minutes later with blankets and three kinds of Cheetos. Ash brought a vodka-filled water bottle and the latest copy of the *Jersey Journal*, with the headline "Westside Socialism: Mystery Figure Redistributes School Funds."

Rosie took the paper immediately and started reading Ordena's statement.

"Due to the current legal proceedings, I am not at liberty to disclose any further information regarding that alleged list. But I am not a villain, nor are the police. Our purpose is to keep this school safe and productive, so we do keep track of which students are in most need of help."

"Safe from who exactly?" Ash interjected. "Ugh, they're probably just gonna transfer him to another shitty school, watch."

Though, Rosie held a twinkle of optimism in her eye. If I didn't know any better, I'd assume she was high. She turned the page around to show his picture in black and white. He was mid-speech, with his open mouth in a frown.

"Would it kill him to smile?"

Caro arrived last and, of course, brought some greens. My good sis. She and I were the only ones partaking. My rings, her bat, and Rosie's jacket made us untouchable against the prospect of any sirens appearing. I was even arrogant enough to try and smoke lying down. My lungs humbled me real quick. I emerged from my coughing fit with only one thought on my mind. The same one that had been haunting me while I stared at the walls at night lately. That I'd been writing in circles about in my Moleskine journal. I still wasn't getting anywhere. Maybe I needed advice.

"I kissed a boy last week," I said.

"You WHAT?" Rosie sat up and turned to look at me.

"How was it?" asked Ash.

"It was alright, I mean . . ."

"You kissed a boy. A real one. Last week? A boy from school?"

"Normal people kiss boys, Rosie," Caro giggled.

"No, I met him online. I thought maybe he was a serial killer, but then I was like . . . eh. That's also pretty hot. Either way a win."

"Stop. That's not even funny. You're mad stupid," Ash said as she shoved my shoulder.

"A fucking dumbass," Rosie concurred. "It was Rishi, wasn't it?"

I shrugged, feeling my face get hot.

"Back to quality. Was it like a good alright or a bad alright? On a scale of one to me," Ash continued. Suddenly I was Carrie in *Sex and the City* (if Carrie and Miranda had shared a drunken makeout session one night).

"I dunno . . . I guess it was . . . okay?" Considering I'd been hanging out at 2Moons every day trying to get it to happen again, "okay" was the understatement of the century. If that was the only kiss I ever got again, that would be enough.

"A good okay or a bad okay?" Now Caro had jumped on the train. "Tongue or no tongue? Show me with your hand."

"Enough! Leave the boy alone," Rosie said, in a surprisingly protective tone. She lay down next to me, resting her head over my shoulder and closing her eyes. I passed my blunt to Caro and watched the smoke disappear into the Hudson River.

Alone was the last place I wanted to be. I'd had enough alone for two lifetimes. Not that I didn't appreciate it. Alone had been there for me when I needed her. When I got lost, alone was the home I always had to turn back to. I'd done up all the furnishings and set out enough lush pillows so that it was a comfortable home now. But through the echoes of purposeless nights, I saw how, like a home, her beauty was only amplified by departure and return.

Chapter
Fifty-two

On Release

– Rosie

I t was the kind of spring night where it felt like nature was playing games. A sneak preview of warmer days to come. I grabbed a fistful of grass and tossed out my idea of us all getting rose tattoos when we turned eighteen, like Mami and Yolanda and the badass group of women in the old picture I found. I already knew Caro would be on board, but it was the kind of idea I expected Ash and Zeke to ruminate over for a while. Instead, they were both immediately down. Zeke, with the caveat that his would only be a tiny rose because he was scared of needles. In my notebook I'd doodled some options and I felt lucky. A tattoo meant a bond for life. And I now had bond-for-life kind of friends.

"I can't believe we fuckin' did that shit, for real, though. We boutta be legends." Caro reached out above her. I nodded. But it was hard to imagine that anyone would ever know who I was after I left this place.

"Y'all ever notice how bomb water tastes at night?" Zeke, as usual, was on his own planet.

"Yo, you gone gone, huh?" Caro laughed.

"No, I'm serious. Like, it just tastes better . . . right? I can't be the only one."

"Bruh, you might be. What is this, some pisces water sign mercury thing?" I said.

"You were actually really close that time. I'm glad you're learning. Proud of you. But no, I mean like for real. Go get some water right now. Go on!"

"No! Where imma get water from?" I hissed.

"Just do it. Please."

"There's a water fountain over there. Just do it so he'll shut up." Ash chimed in. We couldn't help but giggle. I walked to the fountain with an empty water bottle, filled it up, and came back to our blanket to present it to my audience. Zeke's bright eyes looked up at me.

"You're so fucking weird. I don't know why I'm best friends with you." I shook my head. I could see his smile spread even in the dark. And those damn dimples.

"I think you're my best friend, too."

"Shut up." I quickly took a sip of the water and felt the cold slip down my throat.

"It tastes better, right?"

I thought for a moment, savoring it. "Tastes like vodka."

Ash was the first to break. She held onto Caro who started on her bird noises. Until the joy spilled out of all of us and reached for the stars in the sky. And I laid my head down, chin up, smiling and thinking. Thinking about how the sky we see reflects the light of stuff from hundreds of years ago. And I wondered if the stars a hundred years from now would ever know we existed. That we were once here, in Liberty Park. Laughing our asses off.

✿ ✿ ✿

Caro and Ash left us to go make kissy faces at their phones beneath a park lamp. Zeke turned to me, lying on his stomach, bouncing his feet in the air. He looked like a little kid.

"You're coming with me to my Confirmation next month. As my date," I told him. His face twisted in confusion and then he shrugged.

"I guess I am."

"Great. Now that's done, I was thinking . . ." I started.

"That's your problem, always thinking," Zeke said. I ignored him.

"For the rest of the money, we need to find a way to spend it on what everyone needs the most. Like, what would help the most amount of kids? Right? I think–"

"Can I ask you something? How come you don't talk about, like, teenager stuff?"

"Like what?"

"Like about boys you like . . . or people or whatever. You never talk about it. I feel like that's all anyone our age talks about. It's so fucking annoying. I mean, I'm not any better, over here catching bummy ass feelings for a dude only half an inch taller than me. Meanwhile you're over there icy as fuck. Your turn, spotlight on Rosie. Spill. You don't got anyone you look at and you just wanna like . . . ugh . . . like merge souls with them?"

"You wanna merge souls with Rishi?" I smirked. Zeke glared at me. "I don't like anyone, no. I'm only a child of God." My eyelashes fluttered, feigning innocence.

Zeke glared some more. Would it kill him to laugh at my jokes?

"You never liked nobody never?"

I couldn't tell what he was getting at, but it was making me slightly uncomfortable. If I really thought about it, I think I maybe had a crush on a boy in kindergarten, but I didn't know if I actually liked him or if I thought I was supposed to like him because everyone else liked him. Or if it was just that he had green eyes. But it didn't matter because I found out he picked his nose and that was the end of that. Even if I wasn't caught in the orbit of Caro and her troubling boyfriend selections, or Mami and Papi's whole . . . situation, there was this feeling within me that knew I wasn't capable of the elusive thing they kept searching for. Which was its own kind of terrifying. A locked jar for another day.

"I dunno, bruh. Honestly I kinda . . . don't care that much?" I started to roll my eyes but I caught myself.

"There she goes," he pointed.

"Oh, fuck off! I'll roll my eyes when I want to roll my eyes." Zeke laughed. I continued. "Anyways, all that merging souls shit seems kinda time consuming. I got shit to do." I showed him my color-coded calendar.

"Ah, Rosie, Rosie, Rosie. I envy you, girl," Zeke sighed. He turned to his side, cheek in hand, looking dreamy. "Liking boys is a curse. Almost as bad as liking girls."

"Which is why I focus my energy on money. Money never lets me down." I was only half joking this time.

"I don't think we have time to unpack how wrong you are."

"I'm never wrong."

"Right." Zeke shook his head. "So you still going to I.T.I to be a civil engineer, then?"

My mouth hung open, searching for a reply. It almost felt like a betrayal. I'd told him about my mid-teenage crisis in confidence, and here he was throwing it back at me? And with that stupid smug look on his face. Insufferable.

"I am never wrong in the present. Past me doesn't count."

He laughed. Then I couldn't help but laugh at myself, too.

"You wanna know what I think, Rosie Rojas?"

"Do I wanna know?"

"I think you should keep drawing. You're really good."

My first instinct was to brush off the compliment, but I swallowed that instinct. And I nodded. He was right. I was really good and it was really fun. When I was surrounded by my markers and colored gel pens was when I felt most at ease. There was only one problem . . .

"Too bad there's no money in doodling."

"Disagree. You're more than a doodler. You could be a creative director or a boss ass magazine editor like that lady in Devil Wears Prada. Or have your paintings on taxi cabs like Kehinde Wiley."

Ash had introduced us to Kehinde Wiley and his insane portraits wrapped in ornate patterns and bright colors. She had a whole rolodex of Black artists and activists stored up and ready to go for spontaneous debate. I felt my world widen just being around her sometimes.

"I'm not Kehinde Wiley, though," I concluded. I was just a regular person. Just Rosie. I squandered the hope that was building in my chest like a ball of light. There was too much at stake outside of myself to waste time on a hope like that.

Zeke sat up and took both my hands in his. His face got really serious. I braced myself.

"If there's one person who can figure out how to be Kehinde Wiley, it's you."

I bit down my lip. This fucking guy.

"And you?" I hit the uno reverse before my face revealed more than I wanted it to. "Who are you gonna be? Billie Holiday?"

"Psh, don't worry about me. I'm finna be Beyoncé."

This time our laughs crashed and returned, like the waves that flowed over the rocks beneath us. Filling me up until I felt my lungs exhale into the city lights. I was flying without a map now. And it was probably the secondhand smoke, but for once it felt like things might actually be okay. Despite the obstacles, there was one thing I knew for sure: I trusted me. To find a way. There was no one I trusted more, actually.

THE END

Acknowledgments

Writing a second book is hard. Writing your first full-length novel is even harder. I hope I did okay.

It has been a bizarre experience, being a baby debut author just a year ago. Especially when I just tripped and fell into this profession and happened upon the most wonderful publisher that chose to support me along the way. So first and foremost, thank you for the millionth time to Nick Thomas at Levine Querido for falling for my scams again and buying this book during a brunch where I mentioned the idea (with no intentions of actually writing it). You keep taking chances on me and I don't know where I'd be without your unbridled, annoying positivity to balance my pessimism. You changed my life.

Shout out to myself for doing the scary things. And big shout out to my therapist, Tia, for helping ease the anxiety that ensued immediately after signing the contract when I realized I had no idea how to write a book. We made it to the other side, girl.

Thank you so much to Irene Vázquez, the best and most multi-talented publicist. Thank you to Antonio Gonzalez Cerna and the LQ marketing team. Thank you to Chronicle Books for getting my books into the hands of readers. And to Freesia Blizard on Chronicle's production team for making both my books look so pretty.

Always grateful to my parents, Nilsa Tavarez (aka my publicist, manager, assistant, and translator) and Bernardo Gomera for raising me between two worlds. Thank you to my Tía Rosita and my Abuela Neris for your support and sharing your stories. I want to also thank all my ancestors and tíos and tías and cousins and nieces and nephews throughout Santo Domingo, Pedernales, Madrid, Boston, New York, New Jersey, and the Bronx. Especially Laura and Wildre, for answering my questions about sisterhood. And thank you to my brother, Diego, for letting me bother him from time to time.

A very special thanks to all the artists I've had the privilege of being in community with this past year. To my friends Amir Khadar and Moses Jeune for indulging in my ramblings about this story and letting me interview them. To the Maryland Institute College of Art where this story and *High Spirits* were born. To Donna Barba Higuera for being the first person to interview me and for offering your mentorship. To the amazing ladies and they/thems at the Las Musas writing collective. And to my critique group at Tin House 2023 for your invaluable feedback and conversation. Especially our amazing instructor, Jeanne Thornton.

And finally, the biggest thank you to the state of New Jersey and my alma mater, Clifton High School, for serving as inspiration and opening my eyes to the injustices of the world. Thank you to my teachers, Mr. Rogers, Mr. Henry, and Dr. Greenwald, for being truth-tellers and pushing me to be more. As a teen, a fire of anger burned within me at the fact that some kids are granted more resources than others, but I wish all students the quality of education these teachers were able to cultivate within an underfunded, overcrowded public school.

To the CHS Class of 2015. My homies. My day ones. I may never reach the same high I felt during my graduation day on that football field on June 26, 2015 (the same day same-sex marriage was made legal in all fifty US states) where 750 students threw blow-up dolls and giant dildos in the air as teachers frantically tried to stop us. From our time organizing against the school's harmful testing programs as students, to the summer of 2020 where my graduating class organized one of the largest Black Lives Matter marches in the state. I am so, so proud of *us*. There are some people out there who describe their high school experience as "boring" and, honey, I could never.

Reader, if you have never tuned in to a local school board meeting, this is your sign to start. Listen to the kids. They know what they talkin' about.

To the current students at CHS, you are magic and you are the future. ★

About the Author

Camille Gomera-Tavarez is an Afro-Dominican graphic designer, illustrator, and authoress from Clifton, NJ. She graduated with a BFA in Graphic Design and a minor in Creative Writing from the Maryland Institute College of Art. Her "soulfully crafted debut," *High Spirits*, won a Pura Belpré Honor, was a *Publishers Weekly* Flying Start, and earned three starred reviews. Visit her at www.cgtdesign.net.

Some Notes on this Book's Production

The jacket was designed by Dotun Abeshinbioke, who was inspired by her graphic design style and love for mixing patterns and colors to create a layered and playful look. The text was set by Westchester Publishing Services, in Danbury, CT, using Aila, a slab serif designed by Francis Requena for TipoType, the first foundry to ever call Uruguay home. Aila is built on the structure of a realistic Roman but with particular organic features to highlight the tension between structure and rhythm. The display was set in Coconat, a typeface designed by Colllettivo with a unique extended bold style. The book was printed on FSC™-certified 78gsm Yunshidai Ivory paper and bound in China.

Production supervised by Freesia Blizard
Book case and endpapers designed by Camille Gomera-Tavarez
Book interiors designed by Xena Brar
Editor: Nick Thomas

LQ